The King Who Disappeared

By Hank Quense

Other books by Hank Quense

Fiction:

Princess Moxie
Moxie's Problem
Moxie's Decision
Queen Moxie

Gundarland Stories
Tales From Gundarland
Falstaff's Big Gamble
Wotan's Dilemma

Zaftan Troubles
Contact
Confusion
Combat
Convolution
Sam
Klatze
Gongeblazn

Non-fiction:
Complete self-publishing Guides
Creating Stories
Planning a Novel, Script or Memoir
Manage Your Story Design Project

Acknowledgements
The awesome cover was produced by
Gary Tenuta. Visit Gary's website:

http://garyvaltenuta.blogspot.com

ISBN:978-0-9978224-7-2
Published in the United States of America.
Published by Strange Worlds Publishing
http:// strangeworldspublishing.com/wp

Part One: A Long Time Ago

Chapter One

Jerado, King of Gant, entered his throne room and surveyed the officers assembled there. The five generals with a few staff officers represented each kingdom he had conquered. They sat at a table facing the throne.

Jerado was a dwelf, a detested combination of an elf mother and a dwarf father. He had inherited all the bad qualities of both races and none of the good ones. He was shorter than most elves but taller than all dwarfs. He was stockier than the elves but thinner than most dwarfs. Jerado had reddish-blonde hair and a scraggly beard and brown eyes. He was forty-five and had been forty-five for the last six years thanks to an anti-aging spell he used monthly.

His hooded robe was black and shot through with silver threads and cabalistic signs. The large deep hood was usually pulled forward, keeping his face in shadows.

Jerado ascended the dais and sat down on the throne. His first act as king had been to have the legs shortened so his feet touched the floor when he sat on it. He glanced at the generals. They looked uneasy but not very uneasy and that made Jerado uncomfortable. He wanted people to be nervous in his presence. He decided the general on the left looked the least uneasy. Jerado cast a quick spell that snapped a rear leg of the general's chair. With a crash, the general tumbled away from the table and smacked his head on the tile floor. Woozy, the general stood up and looked at the chair in puzzlement. A staff officer ran over with a replacement chair and the general sat down. The other four generals now looked tense, a big improvement.

"We are here," Jerado said, "to finalize our plans for the attack on Sulvaria. All is ready for the final step. You will march your soldiers to the assembly point on the Sulvaria border and be there ten days from today. We'll let the troops rest for a day and, twelve days from now, the attack will begin." Jerado paused briefly and said with a smile, "Whichever army shows up last at the assembly point will be the rear guard on our march into Sulvaria. That army can eat road dust for the entire journey."

The generals shifted in their chairs and one raised a hand. When Jerado acknowledged him, he said, "Do we have any information on what Sulvaria will do?"

"My spies report all is quiet in Sulvaria. I'm sure Bohan also has spies and they will tell him when we approach the border."

"So we won't have surprise on our side?"

"I doubt it and we won't need it. We have a numerical advantage because Sulvaria is a small country with a small population."

"What about Bohan's heroes? They're tough fighters."

"Bah! Forget about the heroes. They're just more enemy soldiers. And by the way, I want Bohan and those heroes taken alive, if possible. I'll get everyone to watch as I torture Bohan to death. Then I'll kill the heroes one by one. After that, other kings will think twice about standing in my way." Sulvaria was one more waypoint in his plan to conquer all of Gundarland.

Jerado stood up and pounded one fist into the other palm. "We will crush Bohan's army and then march on the city of Centi. Once we snatch the capital, there will be rewards for all the soldiers. And the tax revenues from Centi's docks will fund further expansion of my empire."

Jerado sat down again. "We stand on the cusp of glory. Together we will build the greatest empire Gundarland has ever seen. But first, we need Centi. Go and prepare your armies. In twelve days, we attack. In fourteen days, we'll celebrate victory in Bohan's castle in Centi. You are dismissed."

Jerado watched the officers file out of the room. He fought the urge to destroy something to celebrate his excitement. He had grown up in Centi and suffered hatred, bigotry, hunger, isolation and other indignities because he was a dwelf. His mother only knew his father was a dwarf solider, one of many at the time. She worked at menial jobs for little money. Most of her wages went to drink, which left few coins to feed her child.

Jerado planned to visit his old neighborhood and find people who had insulted or ignored his childhood plight. Those wretches would pay for his difficult childhood.

After that, he would visit the University of Wizardry and Sorcery. He would recognize those who denied him entrance to the school because of his low birth status. Jerado visualized those wizards standing on the stage of the school's assembly hall where he would demonstrate that one didn't have to attend university courses to become a powerful wizard. The university staff would be astonished at the power and creativity of the spells he would use to torture those who believed a dwelf had no right to enter the school.

Ruling Gundarland would further show those who had dismissed him as a useless bastard half-breed how wrong they were.

Jerado smiled and pushed the dreams of vengeance aside. Royal matters needed to be dealt with.

~ ~ ~

Bohan, King of Sulvaria — a kingdom located in southeastern Gundarland — rode with a hawk on his right wrist. A tall man with big shoulders, dirty blonde hair and pleasant features, he was twenty-five and had been king ever since his father died three years ago. He wore leather pants and a linen vest open to allow the spring breezes to cool him.

Ansgar, a wizard and Bohan's chief advisor, rode alongside. Tall and scrawny, Ansgar wore a gray hooded robe over a pair of gray pants. Dozens of patches covered his robe, each with a symbol from alchemy or astrology. He had long black hair and was clean-shaven, thanks to a daily spell that was much safer than a knife blade.

On Bohan's other side rode Bianca, a female elf archer. Dressed in a hooded, forest-green shirt and matching trews, she was as tall as Bohan and her long, green hair was plaited into a single braid. She had amber eyes, always drew attention with her attractive looks and was a dead shot with a longbow.

They rode along a dirt road with newly planted fields on both sides. In the distance, they could see a small collection of huts and farmers.

"I miss riding out like this," Bohan said, "traveling to tournaments and seeing the country." Before becoming king, Bohan had been the most famous knight in Gundarland. He had won tournaments all over the country, including the biggest one held every year up north in the city of Dun Hythe.

"I imagine ruling a country is quite

different than being an itinerant knight," Ansgar replied. "Responsibilities, for one thing."

"I also miss the tournaments," Bianca said with a sigh.

"Speaking of responsibilities, here comes trouble," Bohan said and pointed toward a rider pounding down the road toward them.

The rider pulled up, greeted the king and said, "Our spies report that a large army is marching in our direction."

Bohan sucked in his breath, Bianca turned pale and Ansgar groaned.

After a few moments of silence, Bohan asked, "From Gant, no doubt?"

"Yes, Lord. From Gant."

Bohan ran a hand over his chin before saying, "Return to the castle and alert my staff officers to await my return."

The messenger knuckled his forehead, turned his horse and galloped back the way he came.

"Have your wizardly contacts sent any news about Jerado?" Bohan asked Asgar.

"None. Every time Jerado conquers another kingdom, he murders the wizards who don't flee. He doesn't like other wizards around him, possibly because he was never licensed by any Wizards Guild. Anyway, it's difficult to collect news and gossip when there are no wizards around to use our scryer network."

Scryers were magical devices used to communicate short messages over long distances.

"So, at last count," Bohan said, "Jerado has conquered four other kingdoms. His army must be getting quite large, don't you think?"

"I'm sure it is," Ansgar replied. "Jerado must be lusting after Centi's revenue." He adjusted his position in the saddle. "He conquered the other kingdoms with an eye towards building an army big enough to attack us and take the city."

"We'll be ready to meet him." Bohan moved the hawk a few inches up his wrist. "I really detest wars. So much bloodshed. So many killed. Nevertheless, I can't let Jerado conquer Sulvaria, so I'll have to fight a war."

"We'll have to make more arrows," Bianca said. "There is no such thing as having too many arrows."

They neared the Centi city walls. Centi was Sulvaria's capital and was the second largest port in all of Gundarland.

The custom revenues made Sulvaria a wealthy kingdom and a target for other greedy kings.

Once through the city gates, they turned right and dismounted in the castle forecourt. Bohan handed over the hawk to a servant and strode up the steps to enter the small dining hall where his heroes ate and slept. Bohan's heroes numbered eight including Ansgar and Bianca.

Barrow, the group's quartermaster when in the field, played dice with Luc, a half-pint berserker, at a table. Barrow, a human, was a barrel-shaped swordsman with partially bald, dark hair. Luc, a short and scrawny half-pint, wore a brown vest and a kilt. Half-pints preferred to be called halflings but no one ever called them by that name. Luc's bearskin cape was thrown on a bench along with his war hammer He was inordinately proud of his groomed, six-inch toe hair.

Tibbs, a spearman, looked bored while he watched the dice game. Bohan looked around the room. "Where are the others?"

"They didn't have any duties so they went into town," Barrow replied.

Bohan grabbed Bianca's forearm.

"Send a messenger to find the others and have them return immediately."

Bianca nodded and left the room. She was the sergeant of Bohan's heroes and second in command. She also kept the lists for the roster, guard duty and cooking assignments.

"What's up?" Tibbs asked. "We gonna get some action?"

"We'll get plenty of action. Jerado is marching on Sulvaria."

Bohan loved his heroes. Some, like Barrow, Bianca and Luc, he had met while on the tournament circuit. Tibbs and the others showed up as heroes looking for a job. Ansgar came to court with a reputation for honesty and a refusal to use magic to increase the riches of the privileged few.

Ferocious fighters all, Bohan and his heroes could change the outcome of a battle.

"Right now, I have to meet with my staff officers and put out a call for the militia. Prepare yourselves for battle."

Bohan left the room.

~ ~ ~

Gundarland was an unusual planet. Populated by numerous races such as humans, dwarfs, elves, halflings, trolls and yuks, racial tensions ran high in the more the conservative areas.

The largest land mass on the planet was also called Gundarland.

Religion played a part in many people's lives and the largest sect was Snotism. Snotists worshiped Gundar, the god who created the universe with a might sneeze after snorting His favorite recreational drug. Spittle flew through empty space and solidified into suns, planets and comets.

This event was called the Big Achoo by scientific authorities and was celebrated by Snotists with the Sacred Snot-fest. This ritual culminated in all the believers simultaneously inhaling crushed pepper to generate a giant sneeze that spread infectious diseases to an alarming extent.

Magic intrigued the population and wizards were held in high regard. Even incompetent wizards could make a decent living by bluffing their way though simple spells. Kings and dukes tended to appoint wizards as their principal advisors, a practice that often proved catastrophically wrong.

Historically, the country was carved into twenty-three small provinces ruled by kings and dukes and occasionally a madman. Sulvaria and Gant were two of those kingdoms. Waging war on their neighbors became the main occupation of most of the rulers. This led to high employment as each ruler strove to build a bigger army. Dwarf axe warriors were especially in high demand, and many clans prided themselves on loyalty to one ruler or another. These families pointed to generations of warriors fighting for a single royal family, ignoring how many of those warriors died unnaturally young.

Another part of the country was called Yuklandia. It occupied the southwestern corner. Yuks despised all other races and lived separate from the others in a land filled with marshes and mountains.

One city in Gundarland was different from all the others. Dun Hythe in the far north, was an open city and independent of all the kingdoms.

~ ~ ~

From Barrow's Journal: *Battle in the morning. Everyone has pre-battle jitters. Sword and dagger sharpened. Nothing to do but wait. I hate the wait.*

Bohan paced around his headquarters, a large tent. He expected to face battle in the morning. Candles provided light and threw grotesque shadows as the King walked around. Jerado's army was three miles away, and Bohan knew he'd see it lined up in battle formation when dawn broke. He wouldn't sleep tonight. The best he would be able to do was to lie down and rest for a short time.

Some of the heroes sharpened swords and axes while Bianca straightened the feathers on her arrows.

Angus and Maggy, dwarf axe warriors, sat together at the table and concentrated on ignoring each other. The two looked like identical twins although they weren't related. Both had long black hair, dark eyes, full beards and broad noses. The others insisted Maggy wear a colored ribbon in her beard so they could tell her apart from Angus. The heroes suspected that Angus occasionally wore the ribbon as a dwarfish joke.

Colbert, another half-pint, whittled a piece of wood with his assassin's blade. Colbert was also the bugler and sounded signals during battle.

Colbert put down his knife and picked up his bugle. He buffed it with his shirt sleeve, then blew a sour test note.

"Don't start in with that noise," Barrow snarled and shook a fist in Colbert's direction.

"Is this the guy you were talkin' about?" Luc asked. The half-pint berserker had been taking practice swings with his war hammer.

A tall, broad-shouldered man stood just inside the tent flap.

"Come in," Bohan said, "come in. Look everybody. Doesn't he resemble me?"

"He's not as ugly," Ansgar replied. He was the only hero who could openly insult the king.

The group chuckled.

"Hah! You should talk about being ugly, Ansgar," Bohan said as he clapped the stranger on the shoulder and tugged him closer to the table where he had his helmet. "Try it on."

The man slipped the helmet over his head and looked around. It covered most of his face and had a gold circlet on top representing a crown.

"Splendid," Bohan said. "With the helmet on, can any of you see that it's not me?"

The heroes tilted their heads, stood up for a better look and agreed they couldn't tell the stranger wasn't the king.

Fine," Bohan said. "You can take it off now. Tomorrow at dawn come back and get it to wear during the battle. My staff officers will give you directions on what to do."

The man bowed and departed.

"Is everyone clear on what we will do in the morning?" Bohan asked.

The heroes nodded and said, "Yes."

"Then we're all set for a victory tomorrow." Bohan smiled for the first time since the sun had set. "And the end of Jerado."

~ ~ ~

Jerado stood at his command post and watched the last of his troops form up in their battle line. Battalions of spearmen, dwarf axes, elven longbows and half-pint slingers filled the line. In the exact center, a company of released prisoners prepared to try to win a pardon through combat bravery.

His lines of soldiers stretched across a meadow and faced similar but thinner lines of Sylvarian troops. His right flank was anchored by a forest.

A squad of swordsman were posted nearby to protect Jerado as was a troop of lancers. Several mounted messengers awaited Jerado's orders.

Beyond the enemy battle line, Jerado saw Bohan sitting atop a horse. A number of aides stood with him. Bohan was easy to spot with his helmet and the gold crown attached to it. The helmet would make a nice addition to his memento collection, Jerado thought, with or without Bohan's head in it.

Jerado flapped a hand at a general who ordered a blast of trumpets and roll of drums to signal the start of the battle. Jerado's heart swelled with pride as he saw the soldiers step off and approach Bohan's stationary lines. He was sure the battle would be over in a few minutes. Then he would wreak havoc in Centi.

Instead, it dragged on. Bohan's army fought savagely and bravely and Jerado's troops weren't able to force a breakthrough. Jerado started to get bored and wondered if a few spells would speed things up. From the corner of his eye, he noticed a group of nine horsemen emerge from the forest and ride behind his lines.

Curious, he wondered where they

had come from and what they were doing. The horsemen rode straight toward Jerado. He glanced over the battle lines and saw Bohan still sitting on his horse.

With a jolt, he realized it was a false Bohan on the other side of the lines. The real Bohan had concealed himself in the forest and now charged toward his command post.

Jerado slapped an aide on the shoulder. "Tell the lancers to attack those horsemen. Be quick about it."

Within minutes, the lancers formed up and trotted forward.

Bohan saw the threat, stopped his horses and dismounted. The heroes spread out in a single line carrying shields and weapons.

Jerado chuckled. His lancers would skewer the whole lot. In one pass. Too bad he wouldn't be able to torture Bohan to death, but battles are unpredictable. As long as Bohan was dead, it didn't much matter how that came about.

The lancers rearranged themselves into four ranks of nine to match the number of enemy targets. The first rank increased speed as they neared Bohan and reached a full gallop just before impact. Bohan and the heroes raised their shields, tilted them to the right and awaited the lancers.

Jerado frowned. Something wasn't right. Why did Bohan just wait to get killed?

Jerado watched in disbelief as the lancers attacked and then screamed in agony. Two lances flew into the air and nine riders were knocked to the ground.

Bohan and his heroes stood untouched and awaited another charge. The second rank of lancers, determined to avenge their mates, charged Bohan.

Jerado shook his head. Another nine lancers ended up dismounted or wounded. A pile of bodies lay around Bohan. The heroes disentangled themselves and stepped forward a few paces to clear ground.

A third charge ended the same way as the first two.

The fourth rank of lancers turned their mounts and trotted away from Bohan.

Bohan's heroes caught their horses and jumped into the saddles. They spurred toward Jerado's location with swords, axes and spears dripping blood.

Jerado's guards quick-stepped in the opposite direction.

Behind Bohan and his heroes,

Jerado saw mounted soldiers emerge from the forest and attack his right flank from the rear. Already, that part of his army began to fall apart, his soldiers fleeing the mounted troops.

Knowing the battle was lost and facing an attack by Bohan, Jerado decided it was time to decamp. He cast a spell and disappeared.

Bohan reached Jerado's command post and looked around. "Ansgar! Where did he go?"

"He's either invisible," Ansgar replied, "a spell of concealment possibly, or he transported himself to someplace else. I'm guessing he transported."

"Wizards can do that?" Bohan asked.

"It is rumored that Rhinehard the Malodorous developed such a spell."

"Rumored?"

"Rumored. Rhinehard was murdered and his spell library stolen. Jerado is the most likely suspect and, if Rhinehard really had developed a transport spell, Jerado knows what it is."

Bohan looked at the battle lines. "We have to get out of here before the retreating soldiers overrun us." He turned his horse and rode back toward the trees, followed by the others.

Once they reached safety, Bohan said, "After we clean up the battlefield, we're going to hunt down Jerado. We'll start with his capital in Gant."

"Hey," Tibbs said, "ain't we gonna celebrate our victory inna tavern tonight?"

"We'll celebrate after we track down Jerado," Bohan replied. "We'll leave in the morning, so there won't be any tavern visits tonight."

Chapter Two

Jerado transported to a small valley in the Lestat Mountains in the northern part of Sulvaria. He knelt until the dizziness that accompanied a transport spell passed, then climbed out of the valley to reach the cave he used as his secret lair. Boulders and shrubs concealed the entrance and it could only be approached or seen from the east. The cave was also hidden from the road below that ran past the edge of the mountain.

Jerado was still shaken by his narrow escape from Ansgar and Bohan. He had left the battlefield only a minute or two before he would have been captured. Ansgar certainly was capable of casting a spell that would have incapacitated him and left him vulnerable to Bohan's weapons.

Jerado entered the cave, which was lit by an occasional torch fueled by magical spells. It was large and airy thanks to two natural air shafts. A fireplace filled part of the wall on the left. A padded chair sat in front of the fireplace. The back of the chair held a thick iron plate. To the right was a laboratory with a table filled with retorts, bottles and flasks, some full, some empty. Beyond the table was a shelf with supplies. In the rear, the cave opened up into more chambers that served as living quarters.

Jerado called out, "Remy! I'm back." He waited a few seconds and heard shuffling sounds as Remy emerged from the back.

"G . . . greetings, Master."

Remy was an undead half-pint. Jerado had come across Remy's freshly dead body by the side of a road and, on the spur of the moment, tried a reanimation spell he had recently learned. The spell worked and Jerado picked up a new servant, one that didn't have to be fed.

Remy was middle-aged, short, scrawny and bald. His head looked lopsided from the killing blow that partially caved in the left side. He wore a gray tunic and brown pants, both patched and stained. His toe hair had fallen out after his reanimation and had never grown back.

"D . . did you win the b . . .battle?" Remy asked.

"No, I lost and Bohan almost captured me. When word reaches Gant, someone will snatch my throne and the client kings will declare independence. So, my kingdom is no more. I must start anew. Before that, I need to develop a plan that includes getting rid of Bohan as the initial step. He'll try to take revenge on me for attacking Sulvaria. If he learns of my presence, he'll come after me, so I'll not be safe until Bohan and his wizard Ansgar are destroyed."

"I . . . I wish I c . . . could help," Remy said.

"Oh, you can. Hmm, do you have any lead and gold?"

"I . . . have some of each, but the apparatus is out of magic."

"Whatever plan I devise, it will require plenty of gold pennies to recruit mercenaries. So your first job is to produce gold pennies. As many as possible."

A wizard called Conrad the Shifty had developed a spell that, when used in conjunction with a bit of apparatus, could place a layer of gold on a base metal such as lead. Jerado had heard of the spell, tortured Conrad until he gave up the spell, then murdered the wizard.

To make the counterfeit gold

pennies, Remy used an iron press to form a slug of lead into an imitation of a real penny. Once the gold had been plated onto the lead copy, it passed for a real gold penny.

Throughout Gundarland, a gold penny equaled ten silver pennies and a silver penny equaled a hundred copper pennies. Copper pennies were the currency of the peasants, silver pennies were used by merchants and gold ones, by the nobility.

"Start making lead blanks. I'll cast a spell on the apparatus then I'm taking a nap. Losing a battle is tiring work."

~ ~ ~

At mid-morning on the next day, Bohan and the heroes mounted up to leave the battlefield to search for Jerado. Two squires cared for a spare mount for each of the group.

Bohan wanted to find Jerado before the wizard started more trouble. He knew the odds of finding Jerado were daunting, but he had to try.

"Tibbs," Bianca said, "You're the scout. Move out."

"I'm not feelin' all that good. Get someone else to scout."

"I will," Bianca said. "But it will be tomorrow. Today it's you. Move out."

Tibbs shot her a look of disdain and rode away from the others.

Once Tibbs was a half-mile in front, Bohan waved his arm for the heroes to follow.

During the second afternoon, Barrow, riding in advance of the others, paused as he crested a hill. He looked ahead briefly, then backed down from the top of the hill. When the rest of the heroes joined him, Barrow said, "Yuks. A big raidin' party. Goin' south, so probably headin' back to Yuklandia."

Yuks averaged five feet tall. They were heavily muscled, especially in the chest and arms. Green-skinned, they were bald but had tufts of black hair scattered randomly around their body. Their black, beady eyes exuded cruelty. Almost all yuks dressed the same: a pair of canvas pants held up by a rope and nothing else.

Bohan dismounted and climbed to the top of the hill to scout out the situation. He counted sixteen yuks. Each carried a sack on his back, an indication of a successful raid. Somewhere to the north there had to be ruined villages and a lot of dead people.

If this raiding party made it back home with bags of loot, it would encourage more yuks to make raids.

Bohan slid back down the hill.

"Bianca," he said, "take your squad and cut them off. I'll attack from their rear with my squad." Bianca's squad had three heroes besides herself: Tibbs, Barrow and Maggy. Bohan's squad had Ansgar, Colbert, Angus and Luc.

"They're in the middle of an open meadow," Bohan said, "so we'll have easy riding while we run them down." He pointed to the squires. "You two stay here with the spare mounts until it's over. Let's go."

Colbert brandished his bugle and looked at Bohan who shook his head.

"We don't need to warn them."

Bohan mounted up and led the heroes as they rode over the crest and started down the hill. At the bottom, Bianca took her squad on a different tack and increased speed while Bohan's group continued at a modest trot until she got into position.

A yuk saw the riders and gave an alarm. The raiding party broke into a run but they were too far from woods that would offer them a measure of protection.

Minutes later, Bianca's squad cut off the yuks and attacked while Bohan's squad charged from the rear.

The fight was over in less than two minutes. Afterward, the heroes dismounted and opened the leather sacks the yuks carried.

"Whoa!" Barrow exclaimed. "This bag is filled with treasure." He picked up a handful of coins and jewelry and held out his hand for the others to see.

"Hey, so is this one," Luc said.

"And this one," Angus added.

"Let's get the loot collected in one spot," Ansgar said, "so we can see what we have."

When the sacks were emptied, a substantial pile of treasure stared at the heroes. Coins, silver candlestick holders and jewelry glittered in the sun.

Ansgar held up a silver penny. "Minted in Gant," he said.

"We're rich," Maggy said. "Let's get it loaded on the horses."

"We can't take it with us," Bohan said. "Our saddle bags are filled with food and supplies. Even the spare mounts carry food. We'll have to leave the loot behind."

"What?" Colbert said. "You want us to abandon all this treasure?"

"Uh-uh." Bohan shook his head. "We'll bury it and pick it up on our way back when our saddle bags are empty. But we have to do it quickly. We need to find Jerado and we're wasting time."

"Findin' treasure ain't exactly wastin' time," Tibbs said.

"Angus! Maggy!" Bianca said. "Dwarfs are good at diggin'. Make a hole for us to bury the stuff in. Hide it good so no one sees it."

"I'll make a map," Ansgar said with a smile. "Just in case we forget where it is."

"As if!" Luc said.

"The rest of you spread out and stand guard," Bohan said. "If you see anyone approaching, scare them off. We don't need anyone seeing us bury the treasure."

Bohan was happy the yuk raiding party had been dispatched. It was one less group of lawless yuks to worry about, but he fretted about wasting time while Jerado was still free. He strode around the area with his hands behind his back until the treasure was buried and the site restored to look undisturbed.

"All right, mount up. We have work to do."

~ ~ ~

Near Gant's capital, Ansgar expanded his mind, hoping to detect a trace of Jerado's magical aura.

Bohan had initiated the search because of Ansgar's ability to detect Jerado's presence. All wizards emitted a magical aura that other wizards could detect — unless the aura was masked. Jerado's one weakness was that he hadn't learned about auras and how to mask them.

Ansgar thought back to his days at the University of Wizardry and Sorcery where he talked to Jerado for the first time. He had often seen the dwelf janitor mopping the floor outside a lecture. Jerado endlessly mopped a small patch of floor, seemingly just killing time.

One day, after a particularly knotty lecture, Ansgar remained behind in the back of the lecture hall to ponder a tricky spell characteristic. To his surprise, Jerado entered and took a seat in the front. He copied the lecture notes written on a blackboard into a small notebook.

Jerado heard a noise or sensed Ansgar's presence and turned around.

He glared at Ansgar, who got up, went forward and introduced himself. "Want to be a wizard, do you?" he added.

Jerado nodded. "But the university won't admit a dwelf, so I'm forced to learn the hard way, by overhearing lectures. Please, don't tell on me."

Ugly was the only word that could be used to describe Jerado. He had a broad, bulbous nose, heavy eyebrows, a square jaw and a pair of brown eyes that didn't quite move together. His lank reddish-blonde hair looked like it hadn't been washed in a long time.

Ansgar took note of the strength of Jerado's aura. He was surprised others hadn't noticed it or remarked on it. He knew students were full of themselves and didn't notice anything unless it affected them personally. As for the instructors, while they were all wizards, most of them had anemic magical powers. Perhaps they couldn't detect the strong aura emanating from the janitor. Either that or the instructors didn't care.

Ansgar concluded that Jerado hadn't attended the Wizards Academy, a mandatory pre-condition for acceptance to the university. One of its first lectures in the Academy covered how to mask the aura. This was essential if a wizard wanted to travel or live without other wizards discovering him.

"I won't tell on you." Ansgar pointed to the lecture notes. "A difficult lecture."

"Yes it is, but the part about the spell characteristic makes it all worth while."

"You understood that part?" Ansgar asked.

"Yes, I did," Jerado replied and proceeded to explain it in a way that was different from what the instructor said, yet easier to understand.

Ansgar marveled at Jerado's ability to comprehend complicated magical theory and concluded that some day Jerado would become a formidable wizard.

After that, the two often chatted but never became more than acquaintances.

Bohan interrupted Ansgar's reverie. "Can you pick up any trace of Jerado?"

"There's nothing here. Either he isn't in the area or he's found a place that shields him."

"Like what?"

Well, a cave would do that. Or a dungeon. If he's holed in such a place, I wouldn't be able to detect him."

"There are no mountains or caves around here and I doubt if there's a dungeon. Let's move on." Bohan waved his arm forward.

~ ~ ~

Jerado paced the cave searching for a plan to eliminate Bohan and Ansgar. He had been at it for a week. Finally, he said, "Remy, I need to work on something different to clear my mind. I think we'll try the experiment Ming the Unstable described in a scroll I obtained in Gant before I left to do battle. I'll set up the apparatus and you can mix the ingredients."

"A . . . All right, Master."

"Once you mix the ingredients, we'll place it outside in the sun and let the liquid evaporate. The residue in the bowl will be a powerful explosive, according to the scroll. We'll see if that is so. If it is, it could be a useful tool."

On the laboratory table, Jerado set out a mixing bowl half filled with a clear liquid, two small jars and a chunk of metal. "After I sit down I'll call out instructions to you." He went to the padded chair by the fireplace and moved it so the metal plate on the back faced the table. He sat in the chair and hunkered down so the plate protected his back and head. He opened the scroll and said, "Place two spoonfuls of white powder into the bowl and stir slowly and carefully until the powder is dissolved."

"D . . . Done."

"Now mix four spoonfuls of blue crystals into the bowl and stir until they dissolve."

"D. . . Done."

"Now, slowly and very carefully lower the piece of metal into the liquid."

"Y. . . Yes, Master. . . . Oops!"

Jerado heard a splash followed by the roar of an explosion. Bits of equipment, glass and wood splattered against the metal plate on the chair. A large chunk of table whizzed past his head and smashed into the cave's wall.

Ears ringing, Jerado sighed and waited for what he knew would happen next.

"M . . . master?"

"Yes, Remy?"

"C. . . Can you sew my hand back on my wrist?"

"Remy, Remy, Remy. You know how I hate doing mundane chores."

"B . . . but I can't clean up the mess with only one hand."

"That is true. All right, fetch a needle and thread and I'll repair your hand."

"A . . . And I need a new tunic. This one is in tatters."

Chapter Three

A frustrated Jerado groused at Remy and devised multiple plans only to discard them.

Toward the end of another week, Jerado told Remy, "Finally, I have a plan. One that will spell the end of Bohan and Ansgar. I hope."

"C . . . Can you tell me about it?" Remy held a new counterfeit gold penny.

"Before I found this cave, I used one further east, close to the sea coast. But it was too near a village at the base of the mountain. I was sure a villager would see me before too long. So I kept looking and found this one. My plan is to trick Bohan into that first cave and seal it up so that he's trapped. Yesterday, I went there and stocked the cave with supplies so I can stay awhile until I can lure Bohan to his death."

"G . . . Good plan, Master. I wondered where you went."

"The toughest part of the plan is how to get Bohan into the cave. To do that, I'll tell the people in that village that I may have seen the wizard Jerado.

They'll spread the word and it will reach the castle.   Once Bohan hears it, he'll coming running."

Jerado went to his living quarters and donned clothes that a traveler might wear: trousers and a linen shirt with a long cloak. He also carried a shoulder bag and a walking stick.

"I don't know how long I'll be away, Remy," Jerado said as he left the cave. He climbed down the mountain and turned east on the road that ran along the base of the mountain. By late afternoon he reached the village. Jerado went to the village's only tavern and rented a room.

That night at supper in the common room, Jerado engaged a villager in a chat. "I've been up north, but I heard there was a big battle around here recently."

"Aye," a middle-age man replied. "Sent an evil wizard packin', our King did."

"Killed the wizard, no doubt."

"Uh-uh," the man said. "The wizard got away. I heard the king is out lookin' for him right now. Wouldn't want to be that wizard when King Bohan gets him."

"Hmm," Jerado stroked his chin.

"Strange that. On my way here, I saw a man dressed in black up on the mountain. As I watched, the man disappeared. Into a cave, I'm sure. I wondered what the man could possibly be doing up there. You don't suppose it could be the missing wizard, do you?"

The man goggled at Jerado.

"Mind, I'm thinking a cave would be a good place to hide out for a while. Who would think of looking for that wizard in Sulvaria?"

"Be right back," the man said as he left the table and walked to the bar where several men stood drinking. The man returned with a second man in tow. "This is the bailiff. Tell him what you told me."

Jerado repeated his story.

"Sounds right," the bailiff said. "It would be a good place to hide out. I hear the King is out ridin' west figurin' Jerado would go back to his kingdom. Where did you say you saw the man?"

"Up the side of the mountain," Jerado replied. "I was about a quarter-mile from here when I saw him." Jerado pointed to the west. "It was by an oak tree that had been blasted by lightning. If you went there and watched, you may see him going in and out of the cave."

"I know where that tree is. I'll get one of the lads to go watch while I send a message to the castle in Centi."

After spending the night in the village, Jerado left and made his way to the cave where he intended to spend time puttering around outside the cave hoping someone would see him. That should increase the credence in his story that a wizard was living in a cave.

Jerado made himself comfortable in the cave. He was sure Bohan would take the bait. The only question was how long it would take.

~ ~ ~

From Barrows Journal: *Exhausted. Almost too tired to write in this journal. Not used to riding all day, every day for weeks. Damn that Jerado. I hope we find him just to see him get killed for making us take this journey. May fall asleep and topple out of the saddle.*

Bohan fought to keep his eyes open and stay in the saddle. So did the heroes. After fifteen days of riding around southern Gundarland, they hadn't found a trace of Jerado. All they could show for their efforts was wasted time and worn-out horses. Their saddle bags were empty of food, forcing them to hunt and scrounge for food, wasting even more time.

Except for Tibbs who complained about his health, the heroes were quiet, an indication of their state of exhaustion. If they were in a good shape, they would be singing, insulting each other and telling stories, mostly made up of exaggerations about their exploits. The heroes were mad at Sergeant Bianca with her never-ending duty rosters, and they were also mad at Barrow, the quartermaster, for running out of food. Barrow's response was that the heroes were all gluttons who ate too much.

With nothing else left to do, Bohan planned to pick up the buried treasure, go back to Centi and hope someone had news about Jerado.

"Rider comin'," Bianca called out. The elf sergeant had the best eyesight in the group.

Bohan turned in his saddle and looked at her. Bianca pointed to her right. Bohan raised a hand to shield his eyes from the sun and saw a lone rider pounding down a slight rise toward them.

Within minutes, the rider pulled up

and addressed Bohan. "Lord, I'm glad I found you. We have a dozen messengers out looking for you."

"Why?" Bohan asked. "What's the message?"

"We know where Jerado is hiding."

"Where is he?" Bohan's exhaustion disappeared.

"He's hiding in a cave in the Lestat Mountains just north of the village of Abona."

"And you're sure it's Jerado?"

The messenger patted his horse's neck. "The town bailiff reported a strange man dressed all in black has been seen several times entering and leaving a cave. Who else could it be but Jerado?"

Bohan sensed a trick. This was too easy. Why would a powerful wizard be living in isolation? And in Sulvaria? The Lestat Mountains formed Sulvaria"s northern border. And what would a bailiff in a small village know about Jerado?

"What do you think, Ansgar?"

"It sounds plausible," Ansgar replied. "We should check it out, even knowing it may not be Jerado."

"Why would Jerado still be in Sulvaria?" Bohan asked. "That doesn't make sense."

"Jerado is wily," Ansgar said. "With him, one has to expect the unexpected."

Bohan frowned and thought through his options. The list wasn't very long. "All right. Let's ride to Abona and see who is living in that cave."

"What about the treasure? Tibbs asked. "We gotta go get it."

"We'll get it later," Bohan replied. "It's not going anywhere. It can wait."

~ ~ ~

Before reaching the village, Bohan sent the spare mounts and the squires back to Centi. He and his heroes rode into Abona to the shock of the villagers who never thought they would ever see a king. After listening to the bailiff's story, the villager led them to the place where the stranger was spotted.

"Right up there." The bailiff pointed vaguely up the side of the mountain. "A couple of my watchers have seen this guy all in black. We see him early inna mornin' and just before sunset. Just walkin' around, he was."

"Describe him," Ansgar said.

"Umm, medium height and build, red or maybe blonde hair and beard."

"He has a cave up there?" Bohan asked. He was tense with anticipation.

"Guess so," the bailiff muttered. "Where else would he stay?"

"No one went up there to check on this stranger?" Bohan glared at the bailiff.

"If it is a powerful wizard up there, he'd change us into toads if we came close."

"The bailiff is right." Ansgar placed a hand on Bohan's forearm. "Ordinary folk have no business dealing with wizards. That's for us to do."

Bohan sighed. "My apologies," he told the bailiff. "We'll take it from here. Thank you for you service. Give your name to Bianca. She's the elf archer. We'll send you a reward when we get back to Centi."

Once the bailiff returned to town, the group spread out in a line and climbed the side of the mountain. Bohan and Ansgar walked together in the middle.

"Clever bugger, this Jerado," Bohan said. "Who'd ever think he would hide out in Sulvaria?'

"Jerado is very clever," Ansgar replied. "That's why this smells like it could be a trap. It isn't like him to let himself be seen by locals, even if it is from a distance. I wouldn't be surprised if he tricked us into wasting time while he goes about his business elsewhere."

"Do you think it was Jerado the locals saw?"

"Oh, yes. I can sense that Jerado was here. Or maybe is still here. Can't tell which."

Barrow, at the right side of the line, waved his arms. When Jerado and Ansgar looked at him, Barrow pointed to a spot close by where he stood.

When they joined Barrow, they saw a cave hidden below the crest of a small rise.

"Ahh," Ansgar said in a whisper. "The villagers couldn't see the cave from down below. I doubt if Jerado is inside, but let me go first. If he is in there, there's going to be a spell fight."

The wizard lit a torch and climbed to the cave's entrance. He paused and listened for a short time, then crouched and entered the cave. After a minute, he reemerged and waved Bohan forward.

Bohan entered the cave followed by the rest. Light from the entrance illuminated a few feet of the cave. The rest was in darkness except for a puddle of light from Ansgar's torch.

"Jerado definitely was in here," Ansgar said.

The cave held remnants of meals, a few bottles and mysterious pieces of apparatus.

"He must have been conducting research," Ansgar added.

"If this is how wizards live," Luc said, "I'm glad I'm a berserker."

"It's not a very big cave." Bohan thought Ansgar was correct. Jerado had tricked them into wasting time. He made a face in frustration.

"No it isn't very big" Ansgar replied. "I checked the rear and it doesn't go very far back."

The sound of a rolling rock filled the cave and the light from the entrance disappeared.

"What happened?" Bohan turned to see the entrance blocked by a boulder. He took a few steps and hurled his shoulder against the rock. The others joined him. No matter how hard they heaved, the rock didn't budge.

From outside the cave, they heard laughter. "Good-bye, my friend Ansgar. The rock is sealed by a spell I developed especially for this occasion. You'll never get out of the cave. Have a nice death."

"Dig," Bohan ordered as he pulled

out his sword and attempted to dig under the rock. Others joined him.

"It's no use," Colbert said. "The cave floor is solid rock. We'll never be able to dig out."

"Great," Angus said. "Our choices are to starve, die from thirst or kill ourselves."

"Drat!" Maggy stamped her foot. "I don't like those choices."

"Hmm," Ansgar said. "There is another choice."

"What's that?" Bohan asked.

"I can devise a sleep spell that will last as long as the cave's entrance is blocked. Once the entrance is open, we'll wake up."

"How long'll that take?" Bianca asked.

Ansgar shrugged in the dying light from his torch. "Who knows, but it gives us a chance to survive. Best find a spot to lie down while my torch is still lit."

"Sleepin' on a rock floor is gonna kill my bad back," Tibbs said.

"I think Ansgar's spell is our best option," Bohan said. "It gives us a chance to fight another day." He sat down with his back to the wall of the cave. "Do it, Ansgar. I only hope that when we get out of here, Jerado is still alive. I want to return the favor."

~ ~ ~

Jerado couldn't believe his luck. Bohan and Ansgar both searched for the cave. And the heroes also. Sitting under a pine tree and waiting had paid off. He'd spent the time devising new spells and planning his conquest of Gundarland. Except for when he wanted to be seen, a simple ward of concealment kept other eyes from noticing his presence. Now, he was about to eliminate his archenemies. He fought the urge to giggle.

A spearman passed within ten feet of Jerado and didn't see him. Jerado experienced exhilaration for the first time when Ansgar entered the cave. Jerado waited with bated breath until Bohan and the others entered. He sprang up and hastened to the cave. He pushed the boulder and rolled it until it blocked the entrance. Jerado chanted a spell of sealing and the job was done. He danced a few steps and laughed.

Jerado leaned forward and shouted, "Good-bye, my friend Ansgar. The rock is sealed by a spell I developed especially for this occasion. You'll never get out of the cave. Have a nice death."

He transported back to his lair and entered the cave.

"M . . Master! You've returned," Remy said.

"Indeed. My plan worked to perfection. The king and his wizard are no more. Neither are his heroes."

"C . . . . Congratulations."

"Thank you, Remy. By the way, exhilaration is overrated. I much prefer annoyance. But, to business, how many gold coins did you make?"

"I . . . . have thirty-nine."

"Wonderful. I can hire an army of mercenaries with that many coins. I'll be back in Gant in a matter of weeks."

Jerado sat down in the chair by the fireplace. "Fetch me a glass of wine."

When Remy returned with the wine, Jerado said, "Do you remember how to write?"

"I th . . . think so."

"Good. I want you to practice. When I return to Gant, you will go with me. I have a job for you."

Jerado closed his eyes and sipped the wine. Remy would be an ideal foil to handle the many demands for appointments with the king. His undead synapses still worked, but they worked slowly. So slowly, that Remy would try the patience of many of the people hoping to secure their fortunes by impressing a king. Jerado was sure many of them would leave in disgust rather than deal with Remy.

The last obstacle to his plans had been removed. Now, he could go back to working on conquering other kingdoms and becoming the King of Gundarland.

Part Two: Time to Hit the Road

Chapter Four

"Hey!" Barrow snarled. "Put out the candle! I'm tryin' to sleep!"

"Wait a minute," Angus said as he yawned. "It's not a candle. It's moonlight. The rock is gone!"

Gradually, Bohan and the others awoke. He and Ansgar inspected the opening.

"The shelf the boulder rested on fell away," Ansgar said. "That's why the cave is unsealed. We're free!"

"How long have we been in here?" Maggy asked.

"That we can't tell," Bohan replied, "but it must be a long time. That small village at the bottom of the mountain is now a town." He pointed to the many houses illuminated by an almost full moon.

"My back is killin' me from sleepin' on the rock floor," Tibbs said.

"Oh, shut up," Bianca said. "I don't wanna hear your whinin' this early in the mornin'."

Bohan looked back at his heroes.

All were incredibly shaggy, except Bianca. Their full beards covered their stomachs and their hair flowed in all directions and reached below their shoulders. He touched his own beard and discovered it was the same as the others.

"I could use a beer," Luc said.

"I could use some food," Colbert added. "I feel like I haven't eaten anythin' in years."

"Let's go into the town and find a place to eat," Barrow said.

"No! We can't do that." Bohan's mind filled with confusion. He knew they had spent years in the cave. Had anything changed? If so, what? Were they still in Sulvaria, or had that country become something else? How could they find out?

"Why can't we?" Barrow asked.

"We don't how things have changed," Bohan replied. "We're armed, which may not be allowed anymore. Our clothes are surely outdated and our coins may not be any good."

"We got weapons," Tibbs said, checking his spear. "We can go inna town and take what we need."

"Stealing is stupid, Tibbs," Ansgar said.

"What are we gonna do?" Bianca said. "We need a plan."

"Hmm." Bohan ran a hand through his beard. "The coast isn't far away. Let's go there. There is — or was — a road there. We can say we got off a boat if we come across anyone."

He thought the rationale was weak and not very convincing, but it was the best he could do with a mind still foggy from sleep.

"I need feathers," Bianca said. "None of my arrows are any good 'cause the feathers fell apart."

"How are we gonna get food?" Colbert asked.

"Perhaps I can trap some fish with a spell," Ansgar replied.

"All right, let's move out." Bohan stepped out of the cave. "Single file. I'll lead. Try not to make too much noise in case someone is awake in the town. They may sound an alarm, and we want to stay out of sight until we understand the situation we're in."

"I wonder what year it is?" Ansgar asked.

That was another good question, Bohan mused. How long had they been trapped in the cave? What happened to Sulvaria in that time? He doubted if he was still considered the king, but who had taken his place? What would happen if he suddenly showed up at the palace? And where was Jerado?

So many questions!

~ ~ ~

In order to appear accessible, President Jerado began a process that allowed citizens to petition for a short private audience with him. Applicants could apply for an audience once every two weeks.

To ensure that no one was ever granted an audience, Jerado put Remy in charge of the interview process.

Remy entered the interview room on the first floor of the Presidential Palace. Along the way, he walked past two pike-carrying guards. The small, drafty room was lined with benches on three sides broken only by the door the petitioners used.

Remy walked to the desk in the front of the room and sat down. At Jerado's insistence that he look presentable, he wore a rust-colored robe over his threadbare, heavily-patched clothes. He glanced around. Most of the applicants had been here a few times before.   He noticed two new ones and pointed a finger at one. The man moved forward and stood by the desk.

Remy questioned the man and wrote his name and address on a sheet of paper. He wrote the runes very slowly and precisely, more slowly than he normally would. The objective of the process was to get people to leave in disgust because of the delays.

"W . . . hat do you want to talk to the President about?" Remy asked.

"I've developed a way to make inexpensive cloth. I want to build a factory and I'll need steam engines. If I can get the President's approval, I'll be able to get bank loans and the steam engines."

Steam engines, recently developed, were a government monopoly.

"H . . . have a seat. Next?"

A young dwarf presented himself in front of the desk. After stating his name, he said, "I just graduated from college and I'm hoping for a job."

"W . . . what did you study?"

"Art and literature."

"W . . . hat type of job are you looking for?"

"I don't care. Anything that pays

well and has decent hours."

"H . . . ave a seat." Remy picked
up the two applications and started to
stand when the door burst open and a
tall, obese man in a green cassock
entered. "I demand an audience with
the President." He strode to the desk
and glared at Remy. "Immediately. I'm
a busy man."

"N . . . ame?"

"I am Bishop Connors of the
Snotish Church. Where is the
President?"

"W . . . hat do you want to see him
about?"

"I don't discuss church business
with minions. Are you dead?"

"I . . . 've been dead for a long
time."

"The Snotist Church has vowed to
destroy abominations like you."

"Th . . . ank you for sharing that.
W . . . hat do you wish to discuss with
the President?"

The bishop growled under his
breath and said, "I wish to build a temple
in town and it's the government's job to
fund the construction."

Remy wrote the information on a
paper, stood up and left the room.

He went to his office on the fifth

floor. Sitting at his desk he filled out two forms and then played a few games of Tic-Tac-Toe. Playing the "X's", he lost a seven game tournament four games to one.

After a while, he returned to the room and pointed to three folks who had been there before. "T . . . he President has denied your requests for audiences. You may leave."

He beckoned to the inventor and said, "H . . . ere is an authorization to buy steam engines. T . . . his is a grant of twenty-five silver pennies to help you along."

"What about me?" the bishop demanded.

"T . . . he President is considering your request. H . . . e wants to see a plot plan and an estimate of construction costs."

"What! I don't have either of those documents."

"W . . . ell, you have two weeks to get them before the next audience session. O . . . therwise, your audience request will be denied."

Remy then announced, "The President will not hold any audiences today. P . . . lease leave and return in two weeks if you wish."

'More bureaucratic nonsense." The bishop took a step toward the door by the guards. "Where is he? I'll see him now."

"T . . . he guards will prevent you from passing through the door."

"Nonsense! I'm a bishop. My person is inviolate"

"G . . . o near the door and the guards will use their pikes. T . . . hey don't care who you are."

The bishop left, barging past the folks crowding around the door.

Remy watched him and grinned. He planned to jerk the bishop around for months; the young college graduate not so long.

Remy loved his job.

~ ~ ~

Jerado hated his job.

Running a large country was tedious and demanded an excessive amount of time dealing with petty issues. He, a wizard *extraordinaire*, spent time with greedy citizens looking to get a free government handout.

Back when he first entered Dun Hythe at the head of a victorious army and declared himself King, it was different. Back then the job was fun: unlimited power and endless opportunities to steal money. But that was 196 years ago and after a while, robbing people became uninteresting. Besides, the five jail cells in the Palace dungeon were filled with his loot and couldn't be used to house prisoners. To his surprise, he discovered there was a limit to how much he wanted to steal. He preached that lesson to his two children, but they ignored him.

He wore a black silk hooded robe with a yellow sunburst on his left breast. The sunburst had no symbolic meaning, but Jerado liked it and it kept people guessing about its meaning.

The anti-aging spell he used every month kept him alive for the most part. Facially, he looked like a forty-five year old; physically, he was a wreck because the spell was defective. All his teeth had fallen out years ago and he now used a set of ill-fitting wooden dentures. He was bald and wore a cheap reddish-blonde wig that often slipped if he turned his head suddenly. It also had a tendency to take flight in a breeze. His knees were creaky and often ached, and his eyesight had deteriorated.

Seventy years ago, he had

abolished the kingship and became the President, re-elected every ten years by a small group of very rich voters who owed their wealth — and their health — to Jerado.

He entered a richly appointed combination dining and sitting room. Off to one side, a large fireplace was built into the wall. A chair and a couch sat in front of the fire. Light came from three large chandeliers holding a hundred lit candles each. The table, covered by a spotless linen cloth, could seat a dozen. Only three place settings were laid out in the middle, a single setting on one long side of the table and two settings opposite.

His son Lithgow, and his daughter, Flavia sat at the table sipping wine and frowning at each other. The dinner was a weekly event.

Both children appeared to be around thirty even though both were over seventy years old. On their thirtieth birthdays, Jerado had taught them the anti-aging spell.

Despite having a family, Jerado had learned the meaning of loneliness. As ruler, he had no friends, only acquaintances. He had no one to confide in except Remy, and confiding in an undead wasn't exactly therapeutic.

Once he had settled down in Dun Hythe, he was surprised to learn it was much more liberal than Centi and the other provinces down south. No one cared a bit about inter-racial relationships and he used it to his advantage.

Lithgow's mother was a dwarf mistress, and he had many dwarfish features such as the broad nose, short and bulky build and thick, dark hair and beard. Today he wore the uniform of the elite Victory Regiment, spearmen unit. It consisted of a dark blue tunic and tan pants with calf-high leather boots. Lithgow was Gundarland's Minister of War.

Flavia's mother was an elf and, like her mother, she was tall and slender, with pale green hair and eyes. She wore a yellow gown with green slippers. Her long silver hair was done up in a single braid that reached half-way down her back. Flavia was the Secretary of the Interior.

Long ago, Jerado had decided to retire after ruling for two hundred years. He planned to appoint one of his children as his successor and that presented a problem: Whom to select? Both Lithgow and Flavia were poor choices. And there were other issues to be addressed. How would he extricate himself from the government? Where would he live? What would he do? How would he get his stolen treasure out of the Palace dungeon without being seen?

After a quiet dinner, Jerado said, "Well, Lithgow, what have you been up to in the last week?"

"I'm almost finished with the design of a new uniform for my archer regiments."

Flavia laughed. "Such a warrior!"

Lithgow scowled at his half-sister.

Jerado kept a stolid expression as he despaired of Lithgow ever achieving anything meaningful. His only ambition was to start a war and become a famous general. He nagged Jerado to let him invade Yuklandia, the only country in reach of his army. Jerado was sure the yuks would destroy Lithgow's forces and invade Gundarland in retaliation.

"And you, Flavia?" he asked.

"Soon we'll have the inaugural run of the peat train from Yuklandia. I've arranged a big ceremony to take place when it arrives here."

"Wonderful," Lithgow said, "only two years overdue."

Flavia turned on Lithgow. "For your information, it's the first time anyone ever put a steam engine on wheels. We had to make a separate road for the engine. That's why it took so long."

"Poor planning I say," Lithgow retorted.

Flavia glared at her half-brother.

Jerado observed the difference between his two children. Lithgow worked on small, inconsequential projects while Flavia attacked and conquered huge problems. Steam engines had been developed ten years ago. The big problem with the engines was fuel. Cutting down forests wasn't the answer, but peat was. The only substantial peat deposits were in Yuklandia, and wagon carts took two weeks to haul a load of peat to the city. During that time, the mules ate more food than the peat was worth. Flavia had solved the problem, although it turned into a complicated and expensive project. It was made more expensive because of her greed. She typically padded all contracts by at least twenty percent and stole the padded amount.

Lithgow also padded his contracts but his grafts were tiny compared to

Flavia's.

What they had in common was hatred. They hated each other and always had. Jerado often thought if he had more children he would have probably killed himself a long time ago.

"Anything else?" Jerado asked.

"Oh," Flavia replied. "There was an earthquake down south last night."

"Where.?"

"North of Centi, in the Lestat Mountains. I received a scryer message from the governor"

"Was anyone hurt?" Lithgow asked.

She shook her head. "No one was killed or injured and no property damage has been reported."

The news about the earthquake touched a nerve in Jerado, but he didn't understand why.

~ ~ ~

After dinner, Jerado returned to his office in the top floor of the Presidential Building. The area was quiet and empty except for Remy's office. As Jerado's chief-of-staff, Remy had a large corner office with interior windows facing Jerado's desk. Remy rarely left the office and Jerado suspected he often slept at his desk.

Jerado passed Remy's office and said, "Come." He entered the Presidential Suite, pulled off his wig and tossed it on the sofa. Next he sat at his desk, stuck a hand in his mouth, took out his dentures and put them on the desk.

When Remy approached, he said, "Flavia has a report of an earthquake last night in the Lestat Mountains north of Centi. Why does that bother me?"

"P . . . erhaps because people were hurt?"

"No, that's not it. No one was hurt. Even if folks were hurt or killed, that wouldn't bother me."

Remy snapped his fingers. "T . . . hat area was where you had a cave a long time ago."

"Ahh, that's right."

"A . . . nd where you trapped Bohan and the others."

Jerado smiled at the memory Remy had conjured up. "Of course. That's what bothered me. An earthquake might have unsealed the cave."

"I . . . s that a danger to you?"

"No, not at all. Bohan is long dead. Even if the cave is open and someone finds it, all they'll see are bones. Maybe they'll be able to identify Bohan from his armor and weapons, but who cares about him after all this time?"

Jerado stood up. "Thank you, Remy. I'm going to bed. Freshen up the wig and clean my dentures."

"Y . . . es, Master."

I'll see you in the morning."

~ ~ ~

From Barrow's Journal: *Horse and saddle gone, naturally. Most of my armor also. Still have my journal, but the ink is faded and can hardly be read. Can't write because the ink bottle dried up and the quills fell apart. Fortunately, Bianca bought ink and quills in town.*

By the time they reached the coast, the sun had risen.

Black boulders and driftwood sculptures in fantastic shapes festooned the sand-covered beach. Lines of seaweed marked the last few high-tides and squadrons of seagulls soared and squawked while on their food patrols

Ansgar used a spell to attract fish and trap them in a shallow tidal pool. While the fish cooked, the heroes hacked away at their beards and hair and pared their nails. Colbert found a stream with clear water and they washed away unknown years of dust.

With the meal finished, they walked south toward the village that had grown into a town. Bohan worried about not knowing how a group of warriors would be received. Would they be attacked or welcomed?

"At least we know it's spring," Colbert said pointing to a field of blue wildflowers.

"Suddenly, you know about flowers?" Tibbs sneered.

"I know these blue ones only blossom in spring," Colbert retorted.

"Colbert is correct," Ansgar said. "Now that we know the season, it would be nice to also know the year."

They walked a few miles on the dirt road that followed the coast line with Bianca a hundred paces in front because of her great eyesight.

She climbed a steep hill and suddenly stopped once she could see over the top. She walked backwards and signaled to the others to stop.

Bohan trotted forward followed by Ansgar while the others sat down.

"Someone's comin'," Bianca said.

"A woman. By herself."

Bohan thought for a moment then ordered, "Everyone stay here, out of sight. Bianca and I will talk to the woman."

He unstrapped his war belt with its sword and dagger and dropped it to the ground. He removed his helmet and greaves.

"Leave your bow and arrows behind," he told Bianca.

"Might as well," she replied. "All I can use the arrows for is to stab someone."

Together they breasted the hill and approached the woman, who was only a short distance away. In the distance, not too far away, the town shimmered with smoke from cooking fires.

When the woman came closer, Bohan noticed she was tall and pudgy and dressed in a tan shirt and pants with heavy boots. She had a muscular build, brown hair cut short and azure colored eyes. She carried a hefty truncheon in a holster on her waist and wore a white sash over her shoulder.

"Good morning," Bohan said. "My name is Bohan and this is Bianca."

The woman stopped and examined them before responding. "I'm Leticia.

I'm the constable for this area. Where did you come from? How did you get way out here? I think I would have noticed if you passed through Abona on your way north."

"We're, er, travelers. We and our companions were on a quest in a foreign country for many years and we just returned yesterday. The . . . boat captain landed us on the coast back there."

Bohan pointed to the north.

"Why did he do that?" Leticia made a face. "Why didn't he drop you off further south in the port of Centi?"

"Well, er, that was the plan. But the captain saw another ship and believed it was a pirate. So he dumped us on the coast."

"And," Bianca added, "he didn't give us any food or water. May he die a horrid death."

"That's terrible." Leticia shook her head. "You can get food in town. Do you have money?"

"We have some old coins, but I don't know if they're any good," Bohan said. "Besides, I don't think we should go into town. We're a war band, you see. The rest of my warriors are on the other side of the hill."

"How many? And what country did you come from?" Leticia had a worried look on her face.

"There are nine of us and we came from, er, Q'aundum."

"Where is that? I never heard of it."

"Far away," Bianca replied. "Across the ocean and past a vast desert."

Bohan gave her a fleeting smile.

"Well, let's get the rest of you here and let me take a look. Then we can decide what to do."

Bohan whistled and soon the rest of the heroes assembled around the king, who introduced them to Leticia.

"Oh my," Leticia said, "a rough looking group. If you walk into Abona, the people will panic, thinking it's a bandit raid."

"That's our problem, you see," Bohan said. "But we need supplies."

Leticia pulled a face. Hands on hips, she tapped a toe while she thought. Finally she said, "Let me see your coins. Perhaps I could buy some food for you."

Bohan took out a gold coin from a pouch on his hip and handed it to her.

Leticia examined it. "This is old, but it's still a gold penny. I should be able to use it. Let's get closer to town so

I don't have to lug the food too far. I know a stand of trees where you can stay and no one from town will see you."

"I'll go with you," Bianca said. "I'll help you carry back the supplies."

Bohan felt a heavy load lift off his shoulders. Leticia must have been sent by the gods.

Chapter Five

The Godmother entered the conference room for her weekly staff meeting and everyone stood as a sign of respect. She sat down at the head of the table and flapped a hand. Everyone sat down and made themselves comfortable. A servant placed a cup of tea in front of her.

The Godmother was a middle-aged elf, slender, with green partially gray hair and green eyes. She had been the Godmother for ten years. Her mother and grandmother had been Godmothers before her. Her claim on the position came from both lineage and talent. She had learned pickpocketing at the age of five and assassination at fifteen.

The Godmother looked around the table at her seven executives, checking to see if anyone seemed nervous, a sign of incipient betrayal. They all seemed calm. All were elves, except for one half-pint.

"Let's get started," she said. "Vinny, what's going on?"

Vinny cleared his throat. He was muscular and wore his brown hair in a crewcut. He ran two local guilds in the city.

"Ain't got any big problems. The Pickpocket Guild has an openin' 'cause one of the members got run over by a wagon, so one of the territories ain't got anyone servicin' the clients and now I gotta recruit another pickpocket."

Everyone chuckled over his use of the word 'servicing' to depict stealing. The Guild assigned territories to each member. The more lucrative ones went to pickpockets with talent and seniority. Becoming an authorized pickpocket was a coveted position. A new recruit started in a poor territory and, over time, moved into richer ones.

"The Brotherhood of Assassins," Vinny continued, "completed a big contract the other day. They whacked a rich banker at the request of another banker."

"I saw that in the morning broadsheet," the Godmother said, "and wondered if it was a natural death or one of our jobs."

The Godmother pointed to a female elf. "Gina, tell us about Special Services."

Gina smiled at the staff. She wore a light blue revealing dress, had ruby red lipstick and long hair colored blonde with streaks of purple.

"The brothels are working full bore. Gambling had a great week, thanks to a maritime convention the city had. It brought in a lot of heavy gamblers. The saloons are doing all right, but we don't get many locals anymore 'cause of the wage restrictions. Workers can't afford to drink in our saloons any more."

Gina referred to the wage restrictions enacted by the Secretary of the Interior. The restrictions affected the working poor more than anyone else. Wage restrictions for workers had been enacted years ago, but Flavia had recently lowered the allowable wage to a draconian level.

"Sal?" The Godmother said.

Sal was in charge of security and enforcement. His face was a mess of scars and permanent bruises.

"Had a welsher last week. Fell behind on his loan payments. He's caught up now, but he needs crutches to get around. We caught another government agent tryin' to infiltrate us. He ain't a problem anymore."

"I suppose it was Flavia again?" the

Godmother asked.

"Yeah, the guy was from the Interior Department."

The Godmother pointed to Luigi, the head of accounting and tax dodges. He had slicked back blue hair and wore a black expensive silk suit and tie.

"I don't really have anything to report. Revenues are steady as are profits, except for liquor sales as Gina explained."

"We may have to do something about these wage restrictions," the Godmother said. "If folks don't have money to buy a drink, things have gone too far. Pierre?"

Pierre was a half-pint. They made the best lawyers and Pierre was the best of the best. Only his luxurious toe hair with diamond and gold brooches told of his status as a rich lawyer.

"The case against two of Sal's workers for murder has been thrown out of court thanks to a legal technicality I uncovered."

"That's why we pay you so much, Pierre," the Godmother said. "Rocco, what's up with the government?"

Rocco was in charge of government coordination, a fancy name for lobbying and interference. He was handsome and smiled a lot.

"On the local level, the City Council wants permission to close off a section of road in the middle of town to replace some old water pipes. It'll disrupt some of Vinny's pickpocket operations. I told the Council I'd get back to them."

"How long will it take?" Vinny asked.

"About a week the Council says, but they don't know what they're talking about. It could be a few days or a few weeks."

"We should let the work take place," the Godmother said. "We need to maintain water supplies. Rocco, tell the Council they can do the work, but they have to compensate the Guild for lost wages. Get a number from Vinny. What about the President?"

"Jerado is quiet and hardly ever gets seen anymore. Nothing new there. Flavia's Interior Department is all excited about the peat train we keep hearing about. Lithgow supposedly has designed another new uniform. That's about it."

"What about that guy from Treasury? What's his name . . . Maurice? Did we ever get any dirt on him?"

"Maurice Girard," Rocco said. "We can't find anything on him to use. All we got is the usual background stuff. He graduated from Dun Hythe University with degrees in wizardry and finance. He's a member of the Wizards Guild. He went to work inna Palace right after graduation and gotta lot of promotions. Now he's the Treasurer. Oh, and the bankers hate him. He keeps breaking their chops. The guy is clean."

"Well, he can't be an honest bureaucrat." The Godmother pulled a face. "There's no such thing. I don't want to meet with him as equals. I need an advantage. Something to threaten him with. Keep on digging."

"Vito, what's going on with the docks?" the Godmother asked.

Vito looked like a brawler. He was large, heavy and scarred. He ran the Maritime Guild, the largest one in Gundarland. Its members worked the docks, built and repaired ships and crewed the cargo ships that used the port. He also ran the Teamsters and the Laborers Guilds

"Everything is pretty quiet," Vito replied.

The Godmother turned to the last member of her staff, her daughter Sophia. "Anything to add?"

Sophia was beautiful and talented.

In her early twenties, she was already tagged as the next Godmother. A year before, she had graduated from Dun Hythe University with a master's degree in business planning. Prior to that, she had served in the Pickpocket's Guild, tended bar in a saloon, dealt poker at a table and passed the Brotherhood of Assassins initiation course.

"You all know I think we should invest and branch out into legitimate activities. We have excess cash that isn't growing or even earning interest. I'm working on a strategic business plan that I should be able to present to you in about a month."

"I'm looking forward to seeing it," the Godmother said, "as we all are." She glared at the others, daring them to make a negative comment. She knew Sophia's concerns on legitimate businesses made most of the executive staff very nervous.

The Godmother nodded to the others as an indication that the meeting was over.

While Jerado ruled Gundarland, the Godmother ruled Dun Hythe.

Jerado possessed an overwhelming military force and could wipe out the Godmother's family at any time. The

Godmother possessed an overwhelming economic force that could drive the city and even the country into a crisis. She could call a general strike that would cripple Dun Hythe. The port would close down; the wagon drivers would stop driving. Carts filled with goods would pile up on the docks and on the roads leading to the city once the city's gates were blocked by the workers. The strike's ripple effect would spread through the country causing misery everywhere.

The Godmother and Jerado co-existed in an uneasy peace. Jerado kept his soldiers outside the city wall, except for palace guards, and the Godmother kept the workers quiet and the city functioning.

~ ~ ~

When Dun Hythe was nothing more than a muddy fishing village, the first elves came from a forest and settled down to sell fish. Later, these elves became the forerunners of what would be know as urban elves.

The small village was lawless and the inhabitants used their own initiative to settle disputes or crimes. A female elf noted that a few of the half-pints earned a living by picking the pockets of the folks who came to buy fresh fish. She also noted that a few strong-armed men bullied the fishermen into giving them fish in return for not destroying the boats.

Since the elf had a few strong sons, she decided other businesses could be more lucrative than selling fish. Her sons, all experts with longbows and daggers, eliminated the bullies and cowed the fishermen into paying protection to keep other bullies away.

She also organized the pickpockets, assigned operational areas to each one and offered protection from irate victims, all in return for a piece of the action.

As the village grew into a town because of its fine harbor, so did the elf's influence and connections. Soon prospective politicians came to her for advice or loans in return for a promise to help her out in the future. Within a few years, the elf became the most powerful figure in the thriving, growing town.

Over time, the female elf became known as the Godmother because of the 'favors' she granted. More elves moved into Dun Hythe and her business expanded into extortion, assassination, graft and trade unions.

When the original Godmother grew too old to control the various business lines, she handed over control to her daughter, who in turn gave it to her daughter and a tradition was born: the head of the crime organization had to be a female elf.

Over time, it became apparent that no matter who ruled Gundarland, the Godmother ruled Dun Hythe.

~ ~ ~

The object of the Godmother's interest — Maurice Girard a half pint in his late forties — worked in an office on the second floor of the Presidential Palace. A graduate from the prestigious University of Wizardry and Accounting in Dun Hythe, Maurice had a reputation of honesty and innovation, especially in developing new spells.

When Jerado promoted him to Treasurer three years ago, he gave Maurice two assignments: keep the country's economy in good shape and reduce government corruption.

Maurice knew the more corruption he eliminated, the better the economy would be. He also knew, after twenty years working in the Palace, that the source of much of the corruption was Jerado's children, Lithgow and Flavia. That fact made rooting out corruption more than a bit tricky.

To assist his efforts, he modified his office to add a secret room hidden behind bookshelves. In the room, he installed two scryers. Using a specially designed spell, he modified the usual magic that operated one scryer so it monitored and recorded all traffic to and from Flavia's scryer. The second scryer did the same for Lithgow's scryer. In a decision he never could explain, he installed a third secret scryer and used it to record Jerado's scryer. He justified the third one to himself by recalling Jerado's great secrecy. Maurice needed to know what Jerado was up to in order to propose economic projects that supported the President's intentions.

Only later did he realize the third scryer was a death sentence if it was ever discovered by Jerado.

Maurice dressed simply and declined to buy expensive clothing. He always wore traditional half-pint garb: brown linen breeches and a white pullover tunic. His only obsession was his toe hair. He spent an hour each day grooming his four-inch long toe hairs. Besides washing and brushing, he wove the hair into intricate braids and designs.

Maurice's parents owned a small house in the Half-pint Quarter. At an early age, he showed magical talent, much to the discomfort of his grammar school teachers. His raw spell-casting ability won him a scholarship to a prep school attached to the university. Later on, he attended the University, also on a scholarship.

Maurice strongly believed governments should be run for the benefit of most of the people, not just a small special subset of rich or powerful individuals. When he accepted the job as Treasurer, he believed he could steer the government in that direction and away from the subset favored by Flavia. Although he enjoyed a few minor successes, she fought him relentlessly to protect her favored friends and businesses.

~ ~ ~

Several hours later, Leticia and Bianca returned from their trip to town.
Bohan's mouth started to water.

More food would convince him he really still lived. He greeted them and took two heavy string bags from Leticia. Bianca carried a wineskin and led a large goose by a rope tied to its neck.

"I bought back three cooked chickens, bread and cheese," Leticia said.

"And Bianca brought back a new pet," Angus said.

Bianca rolled her eyes.

"The goose is dinner and I need its feathers for my arrows. And to make quills for my lists. I also bought glue and ink."

"Bugger your lists," Tibbs said.

"When I get around to makin' lists, Tibbs, your name is on the top of every one of them." She turned to Barrow. "Catch." Bianca tossed him a bottle of ink. "For your journal."

"Thanks," Barrow said.

"Bugger his journal, too," Tibbs added.

"Tibbs," Barrow said, "you're just jealous 'cause you can't read and write."

"I can so read," Tibbs retorted. "Some stuff anyway."

"I hope you have wine in that skin," Ansgar said.

"Yeah, it's red."

"Red wine gives me headaches,"

Tibbs said.

"Good," Ansgar replied. "More for the rest of us. And after we finish the wine, I'll rinse out the bag, fill it with clean water and turn it into beer for our trip."

Once everyone was seated in a circle eating food, Leticia said, "On the way to town, I wondered why the name Bohan seemed familiar to me. It's an unusual name. I finally recalled where I heard it. Bohan is the name of the King Who Disappeared long ago. I read about him in school."

"'The King Who Disappeared'?" Bohan replied. "That sounds interesting. Tell us the story." Bohan was surprised his name was taught in schools. However, getting trapped in a cave wasn't exactly what he hoped to be remembered for.

"Well, at the time, Bohan was king in these parts. We're now in the Province of Sulvaria, but back then it was a kingdom. One day, Bohan and his guards set out to capture a wizard and they climbed into the mountains somewhere around here. After that, they were never seen again. They just disappeared. The whole lot of them."

Leticia looked around, wide-eyed.

"With the king was a wizard name Ansgar," she said looking at Ansgar. "Just like you and there was a berserker named Luc and a female elf archer named Bianca."

Leticia squirmed in her seat and stared at Bohan. "You're the King Who Disappeared, aren't you?"

Bohan grinned and nodded. "It's nice to be remembered."

"What happened to you?" Leticia asked in a voice filled with tension.

Bohan told her the story of tracking the wizard, getting trapped and Ansgar's sleep spell. "For some reason the cave was unsealed last night and here we are."

"There was an earthquake last night. The boulder must have fallen away. That's why I came out here. To see if the road was damaged or if anyone was hurt."

"Tell us, my dear," Ansgar said. "What year is it?"

"It's 1536."

"That means . . . we were sealed up for 211 years," Ansgar replied.

"No wonder I need a beer," Luc said. "That's a long time to go without a drink."

"That explains why my back hurts

so much," Tibbs said.

"Do you know what happened to the wizard we were chasing?" Bohan asked. "His name was Jerado."

"That's a strange thing," Leticia said. "The President of Gundarland is named Jerado."

"What's strange about that?' Ansgar asked.

"I remember my grandfather, a really old man, complaining about a Jerado. He said Jerado had been around as long as he was alive. And he said his grandfather also complained about a Jerado who lived in Dun Hythe."

"Whoa!" Colbert exclaimed. "That wizard guy is still alive?"

Bohan and Ansgar exchanged looks.

"Jerado was a wizard," Ansgar said. "It's possible he knew of a spell that would prevent aging and postpone death."

"So, he's still alive," Bohan said. "I remember hoping he would be just before you cast the sleep spell."

"We oughta go and capture the guy and let me torture him," Tibbs said.

Bohan curled his lips as he mentally listed the reasons he had for revenge. First, Jerado attempted to invade and conquer Sulvaria. Second, the wizard trapped him in a cave and left him for dead. Third, Bohan's family died without ever finding out what happened to him.

Leticia cleared her throat. "My job as constable is to enforce the laws and regulations that come out of Dun Hythe and —"

"Uh-oh," Bianca interrupted. "You're gonna tell us somethin' we don't want to hear. Right?"

Leticia nodded.

"It's against the law to carry weapons in Gundarland. Only soldiers are allowed to do that. So will everyone please pile up your weapons and armor over there."

Bohan's face turned red. "We can't do that." He pounded a fist onto his thigh. "We'll need them."

"Why can't you?" Leticia asked. "What do you need them for?"

"We're going to Dun Hythe and when we get there, we'll kill Jerado."

He was confident that killing Jerado would even the score.

~ ~ ~

Lithgow sat at a table in his War

Ministry office and studied the formation in front of him. He wore a sand-colored camouflage uniform he had designed for a new unit of special forces he planned to recruit.

On the table, a toy squadron of archers backed up squadrons of lancers and swordsmen. Facing these troops was a horde of yuk troops. Lithgow stroked his chin while he decided on his battle strategy. The right choice could spell victory over the yuks, while a bad choice could mean defeat.

Lithgow loved organizing battles. If only his father would allow him to invade Yuklandia, he could demonstrate his military genius and organizational talents. Yuklandia was a small kingdom in the southwest corner of Gundarland. Its only resource was peat, and Dun Hythe bought peat by the ton to fuel its industry. If Yuklandia was conquered by his troops, Lithgow could get peat almost for free by using the conquered yuks as slave laborers. Lithgow couldn't understand his father's insistence that he leave Yuklandia alone.

Lithgow moved the lancers to the right, the swordsmen to the left and placed the archers behind them. He pushed the lancers ahead in an all out charge while the swordsmen strode forward at a slower pace. His archers poured arrows on the doomed yuks. The lancers smashed into the yuk line, collapsing part of it. Into this mass confusion, his swordsmen carved a path through the enemy lines. Victory! Again!

Lithgow was sure he'd get the same result from a real war.

A water clock chimed, ending his war games. Lithgow left the office and joined a tailor in a different room. The tailor had set up a clothing dummy to display Lithgow's latest uniform design, one for his beloved Swine Riders — a lancer regiment consisting of dwarfs mounted on war swine.

Lithgow inspected the blue tunic on the dummy. "Hmm, No, the brass buttons must be bigger. At least twice as big. And the pants? I want a white stripe on the outside of the leg. It will match nicely with the color of the lances."

The tailor scribbled notes on a scrap of paper. "Of course, Minister."

"How much will the uniforms cost?'

"I can do them for . . . twenty silver pennies each?" The tailor held his breath.

"So five hundred will cost ten thousand, right?"

"Correct, Minister."

"All right. When you submit the bill, make it out for twelve thousand silver pennies."

"What?"

"You will get paid that amount. You will also get a bank account number in which you will deposit the extra two thousand silver pennies. Do I make myself clear?"

The tailor gulped and nodded.

"If you ever disclose the account or the payment, you will disappear and die an unpleasant death. Understand?"

The tailor nodded again.

"Good. I'll expect the uniforms within two weeks."

~ ~ ~

For the first thirty-five years after becoming King, Jerado ignored the Wizards Guild in Dun Hythe even though it was the most prestigious Guild in all of Gundarland. Its members were among the most renowned, the most reviled, the most inept and the most powerful wizards. There was also a few perverts.

Once Jerado became tired of

governing and stealing, he gave the Guild a try. To his astonishment, his membership application was rejected because he hadn't graduated from an accredited university. Jerado responded by promising to buy the buildings adjacent to the Guild, knock them down and use the land as garbage dumps. He also promised to have an accountant-wizard review the Guild's tax status. The Guild quickly approved his membership and granted him a seat on its most prestigious committee, *Philosophical Wizardry*. Jerado found the wizards and the committee to be useless gossips and he stopped attending meetings.

The one aspect of the Wizards Guild he liked was its library — the biggest one in the country. It contained many old spell scrolls, some dating back hundreds of years. He loved to spend a few hours reading these spell scrolls. Occasionally, he would find one that he could use and would copy it down in a notebook he carried.

One day, he found an ancient scroll hidden behind a shelf where it had apparently fallen. Jerado carefully opened the scroll hoping it wouldn't crumble. Once opened, he was stunned to find it was a treatise on black magic.

He was so surprised his wooden dentures fell out and bounced around the table. He scooped them up and re-installed them.

The scroll argued that black magic was as real as white magic, albeit rarely encountered. It also claimed a white magic wizard could convert to black magic by following the procedure outlined and by using the spell that followed the procedure.

The scroll went on to say that black magic was the antithesis of white magic and the two magics, if somehow mixed, would annihilate each other with unpredictable results. Further, it stated that black magic didn't have its own unique spells or method of casting the spells. Simply put, a black-magic wizard could cast a white magic spell, but the spell would have the opposite effect. Thus, a white magic *open door* spell would produce a *close door* effect if cast by a black-magic wizard.

Jerado rolled up the scroll, stuffed it up the sleeve of his robe and left the library. On the way back to the Presidential Palace he pondered the implications of the scroll. Perhaps, he could gain an advantage over white magic wizards by converting to black magic. Certainly he'd be able to surprise other wizards. Not that he anticipated being confronted by another wizard; nevertheless it paid to be prepared.

The biggest attraction of the change was it could alleviate his boredom.

~ ~ ~

Besides running the audience program, Remy also gave occasional press briefings to confuse the reporters. Another responsibility was to go through Jerado's incoming mail and eliminate the unessential material. Whenever an unusually complicated document showed up, Remy shared it with Maurice, who explained it to Remy. Over time, the two became friends, and Maurice told him how Lithgow and Flavia stole money from the government by padding contracts and pocketing the excess money as kickbacks.

As a former estate manager when still living, Remy believed in basic honesty and was appalled at what Flavia and Lithgow were doing. He joined Maurice in his guerrilla warfare against the actions of the brother and sister.

One day, he came across a

proposal from Lithgow for a budget increase to re-equip an archer company with newly invented crossbows. Remy modified the requested budget amount by adding two zeroes to it and sent the proposal into Jerado for approval.

The sounds of Jerado's wooden dentures clattering across the desk was most satisfying to Remy. Soon after, Jerado sent Lithgow a strongly worded notice to leave the archers alone.

Flavia often sent in contract negotiation requests. Most of these were for tax breaks she could use during the negotiations. Sometimes the approval was needed immediately to break a negotiation deadlock. Remy simply 'lost' those requests. That always resulted in a furious Flavia storming in to complain about a lost business deal.

Remy was proud of his contributions to a healthier Gundarland economy.

~ ~ ~

Leticia's mouth dropped open when Bohan said he planned to go to Dun Hythe and kill Jerado. Two mutually exclusive loyalties surged through her mind. One was her loyalty to her job as constable and her oath to uphold the law. The second was her loyalty to her family. For a second or two she hoped she could reconcile the two, but she realized she had to make a choice. She couldn't manage both. She could only adhere to one loyalty.

"I'm going with you to Dun Hythe," she told Bohan. "It's a long trip, you know."

"I know," Bohan replied. "I've been there a few times." He gave Leticia a smile. "But not recently."

Leticia had been born in Dun Hythe and had lived there until she was thirteen. Soon after her mother died, her father suddenly packed her up and moved south. She assumed her father was in some sort of trouble, but he refused to talk about it and his reasons remained unknown to Leticia.

Bohan's eyebrows rose up. He smiled at Leticia and said, "Really? When we get there are you going to arrest us for planning to kill Jerado?"

"I hate to see anyone killed, but I have my own reasons for going to Dun Hythe. And, yes, killing or trying to kill anyone is against the law, but I don't see how I can arrest your whole gang." Leticia gave Bohan a wan smile.

"Why are you going with us?" Bohan asked.

"I have an important reason," Leticia said. "One that is more important than enforcing the law."

"And that is?" Bohan asked.

The wineskin stopped getting passed around and the heroes leaned closer to hear what Leticia was about to say.

"In Gundarland, it's against the law to say bad things about President Jerado."

"What? We can't even bad-mouth Jerado?" Colbert asked. "That's not fair."

"My father, who lived north of here, was in a tavern one night about a year ago. He had a few ales and complained about the wage restrictions Dun Hythe imposes on everyone. Someone in the tavern fetched the local constable and my father was arrested. The next morning he was sentenced to five years in prison and no one will tell me where he is so I can visit him."

"That's nasty," Maggy said. "Everyone should be able to visit their family."

"Finding out about my dad is the most important thing I can do now. If I go with you to Dun Hythe I'll be able to talk to Flavia, the Secretary of the Interior. She's my big boss. She'll be able to tell me where my father is."

"And if she won't tell you?" Ansgar asked.

Leticia gripped her truncheon. "I'll make her tell me." Leticia spoke through clenched teeth. "Even if she is a wizard and Jerado's daughter."

"I like this one," Barrow said. "She's feisty.

"Why can't you go to Dun Hythe by yourself?" Bohan asked. "Why go with us? You could get in trouble traveling with us."

Leticia shook her head. "No one can travel more than ten miles from their home without first getting a travel permit. And they're hard to get and I doubt if they'll give me one. I don't think I'll need a permit if I go with you."

"All right, then," Bohan said. "Your knowledge of current customs and other stuff like money and what towns to use and which ones to avoid will be a big help."

Leticia felt a ton of guilt lift off her shoulders. Ever since her father had been imprisoned, she had felt like she should be doing more to find him. A new guilt replaced the old one. Now, she felt guilty about violating her oath as a constable.

"I can't walk all the way to Dun Hythe," Tibbs said. "I gotta bad back, you know."

"Tibbs is correct for a change," Bianca said. "We need horses."

"Oh!" Leticia put a hand in front of her mouth. "You aren't going to steal them, are you?"

"Before we were trapped in the cave," Bohan said, "we ran across yuk raiders. They had a pile of loot and we buried it with the intention of digging it up later. Later is now. If it's still there."

"It'll take us a week to walk to where the loot is buried," Bianca said. "Or was buried."

"How we gonna find the exact spot after all this time?" Angus asked. "The area could have changed."

"I made a map," Ansgar replied. He opened a wallet and unfolded a piece of parchment now in four parts, but still readable.

Leticia thought of something. "I have to go home and get different clothes. I can't go with you wearing a constable's uniform. It'll be recognized."

"Go now and hurry back. I want to leave first thing in the morning."

Leticia nodded. "If you have more coins, I can buy supplies while I'm in town. Bread, cheese, salted meat, stuff like that."

Bohan handed her two gold coins.

"Leticia can't carry all that much food by herself," Bianca said. "I'll go with her again."

On the way to town, Leticia tamped down her misgivings about abandoning her job. She was about to set forth on a dangerous journey with a bunch of legendary warriors. She pushed aside the probability of getting killed or arrested and tried for treason. The chance to see her dad made it worthwhile.

Along the way, Bianca told tales about Bohan and the heroes, and asked a string of questions about the current situation.

~ ~ ~

After an unannounced visit to Lithgow's favorite bank seeking evidence of corruption, Maurice called it a day and went home. He lived with his wife in the house he was born in. It was in the Half-pint Quarter close to the walls and consisted of a kitchen, a large room with a table, fireplace and chairs, and two bedrooms.

Maurice and his wife Blanche didn't have any children, so they adopted the working class neighbors. The neighbors struggled to survive under the wage restrictions while Maurice's job in the Palace paid him more money than he needed. Blanche went food shopping every day and brought back mounds of food which she used to cook dinner for themselves and five other families every night. She rotated the invitations so that every family in the neighborhood received at least one meal every week. Other well-to-do folks picked up the practice and provided food for the destitute families.

Maurice used these dinners to keep himself grounded in the plight of the common people by listening to their problems and complaints. The dinners also reinforced his self-imposed mandate to fight Flavia and her evil wage restrictions.

Chapter Six

After traveling west for three days, Ansgar believed he was far enough away from the mountains to sense Jerado anywhere in Gundarland. The countryside consisted of rolling hills covered with grass, cows and sheep. Small towns now existed where villages had been two hundred years ago. Villages now existed where none had been before.

Ansgar needed to determine if President Jerado was the same Jerado who had trapped them in the cave. This was important to both him and Bohan. Neither wanted to pursue and kill the wrong Jerado.

Ansgar hoped Jerado was still alive. The dwelf had tricked him into entering the cave. Ansgar fumed over his stupidity and wanted a chance to even the score by eliminating Jerado by whatever means necessary. He opened his mind and let his senses zoom across the landscape. Gradually, he increased the search area. After three hours, his senses approached the capital city and

Ansgar's anticipation increased. He couldn't keep the search up much longer because his magical energies were flagging. He had to find Jerado soon or he'd be forced to abandon the search until another day. He sensed many minor wizards. That puzzled him. Didn't universities teach a wizard how to shield one's identity anymore or were these wizards simply incompetent?

Near the end of his strength, he experienced success.

"Found him!" he exclaimed to Bohan who walked alongside him. "He's in Dun Hythe."

"Is it really Jerado?" Bohan asked.

Ansgar made a face and held up a hand momentarily.

"It is and it isn't," he replied. "He's changed. There is something much different about him. Something I don't understand."

"The important thing is we know where he is."

Ansgar chewed his lip and didn't respond. What had Jerado learned in the last two hundred years? Did he kill more powerful wizards and steal their spell libraries. Could the changed Jerado be more powerful than he was? Could this Jerado even be killed or harmed? Or defeated?

~ ~ ~

After traveling west for three days, Leticia had second thoughts about her decision to go to Dun Hythe with Bohan.

For one thing, her feet hurt. So did her legs and her back. By the end of each day, her backpack seemed to weigh a ton. From all the exercise and small meals she knew she had lost weight. Her white shirt and brown trews were looser now than when she had first put them on.

The first day wasn't too bad. The heroes weren't used to walking after their long sleep and they took frequent breaks. On the second day, they walked faster and took fewer breaks. Today was even worse; the heroes didn't walk, they *marched* and left Leticia breathing their dust. A few times, Bohan had to hold up the group and wait for Leticia to catch up. She knew he was annoyed with her, but he didn't say anything.

Leticia also had doubts about the wisdom of leaving her job. Unanswerable questions surged through her mind. Could she get arrested for leaving? Could it cause more problems for her father? Will traveling with Bohan get her in more trouble with Dun Hythe? Will she get arrested in Dun Hythe and sent to prison with her father? Does Bohan even have a chance of reaching the city? Will the government find out about him and react against him?

As reluctant as she was to travel with him, she was even more reluctant to tell Bohan she'd changed her mind and didn't want to go with him anymore. Leaving the group meant walking back to town by herself. A single traveler could be preyed upon by bandit gangs or wild animals.

Leticia kept her thoughts to herself and decided to keep on trudging after Bohan.

~ ~ ~

Jerado sat on a couch in his office reading a report on the country's economic status. Written by his Treasury Secretary, Maurice Girard was the only government official he trusted. The report discussed the deteriorating monetary conditions and suggested unknown persons or organizations sucked up too much coinage. He knew Maurice referred to Flavia and her unbridled greed.

Sheets of rain beat against the windows and shutters, leaving the room in a gloomy state despite the many candles lit throughout the office.

Bored by the report, Jerado's head lowered and he dozed off.

He suddenly woke up, startled by an unusual sensation. Instinctively, he placed a hand over his mouth to keep his dentures from shooting across the room.

Jerado analyzed the sensation and realized some other wizard had sensed his presence. That hadn't happened in such a long time, he barely recognized it. Who could it be?

With a jolt, he recalled the last time it had happened. Ansgar did it, many, many years ago. Could Ansgar be alive? He shook his head to remove that ridiculous idea. Ansgar and Bohan had died years ago.

Jerado went back to reading the report but couldn't concentrate. His mind wouldn't let go of the idea that Ansgar had just probed him.

He put the report aside and walked to a locked room adjacent to his office. Inside, he kept magical paraphernalia and instruments. He took a far-sight device off a shelf, placed it on a table, sat down on a chair and activated it. He tapped a finger on the table. Where to start? If Ansgar was still alive, and if the recent earthquake had opened the cave where he and Bohan had been trapped, then they would be in southern Gundarland in the vicinity of the Lestat Mountains.

He adjusted the device, a transparent globe, telling it to seek a powerful wizard and began scanning the area.

An hour later, Ansgar's image appeared in the globe.

Jerado groaned aloud. He continued to watch the globe and saw Bohan, all of his heroes and an unknown woman. Ten people in all.

He shut down the device and leaned back in the chair. What to do? Clearly, Ansgar, Bohan and the others couldn't be allowed to roam around free. They would be after revenge and Ansgar's probing had undoubtedly confirmed that he, Jerado, still lived. That meant they would head toward Dun Hythe.

After a moment's reflection, he realized Bohan and Ansgar offered a minimal threat when compared to all the resources he commanded. Nevertheless, their appearance would be an embarrassment.

He would just have to kill them again. And he'd have to be more thorough about it this time. He would demand dead bodies as proof.

~ ~ ~

Flavia sat in her corner office on the third floor of the Palace. She wore a translucent green-blue gown embroidered with images of flowers. Each of her long fingernails had a hand-painted picture of a different flower in bloom. She wore sandals to show off her toenails each with a painting of a different gemstone. Once a week, Flavia sat for three to four hours while a local artist painted her nails.

Flavia's large office had windows facing south and west. The other walls had paintings of woodlands and flower beads. In each painting, the plants leaned into the sunlight and changed positions as the sun moved from east to west.

Today was Flavia's favorite day of the month. Today, she set aside all the problems and issues with the multitude of businesses she controlled and spent the morning figuring a way to screw her brother, Lithgow. She had six spies in his department and they told her what he intended to do.

An ideal plan involved three phases. In phase one, she created a huge problem for Lithgow. In phase two, after letting him flounder for a while, she fixed the problem. In phase three, she received praise from Daddy while Lithgow got chewed out for being so stupid. Granted, such a plan was difficult to develop, but it still remained her goal. So far, she had achieved that goal twice, and the look on Lithgow's face when Daddy yelled at him was priceless.

After musing for over an hour, Flavia couldn't come up with a grand idea. She decided to simply bust his budget, something she did with regularity. She knew Lithgow planned to purchase new uniforms for all the regiments and naval crews in the military. Naturally, all the uniforms would be designed by him personally. The wool and cotton cloth used in the uniforms came from only three companies and she controlled all three.

With a smile on her face, she sent a scryer message to the head of each company.

Effective immediately the price of all cloth shipped to the military will be increased by 33 percent. . .

. . . This new price will remain in effect indefinitely.

Flavia sat down at her desk and giggled as she thought of the hissy fit Lithgow would throw when he found out about the price increase. She was sure his budget wouldn't be able to absorb the increase. That left him with two distasteful options. In the first, he could cancel buying new uniforms for some regiments. Or, he could plead with Maurice, at Treasury, for a budget increase. Whether Lithgow got the increase or not, Maurice would tell Daddy about Lithgow's problem and Daddy would chastise him.

With that pleasantry out of the way, Flavia turned her attention to her biggest project: the arrival of the first peat train. Steady supplies of cheap peat would lead to an explosion of industrial growth in northern Gundarland. Much of that growth would be experienced by the businesses she controlled.

Life was good.

~ ~ ~

Jerado saw Remy standing in the entrance to the apartment. He waved the undead half-pint forward. Remy carried a cloth purse and wore his usual gray tunic and brown pants. The quantity of patches and stains had grown until they merged into a single color.

"Come over here, Remy."

Jerado sat at the dining table in his apartment.

"Sit across from me. Are you sure you recall how to play cards?"

"Y . . . yes, I remember playing cards when I was in school."

Remy sat down and plunked the purse on the table. It clinked.

"Ahh, you remembered to bring coins. Wonderful."

Jerado planned to take his mind off his many problems by taking Remy's money. It would be a refreshing break from ruling the country and would offer a bit of companionship. While learning magical theory and practice by overhearing lectures, Jerado earned money by fleecing rich students at cards. Remy should be an easy mark.

Jerado shuffled a deck of cards and Remy spilled his coins onto the table.

"They're all copper pennies!"

Jerado exclaimed.

"Y . . . ou pay me ten coppers a week."

"Still?"

"S . . till. Ever since you brought me to Dun Hythe, you've paid me ten coppers."

"Hmm. Write a memo tomorrow to Maurice. Tell him your new wage is a silver penny a week. I'll sign it."

"T . .hank you, master."

Jerado shoved a small stack of silver pennies across the table.

"And here is a bonus."

Remy counted out seven silver pennies, more than he had ever owned at one time.

"We'll play with five cards. High hand wins. Bet before I deal."

Remy pushed the stack of silver coins into the middle of the table.

"Are you sure?" Jerado asked as he matched Remy's bet.

"Y . . .es. I feel lucky."

Jerado dealt the cards and they compared hands. Remy won.

After an hour, Jerado said, "That's enough for tonight. I'm tired."

Remy stuffed the fifty-three silver pennies into his purse along with the coppers. The undead half-pint looked as close to happy as Jerado had ever seen him.

"T . . . hank you for a wonderful evening," Remy said.

Jerado waved a hand in dismissal. He was sure Remy hadn't cheated. After all, his undead fingers were too clumsy. Besides, Jerado had dealt every hand, so Remy never touched the deck. It had to be an astounding run of luck.

~ ~ ~

Maurice walked along Dun Hythe's main street after attending a meeting with the Merchants Trade Association. He maneuvered around puddles to protect his well-groomed toe hairs.

In the middle of the day, the traffic was horrendous. Huge wagons drawn by teams of horses, oxen or mules headed to the port area or away from it. Smaller carts tried to squeeze between the wagons to get ahead of them. The smell of dung was pervasive and made stronger by the warm temperature.

Every major intersection had one or two trolls shouting at drivers who cursed back at them.

To his surprise, a burly elf grabbed his right arm while a second elf stuck a knife point into his left side.

"Don't do anythin' stupid," the second elf said. "We ain't gonna hurt ya."

Maurice tamped down his sudden panic and took a deep breath.

"Where are you taking me?" he asked.

"Ya gonna have lunch wid a nice lady. So mind yer manners."

"Lunch?"

"Shut up and keep walkin'."

The elves guided him down a side street and into a restaurant that displayed no name.

Inside, a waiter nodded to Maurice and said, "Follow me, please."

The elf led Maurice past several tables with customers eating lunch and into a separate room where a middle-aged female elf sat a table. She smiled at Maurice and held out a hand to an empty chair.

His two elf escorts came behind Maurice, shut the door after the waiter left and stood against the wall.

"You are Maurice Girard, am I right?" the female said. She was attractive but hard-looking, with shoulder-length green hair partially gone grey and green eyes.

"I am. And you are?" Maurice's

initial fear gave way to curiosity.

"I am called the Godmother, and I want to discuss a few issues with you."

Maurice's heart raced. The Godmother had an infamous reputation. She was a shadowy presence throughout the city and Maurice ran into her influence everywhere. Jerado hated her. Maurice hoped the President never found out about this meeting.

"You have an unusual way of sending an invitation," Maurice said.

She frowned momentarily.

"Oh, those two." She flapped a hand at the guards. "I didn't think you'd accept a written invitation, so I asked them to escort you here."

One escort opened the door in response to a knock. A waiter brought in a bottle of red wine and two glasses. He poured the wine and left the room.

The Godmother held her glass out to Maurice, who clinked it with his own glass. "You are," she said, "either the only honest official in Dun Hythe or the most careful one I've ever come across."

"You've been checking up on me?" Maurice raised an eyebrow.

"I'll be honest with you. I hoped to uncover some dirt on you so you'd agree to my demands to keep the dirt secret.

However, my investigators didn't come up with anything useful, so I'll have to propose a mutually beneficial deal instead."

Maurice sipped his wine and watched the Godmother. He wasn't accustomed to hear people admit they tried to blackmail him. "As long as I'm here, I may as well listen to your proposal."

"Very well. I don't trust Jerado and I don't trust Lithgow or Flavia. Right now, Jerado and I have a working agreement. He doesn't attack me and I don't make labor trouble in the city. I believe it's only a matter of time until he decides to cancel the agreement."

Maurice understood the Godmother's concern. Jerado often raged about her, especially when she ignored one of his decrees. Maurice knew she controlled the labor guilds and probably the city officials as well and could cause economic havoc by calling a general strike. Fear of that strike was the only reason preventing Jerado from acting on his anger.

"Likewise, I'm sure Jerado sees you as a useful tool," the Godmother continued. "Sooner or later, you'll wear out your welcome and be discarded."

"All right. I understand your concerns and I think you're correct on both counts. So what is it you're after?"

Another knock came from the door.

"That'll be lunch." She gave him a smile. "We'll continue after we eat."

The waiter brought in a mixed seafood grill and fresh vegetables.

After the dishes were cleared away and a liqueur served, the Godmother continued. "Since we agree that we both face substantial and possibly fatal dangers, I propose we share information that could be useful to both of us."

Maurice waved a hand in a tell-me-more gesture.

"If you share advance information that can affect my business or my health, I'll provide you with cover and concealment if and when Jerado turns on you."

Maurice blinked. "You want me to disclose secret information that will benefit you alone?"

"Precisely." The Godmother nodded. "If Jerado attacks me, the city will dissolve into chaos. My instructions are already in place. If I learn of the attack beforehand, I may be able to prevent it by giving Jerado a small sample of what he faces. Similarly, I may be able to influence damaging new regulations if I know about them in advance."

She drained her liqueur glass.

"In return, I can hide you so deeply that Jerado's troops will never find you. Later on, I can get you out of the city to wherever you want to go."

Maurice tapped his fingertips on the table. The offer went against his policy of strict honesty in all his dealings. On the other hand, he had a sense that Jerado would someday no longer want or need his services. Flavia especially wanted him disposed of. Since he knew all about the family's corruption, he was too dangerous to be allowed to simply walk away from the Presidential Palace. Having a bolthole could be extremely useful. And life saving.

Maurice nodded. "Deal. As long as the bolthole offer includes my wife."

"It'll even include your children. I know how vindictive Jerado and his family can be."

"My wife and I don't have any children or other family."

Maurice held out a hand and the Godmother shook it.

"I'm glad we met," she said.

~ ~ ~

Jerado traveled to Dun Hythe's golf course in the Wagon of State, a huge gilt-laden wagon pulled by four horses. Remy accompanied Jerado but wasn't allowed to sit inside. He rode atop the carriage and held onto the luggage rails. Jerado played golf once a month with three other golfers chosen by Remy from a list with more than fifty names on it. It cost twenty-five gold pennies to get on the list. Remy used the money to pay clerical salaries and provide the Palace with supplies.

The course, located south of Dun Hythe near the army camp, was the country's only fifteen hole course. All the others had a smaller number of holes. Golf had been developed by a sports-crazed half-pint fifty years ago and had caught on when Jerado became interested. It gave him a chance to practice black-magic spells.

Jerado alighted from the wagon near the first hole while Remy scrambled down the side and untied a bag from the side of the coach. It held Jerado's six golf clubs.

Remy looked at a cloud formation to the south and said, "I . . . . I hope it don't rain."

The bag also held an umbrella made of iron and cloth. In effect, the umbrella was a lightning rod. Whenever it rained, Remy's job was to hold the umbrella over Jerado's head. So far, Remy had been struck by lightning three times, while Jerado, protected by a spell, remained safe and dry.

The President wore a black robe with silver piping and a sun cap, also black and silver. The cap kept his wig from flying away in a wind gust. It was a mild, overcast day and the air held the smell of newly cut grass.

Squads of spearmen from the army camp lined the perimeter of the course and turned away anyone who approached.

Three other players stood by waiting. Remy introduced them and described their occupations. One was a banker, the second a lawyer and the the third a factory owner.

"Shall we make this interesting?" Jerado said. "Say ten gold pennies to the low scorer?"

"You going to use magic today?" the lawyer asked.

"I use only skill and luck. You should know that since we've played together before." Jerado chose a club and took a few swings to loosen up.

"I'll shoot first if no one minds." He dropped a ball on the ground. It was a small wooden pellet wrapped with leather. He whacked the ball and it flew in the air toward a grassy circle with a flagpole sticking out of a hole. The ball started out true, but faded to the left. A puff of wind blew the ball on course and it landed on the green.

The lawyer groaned. "That was luck, I suppose?"

"Exactly."

To the factory owner, Jerado asked, "How's business?"

"It's been great ever since the new, lower wage restrictions went into effect. Once I cut back the workers' pay, my expenses went down and my profits soared."

"What about the workers?"

"They're surly, of course. But they're always surly."

"My company actually was hurt in a small way," the banker said. "Nothing to worry about."

"How so?" Jerado took a club from Remy's bag and waggled it a few times.

"Many workers used to deposit a few coins in an account every week.

Copper, of course. After the new restrictions went into effect, that stopped. None of them make deposits any more. Actually, they're making withdrawals now."

On the fourth hole, after Jerado made a bad shot that left the ball far short of the green, a squirrel picked up the ball and carried it to the green before dropping it a foot from the hole.

"Well," Jerado said, "my luck is strong today." He grinned at the other three players, who rolled their eyes. "You'll need a great game to beat me."

By the end of the game on the par 75 course, Jerado's score was forty-one. "I wasn't at my best today, but the score isn't too bad. You can give Remy your bets."

Remy collected ten gold pennies from each player along with an envelope. He put the coins in a leather bag and pocketed the envelopes. Each envelope contained a request. Mostly the requests were for tax relief but sometimes asked for a favorable regulation or an imposition on a competitor.

Remy honored the requests as long as they weren't too outrageous.

Chapter Seven

Maurice's large second floor office feature windows on two sides. One window looked south giving a view of the main road with all its heavy cart and wagon traffic. The other window, facing west, gave a view of buildings and, in the distance, the city walls. Bookshelves filled with scrolls lined one wall. Maurice collected and studied texts on government issues, monetary practices, societies and other topics. He noted that many of the 'experts' who authored texts had no credentials to justify the expert label. He ignored the advice in those texts.

Twenty years ago, Maurice was an accountant-wizard, fresh out of university, when he was hired by the government. His job, along with dozens of other accountant-wizards, was to check contractors' vouchers. The job was so simple that only a few wizards were needed to handle the work load. This left Maurice with plenty of time to fill. He wandered about the Presidential Palace and noticed that certain areas had a high level of loose magical power floating about. All wizards naturally and continuously produce magical power, but they have limited storage capability, and the excess power leaked into the atmosphere where it dissipated over time and was lost.

Maurice wondered if the lost power could be put to a practical use.

Over the next few months, he developed a proposal to vacuum up the loose power and use it to heat the building during the cold months. He submitted the proposal to his boss, whose first instinct was to fire Maurice as a trouble maker. Instead, the boss passed the proposal up the line where it terrified every layer of management. None of them wanted to call attention to themselves by sponsoring a radical proposal or even acknowledging its existence.

Eventually, it somehow landed on Jerado's desk. Intrigued by the innovation and novel thinking, Jerado ordered Maurice to come to his office. Maurice's self-assurance and his obvious ability impressed Jerado. Promotions quickly followed, and three years ago Maurice was made Treasury Secretary.

Around the same time as that

promotion, Maurice developed a small device that would show the loose power in an area measured in necroms, the standard measure of magical power. He used the device to tinker with the heating system and make it more efficient. He discovered the device could also measure the leakage from an individual wizard. The more powerful the wizard, the higher the leakage would be. The most powerful wizards measured a ten, the highest level. His own leakage was a modest three. He surreptitiously measured Jerado and his children. Lithgow's was so negligible that it didn't measure on the device. Flavia's leakage was two.

Most disturbing was Jerado's measurement: it was a negative ten. For a long time, Maurice couldn't fathom the possibility of a negative number. Finally, he reasoned it must be an indication that black magic wasn't mythical at all. It must exist. This shook Maurice to his core. It went against the fundamental magical principles taught at the university.

Maurice, now a powerful minister, used his position to gain access to the most respected wizard-philosophers and wizard-researchers in the Wizards Guild who routinely refused all interviews. Since Maurice had the power to approve research grants, the Guild made special accommodations for him.

From the interviews, Maurice learned that a few master wizards believed black magic really did exist although it was rare. One researcher held that a wizard could control and use black magic just as all wizards routinely controlled white magic. A philosopher told Maurice black magic was simply anti-white magic. If a white magic spell and a black magic spell collided, the spells would annihilate each other with bizarre consequences.

When pressed for an explanation, the philosopher said, "Assume a wizard cast a white magic spell using a power level of five necroms and another wizard cast a black magic spell of ten necroms. If the two spells touch, they will interact and annihilate each other but the resultant reaction won't be at a power level of fifteen necroms. It will be *much higher*. In other words, it will be far beyond what any individual wizard could do. The result will be spectacular, bizarre and will have unpredictable consequences, probably not beneficial."

The interviews left Maurice shaken.

He was convinced Jerado used black magic. How the President achieved that was a mystery. Since Jerado never mentioned his black magic powers, Maurice possessed a state secret, one that would probably get him killed if Jerado learned he knew it.

~ ~ ~

Jerado walked across his office to the far corner. On a small table sat his scryer. All high government officials had a scryer and so did most wizards. The scryers allowed people to communicate at a distance. Jerado's scryer connected to scryers installed in the governor's office in each province. It also had a few secret connections, and Jerado needed to talk to one of those connections. The scryer was a pewter bowl a foot-and-a-half in diameter filled with silverish liquid. The discovery that Bohan lived still rattled his nerves, but he had a solution to that conundrum.

Jerado stood alongside the bowl for a moment while he tapped his fingers on the table. Finally he picked up a stylus and began to etch runes on the surface of the liquid. Each message could only hold one-hundred-forty runes, including the address.

To Alik From Jerado. Small war band needs to be eliminated.

Alik was a powerful yuk warlord who controlled a large piece of the Yuklandia border. He also took care of local problems for Jerado. A short time later the scryer dinged to announce an incoming message.

To Jerado from Alik. How many and where?

To Alik from Jerado. Nine warriors and a civilian. Near the border. Exact location to follow.

To Jerado from Alik. 5000 silver pennies each.

To Alik from Jerado. Nonsense. 1000SP each

To Jerado from Alik. Get some one else.

To Alik from Jerado. 1500SP each. I have other resources.

To Jerado from Alik. Soldiers in pretty uniforms? Look nice. Can't fight. 4000SP.

To Alik from Jerado. 25000SP total.

To Jerado from Alik. Done. 25000SP to eliminate 10 people.

To Alik from Jerado. And dispose of the bodies.

To Jerado from Alik. 500SP each burial costs.

To Alik from Jerado. Just do it.

To Jerado from Alik. Total bill 35000SP. Full payment requirement up front

To Alik from Jerado. Half up front via usual bank transfer by end of day. Report when finished. Out.

Jerado smiled. Negotiating with Alik was always fun. Now that Bohan and the others were about to be positively eliminated, he could stop worrying about getting probed by Ansgar. "Remy!" he called out.

"Y . . . Yes?" Remy walked out of his small office and looked at Jerado.

"Go to my bank and transfer 17,500 silver pennies to Alik's account."

"S . . . omeone gonna get whacked?"

"You don't need to know, Remy. On your way."

Remy left the office and Jerado sat down at his desk. Too bad Bohan wouldn't be around much longer. Bohan and Ansgar could have relieved his boredom, but he didn't need to take the chance that they would succeed in reaching Dun Hythe and cause trouble.

~ ~ ~

From Barrow's Journal: *Boots are falling apart. Paid a fortune for them. I wonder if the boot maker's family still runs the business. Maybe I can get a refund.*

Leticia believed in Snotism. Every morning she began the day with a prayer to the Great God, Gundar. Today was no different. While most of the heroes still slept, she recited the prayer, then took out a small vial and spilled a few grains of crushed pepper into her hand. Holding her palm under her nose, she snorted the pepper. A second later, she let go with an explosive sneeze. Angus, still groggy from sleep, leaped up, axe in hand and glared around the camp site.

Bohan shook his head while feeding the fire. "Leticia, you have to stop with the sneezes every morning. It can give away our location to enemies. And it spooks everyone who is still sleeping."

"Oh," Leticia replied. "I hadn't thought about that. I won't do it anymore."

While the heroes ate cheese, a

hunk of stale bread and washed it down with a cup of beer from Ansgar's beer bag, Bianca read the day's duty roster.

"Tibbs is the cook for the evening meal. I'm the scout and Colbert, Angus and Ansgar have guard duty tonight."

"Tibbs?" Maggy mimicked throwing up.

"I'll have anti-poisoning spells ready for whoever needs one," Ansgar said."

"We're runnin' outta food supplies," Barrow the quartermaster said, "so you better do some huntin' today, Tibbs."

"And catchin' a squirrel won't feed all of us," Maggy said. "You need to catch something big."

Tibbs made an obscene gesture with his right hand. "A decent quartermaster wouldn't run outta food."

"Hah!" Barrow replied. "This quartermaster runs outta food 'cause you pigs eat too much."

"Enough!" Bohan said. "I hear this argument every time Tibbs has to cook."

Once they cleaned up the camp site, Bianca grabbed her bow and quiver and set out. The others followed after she was a half-mile in front of them.

By now, her feet didn't hurt and she could keep up with the others. She knew she had never been in such great shape and she enjoyed traveling with the group.

Leticia had also gotten to know the individuals in the group. Bohan was regal and rarely gave orders. It was enough for him to indicate what he'd like done. He ignored most of the group's comments and jibes. He also looked at Bianca with longing in his eyes. She wondered what that was all about.

Ansgar liked to throw out sarcastic remarks and had an air of self-assurance about him.

The elf, Bianca, was quiet and serious and the most friendly. As sergeant, she had the responsibility of organizing the duty rosters.

Angus and Maggy were a strange pair. They were always together, side by side, but went to great pains to ignore each other. They rarely talked to each other.

Barrow was tall and pleasant. The man practiced with his sword whenever he had time. Bianca told her that Barrow was an accomplished thief, a useful trait for the group's quartermaster. He was also handsome, and she thought he liked her because he kept glancing at her

Tibbs was an unpleasant man.

Surly, he tried to shirk whatever assignment Bianca gave him. He also complained a lot about not feeling well.

Luc was everything she had imagined a berserker would not be. He was short and scrawny even for a half-pint. He practiced making faces to convince people he was fierce. Every morning he groomed his toe hairs and pinned the six-inch long hairs with silver brooches.

Colbert was a hard working half-pint and always fulfilled his duty. She had learned he was a trained assassin. Unlike Luc, Colbert trimmed his toe hair close and never groomed it.

Toward mid-day, Bianca crested a small rise, stopped for a second then turned and jogged back to the group.

"I think we're about to have some fun," Luc said.

"Good," Maggy said. "I'm bored."

When Bianca reached them, she said, "There's a yuk war party headin' this way. About twenty of 'em."

"Twenty?" Angus said. "That's two each if Leticia wants a couple."

"Light exercise," Colbert said.

Leticia couldn't believe the reaction of the heroes. They dropped their packs, took out weapons and started stretching and limbering up.

"What are you doing?" she cried. "We have to get out of here! There are too many yuks! We have to run back the way we came!"

"That won't do any good," Bohan replied. "We can't outrun yuks. They can run all day long and still won't be breathing hard. Do you have a dagger?"

Leticia nodded. Her hand shook as she grasped the hilt of the dagger at her hip.

"If it looks like the yuks are about to capture you, plunge the dagger in right here." Bohan pointed to the left side of her chest. "It'll be over quick and won't hurt that much."

"Why?" Leticia raised an eyebrow at Bohan's suggestion she kill herself.

"After a day of raiding, yuks entertain themselves by torturing any prisoners they have."

"Oh." The news did nothing to lessen Leticia's fears. Nether did the appearance of the yuk war party. Once the yuks reached the top of the hill and saw the heroes, they hooted and cheered. Each carried a shoulder bag of supplies. They dropped them in a pile and ran forward.

The heroes formed a line with

Bohan in the middle. Bianca and Ansgar stood behind the line ready to launch arrows and spells.

The yuks were repulsive looking. That's the only way Leticia could describe them. They were green-skinned, with ugly features, heavy shoulders, thick chests and arms rippling with muscle. They were bald with clumps of black hair randomly scattered over their bodies. All wore a uniform of sorts: tan pants belted with a rope, no shorts, no shoes. All of them carried a shield and a curved sword.

The yuks stopped a hundred feet away and one who wore a blue sash gaudy with colorful emblems and patches strode forward.

"Name's Alik. I'm a warlord."

"Never heard of you," Bohan replied.

Alik grimaced at Bohan.

"Throw down yer weapons and we'll kill you quick right here. If we have to fight ya, then we gonna capture a bunch of ya and have some fun with ya tonight."

"Cut the crap and let's get started," Tibbs said. "I challenge your best fighter to one-on-one combat."

"Oww, this gonna be good to

watch," Alik said. He turned and pointed to a large yuk. "Kill this guy."

The yuk stepped forward and both groups moved to give the combatants plenty of room.

"Ya ain't gotta sword," the yuk said. "Dey afraid ya cut yourself?"

"Shut up and fight," Tibbs said. He held his spear shaft near the bottom giving his weapon a much longer reach than the yuk's sword.

The yuk charged and swung his curved sword. Tibbs blocked it with his shield and danced backward.

"Stay still and fight," the yuk snarled and swung his sword.

Tibbs stepped back two paces and the sword whistled through empty air.

Tibbs jabbed his spear point into the yuk's left shoulder. He twisted the spear and pulled it free. Blood flowed down the yuk's shoulder and his shield arm dangled uselessly.

Enraged, the yuk charged again. Tibbs moved back and jabbed the spear into his opponent's right thigh. More blood spilled onto the ground. The yuk groaned in pain and tried to walk forward but could only move a few inches at a time.

Tibbs watched the yuk and, with a

quick move, the spear point darted forward and struck the yuk in the chest. He gasped aloud and crashed to the ground.

Alik frowned and the heroes cheered.

Luc pushed forward from the battle line. "I'm next. Who wants a piece of me?" The half-pint threw off his bearskin cape, dropped his kilt and removed his vest. Buck naked, he swung his war hammer a few times.

A burly yuk giggled and stepped forward.

"Ya ain't gonna need to get buried 'cause I'm gonna pound ya inna the ground."

"Try it."

Luc stepped forward and faced the yuk, who was twice as tall and three times as heavy.

The yuk swung his sword downward and landed a solid blow on Luc's shield which the half-pint held over his head.

An expression of surprise and pain filled the yuk's face as Luc's hammer destroyed the yuk's left knee.

Leticia winced at the sound of cracking bones.

While the yuk stood stunned, Luc

crushed his right instep with another blow.

Howling in pain, the yuk collapsed to the ground and Luc finished him off with a savage blow to the forehead.

Alik pulled a face as a third yuk ran forward. "Me next," he yelled. "I want the old skinny guy." He pointed his sword at Ansgar.

"What!" Ansgar exclaimed. "Are you insane? I'm a wizard."

"Ya ain't gonna cast any spells after I cut off yer head, are ya?"

Ansgar sighed and snapped his fingers.

A lightning bolt struck the yuk. All that remained of him was a pile of gray dust. His armor and weapons lay on the ground. The leather straps on the armor smoldered.

"Mind," Ansgar said. "Don't touch the metal parts. They're hot."

Alik had a worried expression his face. "Ahh, I just remembered I gotta appointment inna little while. We gonna pick this up later."

He waved his arm and the yuks retreated after picking up their supply bags.

"Wait," Colbert called out. "I didn't get a turn."

"Don't go," Angus yelled. "Let's have a melee first."

The yuks walked backwards for a dozen paces, then turned and ran.

Leticia was appalled at the casual way the heroes killed and maimed the yuks. It was as if the yuks weren't worth caring about. Of course, the heroes were trained warriors, so they had been fighting and killing for a long time. Still, she had never seen anyone killed before and it was a shock. So was a naked half-pint. She had seen naked men before, but always in a darkened bedroom, never in the middle of the day and out of doors.

After witnessing the fight with the yuks, it occurred to her, for the first time, that she could be killed accompanying Bohan. The government had forts along the border with Yuklandia and many soldiers were bivouacked in the forts. Surely, Jerado had more troops in Dun Hythe. How could the heroes defeat a large contingent of trained soldiers? If the heroes were overrun, would the soldiers spare her or would she be killed just like the heroes?

Leticia regretted her hasty decision to join Bohan, but she couldn't see any way to undo the decision.

Despite the dangers, her hope of finding out about her father still outweighed all the counterarguments.

~ ~ ~

Jerado tapped a quill on the desktop while staring out a window. After a minute or two, he stood up and paced the office. In disgust, he snatched his wig and threw it on the couch. No matter how hard or long he pondered the problem, he could never come up with a satisfactory solution. Despite dealing with the reappearance of Bohan, he still had to face up to his successor.

Jerado planned to retire after his two hundredth year in office and that was only four years from now. He needed to decide on a successor: Lithgow or Flavia. Unfortunately, both choices were bad.

Tradition called for the oldest son to gain the throne. However, Lithgow was a dunce who only dreamed of gaining military glory by leading an army to victory. The only possible enemy was Yuklandia, and the yuks were vicious fighters who would overwhelm Lithgow's army and, in revenge for the invasion, pour into Gundarland looting and killing.

Within weeks, the yuks would be in Dun Hythe.

Jerado knew firsthand how difficult it was to fight a yuk army. The yuks were completely undisciplined and that made it tough to plan a battle against them. They fought for the sheer joy of killing and maiming. An opposing general never knew where the individual yuks would decide to fight. The most the yuk general could hope for was that most of his soldiers moved in the direction he pointed his sword. Yuks didn't move or fight in units; rather, they swarmed over the battlefield. And they fought unencumbered by military strategy and orders. Jerado had actually seen a large gang of yuks sit down to take a lunch break in the middle of a battle.

So to make Lithgow his heir was to doom Gundarland to become a province of Yuklandia. Of course, if Lithgow ruled, he'd have to eliminate Flavia because she wouldn't accept him as her superior.

On the other hand, appointing Flavia to succeed after his retirement would give her a license to steal even more than she did now. Her aim was to become the richest female in the world. It would be only a matter of a few years before she drove the economy off a cliff by stealing every coin ever minted.

Since Lithgow would assume she somehow cheated to gain the throne, Flavia would have to have him assassinated before he assassinated her. Only then could she could feel secure.

Once again, he failed to solve the problem. Rather than get a headache, Jerado postponed a decision until another day. Again!

~ ~ ~

Flavia groused to herself about the unkind fate that made Lithgow a male and the first-born giving, the toad a preferential position for the succession. He was obviously unfit to rule, but still her father considered him for the position.

It wasn't like he had any talent to offer. While her wizardly skills weren't great, they were much better than Lithgow's. She had received poor grades in college in all her wizardry classes, but she earned those marks. Lithgow, on the other hand, only graduated from university because their father both bribed and badgered the school officials to give him passing grades.

Flavia knew she had four years at the most to convince her father to appoint her as his successor. Her strongest argument was her acumen in business and finance. In college, she had racked up the highest grades ever recorded in those subjects. Since graduating, she had become rich and powerful. Yet, even those achievements might not be enough for her father.

Eliminating the competition would do the trick, but Lithgow apparently also had luck on his side. Her two assassination attempts had been unsuccessful.

In the first try, she had a stable hand place a spell-encased burr under the saddle of his war swine. When spooked, the animals were notorious for running towards a wooded area to search for fallen nuts and seeds. Once her spell wore off, the burr would drive the swine crazy with pain and cause Lithgow to lose control. The swine would run towards the closest woods where a low-hanging branch would surely knock Lithgow out of the saddle and kill him.

That was her plan, but it didn't work out that way. Before bolting for the woods, the swine bucked a few times, threw the clumsy oaf out of the saddle and broke his wrist. Naturally, she had to eliminate the stable hand who placed the burr.

Her second attempt used mushrooms, Lithgow's favorite food, and also ended in failure. The poisoned mushrooms were served during a drinking party with a few officers. One of them, as a prank, stuffed the entire bowl of mushrooms in his mouth and swallowed. Once he fell down dead, the others assumed he simply drank too much. His death wasn't discovered until the morning. Regrettably, the servant had to be disappeared.

Those two attempts made Lithgow more cautious and suspicious. Flavia planned to try again after his caution waned.

The next time, she wouldn't fail.

~ ~ ~

Lithgow sat at a table and studied the soldiers arrayed in battle formation. The yuk forces were in trouble and he wanted to wipe them out with a brilliant tactical move, but he couldn't think of one. Should he send his spearmen forward to break the yuk battle line? That move presented a risk in this situation.

The battle was one part of his long-desired invasion of Yuklandia in which he sent three armies surging across the border: one in the east, the center and the west. Right now, he directed the Army of the West, the one who attacked along the coast. His favorite tactic was to send his Swineriders sweeping around the enemy's flank to attack the battle line from the rear. In this case, the yuk line was anchored by the sea on one flank and a mountain on the other.

Finally, he gave up. He couldn't concentrate because his mind kept returning to his father's retirement. When would Jerado do the right thing and appoint him as the successor? After all, tradition called for the oldest male to inherit. His father planned to retire in only four years and Lithgow needed the time to set up his plans, but Jerado refused to announce his appointment.

Lithgow swept his arm over the battlefield and scattered the toy soldiers. He would never achieve his dream of military glory unless he succeeded his father.

Being president or king would be an easy job. As easy as getting through wizardry college. He had graduated while doing the bare minimum of work. Instead of studying, he collected a group of like-minded students and bullied others when not partying. He smiled. Good times back then.

The smile evaporated. There was a chance his father would make a disastrous mistake and appoint Flavia. The best way to deal with that possibility was to eliminate her. He had tried twice, but his sister possessed astounding luck.

Lithgow had discovered that many "volunteers" in the army were actually criminals who were offered a choice: prison or the army. He formed some of them into a small unit called his Special Forces. The unit had diverse talents such as robbers, enforcers, murderers, plain and not-so-plain thugs, and smugglers.

His first attempt occurred after a spy reported Flavia planned to spend a few days at her estate ten miles out of town. Lithgow had one of his Special Forces cut halfway through both axles on Flavia's coach. Lithgow was sure the axles would fail on the open road when the coach traveled at high speed. Flavia was certain to be killed in the crash. Instead, the axles failed when the coach went over a bump while going through the city's gate. That resulted in Flavia getting a bruised shoulder and produced a huge traffic jam until six members of the Troll Patrol picked up the coach and move it to the side of the road.

Naturally, he denied any involvement in the axle sabotage.

In the second attempt, he had a Special Forces soldier drop a bag of cement sand from the roof of Flavia's favorite bank as she entered the building. The soldier waited a second too long and missed Flavia but hit one of her guards a glancing blow.

After that, Flavia increased her vigilance and it became too dangerous to try again.

Lithgow planned to make another attempt in a few months. By then, Flavia's attention would have lessened and she would be vulnerable.

That thought brought a smile back to Lithgow's face.

Chapter Eight

Jerado loved research. In the past, he had devoted much of his time to magical and technological research, but he didn't do the research himself. He had performed magical research by exploring the libraries of other wizards after he murdered them. Rhinehard the Malodorous provided the transport spell that way. Blaise the Braggart developed the anti-aging spell and Conrad the Shifty spent years working on the spell Jerado used to counterfeit the gold pennies in the old days. All three wizards had been faculty members at the Centi's University of Wizardry and Sorcery where Jerado learned magic by eavesdropping on lectures.

Technological research was different. After taking over the government, he encouraged others to work on research and rewarded success. Twice a year, he held technical fairs for researchers, inventors and tinkers to show off their wares. One fair was held in Dun Hythe and the other in Centi.

Devices and concepts that showed

ingenuity or promise were given monetary grants to further their development.

Much of the money ended up getting wasted. Some inventors had no interest in developing a marketable product and spent the money on food, drink and gambling. Others developed a product that had no market. A few, being poor all their lives, spent the money as fast as they could. Those few inventors who fully developed a working and marketable product were shocked to discover the document they signed to get the grant money gave Jerado fifty-one percent of the business.

Jerado often combined companies and products to spawn even more businesses and products.

Over time, Jerado came to own or control almost all of the technologically advanced businesses in Gundarland. Since Flavia controlled most of the financial and commercial businesses, the two dominated Gundarland's economic affairs.

~ ~ ~

The inability to find the treasure exasperated Bohan. Ansgar's map showed the location of the treasure but didn't say exactly where the area was. The heroes spent four days searching for a place that looked like the one described on the map. It rained on one of those days and the group, soaking wet, slogged through mud and ate cold meals. In two places, they had spent fruitless hours digging because the area resembled the markings on the map. Much of the problem stemmed from the numerous changes that had occurred over two hundred years. Forests had been cut back, land had been farmed, roads now passed through wooded areas, and new towns had sprung up. In the back of everyone's mind was the possibility that a road or new construction had uncovered the treasure.

Bohan needed the treasure. Getting to Dun Hythe required money to buy horses and supplies. They restocked their supplies whenever they came across a town, but they were running out of old coins to use for those supplies. The simplest solution to the problem was to recover the yuk loot. If they couldn't find the treasure, they would have to steal food and horses, something Bohan didn't want to do because stealing meant some innocent person suffered. Adding to Bohan's concern were the tracks of a body of yuks estimated to be much larger than a hundred. They had crossed the tracks four times and knew the yuks were close. He wondered if the tracks belonged to Alik's warriors.

"This looks familiar," Ansgar said once again. He and Bohan stood on a slight rise. In front of them was an open plain with forest to the south. Several boulders dotted the area.

Maggy and Angus groaned in chorus.

Colbert wandered off from the group.

"Are you sure this time?" Bohan asked Ansgar.

Ansgar knelt and studied the map which lay on the ground in four pieces.

"Yes, this place matches much of what is on my map. Granted, the area is quite different," Ansgar added. "The forest has receded."

"We buried the treasure near a stand of birch trees," Bianca said. "But there ain't any birch trees here."

"Well, I don't think birch trees last all that long," Bohan said.

"This ain't the place," Tibbs said. "We're just wastin' more time."

"I found it," Colbert yelled to the

others. He stood by a boulder twenty yards away.

"What did you find?" Bohan asked.

"I made my mark on this rock. This is the place."

Everyone gathered around the rock while Colbert grinned.

"The King told me to stand guard while the stuff was buried," he said. "I was standin' here and I got bored, so I used my dagger to scratch my rune on the rock."

He pointed to a rune on the top of the rock.

"It looks like your work, Colbert," Ansgar said. "The rune is backwards."

"Can you recall where the digging happened?" Bohan asked.

"Sort of."

Colbert scratched his beard and looked at the open area. "It was that way." He pointed to the east. "Someone walk that way and I'll tell ya when to stop."

"Maggy," Bohan said, "Angus. Go. Start digging when Colbert tells you to stop walking."

Two hours and seven holes later, the heroes were in a bad mood, especially the sweaty and dirt-covered Maggy and Angus.

Ansgar was convinced someone else had found the treasure and they were wasting time.

All of them cursed Colbert, convinced he was an idiot.

"Rider comin'." Luc called out from his sentry post.

Bohan saw a middle-aged man riding toward them and went to meet him.

"I'm Captain Bohan," he said. "Who are you?"

"I'm the bailiff for the town over there." The man waved vaguely to the west. "Wot are ya doin' out here?"

"Umm, archery holes. We're digging archery holes."

"Wot for?"

"To hide archers, obviously."

"Why do ya need archers hidin' here?"

"To ambush the yuks."

The bailiff's eyes widened and his mouth dropped open. "Wot yuks?"

"We have information about a yuk raiding party coming this way."

"Ya with the army post near Skensfirth?"

"No, we're a special command from headquarters and frankly sir, you are watching a top-secret operation. I hope you know how to keep your mouth shut."

The bailiff chewed on Bohan's statement, then said, "The holes ain't inna line."

"You have a keen eye for detail, sir. If the holes were in a line, it would look suspicious. Scattered about as they are, the yuks won't be alerted to a trap."

The bailiff looked dubious.

"I don't see any archers except for this one." The bailiff pointed at Bianca.

"Sergeant Bianca's archers will be along shortly. She's supervising the construction of the holes. I think it's about time you left, bailiff. And be warned. My general will not be happy if the yuks hear about this trap and avoid it. If I were you, I'd keep my mouth shut and not say a word about what you saw. Am I clear?

"Aye, I understand."

"Then away with you. You're interfering with important work."

The bailiff nodded and turned his horse around.

The heroes waited until the bailiff was out of sight.

"Let's try one more hole," Bianca said. "Dig here." She stood in the middle of a few holes.

"Get someone else to dig," Maggy

said. "I'm tired."

"Tibbs, Barrow," Bohan said. "You dig the next one."

Tibbs, after grumbling about his bad back and getting no sympathy, joined Barrow and dug a hole.

At two feet down, Barrow noticed a piece of leather at the side of the hole. He moved some dirt and uncovered part of a leather sack. "I think I found it," he called out.

"We found it," Tibbs growled. "Not you, us."

Barrow freed the sack and handed it out of the hole.

Bohan opened it and coins and jewelry spilled on the ground. He smiled as Maggy and Angus, suddenly not so tired, widened the hole.

An hour later, the treasure had been uncovered and distributed so each hero carried a portion of the loot in sacks formerly used for food supplies.

"Now for the next step," Bohan said. "Leticia! Where can we buy horses?"

"And ponies," Luc said.

"Right," Bohan replied. "We need six horses and four ponies." He paused and frowned. "You can ride, can't you?"

Leticia nodded and said,

"Skensfirth is the best place to buy the horses. The last time I was there, it had six or seven stables selling horses. It's about two days march from here." She pointed to the west.

"All right then." Bohan stood with his hands on his hips and smiled. "Jerado better look to his defenses."

~ ~ ~

Maurice returned to his office in the Presidential Palace after a surprise audit of the First Urban Bank and Hardware Store.

He stopped at a street corner to watch two members of the Troll Patrol change a minor intersection into a snarling traffic jam complete with cursing wagon drivers, neighing horses and frightened pedestrians. He marveled at the ability of the trolls to screw up any traffic situation and make it worse.

At the bank, one that Flavia frequently used, the stunned bank employees had reluctantly let him look at the account ledgers, but only after he threatened to shut them down for a week. He expected to find evidence of Flavia's corruption and he wasn't disappointed. An anonymous someone had deposited fifty thousand silver pennies in Flavia's account a week ago. She had withdrawn five hundred gold pennies two days later.

Maurice knew where the gold pennies were: in the basement of Flavia's mansion. By now the basement must be filled with casks of silver and gold pennies. Flavia, almost single-handedly, was destroying Gundarland's economy by removing all those coins from circulation. Businesses relied on the silver and gold pennies and both coins were growing scarce.

At his desk he wrote down the details on a sheet of paper. He kept track of Flavia's misdeeds, and they now filled three volumes of notebooks while Lithgow's embezzlements was still on volume one.

Maurice wasn't sure why he kept the records. He could never disclose the contents. If he did, Jerado would instantly disappear him. Still, corruption on this scale outraged him and recording the details was all he could do about it. Perhaps someday the journals would be made public.

He finished up the writing, opened the door to his secret room and placed the paper in a folder on a shelf. Next he checked the scryers. As usual, Lithgow's messages all concerned uniforms. Flavia's messages were sent to the heads of businesses she controlled throughout Gundarland. Jerado sent messages infrequently, but he had sent a number of them recently. They went to someone named Alik, and it directed Alik to murder a group of warriors. Interestingly, Alik demanded a big chunk of money for the job. Few people made demands on Jerado and most of them quickly regretted making the demand.

Maurice was horrified. Murdering a group of people went far beyond corruption. The name Alik seemed familiar and he recalled that Alik was the name of the most powerful warlord in Yuklandia. It followed that whoever needed murdering must be in southern Gundarland near the border.

He had just uncovered another secret that could get him killed if Jerado learned he knew about the transaction. Having a bolthole with the Godmother now appeared to be a brilliant idea.

~ ~ ~

The Troll Patrol was an institution unique to Dun Hythe. Long ago, the city leaders had recognized the need to control and direct the heavy wagon traffic that flowed to and from the port area. They organized a patrol of citizens for this purpose and all went well for a while. No one knows who allowed the first troll to join up, but word immediately spread throughout the troll community that one of their number had a paying job with unlimited donuts. Soon after that, every opening in the patrol attracted dozens of trolls who brazenly persuaded non-trolls to withdraw their applications. Within a few years, trolls had taken over the organization.

Trolls proved to be particularly inept at traffic control. A member of the Troll Patrol could station himself in the middle of a deserted intersection and, within minutes, he would create a traffic-snarling mess. To keep the enraged wagon drivers under control, the trolls relied upon truncheons. A whack or two in the head always knocked a driver groggy and made him a lot less noisy.

The Troll Patrol did prove effective in controlling the riots that resulted from their traffic mismanagement. Trolls had evolved from rocks and they had rock DNA in their systems. That made hitting a troll in his head a waste of energy. All it did was damage the weapon and focus the troll's attention on the head-hitter, much to the head-hitter's discomfort.

Trolls had a unique perspective on bribery. Often a visitor who had been apprehended by a troll on a charge — usually a dubious one — would offer a sum of money to make the charge disappear. The troll always pocketed the money and then added bribery to the charge sheet. The bribed troll scrupulously shared the bribe money with the shift desk sergeant.

Early in the process of changing to the Troll Patrol, politicians discovered that it was impossible to fire a troll and remain alive. The fired troll took the firing personally and considered himself insulted. An insult to one troll insulted the troll's entire family, who then felt obligated to avenge their family honor by slaughtering the insulter.

~ ~ ~

In his study, Lithgow awaited an inventor. Meanwhile, he paced the room and contemplated taking revenge on his sister. He knew she was behind the outrageous price increase in the cost of uniforms. Because of it, he postponed his plans to equip three regiments of foot soldiers with new uniforms.

He dismissed the idea of torching her home. It was too obvious and he would get the blame, no matter how good an alibi he concocted. In similar fashion he rejected hiring thugs to attack and beat her while she walked on the street. The reputation of her guards was so formidable that knowledgeable street felons would never agree to go up against Flavia's guards. He would only be able to hire stupid thugs who would be no match for the guards.

A new possibility popped into his mind. Flavia's Interior Department was responsible for collecting customs duties. What if he invited her to inspect a new navy vessel suitable for chasing smugglers? He could say the vessel was a gift for her because he couldn't use it. And what if the ship sank outside the harbor during the inspection cruise? After a few seconds of thought he discarded the idea. Flavia was a strong swimmer. If she survived the sinking, she'd make life miserable for him. It wasn't worth the risk.

His only option was to rely on his spies to find a weakness he could exploit.

A knock on the door interrupted his planning.

His secretary ushered a dwarf into the room. The dwarf carried a large box and set it on a table. Next he bowed to Lithgow. "MacGregor, sir. At your service."

"Well, MacGregor. I hope you have something useful for me."

"I do, sir! I do!"

MacGregor opened the box and took out models of two different sized sailing ships.

"My development will revolutionize ship building and make Gundarland's navy the strongest in the world."

"How do you do that?" Lithgow moved closer to the models to inspect them. "These seem quite ordinary."

"Aye. They are ordinary except for one detail."

"And that is?"

"They have iron plates instead of wood for the sides. This makes them invulnerable to attacks of any kind. Even ramming them will do no good."

"Iron plates, you say? You fool! The ships will sink from the weight of the metal."

"Nay, sir. The ships are still buoyant and will remain afloat despite the metal sides."

"That's absurd."

"I assure you the ships will be safe. Look, there is a pond outside. I'll demonstrate that these models will float despite having iron plates for the sides."

"Bah. You are a trickster. I"m sure these models have extra thin plates on them. The thicker plates on the actual ships will either sink them or cause them to capsize because they are top-heavy. I am not stupid. I recognize a scam when I see one."

Lithgow stamped his foot.

"Begone before I have you thrown in prison."

Muttering, MacGregor packed up his ship models and left.

Lithgow smiled. Unmasking a crooked inventor always improved his mood.

~ ~ ~

Leticia marched in the middle of the group. Bohan, as usual, marched up front with Ansgar. The heroes used a spread out formation that lessened the chances of the entire group getting ambushed at once. Maggy was the scout for now and was far out in front of the rest, which meant Angus marched alone.

Leticia increased her pace and caught up with the dwarf. After exchanging pleasantries, she said, "You and Maggy seem to be rather close. How did you two meet?"

"Was quite a few years back. Me and some lads went inna tavern for a few drinks. I was getting horny, so I stuck up a conversation with this good-looking gal dwarf named Leslie. After I while, I started to put some moves on Leslie and she objected 'cause Leslie was a guy dwarf, not a gal one. So he punched me inna mouth. Naturally, I punched him back. Next thing I know, everyone inna tavern is fightin'. Even the servin' wenches are throwin' punches. Bottles are flyin' around — empties of course — 'cause you never get a partially filled one back. Chairs are gettin' smashed over heads. It was a real riot. About then, I see a bench flyin' at my head and before I can duck, it hits me and it's lights out."

Leticia tried hard not to smile at the story.

"When I woke up — inna jail cell — Maggy was inna cell with me. I didn't know her at the time and she was a mess. Split lip, broken nose, black eye, knuckles on both hands skinned up. I tell ya, it was love at first sight. When we got out after servin' ten days, we was engaged. Actually, that was the best time I ever had inna jail."

"What a story," Leticia said. "Does a mix-up like that happen a lot?"

"It happens quite a lot. For single dwarf guys and gals, romancin' can be dangerous. Ya see, both sexes have beards and look alike. So if a gal's name ain't somethin' like Mary or if she ain't wearing a dress, it's hard to tell if she's a guy or a gal. Back then, I didn't know Leslie could be used for both a guy or a gal."

"So you and Maggy been together ever since?"

"Yeah, sometimes closer than other times."

~ ~ ~

Within two hours of dividing the loot and marching toward Skensfirth, Bohan found the yuks blocking his path. Led by Alik wearing his blue sash, they stood in a shield wall that stretched twenty-five across and eight deep. A few young yuks stood guard over the pile of supply bags in the rear.

"Drop your weapons and you'll die

quickly," Alik called out.

"Didn't we hear that one before?" Tibbs asked.

"How many are there?" Luc asked.

"Two hundred, at least" Bianca replied.

Luc pulled a face and scratched his chest.

"Twenty," Bianca whispered to him.

"That's twenty for each of us," Luc said. "It'll be a fair fight."

"Maybe not," Barrow said. "We ain't fought inna melee inna long time. We're outta practice."

Leticia grabbed Bohan's arm. "Are you going to surrender?"

"No." Bohan scratched his beard then said, "I'm thinking an arrow formation, lads."

"Right," Bianca said. "Form up."

They dropped the loot bags and grouped themselves into the formation with Bohan at the front and Barrow on his right and Tibbs on his left. Echeloned behind Tibbs were the two dwarfs, Maggy and Angus.

Bianca slung her longbow over her shoulder, drew a short sword, took up her shield and stood behind Barrow. Colbert stood behind her and Luc behind Colbert.

"Leticia," Bohan said. "Stand behind me and hold onto my war belt. Don't let go. Once we hit the yuk line you may have to step over a body or two. Don't trip. If you do, the yuks may grab you before we can get back to you."

Reluctantly, Leticia took her place. She ran her right index finger under her nose and wiped it on her shirt. It was the Sign of the Sneeze, used by Snotists as a short prayer.

Ansgar stood behind Leticia.

The yuk shield wall yelled insults and curses. Alik waved his curved sword.

"All right," Bohan said. "On three, we start forward. Listen to my command to start running."

Once the heroes moved forward, the yuk lines fell silent, obviously not expecting an attack.

"Now!" Bohan called out.

The arrow formation broke into a trot and then into a run. The heroes screamed their war cry, "Bohan! Sulvaria! Bohan!"

Leticia added her own scream out of primordial fear.

Bohan aimed the formation at the left side of the yuk line and hit them while slashing with his sword. He split the yuk line and kept moving forward cutting left and right with his sword. Barrow and Tibbs widened the gap by killing the yuks on either side of the gap. The rest of the heroes carved more yuks out of the way. Ansgar cast fireballs at the yuks on either side of the formation.

Yuk blood fountained into the air, some of it landing on Leticia's hair and face to her horror.

In a few seconds, the formation broke into the clear.

"Left turn," Bohan shouted.

"Left turn," he shouted a second time.

"Halt. Take a few deep breaths and we'll have another go."

The yuk battle line was in disarray. Bodies littered the ground. Those still standing milled about in confusion and fear. Smoke rose from those stuck down by Ansgar's spells.

Bohan's arrow formation now faced the back of the yuk shield wall where the weakest soldiers were stationed. The shield wall broke apart as it tried to turn to face the rear.

"Now!" Bohan roared.

The formation struck the yuk lines again and shattered the yuk formation.

Once clear of the yuks, Bohan

ordered two right turns and halted the group.

Leticia screamed non-stop while the others inhaled deeply and adjusted their weapons and shields.

The yuk line collapsed as the yuks, including Alik, raced to escape from the battlefield.

The arrow formation dissolved without any order from Bohan.

Leticia continued to scream while still holding onto the King's belt.

Ansgar patted her shoulder. "It's all right, dear. The battle is over. You can let go and please stop that wretched howling."

Barrow, the group's quartermaster, said, "After we clean up, search the bodies. We need food and water. All we got left is Ansgar's beer skin."

"I ain't eatin' yuk food," Tibbs said.

"Then starve," Barrow replied.

"That was fun," Luc said. "Too bad the yuks didn't stick around for another go."

Bohan bounced on his toes and grinned, "I haven't had this much fun since I fought in the melee at tournaments. If we find food we'll have a meal, then set out for Skensfirth. I think the way to Dun Hythe is clear."

~ ~ ~

From Barrow's Journal: *That Leticia is quite a gal. Just fought a mob of yuks and she stayed in the middle of our battle formation the whole time. She's quite the screamer also. And good looking.*

Leticia's hands shook and her throat hurt from yelling. The sight of all the yuk bodies, some still some moving, shocked her. Her ears still rang with the sounds of war cries and screams of agony. She recalled the sight of blood and body parts flying through the air and shuddered. Leticia knew she'd have nightmares about the battle for years to come.

It seemed incredible to her. Nine heroes had defeated and routed two hundred yuk warriors. She looked around at her companions. They acted like it was all in a day's work. Some of them stood guard against a surprise yuk attack while the rest searched the bodies for supplies and loot.

"All they have to eat is rice and beans," Barrow said when the search was completed.

"That stuff I'll eat," Tibbs said.

"Got some coins to add to our treasury," Barrow added.

"Come." Bianca took Leticia's arm and steered her away from the carnage. "There's a pond nearby. We'll clean up there."

Maggy accompanied them to the pond. The females stripped off any armor they wore and then, to Leticia's surprise, jumped into the water still wearing clothes.

"Come in," Maggy called out. "It's the only way to get the blood and gore off our clothes."

"We don't have towels to dry off," Leticia replied.

"Don't need 'em," Bianca said. "We'll dry off in the warm air."

Across the pond, half of the males splashed around and tried to drown each other to peals of laughter. The other males stood guard.

Leticia couldn't believe the heroes acted as if nothing untoward happened only a short time ago.

This group of warriors seemed invincible. For the first time since she joined them, Leticia felt that they had a chance of success in Dun Hythe. After all, the heroes, outnumbered twenty to one, barely worked up a sweat in defeating the yuks.

Who could possibly stand against them?

~ ~ ~

After the heroes cleaned up and while they ate the captured yuk food, Bohan beckoned Bianca and Ansgar to walk a short distance away.

Bohan walked with his hands behind his back. "I've been thinking about killing Jerado. It may not be as simple as I originally thought."

"I agree," Ansgar said. "There are bound to be problems with killing a country's leader."

"Yeah," Bianca added. "What if he has a lotta guards around him?"

"I'm thinking more about getting away after the deed. If Jerado is popular, or if he has guards, we'll have to get out of Dun Hythe fast."

"How do we do that?" Bianca asked. "We can't fight our way outta an entire city."

"Exactly," Bohan said. "We have to kill him late at night. Then we make it to the port area and get on a ship that's about to leave in the morning."

"I doubt if a ship's captain will be thrilled to see a bunch of armed warriors show up on his deck," Ansgar replied.

"I think we can persuade him to take us on a voyage," Bohan said.

"Stealing a boat is piracy," Bianca said.

"We're not really stealing it. After the captain drops us off in some foreign country, he can have his boat back."

"So, we'll be traveling to a foreign country?" Ansgar asked.

"Yeah, there's nothing to hold us here. I don't have a kingdom anymore, and there are no small kingdoms looking to hire warriors to add to their army like there were in the old days. Perhaps it'll be different in another country."

"Meeting foreign wizards will be interesting," Ansgar said.

"I'm not sure the lads will like this idea." Bianca pulled a face. "I'm not sure I like it."

"Come now." Bohan put his arm around her shoulders and gave here a squeeze. "Conditions in a foreign land have to be much different than they were in Sulvaria. We can go back to the way we were before I became king."

Bianca's face brightened. "I'd like

that."

"When will you tell the others?" Ansgar asked.

"Right now." Bohan walked toward the camp. Having talked through the problem, he felt more at ease with the formidable task ahead.

Once there, he told the heroes about his plan for Dun Hythe.

"I never been onna ship," Tibbs said.

"Me neither," Luc added.

"We'll have to get supplies onna way to the harbor," Barrow pointed out.

Bohan shook his head. "We won't have time for that."

"Then what do we eat?" Barrow asked.

"Fish," Ansgar said. "We'll be on the ocean. It's filled with fish."

"I hate fish," Tibbs said.

"Good," Bianca said. "Starve."

Chapter Nine

Flavia walked back and forth on the small platform and kept glancing to the south. She wore a hooded gown in pale blue with matching sandals.

The first peat train would arrive from Yuklandia at any time. When it arrived, a long, very expensive project would be successfully completed. While costly, it would prove to be very lucrative. One of her companies owned the exclusive rights to distribute the peat. Another built and maintained the trains and the road. A third hired yuks to extract the peat from the Yuklandia bogs and transport it to the depot.

Executives from several companies involved in the project stood on the platform but stayed out of Flavia's path.

She reached the end of the wooden platform, peeked over the edge and saw a plume of dirty white smoke. Finally! She turned and walked back to the middle of the platform built to prevent her from getting mud on her sandals.

The peat train slowly rounded a bend and came into view. It consisted of a large barrel-shaped boiler, a tall stack and an open cabin for the driver. The contraption rode on eight wooden wheels to better distribute the load on the thick wooden planks that formed a pathway. Four open cars followed the engine, each filled with peat. Flavia estimated the peat at twenty tons.

Flavia's eyes lit up at the sight of the cars. However, she didn't see peat, she saw piles of silver and gold pennies to add to her collection.

Once the train came to a stop in the depot a mile outside Dun Hythe, Flavia addressed the dozen reporters. They stood in the mud because she refused to allow them to crowd the platform.

"Today, you saw history. You saw the first peat train complete its journey from Yuklandia. Already, a second train is down there getting loaded with more peat. As soon as the one here is emptied, it will return to get more peat. An era of cheap fuel is upon us."

A reporter raised a hand. When Flavia acknowledged him, he asked, "Why did it take so long to complete this project?"

"New technology always come with new problems. In this case, during trials, we discovered the train couldn't climb a steep grade. So we had to cut a road through the hills and go around, instead of over, rock formations. That was a major delay."

"Will the trains ever haul anything besides peat?"

"We're working on a plan to haul freight."

"Will the peat be available to everyone or just big companies?"

"The peat will be available to anyone who wants to buy it. I think that is enough questions. I have other appointments to keep."

On the way to her carriage, a male elf approached and gave her an envelope.

"What's this?" Flavia asked suspiciously.

"The Godmother wants to meet with ya. Don't disappoint the lady."

The elf stepped back into a crowd of people.

Flavia almost threw the envelope away. What does that felonious female want? How dare she demand a meeting with the Secretary of the Interior! What could they possibly talk about?

After her initial bust of anger, Flavia decided to accept the meeting. If nothing else, Daddy would want a complete report on what the Godmother wanted.

~ ~ ~

Jerado sat at his desk and tapped a fingernail on the surface. As usual, the office was quiet in the mornings. Last night, he and Remy had played cards again and the undead half-pint won once more. So far, Remy was ahead by five-hundred-thirty-three silver pennies and forty-nine gold ones.

So much for his idea that Remy would be an easy mark. Jerado never heard of such an incredible streak of luck. To make it worse, Remy was a skilled bluffer. Who knew?

Losing touched a nerve and he brooded over it. Jerado could never stand to lose and, many times, losing turned him to violence.

Enough with the cards, he thought. At their next session, he would teach Remy how to play chess. For money. He would recoup his lost coins.

~ ~ ~

From Barrow's Journal: *Bohan told me to find a short sword for Leticia to use. I found one on a dead yuk, cleaned it up and gave it to her. Now, every night after we set up camp, I'm giving her lessons on how to use it.*

Remy entered the press room and shuffled his way to the podium. Reporters from the *Dun Hythe Times*, the *Gundarland Reporter* and several other broadsheet publishers sat in front of the podium.

"G . . . ood morning. T . . . oday, the government issued its annual report on the economy and it's all good news."

Remy paused to see if any reporters were questioning him yet.

"B . . . usiness profits are at an all-time high thanks to the new wage restrictions implemented by Flavia, the Secretary of the Interior a while ago."

A reporter's hand shot up.

Remy sighed and acknowledged the *Dun Hythe Times* reporter, his particular nemesis.

"Remy, how can that be good news? The wage restrictions are crushing the workers. They can hardly afford to buy food."

"P . . . rofits are the lifeblood of the economy." Remy read from a scroll prepared by Flavia. The scroll had answers to the reporters' most likely questions and objections. "W . . . ithout the profits, businesses would go bankrupt and there would be no jobs."

"But people can't eat or afford to buy new clothes," the reporter from the *Gundarland Reporter* said.

The Dun Hythe reporter shouted out, "And what about all the small shops going out of business because the workers don't have money to buy anything?"

Remy scanned the scroll and read, "W . . . orkers only put in ten hours on the job. I . . . f they need more money, they can get a second job."

"That's absurd," another reporter said.

Remy read another part of the scroll. "I . . . f they don't want a second job, they should stop having children."

Sensing the reporters didn't accept Flavia's arguments, Remy said, "T . . . hat concludes today's press conference."

Remy shuffled out of the room while the reporters shouted more questions and curses.

~ ~ ~

Flavia climbed into her coach. It was all black with gold trim. The horses were black with gold harnesses. The coachman wore a black suit with gold buttons and trim. Two of her four guards sat in the carriage with her. They also wore black, but without the gold trim. She rode facing the rear and they faced the front so they could see any threat ahead. A third guard rode up top with the coachman and the fourth stood on a step at the back of the carriage.

Flavia wondered what the Godmother wanted. She intended to teach the obnoxious female a lesson about power: the power Flavia had and the Godmother didn't.

The citizens of Dun Hythe glared at the coach as it moved slowly along the streets jammed with cargo carts. Flavia could feel their hostility. It was there every time she went out in her coach. These peasants needed to be taught how to respect their betters. Perhaps a few arrests would teach them respect. Her guards noticed the mood of the crowds and loosened their swords in their scabbards.

The coach pulled up in front of an unmarked building on a side street. An elegant looking elf stepped forward and opened the door of the coach. One of the guards shoved the elf away while the coachman descended and handed Flavia out of the coach.

The elf recovered his dignity and said, "Good afternoon, My Lady. I am the head waiter. Please follow me."

Another elf opened the door to the building and the head waiter marched through followed by Flavia and her guards. Flavia entered a room filled with tables crowded with bankers and politicians she knew. A few gave her a nod, while others looked away.

The head waiter led her to an unmarked door with burly elves standing on each side with crossed arms. The elves had truncheons stuck in their belts. The waiter tapped on the door and opened it. He stepped aside and beckoned for Flavia to enter.

Flavia felt a sensation of anticipation. She didn't know what to expect and that made her nervous. She still didn't know how she could crush the self-important witch.

The elves blocked the guards from following Flavia and a scuffle took place.

"You won't need guards, dear," a female voice said. "It'll be only us girls here."

Flavia waved her hand and the scuffle ended. The waiter shut the door.

Flavia examined the Godmother and saw a slender, middle-aged elf with green shoulder-length hair, partially gray, and green eyes. The elf looked like someone's favorite aunt, not the demon Flavia's father often described.

"Please sit down. I have your favorite tea here. Would you like a cup?"

Flavia checked a frown. She didn't want to display her feelings, but how did the Godmother know what her favorite tea was?

A tapping sound came from the door.

"That will be lunch. I ordered chicken poached in wine and milk. If you'd prefer a grilled cheese sandwich, I can have that ordered."

This time Flavia did frown. The Godmother also knew her favorite lunch! This elf knew too much about Flavia's habits. How did she get the information? She must have spies in her office. How dare she! A base-born elf spying on her masters! Flavia resisted an urge to slap her.

"Why did you request this meeting?" Flavia asked.

"We have business to discuss. But we'll save that until after dessert."

Business! Was there no limit to her brazenness? "We have no business to discuss. I'm leaving." Flavia started to stand up.

"Oh, but we do, dearie. It has to do with the distribution of your peat shipments. Sit down! Eat some chicken."

Flavia sat back down. The Godmother caught her attention. If the elf thought she could muscle in on the peat business, she would soon find out how wrong she was.

The two ate in silence and by the time dessert was finished, Flavia's jaws hurt from holding an artificial smile.

After a waiter cleared away the dishes, the Godmother said, "You plan to use teamsters to distribute the peat, do you not?"

"Of course," Flavia replied in a strained voice. "How else would I distribute it?"

"Exactly. However, your regulation on how much a teamster can charge means the drivers can't properly feed their families."

"That's not my concern. My concern is to ensure companies can make a profit."

"I think it would be nice if you contributed a stipend to the Teamsters Guild for each ton of peat they have to deliver —"

"What nonsense!"

"Say fifty copper pennies a ton. The Guild will share the money equally among all the teamsters. Isn't that a nice plan?"

Flavia's anger made it hard for her to reply. How dare this churl demand money!

"It's ridiculous. I refuse to pay."

"I think your answer is a bit hasty, dear. Let me explain what'll happen if you don't pay the stipend."

The Godmother's response startled Flavia. She expected an angry reply, not a reasoned statement.

"If you don't pay the stipend, the teamsters will refuse to haul your peat. Your customers will have to pick it up themselves."

Flavia took a deep breath. Now the Godmother threatened her business. "I'll hire my own drivers."

"That's not possible in Dun Hythe. The Teamsters Guild members are the only ones allowed to drive cargo carts. Hiring non-guild members will result in a strike by the Teamsters Guild."

Flavia shrugged. "Let them strike. I don't care."

"Once the teamsters strike, the port workers will strike in sympathy. So will the city's laborers and the building workers. That means no ships will be loaded or unloaded. Cargo will pile up on the docks and on the roads. Some of it will rot. Construction will cease. The city's economy will be hurt and when Dun Hythe hurts, Gundarland hurts."

Flavia jumped up. "I will not be blackmailed by a bawdy house owner. I'll have my father crush you."

"Sit down, you spoiled brat."

The harsh tone of the Godmother caught Flavia's attention. She slowly returned to her seat.

"Your father won't crush me and he'll have a fit when he hears you started a general strike. He and I have an understanding. He doesn't fight me and I keep Dun Hythe open and working."

Flavia's face turned red. Her father hated the Godmother. She never understood why he didn't send soldiers to arrest her and destroy her organization. Now she realized why he didn't.

"Perhaps I should explain more, dearie. You see, your family rules the country and says what goes on in Gundarland. I say what goes on in Dun Hythe. I rule Dun Hythe, not your father."

Flavia stared at the Godmother. She felt the heat of hatred warm her body.

"The Teamsters Guild will have a representative at the depot whenever a train arrives. He'll determine how many tons are in the train and how much your stipend is. Make sure you pay it."

The Godmother rose from her chair. "It was a pleasure meeting you." She left the room by a door in the rear.

Flavia stood up and fought back tears. She had never been so humiliated or so thoroughly defeated. By a peasant no less. Paying the stipend didn't bother her. She would add it to the price of the peat. What bothered her the most was the way the Godmother dared to treat her as an equal.

~ ~ ~

Jerado sat at his desk in the Presidential office studying a manuscript about a white-magic spell that turned a person into a toad and back again. It was easy enough using white magic. But with black magic, he'd have to first cast a spell at the target designed to change a toad into a person even though the target already was a person. To change the toad back into a person, he'd have cast a spell to change a person into a toad. Just thinking about the complications involved gave him a mild headache. He didn't know exactly how to cast such tricky spells. Developing them through trial and error would be costly in terms of people if he couldn't restore them. He could use Remy as a trial subject as he had often done in the past, but the idea of having a toad as a personal assistant was repugnant. It wasn't in keeping with his presidential image.

His scryer pinged to announce an incoming message.

Jerado stood up and walked to the small table holding the scryer. The silver-colored liquid in the bowl quivered, sending small ripples across the surface. He picked up a stylus and touched the surface. A sequence of runes appeared.

To Jerado from Alik. Bugger these warriors. You want them dead, you kill them. Lost 40 warriors killed and wounded...

To Jerado from Alik. I'm keeping the money!

The messages stunned Jerado. Forty yuk casualties! From only nine heroes! Yuks were reputed to be the most ferocious fighters in all the land. How had Bohan defeated them? The situation was a lot more serious than he originally suspected.

Jerado went to his apparatus room and retrieved his far-sight device. After activating it, he ordered it to find the wizard it previously had found. With minutes, the globe showed Ansgar riding a horse. Bohan rode alongside the wizard with the rest of the heroes behind the pair. With horses, they'd reach Dun Hythe much faster. He didn't have much time to come up with a new plan. Suddenly, the globe went dark. Ansgar must have sensed it and cast a spell of concealment on the group.

Jerado put the device away and returned to his desk to ponder his predicament. A secretary came in carrying a parchment. He waved her away.

With Alik out of the picture, he needed another troop of soldiers to solve the problem. Jerado wasn't especially worried about Bohan, but the thought of fighting Ansgar in a spell battle made his blood run cold. Ansgar was a master class wizard and experienced in wizard-to-wizard combat, a situation Jerado always avoided. He was also an amateur when it came to black magic spells, especially combat spells. He now regretted his decision to become a black-magic wizard but he didn't know how to reverse the process.

The only forces close to Ansgar's current location were Lithgow's troops guarding the border with Yuklandia. He dismissed the idea of using those soldiers for two reasons. One, they were on foot and didn't have access to horses. Two, they would be reluctant to get their new, pretty uniforms dirty.

That left Lithgow's troops stationed in their camp outside Dun Hythe as the only other available soldiers. Some of those troops would have to intercept Bohan and Ansgar. Given Lithgow's ability to screw up even the simplest mission, Jerado would have to issue very specific orders. Unfortunately, Lithgow's lack of talent could still screw things up.

As a back up plan, he could seal off Dun Hythe so Bohan couldn't get into the

city.
With the problem addressed, Jerado felt a bit more secure.

Part Three: On the Way

Chapter Ten

At his weekly dinner with his children, Jerado waited until dessert was finished before broaching the subject of Bohan. All during the meal he was quieter than usual, as he wondered how to explain what had happened. After all, failure to kill an enemy was a bit embarrassing. Finally, he decided on a direct approach.

"We have a problem,' he began.

Both Flavia and Lithgow started.

She wore a shimmering pale yellow gown and he wore the new uniform of his Swineriders regiment.

"I'm sure you remember my story about how I trapped an enemy in a cave many years ago. The cave couldn't be opened because I sealed it with a boulder and an enchantment."

Both children nodded.

"Well, the earthquake down south a while back opened up the cave and my enemy, King Bohan, is still alive."

"That's ridiculous," Lithgow said.
"It happened more than two hundred

years ago."

"Are you sure?" Flavia asked.

"I'm sure. Bohan had a powerful wizard with him when I sprang the trap. The wizard must have cast a sleep spell on Bohan and the others."

"What others?" Flavia asked. "How many others?"

"Bohan always traveled with a group of heroes as his bodyguards. I trapped the whole lot of them in that cave. And now they are all alive and headed for Dun Hythe."

"What for?" Lithgow asked.

"To kill me, you ninny."

"Hire someone to kill them," Flavia said. "That's what I'd do."

Jerado paused, lifted his wig and scratched the top of his head, then said, "I tried that. I hired a yuk warlord and paid him a ton of money to eliminate Bohan and everyone with him. He sent me a message the other day saying he lost forty warriors attacking Bohan and he wasn't doing that any more."

"Just how many guards does this Bohan have?" Lithgow asked.

"There is Bohan, Ansgar the wizard and seven heroes. There is also a woman traveling with them. I don't know who she is or what her role is."

"How do you know all this detail?" Flavia asked.

"I used a far-sight device to find them initially. That's when I confirmed Bohan's existence and saw the woman. I used it again yesterday. Now they have horses and they are headed north from the Skensfirth area. I have no idea how they obtained horses. Perhaps they stole them. After a few minutes, the far-sight device went dark. Ansgar must have sensed my observation and cloaked the group from the device."

"What are you going to do?" Flavia asked. "This sounds serious. Is it?"

"Yes, it could become quite serious, but I have a plan. Flavia, I want your constables to watch the Skensfirth-Dun Hythe road and report the location of the group whenever they are sighted. Once Flavia's constables locate the group, she'll tell you, Lithgow, where they are, and you can determine where to set up a roadblock. Send companies of archers and spears to block the road and kill them when they arrive there. And whatever you do, don't try to use lancers against them."

"Good plan, Daddy," Flavia said. "Lithgow, you better not screw this up."

"At last!" Lithgow beamed.

"Action! A chance to demonstrate my military mettle."

"Killing ten people isn't exactly a military action," Jerado replied. "Although Bohan and his guards aren't easy to kill. You'd better send your best troops with your most experienced officers."

"All right, I'll do that. Trust me, I won't fail you."

Flavia snorted. "You better not fail us."

Once the children left, Jerado leaned back in his chair and relaxed. With Flavia and Lithgow using their vast resources, Bohan would soon be dead. Again.

~ ~ ~

After a morning spent at meetings and in reviewing account ledgers, Maurice decided to check on Jerado and his family by looking at their scryer activity for the last week. He didn't consider this as spying. Rather, he felt it was part of his job as Treasurer to keep abreast of events that could affect the economy. In the past, he was able to identify a few of Flavia's more outrageous plans and head them off with well-placed and well-planned comments to Jerado.

In the room with the scryers, he activated Lithgow's scryer. Maurice didn't see anything unusual except a message to several units to prepare for a march. The destination for the march wasn't disclosed.

Flavia's messages proved more curious. She alerted a number of constables, ordering them to watch the main Skensfirth-Dun Hythe road and report any sighting of a band of ten warriors. Maurice wondered what those messages were about. He also wondered if her messages were related to Lithgow's. If so, it would be the first time in his experience the two worked together because they hated each other.

He turned to Jerado's messages, and the hair on the back of his neck rose on end. The vicious yuk warlord hired to kill a group of warriors refused to pursue the assignment further. The yuk claimed he lost forty soldiers to the group and wasn't returning any money.

Stunned, Maurice tried to make sense of the messages. Who were these warriors? Why did Jerado want them dead? Could Lithgow's and Flavia's messages be related to the yuk failure?

What did these warriors want? Were they headed toward Dun Hythe? Is so, what were their intentions?

Maurice wondered if Remy knew anything. It was usually easy to pry information out of Remy, but he often wasn't up on current events. With Jerado out of the building, the President wouldn't see him in Remy's office and get curious or even suspicious.

Maurice climbed the stairs from his second floor office to the fifth floor and entered Remy's office.

The undead, former half-pint sat in a chair behind a desk and looked like he had died again. His eyes were closed and his body was motionless since he no longer breathed. The caved-in left side of his head — the cause of Remy's first death — grabbed a visitor's attention.

Maurice sat down in a visitor's chair and cleared his throat. Remy's eyes popped open.

"G . . . ood day, Maurice."

"Hello, Remy. Is the boss expected back later today?"

"N . . . no, he's out for the day. H . . . he went with Flavia to see a peat train."

"He seems distracted of late. Is something bothering him?"

Remy nodded and leaned closer to Maurice. "K . . . King Bohan is back."

"Who?"

"D . . . id you learn about the King Who Disappeared in school?"

"Of course. Everyone learned that story. Wait! Are you talking about *that* Bohan?"

"Uh-huh. I . . . t seems Bohan isn't quite dead after all. T . . . he President is really upset about it."

"Bohan is undead?"

"N . . .o, he's alive like you are."

"I can see where Bohan could cause some confusion about who is in charge."

Remy made a face. "I . . . t doesn't have anythin' to do with who's in charge. I . . . t's all about revenge."

Incredulous, Maurice stared at Remy while icy fingers ran up and down his skin. After a few moments, he asked in a soft, quivering voice, "Are you saying Jerado had something to do with Bohan's disappearance?"

Remy nodded and replied, "I . . . I'm not supposed to talk about it."

Maurice stood up and turned to leave the office.

"W . . . anna see the President when he comes back?"

"No. It won't be necessary. It's only a small issue and he has much bigger problems to deal with."

Maurice ignored the tightness in his stomach and returned to his office. He recalled what he could about Bohan's disappearance. The king had ruled a small kingdom down south somewhere, had been very popular and a feared warrior. He had a powerful wizard with him and a small number of heroes as body guards.

Maurice ignored his dry mouth. His knowledge of Bohan's existence could be deadly if Jerado learned of it.

If Bohan planned to get revenge when he reached Dun Hythe, there would be chaos, possibly a civil war. A fight between Jerado and Bohan could trigger a blood bath involving everyone in the Presidential Palace.

From the tone of the scryer messages, Maurice knew Bohan was a serious threat. Now, he understood Lithgow's and Flavia's messages. Jerado must have ordered them to eliminate the Bohan problem. Flavia's constables covered the entire country and could send reports about Bohan sightings. Lithgow had thousands of troops to command. Between them, they could locate and crush Bohan.

Given Lithgow's natural ability to mess up anything, Maurice knew it was time to develop a plan to survive a possible upheaval if and when Bohan reached Dun Hythe.

~ ~ ~

From Barrow's Journal: *Luc is such a dunce. He refused to use the stirrups on his pony because they'd mess up his toe hair. So he fell out of the saddle four times today. Now we're camping for the night and he's cutting his toe hair. They were about six inches long. Now they're less than two.*

Bohan took his time going north even though they now had mounts. In Skensfirth two days ago, they had bought horses, ponies, saddles and tack. It cost them more than half of the yuk treasure. Going into town two at a time, they bought the animals and equipment from different stables to avoid anyone getting suspicious about a large mounted gang

Occasionally, they spotted a bandit gang who didn't want to mess with the armed group. At every village and town along the way, Bohan stopped for a visit. His aim was to find out how the people lived under Jerado's rule. Bohan wanted to know whether they barely survived or whether they thrived.

At yet another small town, he, Barrow, Bianca and Leticia rode into the market square. The rest of his heroes waited out of sight. Bohan and Barrow left their armor and shields behind and wore only their swords. Bianca didn't have her longbow, only a small sword.

The four dismounted and tied the horses to a hitching post and wandered among the many stalls. Food was plentiful in the town as evident by the mounds of it on display.

The bailiff, a swarthy, heavy-set man, spotted them and followed along as they moved around the square. Even though carrying weapons was illegal, the bailiff seemed reluctant to challenge a group of tough-looking strangers.

Barrow, as quartermaster, took to negotiating food for the group

Something bothered Bohan. He took Leticia's elbow and pointed to the edge of the market square where a dozen emaciated, ragged women begged for food. A few held infants in their arms.

"Why are there starving people in every town we pass through?" he asked her.

Leticia didn't answer for a moment. "It's like this all over. Even in Abano, many people are starving." Her voice cracked as she spoke.

"Why? Look at all this food. How can the women be hungry in the middle of all this food?"

"They don't have enough money to buy the food."

Bohan shook his head. "I don't understand this."

"Rich people own all the farms and they hire workers to plant, maintain and harvest the land. The government sets the wages the farm hands are paid and it's not high enough for the workers to feed their families."

"And Jerado allows this to happen?" Bohan spoke through clenched teeth.

"I don't know if he knows. Prices are set by the Secretary of the Interior. Her name is Flavia and I heard she's Jerado's daughter or niece or something. Flavia is the one I have to see about my father."

"I think I have to see this Flavia

and get her to explain why she allows her people to starve."

"I have some copper pennies on me," Bianca said. "Should I give them to the women?"

"Will it do any good?" Bohan asked. "Will they be able to buy any food?"

"They can buy bread," Bianca said.

After she distributed the coins, the women howled and sang in gratitude and swarmed the closest bread stall.

The bailiff approached Bohan. Five burly club-armed men backed him up.

"Wot do ya think yer doin'? Ya tryin' to start a riot?"

"We gave some coins to the poor women," Bohan replied. "They're starving."

"If those women wanna starve that's their business, not yers. Leave off and get outta my town. I don't need any troublemakers in here."

Bianca grabbed the red-faced Bohan's arm and pulled him away from the bailiff. "Come on," she said. "Let's leave. Barrow's finished buying food."

On the ride out of town, Bohan digested the news. He couldn't get the image of the women out of his mind. Or they way they ran to the bread stall.

His father had taught Bohan that a king's job was to protect all the people, not just the rich. His father stressed social justice in all his decrees. Oftentimes, he made Bohan sit through the petitions court where anyone could ask the king for mercy or justice. After the petitioner pleaded his case, his father would ask Bohan for a decision. If his father disagreed with Bohan's decision, he would explain why it was wrong. Whether Bohan's decision was right or wrong, his father made Bohan defend it. In this way, Bohan came to understand his father's position on social justice, and it didn't take long for Bohan to adopt that thinking.

What he saw in the towns and villages violated every rule his father had taught him. Jerado's government exploited the workers and the poor in a way that was shameful and cruel. The situation cried out for change, and Bohan experienced a strong urge to do something to alleviate the misery of the workers.

But what could he do? Killing Jerado probably wouldn't change anything. Some one else would take over the government and continue the same policies.

Bohan rode on still troubled by the scene in town.

~ ~ ~

In her office, Flavia plotted the two most recent reports from her constables on a map of Gundarland. Apparently, Bohan wasn't in a hurry to reach Dun Hythe.

She looked out a window and thought about her father's instructions. Her fourth floor view showed Dun Hythe's traffic-clogged main street and in the distance the port and the masts of many ships.

For a few minutes, she watched a pair of trolls bring traffic to a complete stop as they argued with each other and shouted at drivers.

She turned away from the window and thought: Why should her idiot brother get all the glory and the acclaim? Why should Lithgow receive praise from Daddy? Bohan was in the interior of the country and she was the Secretary of the Interior, so why shouldn't she handle the problem and get all of Daddy's praise?

Flavia employed a company of archers and another of spearmen. The troops were stationed in the middle of the country close to the Skensfirth road. The soldiers were her secret army, paid for by a black budget she had established to handle contingencies like this one. Her forces could intercept and kill Bohan before Lithgow's troops even left Dun Hythe.

Such a decisive act would lock up the succession by proving Lithgow couldn't match her ability and talent. Daddy would throw the sluggard aside and anoint her as the heir.

Flavia hugged herself and pondered her actions as the future queen. Her brother, if he was still alive at that time, would never go along with being passed over. So, her first act would be to have him arrested before he could organize his soldiers and lead a coup attempt.

And then there was Maurice. She would have to act fast to catch him by surprise before he could destroy any records. Flavia really wanted to read the records Maurice had accumulated. She was sure she would find the names of many potential enemies in those papers. And who knew what else he had found out. Yes, Maurice's records would make for fascinating reading

Flavia sat down at her desk and

curled a hank of hair while she pondered the implications — all good — and looked at the downside — none. Next she developed a plan. First, she would delay telling Lithgow about Bohan's location. That way, he couldn't tell his troops where to go. Second, she would order her archers to set up a roadblock in Bohan's path and kill him. Third, she would deliver the news to Daddy and bask in his approval. Since the camp wasn't on her scryer network for security reasons, she wrote out an order, sealed it and gave it to a messenger to deliver.

In a rare good mood, Flavia decided to reward all the constables who spotted Bohan with a bonus of a silver penny. Payable sometime in the future.

~ ~ ~

Leticia walked with Bianca toward a patch of woods. Bianca planned to shoot some game for dinner and Leticia didn't want to stay behind with all the male heroes. Their normal conversation consisted of raunchy stories and insults. Maggy didn't seem to mind and often joined in the talk.

"How did you meet Bohan?" Leticia asked.

"Oh, it was years ago, before he became king. We both worked the tournament circuit. After one big tournament in Dun Hythe, the mayor held a feast for the winners. Bohan was the winner in the melee and I won the archery contest. We started chattin' and realized we were both headin' to the same next tournament after the feast. I forget the town it was in. We traveled together to that tournament. And all the ones after that. Pretty soon we started sharin' a room."

Bianca tested the pull on her longbow.

"We made a lotta money bettin' on each other. Bohan'd bet I'd win the archer shoot and I'd bet he'd win the melee."

Bianca chuckled. "Good times."

"What happened next," Leticia asked.

Bianca sighed. "We both knew it wouldn't last, and it ended when he became king 'cause folks in Centi wouldn't stand for a mixed marriage. Or an affair. They didn't even like folks from different races socializing. So when Bohan became king we broke it off. That's when he asked me to join his guards and take over as the sergeant."

"What a beautiful story, but with a sad ending."

Leticia had herself observed the social rigidity in Centi. Oddly, she didn't recall ever seeing it in Dun Hythe when she was growing up. Perhaps she was too young to notice such customs at the time. She also remembered being puzzled by people's attitudes in Centi when she first arrived from up north.

"I miss him," Bianca said. "And he misses me. I can tell from the looks he sometimes gives me."

When they approached the edge of the woods, Bianca said, "No more talkin'. Don't wanna scare the game away. Walk behind me and step in my footprints."

~ ~ ~

Lithgow stood outside his headquarters tent in the campgrounds south of Dun Hythe. He watched units of his army parade past him. His chest swelled with pride as he viewed his mighty forces.

At last, he was about to unleash these warriors and gain military glory! True, the enemy was a bunch of old warriors and there were only ten of them, but still it was a chance to gain a victory.

His Swineriders unit wheeled onto the parade ground and rode past him. The unit was the newest in the army, conceived and implemented by Lithgow. It consisted of a hundred-fifty dwarf lancers mounted on specially bred war swine. The dwarfs looked splendid in the uniforms Lithgow designed for them. They wore dark blue tunics and sky blue pants with a broad white strip. The gold buttons and gilt rank stripes glistened in the sunlight. Each dwarf carried a six-foot white lance held upright to blend into the pants stripe. The Swineriders were his elite unit and the pride of his army. As soon as he could get more swine, he planned to expand the number of lancers.

At Lithgow's orders a company of archers and another of spearmen stood ready to march as soon as Flavia sent word on Bohan's location. It was an indication of his sister's incompetence that she hadn't found the enemy yet.

While this battle didn't exactly fulfill his dream of conquering Yuklandia, it would give his army much-needed battle experience. The last time the army fought a battle occurred generations ago.

A thought popped into his mind. Why not use the Swineriders to destroy his father's enemy? True, Jerado warned him not to use lancers, but surely the Swineriders weren't ordinary lancers and his father couldn't have been referring to them.

In a few minutes, he had developed a plan and sent an orderly running to implement it. He wouldn't wait for Flavia. He would unleash his forces immediately. At sunrise tomorrow morning he would lead fifty Swinderiders out of camp and head out to intercept Bohan. The archers and spearmen would follow on foot.

From his father's explanation, he knew Bohan traveled on the Skensfirth road. He'd be easy to find. All Lithgow had to do was head south on the same road. They'd be sure to meet.

Lithgow hugged himself. He would face down the enemy as the commanding officer of the Swineriders.

Once his father learned of the victory — without Flavia's help — he would be forced to proclaim him, Lithgow, as the successor. He would be The King: no more of this President and voting nonsense. As King, he could finally demonstrate his military genius.

His second action would be to conquer Yuklandia and subjugate the yuks. His first would be to arrest Flavia for corruption and robbery. And even bad taste for good measure.

Lithgow breathed deeply. He stood on the cusp of achieving all his life's dreams.

Chapter Eleven

From Barrow's Journal: *For two days, we rode through dense woods along a narrow track. Great place for an ambush. Bohan made three of us ride scout and the rest rode much closer to the scouts than usual. We carried our shields on our arms instead of tied to the saddle. Very boring ride despite the tension.*

Luc, on scouting duty, turned his pony and trotted back to Bohan.

"Got a company of archers blocking the road," he said. "Can't see 'em from here, but they're over that hill and around a bend inna road."

"Finally, some excitement," Colbert said.

"I hate archers," Tibbs added. "You never know where the bloody arrows will fall."

"Did they see you?" Bianca asked.

"Yeah. As soon as ya get to the top of the hill, they can see ya."

"Let's go take a look," Bohan said. He urged his horse forward and the others followed.

A few minutes later, they stood on the crest of the hill and could see the archers formed up. Each archer carried a bow with a nocked arrow and had a dozen more arrows stuck in the dirt at their right foot.

They wore uniforms of black tunics and pants, an indication that they were a military unit, not a bunch of irregulars. Bohan felt a surge of doubt. These archers were an indication about how difficult his mission was. It was highly probably that, sooner or later, he would face a battle against overwhelming odds.

"What stupidity," Barrow growled. "These archers are gonna get themselves killed someday if they come across cavalry and they ain't got any spearmen to protect 'em."

"They must have really dumb officers to bring archers without the protection of spearmen," Maggy said.

"Well, I guess we have to get past them," Bohan said. "Ansgar? Will you do us the honors?"

"Of course. It'll take me a minute or two to gather the resources I need. Fortunately, it feels a bit like rain today."

Ansgar closed his eyes and stiffened his thin body.

"What's he doing?" Leticia asked Bianca.

"I think he's gonna make it rain on top of the archers."

"What will that do? A little rain won't hurt them."

"It won't hurt the archers, but the rain will wet the bow strings, and a wet string can't launch an arrow very far. The archers will have to replace the wet string with a dry one before they can shoot at us. By then, we'll be past 'em."

"Ansgar can do that?" Leticia raised an eyebrow.

"I've seen him do it a few times. Very impressive."

Nearby, a clap of thunder shook the air.

An officer, off to the side of the archers, looked around at the sky.

Dark clouds blocked the sun and moved toward the archers.

A light drizzle started up.

Ansgar wiggled his fingers to direct the rain over the archers. When the drizzle reached them, Ansgar waved his hand and the drizzle turned into a downpour.

"We'll give it a few minutes," Bohan

said, "then we'll charge."

"Keep the rain goin' until we get past 'em," Luc said. I'm hot and sweaty and the rain will feel good."

The officer seemed undecided whether to move the archers or not. They stood around trying to protect their bow strings without much success.

"I guess that's long enough," Bohan said. "Draw weapons and charge." He pulled his sword, flicked the reins and his horse moved forward. Bohan went into a trot and then a gallop. So did the others.

The archers scurried away while the officer screamed useless orders.

"I like the way these guys move away from the road," Bianca said. "I don't have to worry about my horse trippin' over some clumsy oaf who fell down in front of me."

A mile down the road, Bohan held up a hand to slow everyone down. He didn't like the idea of coming across a uniformed army unit. It implied someone in Dun Hythe knew of his existence and wanted to stop him. It also implied they would meet up with more soldiers. And the next group might have smarter officers.

~ ~ ~

The secrets weighed down on Maurice. He understood that the more secrets he learned, the closer he came to earning a death sentence. The more secrets he harbored, the more likely he would accidentally disclose one of them.

He mentally ticked off the deadly secrets.

Item: Jerado was a black magic wizard, a status he never revealed to anyone. Since he kept the fact a secret, it stood to reason Jerado wouldn't be kind to anyone who knew it.

Item: Flavia had embezzled a considerable portion of the country's currency and kept it in her basement. Flavia's actions affected the economy and already there were signs of trouble as businesses struggled to find the silver or gold pennies they needed to pay bills. While graft and embezzlement were common among government bureaucrats, Flavia had perfected stealing into an art form. Maurice was sure she'd spend a part of her fortune to silence him if she knew he knew.

Item: King Bohan was alive and heading to Dun Hythe. His arrival in the city would generate chaos and destruction if his presence was publicly known. If Bohan tried to overthrow Jerado it could lead to a civil war fought out in the streets and alleys of the city. And how would Bohan's wizard — a white-magic practitioner — confront a black-magic wizard? The results could be catastrophic.

Item: Jerado knew about Bohan and hired a yuk warlord to kill Bohan and the attempt failed.

It seemed to Maurice as if secrets popped up everywhere these days and he was the only one who knew about them. None of the secrets added luster to the regime. They were all negative or evil secrets.

Obviously, the future was about to get very interesting — and deadly.

After pondering the situation for an hour, Maurice decided it was time to make a life-changing decision, namely, which side he would take. Should he defend the status quo and back Jerado's regime? Or should he support Bohan?

Supporting Jerado meant more of the same graft with the addition of economic troubles and starving workers. Supporting Bohan meant an uncertain future. But could that future be worse than one Jerado represented? He didn't see how it could.

Maurice believed a government should look after and protect the majority of the people. Jerado's government failed miserably on that issue. On the other hand, a Bohan future had considerable upside potential while the Jerado future looked pessimistic. Overall, the Jerado future looked especially bleak for himself because of all the secrets he knew.

Maurice prided himself on loyalty. It was a quality Jerado also prized. Loyalty had led to his promotion to Treasurer. To back Bohan meant an end to his life-long tendency for loyalty. From what he recalled of Bohan's history, the man had ruled fairly and supported justice for everyone, qualities missing from Jerado's reign.

His decision came down on Bohan's side, even though he had to suppress a feeling of betrayal. Once made, he began to build a plan to support Bohan. One question seemed immensely important: what did the population think about King Bohan and his return? Maurice wondered what would happen if he leaked the news about the old king?

He needed allies who also supported Bohan. The most powerful ally in the city would be the Godmother. What would convince her to support overthrowing the government? From what he knew, her twin motivations were power and money. He would have to exploit those motivations to gain her support.

Then there was the issue of protecting his own life. He needed a bolthole for when things got interesting. Here the Godmother offered an answer. She had properties all over the city. One of them must be suitable as a hideout.

After all his heavy thinking, all that remained was to begin working on his plan.

The first step was to meet with the Godmother.

~ ~ ~

While riding northward, Ansgar pondering the meaning of Jerado's change. He still didn't understand what he had learned. What exactly had changed about the man? Ansgar only knew Jerado had somehow transformed himself, but he didn't know the meaning of the change. Not knowing your opponent could make for a deadly confrontation. Whatever the alteration consisted of, he knew Jerado would exploit it to make himself more powerful.

Thinking about the wizard brought back a memory about the first time he saw Jerado launch a combat spell.

It was back in their university days. The university had a target practice field behind the building. It consisted of a series of metal targets scattered around a large area and a twenty-foot high dirt wall to protect the citizenry from errant spells. One of the senior year courses taught combat spell-craft, and the students used the field to practice how to control and modulate the spells.

Ansgar came upon an upset Jerado on day at lunchtime.

"They won't let me use the practice field because I'm not a registered student," Jerado complained. "How can I learn how to cast combat spells? If I try it anywhere else, I'll be arrested and thrown in jail."

Ansgar weighed whether he should help Jerado or ignore his situation. In the end curiosity won out. He wanted to see what Jerado could do with combat spells when he never actually attended a class.

"Students are allowed to bring a

visitor to the practice field once a month. Usually the visitor is a parent or a potential employer, but I think I can get you in. Let's do it dinner time. The field will be empty of other students then."

Jerado gave a half-smile and a mumbled "Thank you."

Later that day, Jerado stood behind the firing line and chose a target depicting a spearman located about fifty feet away. He launched a fireball spell. The huge ball of flames overshot the target and crashed to the ground in front of the dirt wall.

"Too much power," Ansgar said. "You have to lower the power settings or else you'll quickly exhaust your reserves of magical power. For a single foe, I'd use the lowest power level possible."

Jerado nodded and aimed another fireball. This one, much smaller, missed the target by ten feet.

Jerado cursed through clenched teeth.

"Take it easy," Ansgar said. "My first time, I missed the target six straight times. That's why we have target practice."

After a few more spell launches, Jerado's power reserve became exhausted. Ansgar noticed his vile mood, as if Jerado suddenly realized he wasn't the all-powerful wizard he thought he was.

A month later, Ansgar again took Jerado to target practice and was amazed at his proficiency. Jerado must have practiced launching combat spells through dry runs: going through the process up to the point of launching the spell. Ansgar could tell that Jerado's fierce determination to succeed would make him a formidable wizard.

Ansgar shook his head to clear the memory. He didn't look forward to a spell fight with such a wizard. But fight they must. There was no other way to clear the slate after more than two hundred years of entrapment.

~ ~ ~

Leticia sat with her back to a tree. The camp was quiet with most of the heroes off practicing weaponry. She could hear the sounds of clashing swords and cursing from the heroes. Only Luc, the day's cook, remained in the camp, grooming his toe hair while watching a haunch of venison roast on a spit. The smell of roasting meat filled the campsite.

"Can I ask how you became a berserker?" Leticia asked. "You don't look like what I expected a berserker to look like."

Luc chuckled. "I get that a lot. Just because I'm not tall and strong, people figure I can't be a berserker. But strength has little to do with it."

"Really? I'd have thought that would be important."

"Naw. Other stuff is more important."

"Like what?"

"I'll tell ya a story. When I was young, I was always gettin' beat up by lads who were bigger and stronger. One day, they were punchin' me around and I couldn't take it anymore. I decided to fight back no matter how much they hurt me. I started throwin' punches. I kept gettin' hit and it hurt, but I didn't stop. Before long, they quit and ran away. They never bothered me again."

"Is that when you decided to become a berserker?"

"That came later on. I learned that soldiers inna battle are really fightin' to stay alive, not to win the battle. So if someone fights because they want to hurt the other guy, they have a big advantage. When I go into a battle, I'm not tryin' to stay alive, I'm tryin' to hurt the other guy. And hurt him real bad. That gives me a big edge."

"I never thought about that," Leticia said.

"It also helps I'm small and scrawny. Everyone thinks I'm an easy target. So I got the element of surprise on my side, also."

"I can see where that helps."

"Now with Tibbs, he likes to fight battles 'cause he loves to hurt people."

Leticia nodded.

"Tibbs used to be a commander inna army up north. Led troops in battles and won 'em. In one battle, his king or duke or whatever, got himself killed and lost the battle. Tibbs escape and went inna exile. Then he ended up here with us.

A sweaty Bohan came back to camp. He grabbed the beer bag, took a long squirt and made a face. "Bah! Warm, stale, flat beer."

"Better than stinky water," Luc said.

Bohan ignored Luc's comment. "Dinner ready?"

Luc poked the venison with a knife. "Not yet. Gotta cook a bit more."

Leticia pondered the Luc's secret.

There was a lesson in it: size and strength aren't that important.

~ ~ ~

Remy took a chair across from Jerado. A chess board and pieces sat in between them.

"Are you sure you remember the moves?" Jerado looked forward to recouping his card game losses.

"Y ..es. I . . . I practiced the moves in my office. I . . . I also read a scroll on playing the game."

"Then you won't object to betting on the outcome of the game?"

"N . . . o. H . . . ow much?"

"Let's bet a modest sum. Say, twenty-five silver?" Jerado pushed a stack of silver pennies into the middle.

"A . . . ll right." Remy pushed a similar stack forward.

"I"ll let you have the first move," Jerado said.

Remy moved a pawn forward to start the game.

Five moves later, Remy said, "C . . . heckmate," and scooped up the silver coins.

Jerado sat stunned for a few moments. "Rematch."

After Remy won four more games — the last for seven gold pennies — Jerado said through clenched teeth, "That's enough for tonight, Remy. I'm tired."

~ ~ ~

The heroes camped for the night on a hilltop in a wooded area.   Bianca fed wood to the fire and cleaned the pan she'd used to cook squirrel fricassee for everyone's dinner.

Colbert came back from guard duty and said in a quiet voice, "Got some bandits trying to sneak up on us. They're making enough noise to wake the dead." He took a plate of fricassee and sat down.

Angus stood up. "I'm next on duty. I'll take care of them." He picked up his axe and took a few warmup swings. At the edge of the hill, he paused. "Hey, Maggy. Wanna help?"

"Umm, all right." Maggy stood up and fetched her weapon, also an axe. "I think this counts as a date."

Angus nodded.

Both dwarfs went down the hill and several minutes later the woods erupted with screams, the sounds of axes pounding into shields and flesh. While attacking the bandits, Angus and Maggy sang a dwarf love duet.

"If those two get married," Barrow said, "I ain't buy 'em another weddin' present."

"How many times will this make?" Luc asked. "Five, maybe?"

"Seven," Bianca said. "Maggy and Angus have been married and divorced six times. So far."

"What?" Leticia was incredulous. "Those too have been married and divorced that many times?"

"That's since they joined up," Luc replied. "Who knows how many times they got hitched before that."

"You know," Barrow said, "when a couple gets divorced, they ought to give the weddin' presents back."

"That's absurd," Ansgar said. "Why, the people getting married would have to make a list of who gave them what. And how they going to find it if they don't get divorced until ten years later. And what if the gift got broken in the meantime?"

"If they can't find the list, or they ain't got the gift anymore," Tibbs said, "then they oughta give everybody some money."

Bohan laughed out loud. "I only wish I had philosophical problems like this one."

"And the weddin' receptions were terrible," Colbert said. "Dwarf beer and raw rabbit. Ugh!"

"And inna dark, damp underground cave," Luc added.

The noise from the bottom of the hill stopped. A few minutes later, Maggy appeared at the crest of the hill and announced, "We're engaged."

The heroes groaned.

"We're gonna get married in Dun Hythe. You're all invited."

The heroes groaned louder.

~ ~ ~

From Barrow's Journal: *Went into a small town today. Got 10 pounds of flour and 50 of beans. A good quartermaster is also a good thief. To keep in practice, I stole the flour. Didn't tell the king because he'd make me go back into town and pay for it. Also bought a lamb. It's cooking and it smells so good. Tonight at least, we'll eat good.*

Bohan continued to think about the

living conditions of the workers. He knew there were poor people in every town, many of them poor because of accidents, disease or other problems beyond their control, but Jerado's government deliberately caused more poverty and starvation. Workers should be paid enough to be able to feed and care for their families. Workers shouldn't be part of the poor and destitute.

Jerado's wage restrictions ran counter to the lessons Bohan learned from his father. According to his father, the king is responsible for caring for those who are too unfortunate to care for themselves. It is also the King's responsibility to ensure all are treated fairly and all have a chance to prosper.

When Bohan worked the tournament circuit, he took a portion of his prize money to pay for his travel expenses and used the rest to feed and clothe the poor. Sometimes he gave the money directly to the poor, but most often, he donated it to a local organization that helped those in need.

Bohan beckoned to Ansgar and Bianca and walked away from the camp site.

"I'm bothered by the situation we see everywhere. All these starving people. If I don't help them, I'll disgrace my father's memory. I don't think killing Jerado will change anything. Someone else will seize power and the workers will continue to starve."

"Hmm, you're correct," Ansgar said. "Killing a dictator and leaving an empty throne will only lead to a new dictator. Whoever is strongest will grab power."

Bianca gave Bohan a shrewd look. "I know what you're doin'."

Bohan pulled a face. "And what am I doing?"

"You're talking yourself into replacing Jerado and becoming a king again."

Bohan sighed. "Probably. I can't think of another way to fix the worker's situation. I'd rather not become king if I can help it, but I can't ignore my responsibility to change things here."

"Once we kill Jerado," Ansgar said, "there maybe several if not dozens of others who think the throne should be theirs. They won't be thrilled with you taking it."

"That's true. It's one more complication I have to address."

"Face it, Bohan," Bianca said while fighting back tears. "Sooner or later, you'll convince yourself it's your destiny to become king just so you improve the lot of the people. So why not stop all the heavy thinking and come out and say it."

Bohan sighed. "You know me better than I know me."

Bianca turned her back and walked away.

"On another note," Ansgar said, "the lads will like the idea of good food and soft beds again."

Bohan ignored Ansgar and watched Bianca go back to the camp.

"Ahem." Ansgar cleared his throat.

"All right," Bohan finally said. "We don't sail away after we kill Jerado. We stay in Dun Hythe and help the people."

Bohan felt one large mental boulder lift from his mind only to be replaced by a different, equally large boulder.

Chapter Twelve

Bohan saw Barrow pull up his horse and wait for the rest of the heroes to catch up to him.   The day was overcast and it threatened to rain before long.

"See something?" Bohan asked Barrow.

Instead of answering, Barrow pointed up the road which ran between two steep hills. A half-mile further on, the hills ended and five lines of lancers sat on their mounts awaiting them.

"Lancers!" Tibbs exclaimed. "If that don't take the biscuit. More than two hundred years ago, we beat Jerado's lancers. You'd think by now they'd come up wid a better way to stick holes inna enemy. Their army needs fresh blood at the top."

"Like you, Tibbs?" Ansgar asked.

"Exactly!" Tibbs replied. "I can teach 'em a lotta stuff."

"They ain't on horses," Barrow said. "They're ridin' pigs, looks like."

"Good," Angus replied. "We don't

have to reach up so high to hit the rider."

"What about Leticia?" Ansgar asked. "She can't stand in the line with us."

"She can stay with the horses,' Bohan replied.

"And ponies," Maggy said.

"She can stay with the horses and ponies."

"W . . .what are you going to do?" Leticia's face was pale..

"Kill 'em," Tibbs grinned while replying. "This'll be easier than fightin' yuks."

"But they have those big long spears or lances," Leticia said.

"The lances ain't no good if the point misses," Maggy said.

"What will I do if one of the riders gets past you?"

"Ain't none of 'em gettin' past us," Luc assured her.

"I don't see any spearmen or archers to back up the riders," Colbert said. "Where do they get these stupid officers?"

"See what I mean about needin' new officers?" Tibbs said.

"I guess the fat guy off to the side is in charge," Maggy said.

"Let's get closer before we

dismount," Bohan said. "We'll stop where the hills are real steep. The lancers won't be able to outflank us there."

Lithgow sat on his war swine and watched the enemy ride closer. He was puzzled. Why did they do that? Why didn't they turn and flee? Then his Swineriders would enjoy a chase. The horses were initially faster, but the swine had more stamina. It was only a matter of time until the swine caught up to the horses and the fun began.

To his consternation, the enemy dismounted and formed a line across the road, from hill to hill. The enemy was actually going to stand and accept a charge from his Swineriders! This was too easy.

Lithgow frowned. Why did the enemy do that? Was it a trick? He examined the line again and spotted a problem. There were only nine enemy in the line and a lancer line had ten. He couldn't have two riders competing to kill one enemy. It just wouldn't do. He chewed his lip briefly before issuing an order. "Leftmost riders will move aside."

The Swineriders shifted and shuffled around for a few minutes before coming to rest again.

"First line only! Lower lancers!"

The riders lowered the lancers until they were horizontal.

"First line only! Move forward!"

The nine Swineriders in the front line walked their swine forward.

"First line only! Charge!"

The Swineriders trotted at first and then changed to a gallop while shouting a war cry.

Lithgow stood in his stirrups to see better. Killing the enemy was even greater fun than he had anticipated. When the Swineriders got close, he could no longer see most of the enemy. He heard the crash of the lances, the screams and then the swine were past the enemy line. Without riders! All his Swineriders had been dismounted while the enemy line remained intact and without noticeable wounds. The swine kept moving and ran up the side of a hill to root around for food.

Lithgow couldn't believe his eyes. His elite unit dismounted without causing any injuries to the enemy. The first line must have done something wrong. He ordered the second line to make ready. Out of the corner of his eye, he noticed the dwarf riders seemed a bit squeamish.

With a roar, he sent them charging

forward. The nine dwarfs rode much slower than the first line and their war cry wasn't as loud. Their screams, however, were just as loud.

Once again, Lithgow was horrified to see nine riderless swine disappear into the wooded hills beyond the enemy line.

"Third line only! Lower lances!"

Lithgow knew battles resulted in casualties and he had three more lines of lancers.

"Bugger that," someone yelled.

"Yeah, I ain't chargin' those guys," another said. "I ain't gettin' kilt today."

"Silence!" Lithgow ordered. "Third line! Prepare to charge."

The Swineriders ignored the order, milled about and turned their swine to face away from the enemy line. Without an order, they rode back the way they had come, leaving Lithgow by himself. He screamed orders, then pleaded with them to return, all to no avail.

Lithgow's disappointment threatened to overwhelm him. All his dreams of martial glory destroyed by only nine enemy warriors. How could he explain his failure to his father, especially when Jerado had forbidden him to use lancers?

"Well, that was fun, "Colbert said,

"while it lasted.

"Hey! We have a prisoner," Bianca said.

They all looked behind at a lancer who sat amid the carnage of his mates. The dwarf groaned and held his right shoulder. His faced was pale as if he was on the verge of fainting.

"Someone must have missed," Ansgar said.

"Yeah, I did," Luc replied. "I missed the second guy to ride by."

The dwarf looked at the heroes. "Ya gonna kill me?"

"No." Ansgar knelt down. "Let me look at your shoulder." His probing fingers caused intense pain in the dwarf who bore it silently. "Broken. You have to hold you arm across your chest until it heals."

"What unit are you?" Bohan asked.

"Wait!" Tibbs said. "Let me torture him before you ask questions. I'll make sure he answers real quick."

The wounded lancer turned even paler.

"Go away, Tibbs. You aren't torturing him. What unit are you?"

"We're the Swineriders."

"You're part of the army?"

"Yeah."

"Who was the fat guy?'

"Our officer. His name's Lithgow."

"Lithgow is Jerado's son," Leticia said. "I think. I know he's somehow related to the President."

"This Lithgow ain't too smart, right?" Barrow commented.

"Where are you stationed?" Bohan asked.

"Outside Dun Hythe."

Are there many more soldiers there?"

"About a thousand, I'd say."

"What kind of units?"

"Mostly spearmen and archers. Some swordsmen."

"Any cavalry?"

The dwarf shook his head. "We're the only mounted troops.

"We saw archers dressed in black a few days ago. Are they part of the Dun Hythe army?"

The dwarf pulled a face. "Don't remember ever seein' archers in black uniforms. They must be from someplace else."

"What I suggest you do," Bohan said, "is catch one of the pigs and ride back to your camp. How far is it?"

"About a day and a half ride."

"Best get on your way. Maybe you

can catch up to your mates." Bohan turned away. The appearance of the lancers meant overthrowing Jerado became a lot harder. Now the Gundarlandian army was involved. Who knew how many soldiers Jerado commanded? He had to assume the city gates would be reinforced with soldiers looking for him. If he couldn't get into the city, he wouldn't be able to find Jerado. Perhaps his mission was doomed to failure. Maybe his heroes faced certain death. Despite the possible dire outcome, he was determined to try and reach Jerado.

~ ~ ~

The Godmother waited at a table with a bag of coins in a saloon in the Dwarf Quarter. Sophia sat at a different table with a pile of papers in front of her. Once a week, the Godmother went to one of her saloons and dispensed favors to needy citizens. Folks lined up outside despite the rain, clutching their cloaks to their bodies.

She nodded to a guard by the door and he let in the first favor seeker. The dwarf walked up to the table, hat in hand, water dripping on the floor, and said, "I'm a tailor and I gotta chance to buy out a competitor. It'll make my business grow like crazy, but I need ten silver pennies to do it and I ain't got the money."

"See Sophia," the Godmother said. "She'll arrange a loan for you. But remember this. You owe me a favor. If I ask, you better repay the favor. Do you understand?"

The dwarf nodded. "Thank you, Godmother."

Next in line was a female half-pint. "My son has two rotten teeth and I don't have the coins to pay a barber to pull them out."

The Godmother pulled a face and tutted. This was the problem with wage restrictions. People spent all their money on food and had nothing left over for life's other problems.

"How much do you need?"

"Seven coppers."

The Godmother opened the bag, took out ten copper pennies and handed them to the female. "This is a gift. You needn't pay me back."

The half-pint clutched the coins to her chest and said, "Bless you, Godmother."

The next person was a young man

with calloused hands. "I work at a lumber company. I plane logs into planks using the tools my father handed down to me. Someone stole my tools and now I can't work. My family is hungry and I ain't got money to buy new tools."

"How much do you need for new set of tools?"

"One and a half silver."

The Godmother reached into her bag, took out two silver pennies and gave them to the man. "Buy food with the rest of the money."

After two hours, the Godmother told the guard to shut the door. She was done until next week when she would appear at a different saloon. Most of the people who showed up really did need help. Occasionally, some ne'er-do-well tried to get free money, but her guards quickly threw him out of the saloon.

It made her feel good to help so many people.

~ ~ ~

From Barrow's Journal. *What a boring journey. Nothing but riding all day, lousy food and sleeping on the ground. Had a couple of battles to break up the boredom, but they were nothing, just light exercise.*

       Leticia couldn't believe her eyes. The heroes had just wiped out a quarter of the lancers. The officer in charge shouted orders and waved his sword, but the remaining lancers ignored him and rode back in the direction of Dun Hythe.

       All her previous doubts about reaching the capital dissipated. Instead, she now believed Bohan could do it. Each battle they'd fought in, they won without any problems or injuries. Tibbs and Colbert actually complained about how easy it was.

       Leticia worked out a plan on what to do once she reached Dun Hythe. First, she had to find out where Flavia lived. Jerado's daughter would likely have guards, so for her second item, Leticia needed the help of a few heroes to defeat the guards. She was sure Bianca would help. The two had become close during the journey. Angus and Maggy would probably help as well. Perhaps the four of them would be enough to force their way into Flavia's home.

       Then there was the advice her

father had drummed into her head. "If you ever needed help," he said, "go to the Godmother in Dun Hythe and tell her you're my girl. Mention my name. She'll remember Casey. She owes me a favor or two."

When asked how she was supposed to find this Godmother, her father said, "Go to the Angry Shoat near the docks and ask my friend Vinny. He'll know how to find the Godmother."

Leticia pulled a face. There was so much stuff her father would never talk about. Like why the Godmother owed him favors or even who the Godmother was.

Another idea popped into her mind. If Bohan did indeed kill Jerado and took over as president or king, would he free her father? The thought jolted her into a state of excitement. It could be her reward for helping Bohan! Maybe she didn't have to worry about finding Flavia.

Leticia had to think about a way to broach the subject and how to phrase her request.

~ ~ ~

Remy, wearing his rust-colored robe, entered the interview request room. As usual, it was packed and, as usual, the Snotist Bishop paced the room and glared at everyone and everything that got in his way.

"It's about time, you showed up," the bishop snarled. "I'm a busy man and yet I'm forced to waste time here. When will I see the President?"

Remy ignored the bishop, saw three new applicants and waved them over to the desk. After questioning each of the three, Remy turned to the Bishop. "The P . . . resident is still most interested in your church. H . . . owever, he says the steeple is too high and must be reduced in size. H . . . e also says the budget needs to be trimmed by a third. W . . . ithout these modifications, he won't approve the plans. O . . . r grant an audience."

"I'll have to pay an architect to make those changes. Is the President going to pay for those costs?"

"N . . . No, he won't pay for them."

After the red-faced bishop took a few deep breaths, Remy added, "S . . . ince you are such a busy man, you may as well leave until you've m . . . ade the changes."

The bishop stomped out of the room, knocking a peasant out of the doorway.

Remy loved his job.

~ ~ ~

From Barrow's Journal: *What I wouldn't give to sleep in a bed again. And to eat a decent meal in a tavern with a few cups of wine. Think I'll dream about this tonight.*

The closer to Dun Hythe he came, the more pessimistic Bohan grew. When first freed from the cave, he thought he could simply go to Dun Hythe, find out where Jerado lived and make the wizard pay for his evil ways even if he ruled the entire country. Now he knew the plan was a pipe dream. The yuks gave Bohan the initial indication that his plan was naive. Since then, two uniformed army units had blocked their way. Certainly, Jerado knew of their location and sent those soldiers. The Swinerider survivor mentioned his camp contained over a thousand soldiers. Jerado wouldn't hesitate to use all of those and more to protect his regime. As tough and as fierce as his heroes were, they couldn't prevail against that many trained soldiers.

He needed a new plan. He beckoned to Ansgar and Bianca. The three walked a short distance away from the camp.

Bohan stood with his arms crossed and his chin down while he said, "How are we to get into Dun Hythe? Jerado will have his entire army watching for us. I'm sure the city has changed quite a bit since we were last there over two hundred years ago."

"Another issue," Ansgar said, "is how do the citizens in the city feel? The folks in the small towns are miserable and would support a regime change, but it doesn't follow that the same is true in the city. We may not have any support in there for getting rid of Jerado. In other words, it's possible no one in the city will help us."

"So what are we to do?" Bohan asked. "We can't just ride up to the gates and ask to be let in."

Bianca nodded. "First, we need to know what the situation is in the city. Why don't we hide out close to the city and I'll go in and poke around. Maybe I'll also find a way for us to secretly get inna the city."

"I like the idea of sending someone

into the city," Bohan said, "but I'll do it."

"You can't go," Ansgar said. "Jerado may see and recognize you. Remember, he know's we're coming and he'll be watching out."

Bohan sighed. "I guess you're right. I'll send Barrow. He's good at getting people to talk to him."

"Leticia," Ansgar said. "We should send Leticia. She grew up in the city and she must know her way around. She probably has relatives or people she knows."

"I can't order her to go into the city. It'll have to be her decision."

"I'll go get her," Bianca said.

When Leticia joined them, Bohan explained their situation and the need to get information about the city.

"Of course, I'll help," Leticia said. "I shouldn't have any problem getting into the city, even if the gates are guarded. I can look up my father's old friends. They can tell me what's going on. And I can overhear folks talking. I'll bet I can learn a lot that way." She paused to take a deep breath. "Afterwards, can you help me find out where my father is and get him released?"

"Yes." Bohan gave her a brief

smile. "That's just one of many tasks I'll have to do, but I'll put it on the top of the list."

"Another thing," Bianca said. "I think we should get off the main road and go cross-country. I'm sure the road is watched."

Bohan and Ansgar agreed with her.

Bohan relaxed a bit. At least now he had a plan, a partial one to be sure, but still a plan. Their chances of success were slim, but he felt a bit more confident than he did a few minutes ago.

"What happens when we find Jerado?" Bohan asked. "How do we approach him?"

"It isn't 'we'," Ansgar replied. "It's me. The confrontation has to be wizard against wizard. You can't fight a powerful wizard as if he was just another ordinary soldier."

Bohan shook his head. "I'm going with you. While you and Jerado trade spells, I'll get close enough to kill him."

Chapter Thirteen

Jerado waved a hand for Lithgow to enter the office. Flavia sat on the couch while Jerado paced the office.

"Why haven't I heard any progress reports about Bohan?" Jerado snarled. "I demand to know what is happening."

Lithgow turned red in the face and stammered, "I . . . I couldn't stop him. I'll try again." He wore the uniform of an officer in the First Spears, an elite unit. The uniform had a black tunic and tan pants decorated with battle badges from a hundred years ago. It also had a lot of gold braid.

Flavia made a clucking noise behind Jerado's back.

"What did you do that failed?"

"M . . . My Swineriders. I was sure they would succeed."

"You idiot! Jerado clapped a hand over his mouth to keep his wooden dentures from flying out. "You used lancers when I specifically told you not to? Where were the spearmen and archers I told you to use?"

Lithgow gulped and sucked in air. "The Swineriders move faster than the spearmen and archers. So they hadn't reached the ambush point when Bohan showed up."

"Let me guess what happened," Jerado said. "You sent a line of lancers to attack Bohan and his guards. After the lancers were slaughtered, you sent a second line who also failed. How many lines of lancers did you waste attacking Bohan?"

When Jerado wasn't talking, his dentures ground together.

"Just two. The others wouldn't attack."

"The Swineriders are smarter than you are."

"Well, she didn't do much better." Lithgow pointed a finger at Flavia. "Ask her what happened to her archers."

Jerado turned to Flavia. "What is he talking about?"

Flavia gave her brother an evil look and said in a low voice, "I had a company of archers nearby so I thought they could do the job."

"Why do you have archers? Do you have any more troops?"

"I recruited them in case of an insurrection. Or a strike. I also have a company of spearmen."

"Those archers and spearmen should report to me," Lithgow said. "I'm the Defense Minister and army units report to me."

"Shut up, Lithgow," Jerado snarled. You're lucky I don't make you Minister of Garbage Pickup." To Flavia he asked, "And they didn't stop Bohan? Why not?"

"A rain shower wet all the bowstrings. Bohan was lucky."

"Another idiot. Bohan has a powerful wizard with him. The shower was no accident."

Jerado paced the office some more while muttering curses under his breath. Finally he said to Flavia, "Where is Bohan?"

"The last report I had from a constable said he was at mile marker thirty-two."

"When was that?"

"Two days ago."

"Bohan hasn't been seen in two days?"

Jerado pulled a face and stared through a window for a minute. "He left the main road. That's why you haven't gotten any reports. So we don't know where he is anymore."

"I have constables riding around

looking for them."

"Lithgow! I want three companies of spearmen and a company of archers. I want the best units you have. I also want your best officer to command them. They will report to me personally, not to you."

"That's not fair. I should command them."

"What's not fair is you being in charge of the army. I never should have put you in command. The soldiers deserve a leader who knows what he's doing. I want the officer in my office before lunch and have the soldiers ready to march by mid-afternoon. Make sure they don't march through the city. I don't need the Godmother calling a general strike right now. Have them go around the walls. I will station a company of spearmen at each of the three land gates backed up by a squad of archers. They will stop and inspect everyone coming into the city. Anyone who looks like a warrior will be stopped."

"If the Godmother calls a strike," Lithgow said, "my soldiers will crush it.

"That's my job, not yours." Flavia slapped a hand on her thigh.

"Get out!" Jerado waved a hand. "Both of you!"

Lithgow and Flavia hastened out of the office.

Jerado could hear them yelling at each other as they walked down the hall.

With soldiers guarding the city gates, he would feel less threatened. He could try the far-sight device again to find where Bohan was, but he was sure Ansgar would have cast a ward over the group.

So there was nothing to do except wait for Bohan to try to get into the city. He'd order the officer to kill any one suspicious trying to enter the city.

Still seething at the incompetence of his children, Jerado left his office to walk off some of his anger. He passed Remy's office and did a double take. Remy sat behind his desk as usual, but he looked different. Much different. Jerado entered the small office and recognized the change. It made him smile.

Remy wore new clothes. After a hundred years! The undead half-pint now wore a white silk tunic with gold piping and black silk pants with a gold strip on the side. Most incredible, the hairless Remy had toe-hair! Four inches long, twisted into braids and held in place by gold and silver brooches.

"Remy, what happened?" an amused Jerado waved a hand indicating the new clothes.

"I. . . spent some of the money I won from you."

"A big improvement. But how did you get toe-hair?"

Remy reached behind his chair and picked up a tangled mess of hair. "I b . . . bought a wig and glued some hair to my feet. Do y . . . you like it?"

"I do. It's quite a change. You almost look alive."

Jerado's annoyance dissipated as fast as it had developed. Having incompetent children really was his own fault. So why be angry with Flavia and Lithgow? They couldn't help screwing things up. It was what they did, the one thing they were good at.

~ ~ ~

To meet with the Godmother, Maurice first entered a bookstore ten blocks from the Palace. Inside, a burly elf beckoned him to follow. They went into the basement where the elf opened a hidden door leading to the next building. The second building had a hidden door leading to the third building.

In the sixth building, they climbed stairs and the elf showed Maurice into an office. The Godmother sat behind a desk stacked with papers.

She nodded to Maurice and indicated a chair by a table.

His stomach threatened to revolt and toss back his breakfast. He needed an ally and the Godmother was the only one in the city powerful enough to be useful. If she turned him down, he would be alone. If his secrets were exposed, his only hope of survival would be to leave Dun Hythe. Fast! If he could escape from the Palace.

The Godmother rose, walked to the table and sat down with him.

"I'm glad you asked for a meeting," she said after ordering snacks and drinks from a servant. "There are confusing events afoot and I hope you can sort them out."

"I hope so, too," Maurice replied. "What events are you talking about?"

"I keep hearing silly rumors about an ancient king who's come back to life. The whole city is buzzing with this nonsense."

"King Bohan. I know about that one because I spread the word by telling my staff about it after I swore them to secrecy. That ensured they would tell everyone they knew."

"Why did you do that?"

"Because it's true. King Bohan is indeed alive and headed this way."

The Godmother made a face, leaned forward in her chair and waved a hand. "What nonsense. Dead kings don't suddenly come back to life."

"In the case of Bohan, he never died. He was asleep. Has to do with a magical spell, I'm sure. Jerado knows about Bohan and has tried to kill him. At least twice. There may have been other attempts I don't know about. So obviously, Jerado believes Bohan is out to kill him. It's revenge, as I understand it."

The Godmother sat back in her chair. She raised an eyebrow and said, "Tell me what you know."

After relating Bohan's story, the Godmother tapped a fingernail on the table. "This is worse than I suspected. If this Bohan comes here, there could be riots and chaos. Neither is good for business."

"This is why I wanted to talk to you. This could be a grand opportunity and we need to decide on a position to take."

"You mean we take a side?"

"Yes, I guess you can call it that."

"Why should we do that? Taking sides is dangerous."

"Because Jerado is dangerous and so are his children, especially Flavia. Her greed is wrecking the country's economy."

Maurice explained about Flavia's horde of coins.

"Flavia!" the Godmother hissed. "Her wage restrictions are causing untold grief in the city. Families can't afford to buy food every day. Children go hungry and get sick. I hear it's worse outside of the city."

"Exactly," Maurice said. "And Jerado won't do anything to rein her in. Believe me, I've tried to get him to remove the wage restrictions."

The Godmother stared at a wall while drumming a fingernail. Finally, she said, "So, what are you asking?"

"I think we should support Bohan's crusade to overthrow Jerado. Bohan can't be worse than our current president and probably will be much better. His history as a king supports this."

"How do we do that? Where is he? Do you know?"

"The last report Flavia received

placed Bohan at mile marker thirty-two on the Skensfirth-Dun Hythe road. Since then he seems to have disappeared."

"How do you know what Flavia knows?"

"Don't ask," Maurice replied with a smile. "Then I won't have to lie to you."

The Godmother smiled back. "What you told me explains why spearmen and archers have taken over all three city gates. They examine everyone who comes into the city. Every wagon is stopped and searched. Jerado obviously must be frightened of this Bohan."

The Godmother stood up, placed her hands behind her back and walked around the table. On her second circuit, she said, "Let's assume I agree to support Bohan. How do we do that? We don't know when — or if— he'll get into the city. We don't even know where he is. I don't see where there is anything we can do to help."

"Actually, there isn't anything we can do right now. If we agree to support him, we just have to sit tight and watch developments. I think an opportunity to help Bohan will occur. And it will be soon."

"What's in it for me? What do I get

for helping him? All I can see is getting into a lot of danger and trouble."

The Godmother sat down.

"You may not gain anything directly — at least not immediately — but there could be benefits for your family. Especially if Bohan removes the wage restrictions."

"Why would he do that? Does he even know about them?"

"There is a good chance that Bohan will need my expertise once he comes to power. After all, he won't know anything about Gundarland's economy or the Treasury."

"Ahh, now that is a good point." The Godmother grinned at Maurice. "It's always good to know someone close to the throne."   She tapped a fingernail on the table. "All right, we agree to support Bohan and we agree to await developments."

"We need a way to contact each other, in case something comes up."

After a moment's thought, she said, "I'll station a bootblack across the street from the Palace. We can pass messages back and forth using him."

"I know many Palace secrets. Perhaps too many. It's possible I'll need a place to hide, especially from Flavia's wrath."

"Go the bookstore. The owner owes me a big favor. He'll let you into the basement and he'll contact my family to come and get you."

"Can you also get my wife?"

"Of course."

Maurice's tension evaporated. He had a bolthole. He also had an ally in the Godmother. Now it was up to Bohan to come to Dun Hythe. How they would contact Bohan remained unclear.

~ ~ ~

Flavia returned to her corner office on the fourth floor with much to think about. Her archers had failed to stop Bohan. So had Lithgow's soldiers.

She looked again at yesterday's note from Lithgow demanding her troops be put under his command. How did Lithgow find out about her archers and spearmen? That was annoying and confirmed her suspicion that her slug of a brother had spies in her department.

A more ominous development was her father. He was obviously scared of Bohan and the wizard Ansgar. Otherwise, he wouldn't have taken control of three companies of Lithgow's troops to guard the city's gates.

No matter what happened between Bohan and her father, there was sure to be a lot of chaos, and chaos wasn't good for business. Or for her wealth. If the citizens of Dun Hythe became unruly or started a riot, they might take out their anger on the ruling family. They might overwhelm her guards, break into her home and find all the money stashed in the basement.

Perhaps, it was time to move the coins to a safer place. Like her country estate. Large, heavily guarded wagons would be conspicuous traveling cross country, but the peat train wouldn't be and the peat train ran close to her estate. If she transferred the coins to the peat station and onto an empty southbound peat train, she could move the coins to safety with no one being the wiser.

Flavia felt relieved now that she had a way to protect her money from the rabble. Just in case Bohan caused trouble.

Chapter Fourteen

From Barrow's Journal: *Close to Dun Hythe now. Everyone's starting to get pumped up over the thought of action. And the end of the journey. And beds. And real food. And real ale, not that crap Ansgar makes.*

Leticia approached the city from the west and got on the end of the line of people waiting to enter. A half-dozen guards questioned people before letting them through the gate.

The walls stood twenty feet high and were made from dressed stone. The west gate had a portcullis, open now, but ready to drop and block the entrance. The road through the gate was paved with stones sprinkled with weeds.

Leticia realized she had changed during the journey. Before, she would have been quaking about the guard's inspection. Now she calmly awaited it. During the trip, she had experienced combat, fatigue, and hunger. She had learned how to defend herself with the short sword on her hip. Her confidence had climbed. After a half-hour, she made it to the front of the line. A rough-looking guard questioned her and examined her backpack. When he finished looking, he nodded and let her move past the barricade. Leticia took note of the barricade details.

Made of sturdy wood posts and boards, the barricades formed a long zig-zag path that ended up at the gate. Anyone running this gauntlet would be attacked along its entire length.

Bohan would be interested in the obstacle since it assured the heroes would have to fight their way into the city or use a different approach.

Once past the gate, she walked along the main east-west street recalling memories of her years in the city. The traffic was still heavy with cargo wagons and a few coaches for rich people. Two trolls mis-directed traffic at a major intersection, causing delays, shouts and cursing.

The poor people surprised Leticia. They seemed to be everywhere. When she lived in town, there were poor but she didn't remember the vast numbers she saw now. The females wore old, heavily patched dresses, and the males wore trews with holes in the knees and all the color leeched out of them.

Another surprise was the way the races intermixed. She saw half-pints walking with dwarfs. She saw a human-elf couple holding hands. A group of males stood on a corner having a conversation. They consisted of a dwarf, elf, human and half-pint. Such mixing never happened down south.

The mild weather made walking a pleasure and when lunch time approached, she searched for a place to eat. She saw two rich-looking women, an elf and a human, enter a tavern and decided it was a safe place for an unattended lady to have a meal.

Inside the busy tavern, she found a small table near the bar, sat down and ordered soup, bread and a beer. She listened to the conversations of folks at the bar. To her amazement, they openly disparaged Jerado and his government. Such talk in Abano would lead to instant arrest. Another popular topic of conversation concerned Bohan. Was he really alive? Was he headed to Dun Hythe? Would he challenge Jerado? Would he be better than Jerado? Leticia noted the people were fascinated by the

Bohan rumors. She wondered how they started. Obviously, someone besides Jerado knew of Bohan's existence.

After leaving the tavern, she walked toward the docks in the eastern part of the city to find her father's friend, Vinny. Maybe he could explain why her father left the city and how the Godmother — whoever she was — could help Bohan, but Leticia didn't think an old female could do much for the heroes.

At the waterfront, she found the Angry Shoat. The tavern was in a dilapidated building that looked like it would blow over in a strong wind. Inside was even worse. The floor was sticky, the air fetid and the furniture scarred and rickety. On the left, a bar stretched the length of the room. The right side held standup tables. A huge fireplace with a roaring fire filled the back of the room.

The bartender, a hefty man with a scarred face looked her over and raised an eyebrow. "Help ya?"

"I'm looking for Vinny."

The man's faced showed surprise. He pointed down the bar at a table in the rear with three old men at it. "Vinny's the one inna middle."

Leticia walked towards the table,

her shoes making strange noises on the sticky surface of the floor. The three watched her approach. She noticed all three were rough-hewn elves.

"Hello. Are you Vinny?" Leticia said.

"Maybe," the middle elf said. "Who wants to know?"

The other two elves walked away from the table.

"My name is Leticia. I"m Casey's daughter."

The elf's face lit up in a gap-toothed smile. "Casey? How is the old dodger?"

"I don't really know. He was arrested for speaking against the wage restrictions and other things and got arrested. I don't know where he is."

"Ahh, what a shame. And the restrictions are so bad. Everybody is hurtin' because of 'em. What brings ya here?"

"My dad always told me to look you up if I needed a favor."

"I do owe yer old man a few favors. He did enough of 'em for me."

"What did my father do on the docks? He would never tell me. Or why we suddenly left."

"He ran the Guild down here and

he fought against the wage restrictions when they were first laid down. He hadda leave 'cause he heard the government wanted to shut him up."

"Oh." Leticia placed a hand in front of her mouth.

"Casey's still a hero down here. What kinda favor ya need?"

"I'd like to talk to the Godmother."

Vinny squinted at Leticia for a few moments. "Do ya know anythin' about her?"

"Only that my father said she'd help me if I mentioned his name."

"Ya want the Godmother to get Casey outta prison? I don't think she can do that."

"No." Leticia shook her head. "I want her to get some friends into the city without going through the gates and the guards."

Vinny did a double-take and stared at her for a while. "I'm havin' trouble thinkin' a nice lady like you is smugglin' stuff inta the city."

"Will you help me talk to the Godmother?"

"Yeah, why not. I can talk to some people about it and probably get you a meetin'."

~ ~ ~

Remy, wearing his rust-colored robe, shuffled into the room used for press conferences and went to the podium. He looked around the dozen reporters, all nemeses of his who constantly tried to trip him up on his explanations of government actions and policies.

Remy placed a piece of paper on the stand and cleared his throat.

"T . . . oday, I want to make something absolutely clear. T . . . he rumor that Bohan is still alive is fake news. I . . . t's a hoax put out by the media. You —"

"Who?" a reporter called out.

"We didn't publish anything about a guy named Bohan," another said.

"Remy? What are you talking about?" a third asked.

"How do you spell Bohan?" still another yelled.

"I . . . I repeat," Remy said. "T . . . he Bohan news is fake news. A . . . nd to say he's headed for Dun Hythe is ludicrous."

"Remy?" a reporter asked, "will you please explain what you are talking about? What fake news?"

"Th . . . is press conference is over."

Remy picked up the paper and shuffled out the door accompanied by shouted questions and curses from the reporters.

~ ~ ~

Leticia made the Sign of the Sneeze before knocking on the open door to the Godmother's office. Inside, she saw two female elves sitting on a couch. Both females looked her up and down before the middle-aged one beckoned her to come in.

The younger one smiled and said, "Hello. I'm Sophia."

The Godmother said, "So you're Casey's daughter? You look like him. How is he?"

"I . . . I don't know. He was arrested for saying bad things about the president and the government and I don't know where he was sent."

The Godmother leaned forward. "I was told you seek a favor. I hope you don't think I can get him out of prison. By the way, what's your name?"

"Leticia. And no, I'm not here about my father."

Leticia knew the success or failure of Bohan's mission could be decided in the next few minutes.   Never before had such great responsibility been thrust upon her. She took a deep breath and plunged on.

"I guess you've heard all the talk in town about King Bohan's reappearance?" Leticia asked.

The other two nodded.

"All rumors," Sophia said. "We have no proof this Bohan exists. No one has ever seen him."

"Now you have proof. I've been with him since he re-appeared down south and together we've ridden north."

"You've seen Bohan?" the Godmother said in a whispered voice.

"Yes, ma'am, I have. Bohan, his wizard Ansgar and the seven heroes he uses as his bodyguards."

"Wait," Sophia said. "You expect us to believe Jerado just ignores this threat and lets Bohan ride around free?"

"No. We were attacked several times as we came north. First by yuks, probably hired by Jerado, then by soldiers. So far, none of us has suffered a scratch. Bohan and his heroes have defeated everyone Jerado sent against him."

The Godmother stood up and went behind her desk. She sat down, picked up a quill and tapped the point on the desktop. "Where is he now?"

"Outside the city. He sent me to find out how things are in here. Then I remembered my father saying to ask you if I ever needed help."

"What does Bohan plan to do in Dun Hythe?" Sophia asked.

"He plans to find Jerado and kill him."

"Who will rule Gundarland after Jerado is killed?" Sophia asked.

"I guess Bohan. We never discussed what happens afterward."

The Godmother pointed the quill at Lucretia. "What's the favor you want me to do for you?"

"I want you to help Bohan get into the city. The gates are packed with soldiers and I don't think he'll be able to fight his way in. Besides, he doesn't want Jerado to know he's in town."

"How many are you?" Sophia asked.

"Ten counting me. With horses. I guess we'll also need a place to hide once we get into Dun Hythe."

The Godmother and Sophia exchanged glances.

"Tell me what you think, Sophia."

"We all know Jerado has to go. His regime is repressive and Flavia's regulations are bad for business. Our revenue streams are decreasing because people don't have any money to pay for our services. Strictly from a business prospective, we should support Bohan."

The Godmother made a face. "I think the risks outweigh the potential rewards."

Leticia's heart sank at the Godmother's words.

"But we don't know what the rewards are," Sophia argued. "And we won't learn what the rewards are until we talk to Bohan and find out what he's willing to give us in return for our support."

The Godmother went back to bouncing the quill point. "You're saying we should help Bohan get into Dun Hythe, then negotiate with him for our further support?"

"Exactly. We risk a little by helping him in, but we don't have to support him if he won't support us. But I think he'll be grateful enough to give us what we want or most of it anyway"

"Wait," Leticia said. "What is it you want from Bohan? He'll want to know and he'll ask me."

"Mostly to be left alone," the Godmother said. "We want to run our businesses without government interference. Jerado leaves us alone, because if he doesn't I'd call a general strike of all the workers. I need assurances that Bohan will likewise leave us alone. And we get a reward for helping him."

"What kind of reward?"

"We'll discuss that with Bohan afterward," the Godmother replied.

"Bohan is a fair man," Leticia said. "He is most upset about the conditions of the poor people. I'm sure — like Sophia says — he'll be grateful for your help, especially if it allows him to help relieve the suffering of the people."

After a great deal of quill bouncing, the Godmother nodded and yelled for a clerk to come into the office. "Get Sal and Vito in here immediately." After the clerk left, she said to Leticia. "They'll help us put together a plan."

When Sal, the head of security and enforcement, and Vito, who ran the docks, came into the office, the Godmother told both elf males what she wanted to do.

"We can go over the wall," Sal said

"but that's risky wid a large group. Sal's face was a mass of scars and permanent bruises. "They're gonna make noise and that'll alert the local police."

"I agree," Vito said. "We should bring 'em in by boat at night." He was large and heavily muscled for an elf. "I can take care of the customs guys so they won't see the boat. But I can't take the horses."

"All right," the Godmother said. "Vito, set it up and then send someone with Leticia to find Bohan. He'll need a guide to get to the boat."

"Good plan," Sophia said. "I think we're onto something big here."

"After I talk to the customs guys and set up the boat trip, I'll go wid her," Vito said. "I wanna see this guy for myself."

"While we wait," the Godmother said, "let's have tea and you can tell me where Casey went after leaving the city."

Sophia grinned and said, "And I want to hear more about Bohan and your adventures in traveling north."

Leticia beamed. The Godmother would get Bohan into the city without Jerado knowing about it. Her mission was a success.

Chapter Fifteen

Maurice opened the door to his secret room and checked the scryers. Lithgow's had nothing important. Jerado's had a message to Lithgow ordering him to send mounted patrols outside the city's walls to look for Bohan.

He found a message in Flavia's scryer to the peat train supervisor. It ordered him to stop the train from leaving until a cargo could be loaded on it during the night.

He puzzled over the message. What could Flavia possibly want to load on an empty peat train?

In a flash of inspiration the answer came to him: her coins! Flavia must be shipping her treasure out of Dun Hythe and was using the peat train to do it. She must fear Bohan's arrival and was protecting her fortune.

A second message from Flavia went to a factory owner. That message ordered the owner to assemble a dozen carts and meet the peat train at a location twenty miles south of the city later on tonight.

Maurice smiled to himself. He knew Flavia had an estate down there. She had ruined the owner's business to snap it up at a fraction of its value.

Could this be an opportunity to strike at Flavia and get all her stashed silver and gold pennies back into circulation? How could he disrupt her plans? He didn't have the resources, but the Godmother did.

~ ~ ~

The Godmother stood by a window watching the trolls sow confusion among the Teamster drivers and the carriages of the rich. A secretary handed her a note. She glanced at the note, sucked in her breath and sat down to calm her palpitating heart. She read the note a second time and called out, "Get Sophia in here, right away."

When her daughter entered the office, the Godmother handed her the note.

Sophia's eyes widened. "What an opportunity!"

"This could be the biggest heist in history," the Godmother said.

"Ma! We can't keep it. We grab it and hold it in custody until Bohan takes over. This is our big break."

"What! You want we should steal this treasure and just give it back?" She glared at her daughter and thought: Maybe she isn't Godmother material.

"Exactly! Only we don't just hand it over. We use it as a bargaining chip when we negotiate with Bohan. With all this money, we can get almost anything we want. It's our chance to diversify and get into legitimate businesses."

"I can't believe my daughter wants to simply hand over a vast amount of money."

"What 'simply hand it over'? We're entitled to a finder's fee along with a lot of other stuff." Sophia smiled. "This is like a dream come true. The finder's fee alone could be the biggest payout we've ever had. And who knows what we can bargain for in addition to that fee."

"That's better, girl," the Godmother said. "You had me worried there for a while." Sophia promised to be a new type of Godmother, one that could take the family and the business to new heights. She didn't understand much of what Sophia was about, especially the economics and financial stuff, but she trusted the girl.

~ ~ ~

From Barrow's Journal: *Today, Tibbs said he hopes we get into few more battles because he loves to fight. Actually, what he loves is hurting people.*

Bohan sat with his back to a tree in late afternoon. He and the heroes camped inside a thick wooded area five miles from Dun Hythe. It was the first time he hadn't spent the day traveling since he left the cave. The others lounged around the fireless camp cleaning equipment or catching up on sleep.

The only sounds came from Luc's axe slamming into trees as he endlessly threw it.

Barrow, on guard duty, entered the clearing and said, "Two riders comin' this way."

Bohan stood up, signaled to Ansgar and Bianca and followed Barrow to the edge of the woods.

"What can you see, Bianca?" Bohan asked.

"It's Leticia and some guy."

"Is she a prisoner?"

"I don't think so. Her hands are

free and she's talkin' to the guy like they know each other."

A few minutes later, Leticia jumped off the horse and greeted Bohan. "We have a way to get into the city without anyone seeing us. This is Vito. He's going to help us."

"Let's get the horses in the trees where they can't be seen," Bohan said. "Then we can talk."

Once the horses were secured with the others, Bohan asked Leticia, "Who's Vito and why is he helping us?"

"I'm a boss in the Godmother's organization," Vito answered. "She said to smuggle ya inna city and that's wot I'm gonna do."

Vito had the air of someone who knew what he was doing and wanted someone to challenge him so he could cause pain to the challenger.

"Why is she helping us?" Bohan asked.

"I don't know that," Vito said. "The Godmother says do somethin', ya do it. Ya don't ask questions.

"I know," Leticia said. "She told me Jerado and his government are treating the people badly and she wants him replaced. She thinks you're the only one that can do that, so she wants to help you."

Bohan nodded. So, it wasn't just the rural people who despised Jerado. The ones living in Dun HYthe also felt that way. That was an encouraging bit of news. With the support of this Godmother, whoever she was, his chances of success improved a bit.

"What does she want in return for helping," Bohan asked.

"To be left alone to run her business without interference and to be rewarded," Leticia replied.

Bohan raised an eyebrow. "Rewarded?"

"She said she would talk to you about a reward afterward."

"How will we get into the city?" Ansgar asked.

"After it gets dark, we'll mount up and ride north," Vito said. "There's a farm up there near the coast. We can leave the horses there. A boat'll be waitin' for us. The boat'll take us inta the city's harbor and dump us off by a warehouse you can use to hide out in."

"There are mounted patrols," Bohan said. "We've seen a number of them ride past. We could run into one of them in the dark."

"Naw," Vito replied. "There ain't

gonna be any patrols after dark."

"How can you be so sure?" Bohan asked.

"My brother commands a company of spearman. He says at dusk, they lock the camp gates and everyone starts drinkin'."

"All right. But tell me, who is this Godmother?" Bohan asked.

"She's the boss lady in Dun Hythe."

"I thought Jerado was in charge of the whole country."

"Jerado may think that, but it's the Godmother who calls the shots in Dun Hythe."

Bohan raised an eyebrow. Vito's claim sounded false.

"Everyone in Dun Hythe looks to the Godmother to tell them what to do," Leticia said. "She really does call the shots in the city. I met with her earlier today when she agreed to help us. She sent Vito to show her support. Once we're in the city, she wants to meet with you to discuss your plans."

"What's it like inside the city?" Bohan asked.

"It's so much different from down south," Leticia said. "In Centi, everyone is race conscious and no one wants to deal with folks from other races unless they have no choice.   In Dun Hythe, all the different races are melded together. No one cares what race you are or who you married. I saw stuff in there that would start a riot down south."

Leticia noticed Bianca staring at her, open mouthed.

Bohan started at her depiction of life in the city and glanced at Bianca.

"I wonder," Bohan said, "if life was like that back when I did tournaments, but I never noticed it."

He scratched his chin beneath his beard while he reviewed his situation. His basic plan was simple: find and kill Jerado. He knew there were many details still to be worked out and the Godmother could help with those. He wondered what the Godmother's support would cost him and if he could afford to pay it. He also wondered how he would adapt to life in a city like Dun Hythe.

~ ~ ~

Sal, the Godmother's head of enforcement, drove the lead wagon to Flavia's house. Two more wagons followed. Flavia and her guards waited outside. As soon as the wagons stopped, muscular servants struggled with iron-bound chests and small kegs, carrying them from the house to the wagons. It was after dark and Flavia and the guards held lanterns to allow the servants to see what they were doing.

Flavia approached the wagon and held up the lantern to illuminate the driver. "I never saw you before. Who are you?"

"I usually work the docks, Miss." He touched his forehead. Sal was middle-aged, scarred, muscular and had brown hair cut short. "A few of the lads are sick so the Guild asked me and my crew to fill in to work yer request for wagons."

"Do you know where the train depot is?"

"I do. I've passed it many times onna deliveries."

"Use the west gate and go directly to the depot. No stops, no detours. Do you understand?"

"Aye. No stops, no detours. Use the west gate."

Flavia wagged a finger at Sal. "Just in case you drivers think you can steal some of the cargo, I'll have a guard on each wagon."

"No need for the guards, Miss. But if it'll let ya sleep better, then they're welcome to ride along."

Flavia sniffed and walked away.

Once the cargo was stowed on the back of the wagons, a guard climbed up and sat down alongside each driver. Sal flicked his reins and the mules pulled away from Flavia's house. Three blocks away on a street shielded from Flavia's house, members of the Assassins Guild eliminated the guards, who were thrown into a small cart, driven to Flavia's house and left to be discovered in the morning.

One block short of the west gate, the wagons made a right turn, followed the curve of the walls and left the city by the north gate.

Once free of the city traffic, they headed north and disappeared into the darkness.

Chapter Sixteen

Ansgar realized that a fight with Jerado was becoming increasingly possible. Up until now, it was just a possibility what with all the roadblocks in the way, including hostile soldiers. But now, within a few hours, the only task left would be to confront the dwelf. Everything else was taken care of or would be.

The reality of the situation was that he hadn't cast a combat spell in over two hundred years. Hitting a standing target with a lightning bolt was simple stuff. So was making it rain on a stationary group of archers. Jerado wouldn't be standing still. He would be moving and attacking him with spells.

Ansgar reviewed the information necessary to cast a combat spell. First, he needed to set a deflection value. That value was the difference, left or right, from north. He looked to his right and saw a tree. The deflection value would be about twenty degrees right. To his left, he spotted a large boulder and it would be ninety degrees left. To hit the tree, he needed an elevation of ten degrees. The boulder, further away, could use twenty-five degrees of elevation. Then there was the power level using the standard measure of magical power, the necrom. A power lever of ten would embed a tenth of his magical power into the spell. A five would specify a twentieth and a one a hundredth. Too high a value wasted power, too low only annoyed the target. So many decisions to be made on the spur of the moment while someone else tried to kill you.

Ansgar changed his thoughts to Jerado. He had over two hundred years to learn new spells and techniques while he, Ansgar, slept in a cave. What did the evil half breed learn during that time? That was a question that couldn't be answered until the trial by combat began, a trial that could prove to be fatal.

~ ~ ~

From Barrow's Journal: *Getting to hate Tibbs and a few others. All he does is complain. The others tell the same stories over and over. Getting real tired of hearing them. Glad this journey is almost over. Bianca says Leticia did a good job in the city. The word is that Leticia got a way for us to get into the city. She's quite a gal.*

Bohan believed his life was about to change. If he survived. There was a possibility Ansgar would be defeated by Jerado. In that case, he wouldn't be able to kill the wizard and, after that, Jerado would hunt them all down.

If Ansgar and he prevailed then he, Bohan, by right of conquest, would be the new ruler of Gundarland, a daunting prospect. A long time ago he had ruled a small kingdom for three years, not exactly a great resumé for taking over an entire country.

Customs and cultures must have changed and evolved over the two hundred years and he didn't know what those changes were. Ignorance of the changes made a misstep easy. Missteps often had strange consequences. Some of them deadly.

Bohan knew he had to alleviate the hunger and suffering of the poor citizens. His time as king taught him that a change in one area resulted in changes in other areas, often unanticipated changes. If he helped the poor, what other changes would ripple through the country? What would be the repercussions of those other changes? He had no idea what they would be. He obviously needed someone who understood Gundarland to help and advise him. Whoever that was should also understand the machinery of government and what made it run.

Where and how could he find that someone? That was a crucial question, and the answer would be the difference between a successful reign and a unsuccessful one. Unsuccessful ones tended to be bloody.

~ ~ ~

Jerado sat by the fireplace in his Palace apartment and reviewed the latest reports. The multiple patrols scouring the area outside the walls found no sign of Bohan. He had disappeared. The gate guards assured him Bohan hadn't entered the city, so he must be hiding somewhere in the countryside.

No doubt Bohan had sent someone to look at the city gates and realized he couldn't fight his way into the city that way. Of course, Bohan could try to go over the walls, but spearmen now patrolled the wall night and day. No, Bohan wasn't climbing over the walls. Nevertheless, he had increased the number of his personal guards on the night shift outside the palace.

Just in case.

As soon as Bohan's location was uncovered, Jerado planned to lead an army out to confront the enemy. This time, Lithgow wouldn't be in charge. It'd be like old times when he had led armies and conquered Gundarland.

Quite possibly, the future held a battle against another wizard. The thought sent a delicious thrill up Jerado's spine. It would put an end to the boredom that plagued his days. He decided to mentally prepare for a battle against Ansgar. He lifted his wig, scratched the top of his head and made a face as he realized he hadn't cast a combat spell in ages. With a bit of reflection, he recalled his last combat spell. It happened before he marched his army into Dun Hythe and that was many years ago. In fact, the only spells he used in the past few years were golf spells or mundane household spells such as open or close a door and start a fire.

He reviewed the steps necessary to launch a combat spell: deflection, elevation, power level. He whirled, cast a make-believe spell at a lamp and frowned. The deflection and elevation values he used were too large for a target so close. He set a goal of casting five imaginary spells every day.

Just in case.

He frowned as a new thought popped into his mind. He was a black magic wizard and he had never cast a black magic combat spell. In fact, he didn't *know* any black magic combat spells.

~ ~ ~

In the morning, Flavia finished eating breakfast and stood up when a servant came in and told her about the dead guards in a cart on the street. She gripped the table edge with both hands. Her skin grew clammy and she fought the urge to lose her breakfast.

After the clamminess passed, she went to her home office and checked the scryer. She saw four messages from the depot manager late last night asking where the cargo was and when would it arrive. She sat down and lowered her head between her knees until the dizziness stopped.

Flavia knew her silver and gold pennies had been stolen   Her fortune, amassed over years of business deals and hard work, was gone. She was destitute. All she had left was the mansion she lived in, two more outside of Dun Hythe and a controlling interest in dozen enterprises.

What would she do of an evening now? One of her favorite pastimes was to dip her hands into a chest of coins and watch them spill back into the chest.

Her despair was soon replaced by anger and determination to regain her treasure. She realized the Godmother had to be behind the robbery. Only she controlled the resources to pull off something this big and brazen. But how did the bitch learn about the coin shipment? Someone told her. Someone in the Palace. But who? Flavia didn't tell anyone about the movement of her treasure so who and how could someone learn of it? Was it the Teamsters Guild when she ordered the wagons? That didn't make sense because she didn't tell the Guild why she need the wagons or where they were going.

After a few minutes of thought,

Flavia was left with nothing more than a mystery and a sense that her world was caving in. First, it was this Bohan business. Now her retirement funds had gone missing.

For the first time in years, Flavia felt helpless. She didn't know how to deal with the changed situation.

Part Four: In Dun Hythe

Chapter Seventeen

Dun Hythe was always a unique city. In the days when dukes and kings controlled the provinces, Dun Hythe remained an open city led by an elected mayor. This status was protected by the same dukes and kings because of the city's seaport, the only one in the north, and the largest in the country. Imports were unloaded from the ships and sent to all parts of the land. Similarly, products were sent to Dun Hythe for shipment throughout the known world. The greatest nightmare of those dukes and kings had been that one of their number would gain control of the city by violent means and use its revenues for all-out warfare against the others.

Within the city walls, two broad boulevards separated the old city into four quarters. These boulevards were paved in stone. All the other streets, roads and alleys were muddy when wet and dusty when dry.

Originally, each quarter was dominated by one race, so the districts were named Human, Elfin, Half-pint and Dwarfen Quarters, but these racial groups refused to be limited by such labels and they melded together, and the four districts became one semi-homogenous population. The Dwarfen quarter clustered around the docks, where many locals worked as stevedores loading and unloading ships.

Over time, many changes had occurred in Dun Hythe. One of the most troublesome was the separation of the classes. The wealthy moved outside the city walls to new suburbs while the working classes, always poor, stayed in the tenements that lined the streets in the old city.

With their tradition of independence, the inner city inhabitants hated Jerado's government. These citizens resented the government's intrusion into their lives. Taxes, restrictive laws and interfering bureaucrats angered all of the city's inhabitants inside and outside the walls. Their favorite way of working off aggravation was to go on strike.

~ ~ ~

Maurice walked down the city's

main street. Without thinking about it, he blocked out the noises of the heavy wagon traffic along with the shouts of the Troll Patrol and the curses of the drivers.

Rich visitors crowded the sidewalks and stared in shop windows. Maurice shook his head at the contrast between the visitors and the citizens. The rich wore elegant clothes while the citizens wore tattered and patched rags. The rich talked gayly while the citizens were mute. The rich were happy while the citizens were morose. He wondered how much longer the citizens would tolerate their miserable living conditions before rebelling.

Nearing the Palace, he approached the bootblack who worked for the Godmother. The elf nodded and waved him closer.

"Gotta message for ya," the elf said. "Straight from the old lady herself.

"The Godmother? What is it?"

"Be at the big warehouse by Dock One at eight o'clock tonight."

"Anything else?"

"Naw. That's the whole message."

Maurice gave the elf a few coppers and walked away wondering why the meeting was at a warehouse. He hoped it concerned Bohan. The burden of his secrets became heavier with time and the list continued to grow.

After Flavia realized her treasure was stolen, her scryer messages threatened dire punishment to anyone involved and huge rewards for anyone who disclosed the thieves. Her messages didn't mention what had been stolen.

Maurice worried that his secrets would lead him to make a fatal mistake. The best solution for his safety involved a change of government, but the longer that took, the more danger he was in.

~ ~ ~

The Godmother puttered around her office, moving stacks of scrolls from one place to another. It was mid-afternoon and she had been at it all day.

"Ma!" Sophia said, "Will you stop it."

"I can't help it. I'm not cut out to be a revolutionary. The outcome is too hazy. I like plans with clear-cut endings. I never should have agreed to support someone I never met. What was I thinking?"

"We had no choice. The people are

suffering slow starvation. It's hurting our business now and it will only get worse. We need to get rid of Jerado."

"What if the new guy won't work with us? What if he wants to drive us out of business?"

"He won't be able to, Ma. We have too many options, too much power. He could maybe shut down the gambling houses. They're profitable, but they only account for a small part of our revenue. A new king or president can't really do anything about the Guilds. As long as the Guilds are intact, our revenue streams are solid. So stop worrying."

"I can't." The Godmother moved a stack of scrolls back to their original place. "What if this Bohan turns out to be a homicidal maniac?"

"Ma! Stop worrying. It's done. We're committed and you'll meet the guy tonight Then we can start negotiating what we want for our support. And what safeguards we need."

"But what if Jerado wins? Then what'll we do?"

"We don't change anything. Jerado won't know we were involved."

"I hope you're right, Sophia." The Godmother gave her daughter a wan smile. "We need to do something to show Bohan how much power we have. It'll make negotiations simpler."

"You're right, Ma. Sophia thought for a few moments. "How about this? We call a general strike and make sure Bohan knows who called it. That'll tell him how things stand in the city."

"Good idea. I'll tell the staff to spread the word. We'll do it tomorrow in the morning. We'll demand higher wages. It'll give everybody a chance to work off some steam and have a bit of fun. Let's make it into a family outing so the wives and kids can join in."

The Godmother stopped moving scrolls about and instead wrote notes to her lieutenants.

~ ~ ~

From Barrow's Journal: *Going into the city tonight. Don't know what to expect. Probably have a battle. Just don't know who with and how many of them will be fighting us.*

Bohan and the others mounted up an hour after dark. The ride through the grassland was easy because of a half-moon. On the ride, Bohan's hands constantly moved. They touched his sword, his shield, his saddle, his horse's neck. He didn't think he had ever gone into a situation surrounded by so much uncertainty, by so many unknowns. He followed a rough-spoken elf he didn't know going to a strange place to sail into a hostile harbor and meet with more people he didn't know.

Despite Leticia's assurances, he was concerned about walking into a trap. Jerado was devious. It would be like him to lure the group into a place where they could be surrounded and killed. Before mounting up, he ordered Bianca to have a quiet word with everyone and tell them to be prepared to fight their way out of a possible trap.

After a few minutes, Bohan rode forward to talk to Vito, who led the group.

"Tell me about the people in the city and what's going on in there," he said.

"It's bad," Vito replied. "People are hurtin' 'cause they can just barely survive. The government says how much us workers can be paid and it ain't enough to eat proper, especially if ya gotta family to feed."

"That's terrible."

      "I hear ya gonna change that. Are ya?"

      "I'll try. I don't know enough about how the government works right now to say for sure."

      "If ya don't change it, ya ain't gonna be around very long."

      "So all the people in the city are poor. That doesn't make sense. How do shops and small business get along? Someone must have money to buy stuff."

      "Some people are rich. Then there's the visitors. Rich visitors. People come from all over to buy the stuff that gets shipped inna port. So ya got the powerful people like Jerado and his kin, the rich visitors, the merchants and then everyone else. Everyone else is the poor people. Except the soldiers. They get food, housing and decent pay. Everyone wants to be a soldier. Every once inna while, a recruiter comes by to enlist more soldiers. If you wanna join up, ya gotta bribe the recruiter. And it's gotta be a really big bribe."

      Bohan thought about Vito's answers. Dun Hythe was just like the farm areas. Everywhere in the country people starved while the rich and powerful enjoyed life. He switched the conversation to a different troubling topic.

"You said the Godmother rules the city. How can that be?"

"She controls the Guilds. Like the teamsters, the dock workers, the pickpockets and thieves. She also owns most of the taverns inna city. If the Godmother snaps her fingers, the whole city goes on strike and nothin' gets done."

Bohan gulped air. Pickpockets? Now he had an inkling about how powerful the Godmother was and where her power came from. He realized he needed to build bridges to her and possibly make an accommodation with her. One that he normally wouldn't think of making, but he needed the Godmother's support if he ever hoped to rule the country. An unruly Dun Hythe was the last thing he needed.

"We gotta go through the woods over there." Vito pointed ahead. "We gotta go single file once we get there 'cause it's a narrow path."

Bohan's hand reached for his sword hilt. Stretched out in a line was the preferred way to get killed in an ambush. If it was a trap, Bohan vowed Vito would be the first one to die, and Vito must know that.

They rode slowly and silently through the woods. Bohan strained to hear any noise indicating the presence of armed assassins. A short time later, they emerged from the woods and Bohan realized he was holding his breath much of the time.

"Relax, will ya," Vito said. "Yer a bundle of nerves. Ya ain't ridin' in to a trap. The Godmother's word is sacred."

Bohan raised an eyebrow and loosened his grip on the sword's hilt.

"The farm's up ahead," Vito said. "We leave the horses there and get inna boat for the rest of the trip."

The closer they came to the farm, the stronger the smell of salt water and rotting fish became. They left the horses in a stable, loaded their backpacks with belongings from the saddle bags, then walked toward the shore. A dock stretched into the water with a single-masted ship tied to it.

"The boat ain't that big," Vito said. "With all of ya on board, I can only take one guy to work the sail. Ya gonna hafta row to get away from the dock and when we get to the city. Can't use the sails then, ya see."

Bohan didn't see. He knew next to nothing about sailing. Getting into a boat and going out into the ocean added to his concerns because he couldn't swim. None of his heroes could either. Vito ordered a few heroes to sit at the oars and told them what to do. The crewman, an elderly elf, cast off the ropes and Vito, at the steering oar, called out, "Row."

He cursed the clumsiness of the rowers when they splashed cold water on him. After a few minutes, the rowers grew more accustomed to the job and the boat moved away from the dock. Immediately, Tibbs and Luc became seasick.

"Lean over the side, you idiots," Vito called out. "Don't get sick inna boat or ya gonna clean it up."

A half-hour later, Vito said, "Get ready wid the oars. We're goin' inna harbor." Vito leaned on the steering oar and the boat turned to the right. "Drop the sail."

The sail dropped with a thud.

"Row."

The boat sailed past a dock with a hut on the end.

"That's where the customs guys hang out. They got told to stay inside tonight."

"What if they don't stay inside?"

Bohan asked.

"Ya screw the Godmother, ya regret it. It's that simple."

Vito steered the boat to a pier and the crewman threw a rope to a dock worker.

"The warehouse is straight ahead. The Godmother should be in there by now. She's probably got food and beer waitin' for ya. Good luck wid yer quest."

Vito shook hands with Bohan, then climbed out of the boat and disappeared into the darkness.

Bohan, still tense, looked about for an ambush as he walked toward the warehouse.

Chapter Eighteen

From Barrow's Journal: *By the end of the day tomorrow, Bohan will be king again or we'll all be dead.*

Bohan entered the warehouse and found a large room filled with crates and barrels. A few widely spaced lanterns provide a modicum of light. A burly elf armed with a cudgel pointed down an aisle.

"Go down that way."

Followed by the others, Bohan walked toward the office, glancing into every nook and dark area he passed. He took deep breaths to try to loosen the knot in his stomach. It didn't work.

In the back of the warehouse, he came to an open area. A table with food and a keg of beer stood on the left against a wall. To the right was a wall with a door and two tough-looking elves.

"All of ya ain't comin' in here," one tough said. "Ya all won't fit."

"The food is yers," the second said.

"Help yerselves."

"Beer!" Tibbs exclaimed. "Just what I need to forget about sailin'."

"Ansgar, Bianca and Leticia, grab something to eat then come with me," Bohan said. He walked to the table and ate bread and chunks of cheese along with a mug of beer. "Go easy on the beer," he told everyone. "We don't know what the rest of the night holds."

When they finished eating, the four walked to the office door. One elf held up a hand. "Leave yer weapons here."

Bohan and Ansgar exchanged glances before Bohan handed over his sword and dagger. Bianca stood her longbow against the wall and dropped her bag of arrows and short sword on the floor. Leticia put her dagger and sword on top of Bianca's weapons.

A guard opened the door and Bohan walked into a room with a large round table. Sitting at the table were two female elves and a half-pint. All of them stood.

"You must be Bohan," the older of the elves said. "I'm the Godmother. This is my daughter, Sophia and this is Maurice Girard. He is Jerado's Treasurer."

"Yes, I am Bohan. With me are my wizard, Ansgar, my squad leader, Bianca, and you know Leticia. I thank you for helping me get into the city."

"Since I don't know you," the Godmother replied, "my help is not personal. It's strictly business. Please sit down."

Once they were seated, she continued. "The rumors have it that you intend to take over the government. True?"

"I came to Dun Hythe to settle an old score by killing Jerado. Once I do that, I become the ruler, but that isn't my initial concern. Jerado is." Bohan nodded to Maurice. "Why is one of Jerado's officials here?"

Maurice cleared his throat. "I've watched the people in the city suffer for too long. I've been told it's the same in the countryside. The suffering is caused mostly by Jerado's daughter, Flavia. She's the Secretary of the Interior and controls much of the country's economy. I've tried to tell Jerado about the problem caused by the wage restrictions, but he won't listen or do anything. It's time for a change. The people can't live like this much longer and I fear a bloody rebellion will happen soon. I'm hoping you're the change agent who will prevent a civil war from happening."

"I agree," Sophia said, "the people won't suffer much longer before they try to overthrow the government. Your way can be quicker and a lot less bloody."

"That's why we helped you get into the city," the Godmother said. "As Maurice said, to be a change agent."

Bohan weighed the information he had just received. His arrival was seen as a relief from an oppressive government. As much as he needed and appreciated the support, he wondered what it would cost him.

"What do you expect to get from me in return for your support?"

"We can negotiate that after the fact," the Godmother replied. "If you survive."

"At the very least, we expect to have a say in the policies you initiate," Sophia said.

"And you?" Bohan nodded to Maurice.

"A government is supposed to help and nurture the people, not work them to death. I want a government that will help people. One that will make everyone's life better, not worse. Perhaps I'm naive, but that is what I believe and that is what I want.

"Also being so close to Jerado, I've

come to discover secret information. Secrets that will get me killed if the family learned I knew about them. It's only a matter of time until I slip up and disclose a secret. I want to save my life."

"What kind of secrets?" Bohan asked.

"Flavia is a genius at embezzlement. She's looting the country and has amassed a huge private fortune. Jerado's son, Lithgow, also practices embezzlement, but he is an amateur compared to his sister. And Jerado is a black wizard."

"What?" Ansgar came out of his seat. "Black magic is a myth. It doesn't exist."

Ansgar sat back down with a puzzled look on his face.

"The Wizard Guild believes it does exist even though it is rare. How Jerado found out about it, I don't know, but I'm certain he's a black magic wizard."

"Let's talk about the deed," the Godmother said. "How do you intend to get rid of our President?"

"My plan is to sneak into wherever Jerado stays at night and get rid of him. Of course, I don't know where Jerado stays, so I'll rely on you three to tell me how to implement the plan."

"Jerado stays in the Palace," Maurice said. "He has an apartment on the top floor. Flavia and Lithgow have their own palaces elsewhere in the city."

"So we have to get into the Palace and up to the top floor?"

"I will help you get into the Palace by distracting the guards," the Godmother said.

"Jerado increased the guards in front of the Palace," Maurice said. "He now has six of them at night. Three are hidden and can't be seen."

"That makes it difficult to distract them," the Godmother said. "I thought to use a few of my good-time girls to do that. If the girls can't find the guards, they can't distract them."

Maurice chuckled. "Jerado didn't increase the guards in the back of the Palace. The rear door still has only two guards at night."

"Ahh." The Godmother grinned. "Those two guards will think they went to heaven when my girls show up." She looked at Bohan. "When?"

"Tomorrow night."

"Good. The city will provide an extra distraction tomorrow."

"What's that?"

"The workers will go on strike at noon. It will be a general strike protesting their low wages."

That comment struck Bohan as strange. "And how do you know that?"

"Because," the Godmother grinned some more, "I ordered them to go on strike."

Bohan kept his face neutral, but he was flabbergasted at how powerful the Godmother really was. She was a force that would have to be reckoned with as he set up a new government.

"I set up sleeping quarters for everyone in this warehouse. You can stay here until you leave tomorrow night. I'll have food sent in and you can watch the strike from here." The Godmother stood up. "I'll bid you good night and I'll see you again after you become the new head of the government." She left the room followed by Sophia and Maurice.

~ ~ ~

In the morning, Jerado left the palace for the first time in years other than for golf outings. Accompanied by two guards, he left through the back door which opened onto a large private park area. He told the guards to stop while he walked further into the park to practice casting spells, especially combat spells. Sooner or later, he reasoned, he and Ansgar would come face-to-face once his army trapped Bohan. Then it would be wizard against wizard and may the better one win.

So far, he had never used a black magic combat spell and he wanted to try several of them.

Despite all his research at the Wizards Guild, he never found a description of any black magic spells. All he could find was a warning that black magic spells were the opposite of white magic spells. He knew if he cast an *open door* spell it would close a door. To start a fire, he cast an *extinguish fire* spell. Presumably, to cast a fireball spell he would have to launch a water ball spell. Today he would test that presumption.

First, he tried a basic protection spell, casting a ward on himself. "Cast a ward." Nothing happened. "Remove ward." That worked! Particles of magic tickled his exposed skin. "Cast a ward!" The tickling stopped.

Jerado selected a tree as a target and thought about the combat spell parameters he needed. "Deflection left 15, elevation 5, power level 1, cast fireball."

He jumped as water soaked his right foot.   Jerado scratched his chin as he reviewed what happened. He called for left deflection, but his right foot got wet. He called for an elevation of 5 but the spell hit the ground at his feet. Obviously, casting black magic combat spells would require some practice. Maybe he had to reverse the parameters instead of using the usual ones.

He tried again using the same tree as a target. "Deflection right 15, elevation minus 5, power lever minus 1, cast fireball."

A small water ball missed the tree by a few feet.

"Close enough." Now, he thought, to come up with a few more combat spells. One of his favorite white magic spells was a lightning spell, but what was the opposite of that? He tried casting a white magic lightning spell and was rewarded by a small rain cloud over the target area with a few drops of rain. Next he cast a rain spell and the dark clouds over the target area disappeared.

He spotted a squirrel and thought about trying to change it into a bird, but decided the unpredictable results could be dangerous. The squirrel may turn into a ferocious beast looking for prey.

He picked another tree as a target and threw a fireball at it by casting a water ball spell. It missed the tree by inches and set fire to a nearby bush. Jerado quickly muttered a fireball spell to send a water ball at the bush and extinguish the fire.

That would have to do for now, but not for the future. With only two combat spells he was vulnerable to Ansgar. He needed to develop more black magic spells.

~ ~ ~

In the morning, they all slept late except for Maggy, who had the final night watch. Last night Bohan ordered everyone to keep their weapons nearby since they were close to Jerado's Palace.

After a breakfast provided by the Godmother, Bohan gathered them around to explain the plan. He was both excited and concerned. Excited that revenge was at hand, concerned that he didn't know the layout of the Palace. Who knew what or who they would blunder into.

"We'll attack in the middle of the night," he said. "I've been told there are only two guards at the back door. The Godmother will distract them somehow. Tibbs and Angus will take out one guard and Barrow and Maggy the second. Don't kill them. Just secure them so they can't make trouble or noise."

"Why can't I kill 'em?" Tibbs asked. "I can do it quiet like."

"I want a minimum of bloodshed. The guards will have family in the city and killing them will make enemies of the families. I don't want that."

Tibbs made a face but nodded agreement.

"You four stay to guard the door and prevent anyone from coming in. The rest of us will go into the Palace. Maurice will guide us once we're inside. According to Maurice, Jerado lives on the top floor, so we'll have to sneak up the stairs. I'll lead with Ansgar behind me ready to launch spells. The rest of you follow but be prepared to fight any guards."

"What about Flavia and Lithgow?" Leticia asked.

"They'll have to wait until the morning."

Maurice walked into the assembly area. He pointed to the docks and said, "The strike is starting."

"How many workers will be on strike?" Bianca asked.

"Thousands. There won't be a single worker at his job in a few minutes."

Bohan shook his head. To be able to bring a large city to a standstill spoke of a strength that couldn't be ignored. The Godmother needed to be involved in developing policies for the new government, but he would have to be careful to limit her involvement. He couldn't let her dominate his decision-making. Bohan didn't want the Godmother to go from the most powerful figure in the city to the most powerful figure in Gundarland.

~ ~ ~

Ansgar chewed his lower lip. He hadn't anticipated facing Jerado inside a building. He had always pictured the fight outdoors where he could use his full range of spells.   Inside a building, launching lightning bolt spells and fireball spells could set the building on fire and turn it into a death trap.

His only usable indoor combat spell was the air hammer. That one sent a mass of compacted air at the target. It could do great bodily damage. But Jerado would use a ward to protect himself. Still, the air hammer would knock him about but the ward would protect Jerado from getting crushing bones or suffering other damage.

Perhaps that was how he would win: keep striking blows on Jerado to keep him off-balance. That would give Bohan a chance to move in and use his sword.

Ansgar made a face. Jerado would certainly strike back and who knew what spells he had devised in his years as a black wizard? Ansgar wondered if he could even protect himself with a ward against black magic spells?

Tonight would be interesting, possibly even fatal, he realized.

~ ~ ~

After returning from spell practice, Jerado sat in his office and worked on devising spells he could use in his anticipated battle with Ansgar. So far, all he had developed was the black magic equivalent for a hot foot, a minor spell that might distract Ansgar.

He tapped the quill point against the desk while he thought. Jerado noticed an unusual street noise growing in volume. He stood and walked to a window. Below, thousands of low-lifers filled the main road and milled about shouting something about wage restrictions. Enterprising workers set up food stands while others opened drinks tables. The strike must be the work of that wretched Godmother. It could only mean someone had broken the unspoken truce: he ignored what she did in the city and kept soldiers outside the city walls. In return, she maintained peace and order.

Wage restrictions were Flavia's doing. The strike must be a reaction to that. Maurice would know how to fix the problem.

"Remy! Fetch Flavia and Maurice up here immediately."

"Y . . . yes, Master." Remy scurried out of his office and disappeared down a corridor.

Jerado went back to watching the mob and noticed many of them carried arms. He saw clubs, swords, daggers, spears and even a pitchfork and realized if someone annoyed them, the streets would fill with blood.

Remy returned and said, "F . . . lavia will be right up. Maurice isn't a . . .

round. His clerk said he's auditing a b . . . ank."

"That means he's causing trouble," Flavia said, walking into the office. "I wish you'd get rid of that troublemaker."

"Nonsense. Auditing banks is what he's supposed to do."

"He only audits banks I use."

"Forget the banks. What did you do to stir up a strike?"

"Me? It's the Godmother's work, not mine. When are you going to get rid of her?"

Jerado ignored the question. "She wouldn't call a strike without provocation. The mob is calling for an end to wage restrictions."

"Send a message to Lithgow and tell him to bring troops. That'll put an end to this strike."

"No!" Jerado shook his head. "I won't let troops enter the city. Besides, the mob is armed. They'll probably defeat Lithgow's troops. What are you going to do to satisfy the strikers? Perhaps a raise in wages?"

"Give in to the rabble? Never. It'll only encourage them. Besides, increasing wages will cut into profits."

"This strike is cutting into profits. All our wealthy visitors must be quaking in their boots and hiding in their rooms instead of shopping."

Flavia didn't reply. She stood with her arms crossed and an angry look on her face.

"I don't want any more strikes. Come up with a plan to placate the mob and prevent further strikes. And don't even think about bringing troops into the city."

Jerado flapped a hand dismissing his daughter.

Chapter Nineteen

In the middle of the night, Bohan opened the door to the warehouse and slipped out followed by the heroes, Leticia and Maurice. The city streets still rang with sounds of strikers now celebrating the end of the event with booze and songs.

"What's with the shield?" Barrow asked Ansgar. "I thought you was gonna fignt with spells.

"It may help protect me by deflecting Jerado's spells."

At the rear of the palace, Bohan heard guffawing from the guards and giggling from the Godmother's girls. He motioned Tibbs, Barrow and the two dwarfs to go ahead. A scuffle broke out momentarily followed by the thump of bodies hitting the ground.

"'Bout time," a girl said. "This one ain't taken a bath inna few years."

"On yer way, ladies," Barrow said. "And thank you."

Bohan and the others approached the door while Maggy and Angus tied up the guards.

"All of you stay here for now," Bohan said. "I'll go upstairs with Ansgar and Maurice. Leticia, if this ends badly, run to the Godmother's house. Jerado doesn't have to know you're involved. Let's go."

"Hold on a minute," Luc said. "I never fought a wizard and I ain't missin' out on this one. Wait until I get rid of my clothes."

"What do we do now, Maurice?" Bohan asked while Luc stripped.

"We go up the stairs to the fifth floor. Mind, it's dark. There are no lights." He took out a small candle and lit it with a flame that leaped from his fingertip. He put a trembling hand around the flame to protect it. "Open the door and I'll lead you up the stairs.

They climbed slowly up flights of uneven wooden stairs.

Bohan was glad he left Tibbs by the door. Jerado would surely hear them coming if Tibbs was here. The man was like a ballet dancer in battle; otherwise he tripped over his feet.

At the top of the stairs, Maurice whispered, "To the left is the office. Jerado's apartment is to the right. I'll wait here for you."

Beyond the corridor to the right, they saw a flickering light from a fireplace and candles.

Bohan took a deep breathe and nodded to Ansgar. The wizard cast a ward on himself and Bohan. The two walked silently down the corridor while Luc followed.

~ ~ ~

Maurice clenched and unclenched one fist as he watched Ansgar, Bohan and Luc move down the corridor. The other hand held the candle with its flickering flame. Within a few minutes, his fate would be decided. If Ansgar and Bohan won, then he would no longer live in fear of divulging the secrets. If Jerado won, the wizard would come rampaging down the corridor and destroy him with whatever kind of spell black magic wizards used.

A drop of candle wax burned his hand and he snuffed out the flame, preferring to wait in darkness. He didn't regret his dangerous choice. Backing Bohan was the right thing to do. But if it didn't work out, he would pay the penalty for betrayal.

So be it.

~ ~ ~

Jerado snoozed in a chair in front of the fireplace in his apartment. To his left was a large couch and beyond the couch, a dinner table and chairs. Light came from the fireplace and the candles in one chandelier. Two other chandeliers were dark.

As he snored away, he dreamed about defeating Ansgar with a new powerful, black magic spell, one he had yet to develop.

A noise jerked him awake. Jerado frowned, trying to identify the sound. He heard it again. It was the sound of someone sneaking down the hallway. At this hour, the guards only allowed Lithgow and Flavia to enter the Palace. It must be Lithgow trying to sneak up and scare him. Well, he'd give the little shit a surprise.

Jerado plopped his wig on his head and shoved his dentures into his mouth. He stood up, smoothed out his robe and prepared to cast a newly developed hot foot spell. To his shock, the intruder wasn't Lithgow. Ansgar and Bohan stood in the entrance of the corridor carrying shields.

Ansgar looked over the room and only saw a fire burning in front of the chair. To his surprise, Jerado rose from the chair and turned to face him, shock written large on his face.

"At last," Ansgar called out. "I've waited a long time to fight you." He cast an air hammer spell at maximum strength just as Jerado set a ward upon himself.

The white magic air hammer slammed into Jerado's black magic ward, knocking him backward against the wall. His wig turned into a pigeon and flew to a chandelier, where it pooped on Jerado's shoulder. Jerado launched a water ball spell aimed near his feet. The fireball bounced off the floor and shot into the air engulfing the chandelier and the pigeon. The smell of roasted meat and burnt feathers filled the area. Before the flames could spread, he bounced a fire ball spell off the floor to douse the flames. It also extinguished the candles leaving the room lit only by the fire.

Ansgar blinked in confusion at Jerado's actions.

Jerado raised an eyebrow when he saw a naked half-pint running through his apartment. What was he doing here? Obviously, the Palace needed new guards. Another question came to mind. Why did the half-pint carry a hammer in one hand and a hatchet in the other? What did he intend to do with the weapons?

The half-pint ran to the right and dove under the table.

Ansgar launched another air hammer spell just as Jerado launched a fireball spell. The two spells met in mid-air. A cloud of thick, multi-colored smoke appeared accompanied by a hideous sound like dozens of fingernails scrapping on pieces of slate.

A confused and angry goat materialized out of the smoke. It saw Jerado and pawed the rug under its feet.

"Leave the rug alone! It was expensive. And get out of my apartment!" Jerado roared.

The goat charged and hit him in the groin area. Jerado bounced off the wall and fell to his knees. He staggered upright while the goat ran around the room. It spotted Luc under the table and charged. Luc hit the goat in the head with his hammer. The goat disappeared.

Luc stared at the business end of the hammer wondering how it had disappeared the goat.

Ansgar wondered how Jerado had

disappeared the goat.

Jerado wondered how Ansgar had disappeared the goat.

"Are all spell fights this confusing?" Bohan whispered.

Jerado, still hunched over from the goat strike, launched a fire ball spell. The flames hit Ansgar's shield and sprayed around the room. Some bits of flame bounced off Bohan's shield.

Jerado followed that with a water ball spell to put out the flames.

Ansgar and Bohan both yelped when sprayed by cold water.

Ansgar didn't understand Jerado's spell strategy. Why was he trying to set fire to the apartment? That would endanger everyone including himself. And why the water ball spells if he planned to start the fire? Was Jerado trying to put him off guard by acting incompetent? Time to put an end to the fight, he thought.

"Bohan!" Ansgar yelled. "Luc! Get ready! Attack on my command."

His next move was to try to remove Jerado's ward. If successful, the enemy wizard would be vulnerable to weapons.

Luc scurried out from under the table and ran behind the couch where he awaited Ansgar's command.

Bohan gripped his sword and shuffled forward.

Ansgar cast the spell to remove the ward.

Jerado's ward shimmered when hit by the spell. He responded by sending a hot foot spell speeding at Ansgar.

"Now!" Ansgar yelled. "Oww!" He hopped around on one foot while trying to put out the fire burning his boot.

Bohan rushed ahead.

Luc threw his hatchet. It hit Jerado in the shoulder on the left side.

Luc ran closer and smashed Jerado's foot.

Jerado screamed as he lurched forward just as Bohan pushed the sword into his chest.

Jerado collapsed without a sound.

Ansgar hopped forward, smoke trailing behind him, ready to launch another air hammer if necessary.

A small black cloud emerged from Jerado's body.

"Catch that!" Ansgar ordered. "Don't let it escape."

He removed his burning boot and tossed it into the fireplace.

Luc and Bohan both dove for the cloud, but it eluded them and melted through the outer wall of the apartment.

"What was that?" Bohan asked.

"Jerado's shade. He managed to free it just before he died. It has to find a new host now before it fades into oblivion."

~ ~ ~

"Jerado escaped?" Bohan couldn't believe the news. He was sure he had gained revenge on Jerado. Now Ansgar told him differently.

They had returned to the top of the stairs where Maurice waited.

"That's not what I said. Jerado's body is inside, dead," Ansgar replied. "His shade fled the body just before he died. If the shade doesn't find a new host quickly, it will fade away."

"Where does it find a new host?"

"The shade has to find an infant or new-born baby to survive. Then it is stuck in the new body. Ten years from now, we should make inquiries if any children show magical talents." Ansgar paused. "But you are now the King. Or President. Or Whatever."

Bohan accepted Ansgar's explanation and whistled for the heroes to come up the stairs.

A grinning Maurice ran in circles and hugged himself.

Bohan watched the heroes laugh and clap each others' shoulders. To Maurice he asked, "All right, what's the first thing I should do as King? The most important proclamation I can make?"

""I never thought I'd have to answer a question like that." Maurice stared at the ground a few moments. "First, you have to arrest Jerado's children and meet with the Godmother. After that, issue a proclamation increasing wages by fifty percent and declare it is the minimum wage, not the maximum. Third, sieze Lithgow's and Flavia's stolen wealth and return it to the Treasury. And Jerado has a stash of loot somewhere in this palace. That also should go back into the Treasury."

"All right, but how do I deal with Jerado's children? What are their names again? Lith-something and Flavia, is it?"

"Lithgow and Flavia," Maurice said. "I can use the scryer in Jerado's office to send them a message ordering them to come here at first light in the morning."

"Good. And the Godmother."

"I can fetch her also in the morning." Maurice couldn't stop grinning.

"Will the strike continue in the morning?"

"I doubt it. Usually, the Godmother calls them for only a single day."

"Colbert, go downstairs and tell them to pull the guards inside the building so the replacements in the morning won't see them.

"Thank you Maurice. Let's see what the Presidential Suite looks like."

~ ~ ~

Jerado's shade hurried toward a hospital. By the time it found the delivery ward it had only a short time left before it faded completely. Jerado spotted an about-to-born baby. Without a moment to spare, the shade slipped into its new host.

As soon as the shade entered the host, Jerado knew something was wrong. The last sound he heard was the mid-wife saying, "I'm sorry, dear. The babe was stillborn."

Chapter Twenty

Bohan faced Lithgow after Angus and Maggy escorted him into the Presidential office .

"Who are these miscreants?" Lithgow demanded. "And who are you?"

"My name is Bohan and you are under arrest. Your father died last night. His body is lying inside if you wish to see him. I'll make an announcement later today."

"Then I'm the King!" Lithgow danced a few steps.

"No, I'm the King. I killed your father."

Lithgow looked shaken by the news, but Bohan couldn't determine if that was because of his father's death or his loss of the kingship.

"Wh . . What are you going to do with me? I did nothing wrong. Why am I under arrest?"

"You embezzled money from the treasury by inflating contracts," Maurice said.

"But . . . but everyone does that.

And I only did it a little bit."

"Put him on the couch for now," Bohan said.

An enraged Flavia showed up a few minutes later escorted by Bianca and Leticia.

"Where's my father? I want these two flogged."

Flavia saw the expression on Lithgow's face and scowled at Bohan.

"Your father died last night."

Flavia's mood brightened. "Did he announce that I'm his heir?"

"I am now the King. My name is Bohan."

"My father would never let you kill him. Where is he?"

"His body is in the apartment. Bianca, take her to look at the body, then bring her back."

A pale, shaken Flavia returned to the office.

"I suppose you plan to kill me, also?" she said. "Even though I didn't do anything wrong."

"Your crimes would fill pages," Maurice said. "You singlehandedly wrecked the economy with your greed."

"And you arrested my father," Leticia added. "Where is he?"

Flavia spit at Leticia's feet. "You

dared to touch me, you peasant. You'll never find your father. He'll rot in prison."

"Oh!" Leticia sobbed. "Please make her tell me, Bohan."

"I'll take care of it," Maurice said. "There are only two jails for political prisoners. I'll find him, have him released and brought to Dun Hythe."

"Good work, Maurice," Bohan said.

"Thank you," Leticia said.

"Actually, I recommend you free all the political prisoners," Maurice said.

"Ahh, yes. That's a splendid way to start my reign."

Flavia gave Bohan a withering look while Lithgow sobbed.

"What should I do with these two, Maurice?"

"Lithgow's rather harmless and he likes military things. Why not assign him to clean out the stables in the army camp? Permanently."

"Good idea. And I need a new army commander. Tibbs has experience leading troops. Where is he?'"

Angus went to fetch Tibbs.

"Why did this maggot wake me up?" Tibbs asked. "I spent the entire night watching those two guards."

"I need an army commander. Want

the job?"

Tibbs' face lit up with a rare smile. "I like commanding troops, so yes, I want the job."

"This one will show you where the camp is." Bohan pointed to Lithgow, then told Tibbs about the stable assignment. "He'll also introduce you to the other officers. Make sure they don't cause trouble over the change in government."

"You won't hear a peep outta the army." Tibbs grabbed Lithgow's arm. "Let's go. I ain't eaten breakfast yet. Yer mess hall better be good."

"And Flavia?" Bohan asked Maurice.

"She's a lot more dangerous than her brother. I think the Wizards Guild can use more cleaning staff. They'll keep a close watch on her."

"I don't clean," Flavia said with a sneer. "I have minions to do that."

"I think you'll learn quickly. The chief wizard over there has a real nasty magic whip spell. I can take her over there later.

"Anything else I have to do?"
"You have to deal with Remy."
"And who is Remy?"
"Remy is Jerado's personal

assistant." Maurice shouted for Remy to stop hiding under the desk in his office.

"He's undead," Maurice explained as Remy shuffled into the office.

"T . . . the master is really dead?"

"He is, Remy," Maurice said. "You're free. What can we do for you?"

"T . . . he Master kept me alive with a spell he used every three months. I w . . . anna buy a nice mausoleum and wait there for the spell to wear off C . . . an some one close the door for me afterwards?"

Maurice and Bohan both nodded.

"I can take Flavia to the Wizards Guild after the Godmother shows up."

"Yes, do that. I need to organize my thoughts on how to break the news to the nation."

~ ~ ~

When the Godmother and Sophia entered the Presidential suite, Jerado lay stretched out on his desk and Flavia, tied and gagged, sat on a chair brought from the apartment.

Bohan, Maurice and Ansgar looked exhausted, as did the rest of the heroes.

"Lovely," the Godmother said. "I see you took care of business.   How nice to see you again, Flavia."

Flavia turned red in the face and struggled against the ropes.

"So, please tell us what happened since I last saw you."

Bohan invited the ladies to sit down and described the events of last night and this morning.

"He'll remove the wage restrictions as his first act," Maurice said.

"Excellent move," the Godmother replied.

Sophia clapped her hands.

"Let's get down to business," the Godmother said.

"Flavia's treasure?" Bohan asked. "Maurice told me about that."

"Yes. After Maurice alerted me that Flavia was moving it, I arranged to have it go missing. We took a lot of risk doing that. If we were caught, Flavia would have had us killed. We're entitled to a reward."

"I agree," Bohan said. "What did you have in mind?"

"Twenty-five percent."

"I think a hundred silver pennies is sufficient." Bohan grinned at the Godmother and Sophia. He loved negotiating and thought it was fun.

"Absurd. Twenty percent is as low

as we go."

"One percent is as high as I go."

"That won't cover the cost of the feed we used on the animals and the wages of the drivers."

"All right. Five percent is my last offer."

The Godmother pulled a face and started to reply, but Sophia stopped her by placing a hand on her arm.

"Flavia owns a lot of businesses," Sophia said. "They must belong to you now."

"Yes I supposed they do. Do you know about these businesses, Maurice?"

"I do. I'll make a list of them later on."

"We'll accept the five percent of the treasure," Sophia said, "if you throw in some sweeteners."

Such as?"

"The entire peat train operation. The engines, the route, the peat contracts, everything to do with the peat."

"What's a peat train?"

Maurice explained the vast improvement the peat train made over mule-driven wagons.

"All right." Bohan nodded.

"I have ideas on how to expand the

operation to include passengers and freight besides peat," Sophia said. "It's the future for travelers. And we want Flavia's steam engine factory."

"What's a steam engine?" Bohan asked.

"It's a mechanical device that makes the peat train work," Sophia said. "Factories are starting to install them to increase output. And one guy claims they can be put into ships and eliminate the need for sails and oars. We want a monopoly on the steam engine production."

"You mean no one else in Gundarland will be able to make the steam engines?"

Sophia nodded.

"If you expect to have the monopoly forever, that's nonsense." Bohan shook his head. "You can have it for five years. After that, anyone can make steam engines."

"Agreed." Sophia bounced in her chair.

"Is there anything else?" Bohan looked at the Godmother.

"One more thing," the Godmother said. "Dun Hythe is and always was an open city. That means you don't station troops in the city. Except for your guards. That's the way it has been and even Jerado followed that tradition."

"That's reasonable. I look forward to working with you in the future."

Sophia and her mother stood up.

"It's so nice having a reasonable person in charge." The Godmother smiled at Bohan and took her leave.

Bohan looked around at his heroes and Maurice. "We have a few more chores before we can rest. Maurice, I need a prime minister. Someone who knows how this government works. Do you want the job?"

"Yes, I do."

"We need someone to replace Flavia as Interior Minister. Do you know anyone?"

"I can draw up a list of possible replacements."

"Good. I think we should put Leticia in charge of the constables and bailiffs since she knows how they work and what should be changed."

Maurice nodded and Leticia grinned her acceptance.

"Now, it's time to let Gundarland know about Jerado. We'll start with the guards. We'll bring them in to look at the body. Maurice, work the scryers to send out messages about the change."

Bohan looked around the room. "Where's Bianca?"

Bianca, who had been dozing on the couch, opened one eye and looked at Bohan, who beckoned with a finger. She stood up and walked over to him.

"We're starting a fresh government in a different time. Dun Hythe is a very liberal town and won't mind a mixed marriage. Bianca, I need a queen. Will you marry me?"

Bianca jumped into Bohan's arms and gave him a passionate kiss.

Once the two broke apart for air, Bohan said, "If that's a 'yes', we can get married and follow that with a double coronation. One for me and one for you."

The heroes applauded.

"Maybe we can have a double marriage," Maggy said.

The heroes groaned.

From Barrow's Journal: *If Bohan lets Maggy and Angus get married with him and Bianca, we won't have to drink that skunk beer the dwarfs serve at their weddings.*

I told Leticia I'd escort her to the Constables office. In case there's

trouble. She said okay. She also told me I can have the first dance with her at the wedding feast.
Things are looking up.

****

If you enjoyed reading this story, please write a review. It's an important way to let others know about the book

About the Author

And now, a few words about the guy who writes this stuff, Hank Quense.

Of late, Hank has been bouncing between fiction novels and non-fiction. Since writing fiction is fun and non-fiction is work, he's dedicating himself to fiction for a while.

On the non-fiction front, Hank has written two series of ebooks. His *Fiction Writing Guides* are aimed at beginning and inexperienced fiction writers. The *Self-publishing Guides* describe the process of publishing and marketing a book.

His *Fiction Writing Guides* consist of *Creating Stories* and *Manage Your Story Design Project* and *Planning a Novel, Script or Memoir.* The first named book concerns itself on fiction writing while the second uses a project management type approach to creating stories. The third describes a process that will enable an author to get control of a long work.

The *Self-publishing Guides are* a

set of four books aimed at authors who need to understand the publishing processes. The book titles are: *Self-publishing a Book*, *Marketing Plans for Self-published Books*, *Manage Your Self-publishing Project* and *Business Basics for Authors*.

There is also a boxed set incorporating all four titles under a single cover. It's called the *Complete Self Publishing Guide*.

On the fiction front, Hank has written and published a number of parodies. If you enjoy humorous and satiric fantasy and sci-fi fiction, you'll enjoy reading his books. You can chose from:

Zaftan Troubles
Falstaff's Big Gamble
Wotan's Dilemma
Tales From Gundarland
Moxie's Decision
Moxie's Problem
Queen Moxie

Better yet, why bother choosing. Get a copy of all of them and lay in a supply of laughter.

You can find all of these books on the websites of many book sellers.

Links? You want links? Here you

go:

Strange Worlds Publishing: http://strangeworldspublishing.com/wp

Hank's blog pages: https://http://hank-quense.com/wp

Hank's Facebook fiction page: https://www.facebook.com/StrangeWorldsOnline?ref=hl

Hank's Facebook non-fiction page: https://www.facebook.com/pages/Strange-Worlds-Online-Non-fiction/439722529522496?ref=hl

Twitter: https://twitter.com/hanque99

Aspects, Bright and Fair

WAUGH WRIGHT

Dedication

To Megan,

Happy Birthday. Thanks for being wonderful. Thanks for being wondrous. Thanks for letting me give you chapter one with a "To Be Continued," as a present eleven years ago. Here's the rest of it. Well, Book One, at least.

-Waugh

CHAPTER ONE

It was a beautiful not-quite-summer afternoon in Philadelphia and a crowd had gathered along the Schuylkill River to look for monsters. Joni Margulis stood on the hill she had just climbed, next to the art museum. She saw the spectators spread out on the field next to the river and gritted her teeth. She turned to the dog at her side.

"Idiots, Bramble. They're such idiots. And they're right in the middle of your spot. Well, that's their problem."

She tugged on Bramble's leash and together they jogged down to the lawn by the old waterworks. They set up on the grass field behind the crowd, which was clustered at the river's edge. A good fifty people were leaning over a marble railing, peering into the murky waters of the river. Bramble ignored them and ran out twenty yards, where she plopped down and stared at her mistress. Joni loaded up her homemade tennis ball thrower and reared her arm back.

"Ow!" someone yelped behind her.

Joni spun around. "I'm so sorry — I didn't see you there."

A guy was rubbing his head where she'd backhanded him. Joni pegged him at a year or two older than she was, around seventeen. Good looking, but smiled like he didn't know that. He was tall and thin, with light brown skin and dark brown hair down to his shirt collar. He pocketed the cell phone he'd been looking at.

"It's all right," he said, with a faint accent that Joni couldn't recognize. "I should have watched where I was going."

"Yes, you should have. But I probably shouldn't have hit you with my atlatl."

"Your what?"

"My atlatl. Isn't it awesome? My godmother, well, she's not really my godmother, but what she is doesn't have a label, well, she's always teaching me about ancient weapons and stuff. The Aztecs used them to throw spears." She considered it briefly. "Or was it the Incas?"

"I know what an atlatl is," the stranger answered. "I've just never seen one used to throw tennis balls before."

"My friend Kelly helped me build it for physics class. She's got a good head for that sort of thing. She's taking calc as a sophomore."

"Just like the Aztecs did."

Joni gave him a look, trying to figure out if he was being a jerk, but decided the comment was on the friendly side of sarcasm. Which is where she usually was. Bramble came trotting over and the stranger got on one knee and started scratching her behind the ears and letting her lick his face.

"You're not looking for Schuylkill Sally, are you?" she asked.

"Who's a good girl?" he spoke directly to the dog. "¡Buena chica!"

"Are you here for Schuylkill Sally?" she repeated.

"No. I'm here for the museum," he answered, tapping a gift bag he was holding that said Philadelphia Museum of Art, next to a drawing of a griffin. "Who's Sally?"

"You don't know? Two weeks ago someone took a blurry picture of something in the river and it went viral. It was obviously just some floating trash or maybe a turtle, but everyone thinks it's a monster. All the tourists keep coming to see it. And Philly natives, who should know better. Kelly, that's the calc friend, is already super obsessed with any kind of animal and she left there like a minute before it supposedly appeared and now it's all she'll talk about."

She shook her head a little and then said, "Watch this," as Bramble walked off a little. "See that bench?"

With a surreptitious glance behind her this time, she swung her arm backwards and launched the ball forwards, straight as an arrow. It hit the bottom of a concrete bench thirty yards away and ricocheted back over the charging dog's head, where Joni caught it smoothly in her left hand.

"Pretty good, unless you're attacking someone with a tennis racket."

Joni guffawed in spite of herself and tossed the ball to Bramble. Just then, the crowd began buzzing and there were excited shouts of "Sally!" and "There she is!"

Forgetting that she didn't believe in the creature, Joni dropped her stuff and ran towards the river, Bramble bounding right behind her, ball in her mouth. Unfortunately, everyone else was doing the same, and in the jostling Joni was knocked down. Finding nothing hurt but her dignity, she sat up and straightened the crescent pendant hanging around her neck, trying to act like nothing happened.

A hand appeared in front of her face, outstretched. She followed it up the wrist and arm, to the face. The museum boy was leaning over to give her a hand up.

She took his hand, but as he pulled her up the satchel over his shoulder opened up and some notebooks spilled out, papers flying all around.

He rushed about, trying to grab them.

"Here," Joni called out, "let me help you, uh…"

"Alejandro. No, no. I've got it. No problem. I got 'em."

The waterworks lawn stretched to a long and crowded railing along the river that led to some Greek Revival columns overlooking the Schuylkill. A gust of wind suddenly sent several of Alejandro's papers over the railing and into the river. Alejandro chased them, frantically. A monster watcher came over (it turned out the phantom Sally sighting was nothing more than a large channel catfish coming to the surface) and offered him a net on a long pole to try to fish them out.

What kind of monster, Joni wondered, were you hoping to catch with a net like that?

She grabbed twenty or so papers and ran back, while Alejandro leaned over the balustrade, reaching into the water with the pole. A few more bystanders were offering him advice.

As she was stuffing papers into Alejandro's satchel, something about a photo on one caught her eye. Something familiar, that made her hesitate. Not quite sure why she was doing it, but trusting her gut, she crammed it and one or two beneath it into her pocket.

A spasm of guilt made her glance quickly over her shoulder. Alejandro was climbing back over the rail, which he had evidently scaled. He was clutching some watersoaked papers and gave a wistful smile at Joni. She forced a grin back, hoping the bulge in her pocket wasn't obvious.

He didn't notice as he clambered back to dry land, handed the net back to its owner, and strode over to her.

"Thanks," he said, grabbing the satchel from Joni. "I'll get that."

"Uh…yeah, I think I got it all."

"Well, thanks. I better run, try to dry them all out back in my hotel room." He gave Bramble one last scratch and walked away.

Once he was out of sight, Joni pulled the paper out of her pocket and looked at the picture. It was a grainy copy of a newspaper clipping, really just a picture with no article. The headline said "Local Girl Shot Dead," which didn't hold her attention, because she was from Philly and all, but then she looked more closely. The girl, the dead girl, had longish, not-quite-black hair, bony shoulders, hips, and elbows sticking out in various directions, and a thin face with expressive eyes and eyebrows, although the graininess of the photo made it hard to read the expression. Bored? Jaded? Exasperated?

And she realized why it was familiar.

It was her.

She stared at it for almost a minute. It wasn't a great copy, but it was her, right? She would swear it was. Probably. What was going on? She looked in the direction Alejandro had gone. Why did he have this? *How* did he have this?

She shivered as a cool breeze disrupted the muggy afternoon. *Local Girl Shot Dead.* There was no caption and no article, just the headline and the picture. A headline that said she was dead. If it was her. It wasn't a perfect picture, but it had to be her. Yeah, it totally was.

Joni felt her gut drop, like it weighed a hundred pounds. But at the same time her mind was racing a hundred miles a second.

What does it mean?

Who is Alejandro?

Is it some kind of joke? Yes, that's it, it must be, it's a sick joke.

No, it's a threat.

I'm being initiated into a secret society.

I'm going to die.

I'm already dead and Philadelphia is purgatory.

It's a prank.

It's for an art exhibit.

I'm being filmed for a reality TV show. Yes! A reality show, that totally makes sense, and Alejandro works for them. She whirled around, looking for hidden cameras, but saw nothing.

She looked at the picture again. Under the headline there was date — almost six years ago. So it wasn't her. Couldn't be her, because she wasn't dead. Obviously. How could she think she was dead? It wasn't her.

It's a mistake.

There. Simple as that. A mistake.

Only, it wasn't so simple. Her gut was fluttering again, telling her what she knew with certainty: The picture was of her. It was how she looked right now, only dead in an alleyway.

Unless it wasn't her. But it was.

Why would someone do this? Do this to her? She'd broken up with a couple of nothing boyfriends in the past year, but she knew they weren't behind it. They weren't creative or offbeat enough to do something like this. Otherwise she wouldn't have broken up with them.

She grabbed Bramble's leash and began to walk home.

She stopped.

"Do they think it's funny?" she asked Bramble. "Cause it's not."

She started again and climbed up and over the hill and waited at the stoplight on the far side. She looked across to the traffic island where the statue of Joan of Arc astride her warhorse was shining golden in the sunlight. When Joni was little, she had thought the statue was of her and she still adored the warrior saint. Young Joni used to climb on it and instruct passersby in the "exploits of the Maid of Orléans." Current Joni crossed the street and ran her hand along the statue's base, while cars whizzed noisily by.

She wanted to ignore the picture. And why couldn't she? It was silly. It's just a picture of a girl who looked like her. It was so random.

But it wasn't random. How could it be? Alejandro must have been spying on me. Is it a message? But what's it supposed to say? Am I in danger? I'm not dead.

"What was it like for you, Joan?" she asked the statue. "The French told you they were going to kill you before they executed you. Or was it the British? Did you believe it? Were you scared? You had faith and talked to saints and stuff, so that probably helped. But I bet you were scared. I'm not scared. Not much. I'm just confused."

She grunted and then pulled Bramble across the street and up the gentle slope into the Fairmount district. They zigzagged through a neighborhood of narrow row houses, past pharmacies, tiny groceries, and small taverns, all in the shadow of the giant gothic walls of Eastern State Penitentiary, a former prison that dominated the area, now open for tourists. She walked right past her street, but Bramble pulled her back. When they reached home, they ran up a few concrete steps, aromas of basil and mint rising from her dad's pots of herbs. The door on the right led to her friend Kelly's house, nearly the mirror image of Joni's. Joni opened her door and released Bramble, hanging her leash on a hook. She dashed up the stairs to her third story bedroom.

"Dinner in ten minutes, Joni," her father called from the kitchen.

"Okay, Dad. I just gotta do something first."

Pulling the sheets out of her pocket, she walked over to a crimson wall tapestry, next to a shelf with an old moon globe on it. Because both her parents were physicists, Joni uncovered things like moon globes in odd places throughout the house. Somehow Kelly didn't have the same problem, probably because she had only one physicist for a parent, and her mother was the mathematical kind, not the interesting kind. Joni whacked the tapestry with one hand, the sound echoing through a hidden door into Kelly's room on the other side of the wall. Hearing no response, she grabbed her cell phone and texted Kelly,

> *we need 2 talk*

There was a brief pause before her friend replied.

> *u see sally?*
> *just a catfish*
> *cool!!! what kind?*

idk we need 2 talk

later I'm about to eat

Joni grunted, but she could hear her own father calling her for dinner. She glanced at the picture one final time before placing the sheets on her desk and running down the stairs.

"How was your day, Joni?" her dad said a bit absentmindedly, spinning linguini around his fork.

"Uh…uh," Joni wasn't sure what to say. "Why do we always talk about my day? How was your day? What did you learn? You guys must learn stuff all the time."

"I wish I learned stuff all the time. I spent half today trying to get the equipment in the lab to work and the other half yelling at it when it didn't."

Joni laughed at her dad's expression and he managed an amused snort back at her.

"Now, Peter," Joni's mother said, "you'll get through it. Tamara called and said she might have had a breakthrough today. I told her to bring George and come by after dinner."

Joni looked up, hopefully.

"Kelly's parents are coming over? Can I go over to Kelly's?"

"Yes, yes," her mother said. "That'll be perfect."

The three of them finished dinner, quietly, all of them too preoccupied to notice how preoccupied the others were. Afterwards, Joni was washing the dishes when there was a knock on the door. She dropped a plate into the sink with a splash, sprinted to the door and opened it. Kelly's parents, Tamara and George Grebe, entered.

Joni tossed out a quick, "Hi," and dashed past them, her hands still wet. Down her front stairs, up Kelly's stairs, through the door, then bolting up to Kelly's room, which was identical to Joni's except that Kelly knew where everything was. It even smelled cleaner.

Her best friend was lying on her bed, under a shelf of her trophies, headphones over her long dark hair, doing her homework. She was jolted by Joni leaping on her bed.

"Joni! You scared me!"

"Sorry, Kell. But I need your help with that picture!"

"What picture?" She reached for her phone.

"No, not on your cell phone."

"Well, good, because my parents confiscated my real phone after I took the fall for you…"

"Look, I've said I'm sorry about that, and I really am, but now we've got to figure out what's up with that picture."

Kelly stared at her friend for five seconds before speaking again.

"So, I'll repeat myself. What picture?"

"The picture at the park…"

"What park?"

"In the newspaper…"

"What newspaper?"

"Uh," Joni faltered. "I don't have it here. I left it in my room."

"Joni, I'm trying to do homework. Like you should be doing. Can we hold off the crazy train for one night?"

"No," Joni paused, not even sure how to begin. "Listen. I was walking Bramble down by the river, and I hit this guy with my atlatl…"

"Of course, you did."

"And then he dropped all his stuff and I was helping him get his papers and he had a picture of me."

"That's weird."

"And I was dead."

Kelly paused again.

"Ok, the train has left the station. I'll see you tomorrow."

She started to put her headphones back on, but Joni jumped on the bed and grabbed them off her. Jazz music spilled out, and Joni covered them with a pillow.

"We've got to go next door." Joni got on the floor and started to crawl under Kelly's desk.

"No way. I'm not sneaking into your room just so you can get me to do your homework for you."

"I'm serious, Kelly. Just come on over."

"Why can't we just go back downstairs the normal way and get it?"

"Our moms are talking math and you know they hate being interrupted for that."

"They'll hate it more if they hear us creeping in upstairs."

"They'll hear nothing. Not if we're quiet."

Kelly paused. Joni was right; once their mothers dove deep into discussing equations, they wouldn't notice much, although their dads might. Kelly sighed and followed her friend.

"I wish I had never found this door. Or told you about it."

"Well, you did, so let's use it."

Joni crawled under the desk, pushing Kelly's neatly ordered cosmetics out of her way. Peeling back a poster of Kelly's favorite soccer player, Joni inserted a loose handle into a hole. After a click, the door opened quietly into Joni's room behind her tapestry.

"Come on," Joni whispered.

The lamplight from Joni's room shone on the open door. Kelly hesitated for the briefest of moments and then scuttled under the desk herself, worming her way into Joni's room. She rose to her feet, sniffed, and took a half-eaten apple off Joni's desk and threw it into the trash. Joni adjusted the tapestry so it covered, but did not close the door. They listened quietly to their parents talking in the living room below, to make sure they hadn't been discovered.

"We're safe," Joni said and then nearly fell over as Bramble ran into the room from downstairs.

They froze for a moment, Bramble at their feet, but their parents' voices didn't change.

"Why didn't you just get the picture and bring it back to me?" Kelly asked.

"Uh, I guess because I didn't think of that till you just asked me."

Joni took the photo and the other sheets off her desk and handed them to Kelly, who silently looked at the photo.

"Well?" Joni asked after a minute, a little nervous, a little excited.

"It's not you."

"What are you talking about? It's totally me."

"This girl's dead."

"I know."

"You're not."

"No."

"And it's from six years ago and you didn't look like this six years ago."

"Exactly," Joni seemed to think she had won a point. "So what does it mean?"

"It means it's not a picture of you. Go to bed."

Joni was not going to give up so easily.

"Someone's stalking me and has this picture and I think you should be concerned."

"Fine. Go tell your parents. They can call the police."

"My parents," Joni said, "think I'm a tad melodramatic."

"No, they think you're a full-fledged drama queen."

"It's so unfair."

"Unfair?" Kelly whispered as loudly as she dared. "You jumped in the river last month!"

"To save a drowning girl!"

"It was your reflection, Joni."

Joni had really thought she had seen a girl in the water before she jumped in, but since she had found no body or anything, it was an argument she was bound to lose.

Kelly had already dismissed the photograph and was looking at the second sheet Joni grabbed.

"What's this?" she asked.

"I dunno. Just some math equations."

The paper was half covered with numbers and symbols, apparently continued on from some pages Joni didn't grab.

"'What if we extend into cyclic symmetry?'" Kelly read a penciled note on the paper.

"Yeah, that was the only part in English and it made no sense."

Kelly looked at it a bit more, but, while her math was good, it wasn't this good. She was about to say something else, when they heard her mother's voice carrying up from the living room downstairs.

"So then I wondered, what if I used cyclic symmetry?"

The girls looked at each other confused.

"What?" Kelly said.

Joni waved her quiet.

They tiptoed closer to the stairs. Their parents' voices could be heard clearly from the first floor.

"It seems to do the trick," Kelly's mom continued. "I wish I could send it to someone, but I can't think of a single researcher who's doing anything remotely like this."

"Let me see it," Joni's mother said.

Joni could picture her mother scrunching her whole face as she concentrated. Then she started muttering something about "n-dimensional geometry" and Joni whispered to Kelly,

"How can this paper talk about cyclic symmetry or whatever while they're talking about it downstairs?"

"A coincidence?" Kelly said, slowly, as if trying to convince herself.

"No way. There's definitely something going on."

"Sshh," Kelly said, leaning towards the door.

"I don't care about the details," Joni's dad interrupted. "Will it help us isolate the branal anomalies on the AGA?"

Joni rolled her eyes at another of his complaints about his machine.

"I think so," Kelly's mom said.

There was another long pause, broken by Joni's mom saying, "Is that someone at your door?"

"Anita Redpoll is dropping something off," said Kelly's father. "Kelly will answer it."

The girls stared at each other wide-eyed and then scurried like crabs back to their secret door, mysterious photos of past or future deaths forgotten for the moment. They threw themselves under the tapestry and ran down the stairs, taking them two or three at a time. Kelly opened the front door just as Joni crashed into her.

Anita Redpoll strode through the entryway. Standing six feet tall, Redpoll was thin and wiry, hoarding energy like a coiled spring. Her hair was dark with a few strands of gray and her eyes were never still, but constantly looking around her.

"Hello, girls," she said crisply. "Hello, Bramble."

The girls swung around and saw Bramble galumphing down the stairs, having followed them through the hidden door. They gave terrified looks to each other, seeing Bramble in the wrong house. Redpoll was already scratching Bramble behind her ears, and the girls didn't know when Kelly's parents would return.

"Um, hello, Ms. Redpoll," said Joni. "We've got to, uh, take Bramble upstairs."

"Why, girls? Sit down a moment. It's been weeks since we've talked."

The girls hesitated, but even friendly requests from Redpoll seemed to demand obedience. Slowly, tensely, they sat down on the edge of the sofa as Redpoll threw herself into a large padded chair and faced them, her finger resting on her chin.

"How are you two doing? How is school?"

"It's fine, it really is, it's fine," Joni answered, then perked up, momentarily distracted. "Oh! I've been throwing tennis balls to Bramble with the atlatl Kelly made."

"I've seen you using it, Joni. You're getting quite the hang of it. It's probably a little safer than when I taught you knife-throwing."

"My wall still has the scars," Kelly said.

Redpoll's lips thinned into what was almost a smile, as she fingered her crescent pendant necklace, just like the one she had given Joni.

"It's better to practice outside. But before I forget, I'm returning a book to your mother. I'll be gone for a bit and wanted her to have it before I leave."

"Where are you going?" asked Joni. "Are you leading another wilderness survival course? Will you be eating rattlesnake liver again?"

"Nothing so interesting this time. Just seeing some old colleagues. I'll be back for us to go backpacking in a few weeks, after your term ends."

"More like boot camp," Joni laughed.

"Nothing more than you're capable of," Redpoll grinned as she rose.

The girls sprang up after her, just as the sounds of their parents walking down the stairs next door could be heard through the thin walls. The girls said good-bye to Redpoll as quickly as they could. Kelly held the door open for her as the Dr. and Mr. Grebe emerged from Joni's house. They greeted Redpoll, but by that time Joni was already sprinting up the stairs, dragging Bramble beside her.

Reaching Kelly's room, Joni grabbed Bramble's collar and thrust her under the desk and through the door. She then snapped the door shut and ran back downstairs. Joni yelled breathless goodbyes to everyone, raced out the door, spun around, and went into her house, where Bramble was already waiting.

"She just came charging down the stairs looking for you, honey," her father said. "Why don't you take her out? I've got some work to do."

Joni, trying to figure out if she was going to die and how cyclic summative something could fit into it all, was mostly just relieved that she had been able to sneak Bramble back in with no one the wiser. And the only response she could come up with was "Okay, dad."

CHAPTER TWO

"It's not you, Joni," Kelly said as they walked Bramble the next afternoon. "It's a picture of a teenage girl with shoulder-length dark hair, a thin body, sharp cheekbones, and barely any breasts worth mentioning. It could be half the girls in Philly."

Joni smirked at her friend, who was clearly not taking this seriously enough. When the girls had gotten home from school, Kelly had scanned the picture at Joni's urging, but an image search on the Internet turned up nothing. Joni then insisted they go back to the park to do reconnaissance.

"You're just jealous. I'm like Joan of Arc, getting orders from heaven to drive out the infidels."

"You know she died when she was like, nineteen."

"Are you sure she wasn't 29? Because that's what I keep telling people."

"I'm sure."

"All right, then I feel like Cleopatra. Yeah, yeah, I know, she was killed too. Whatever, Kelly. That's not the point. The point is that someone's following me."

Joni was peeved at her friend for not believing her. Joni was 95% sure the picture was her. Maybe 90% sure. Kelly should trust her. She wished she could go to her parents, but Kelly was right: Joni did have a reputation as a drama queen.

"No one's following you, Joni."

"It can't hurt to look. Hand me the binoculars."

They had reached the tiny, metal-thatched Mercury Pavilion on the bluff above the waterworks. They faced west Philadelphia, with the river 50 yards in front of them and below them. The air was hotter than the day before, or at least thicker with humidity.

They scanned the area. The crowd hunting for monsters was a little smaller than yesterday's, but there were more people milling about in general.

"Anything?" Kelly asked.

"Nothing suspicious. I mean, it's Philadelphia, so there's plenty of suspicious-looking characters, but none out of the ordinary. I'll take some pictures anyway."

"What about that guy?" Kelly pointed. "The one with the ferret on his shoulder?"

"That's Schmitty," Joni said, gazing at a heavily-tattooed, leathered-clad man. "He's here all the time. We're buds. And I would have noticed if he got near me. His ferret stinks to high heaven."

"How about those girls with the swords?"

Two young women in red velvet skirts and bronze goggles were lunging at each other next to the bike path. Their grunts could be heard, if not the clash of metal.

"They're foam swords, Kelly. And they go to our school. Seniors, I think. Is this the first time you've ever been outside?"

"How about that boy over there?"

"Which one?"

"The cute one," Kelly said, pointing.

"That's him," Joni shouted, ducking down to get out of sight. "It's Alejandro."

Kelly dropped down beside her.

"That proves it," Joni says. "Doesn't it?"

"Not necessarily."

"Whaddya mean? Why else would he be here? Go down and talk to him. Find out why he's here. Interrogate him."

"You go talk. You already met him."

"Are you crazy? He's probably got a butterfly knife on him."

"So you want me to go?"

"He's not going to slice you up. He doesn't even know you."

"No, thanks."

"Just take Bramble with you. He likes dogs. He probably won't even look at you."

Kelly grunted. "All right, but I'm only going because chances are his only crime is getting hit in the head by you."

Joni walked halfway down the cliff path with Kelly and then hid behind some bushes, where she watched Kelly lead Bramble by Alejandro. Alejandro said something to Kelly and she spent a few minutes talking with him. Actually, from Joni's vantage point it seemed that he spent most of the time scratching Bramble. Kelly then took a circuitous route back to Joni, while Alejandro wandered off.

"I got nothing out of him, Joni."

"Did he recognize Bramble?"

Kelly paused.

"He gave a look, but I think it's what you said, he just likes dogs a lot. He says he's just here in Philly for a couple of days."

"He didn't say where he's from? Why didn't you ask more? You should have followed up."

"What was I supposed to say? 'Do you have any mysterious photos on you?' He seemed nice. I don't know."

They both looked around for a minute, hoping for a clue to walk into view.

"Maybe we're following the wrong lead," Joni finally said. "Maybe we should follow up all the math stuff on that sheet."

"I looked at some of mom's notes this morning that she left on the table. It didn't look a lot like the ones you took…"

"It's got to be connected. No one just goes around writing about cyclic symmetry. I asked my math teacher and he had no idea what I was talking about. And now Alejandro's snooping around here again?"

Joni could tell that she was drawing Kelly to her side, albeit slowly. Kelly was always calculating, adding up the pros and cons of Joni's plans, the plusses and minuses, before making a decision. Or before Joni made her do it anyway. And here Joni had enough oddities on her side to make Kelly probe a bit further.

"OK, J. But how?"

"We talk to my dad. If there's anything secret going on, he'll blurt it out without realizing it. We just have to sweet talk him."

The girls told Joni's father that they wanted to interview him for a school assignment about careers in science. He was delighted, happy for any chance to talk about his toys. Luckily their school had a halfday that Friday, so the girls biked across the river for lunch and a tour of the laboratory.

"So, Dr. Margulis," Kelly said, as they ate falafel pitas by the food trucks on campus, Joni's drenched in hot sauce, "how did you get this job? What brought you here?"

"And did you meet any unsavory characters along the way?" Joni added. "Maybe someone who might hold a grudge?"

Kelly glared at her friend, but Joni's dad had spent years ignoring her daughter's random questions.

"Well, I met Petra during my first week of graduate school. 'Peter and Petra' was kind of a joke between us, but then we became an item. We were studying cosmological physics, basically how everything started and trying to figure out how it all goes together. Your mother, Kelly, was already there. I couldn't keep up with the mathematics of either of them, but I did a pretty good job of translating their theory into practice. We all graduated within a year of each other and then came here to Philadelphia as the institute was forming. Your dad had gotten his MBA by then and found a job in center city."

"Are a lot of people doing this sort of research?" Kelly asked.

"I would say that many scientists are asking the same questions, trying to find a Grand Unified Theory of Everything." Joni could hear the capitals in his voice. "Not many of them are looking for the answers in the same way though. Speaking of which, if you're done eating, we can head over to the lab."

Dr. Margulis and the girls tossed their trash away and walked through tiled courtyards and past ivy-covered trellises to a three-story red brick building. They climbed the stairs to the top floor and entered the laboratory. The girls' feet stuck a bit to spots on the gray linoleum floor, although Dr. Margulis didn't seem to notice the mess. There were a few desks at either end, currently occupied by two graduate students wearing headphones, staring at computer screens. Indeed, one was so focused she nearly jumped out of her chair as the girls walked by and quickly tried to hide the game she was playing. Joni's father had an office in one corner, glassed off from the rest of the lab, but instead he took the girls over to the apparatus that was occupying a good two-thirds of the floor space.

Cables and wires stretched everywhere, connecting dozens of machines, and large ducts stretched up into the ceiling. Joni could smell recently soldered wires. There were four chairs in the center of it all, sitting at a bank of computers. Behind the computers was a bluish-gray cube, about four feet on each side. It appeared solid, like marble, and had a flat black disc on top. However, looking closer they realized the disc was more like a conical hole, but it projected an optical illusion, making it appear to move as they moved. Joni's dad was quite proud of it.

"Isn't it great?" he asked, peering into it himself.

"I love it," Joni said, mesmerized. "What is it?"

"We call it the Abelian-Gauge Apparatus, the AGA. It's a sensor, working with supplementary antennae around the building that help channel waves towards it," he answered and pointed towards the ducts.

"Huh?"

"All right, all right. You want to know?" He switched into his teacher mode, with lots of hand motions and gestures. "So, we have three dimensions around us, length, height, and width. Agreed? And we can picture time as another dimension. Yes? No?"

Joni looked back confused, while Kelly nodded.

"Okay, ignore that for now," he continued. "In the last few decades, scientists have come up with various theories, like string theory, that say we could, or should, or might, have more dimensions—perhaps many more."

"So there are other worlds out there?" Joni asked.

"Well, Petra can make the math say that, but no one will publish it. No, no, our idea here is to try to prove the extra dimensions by seeing what bounces off of them. And because they don't exist in our three dimensional space, in a sense, they're simultaneously all distances and no distance away at all."

"Does that mean they're folded up in the dimensions we can see?" Kelly asked.

"Yes, exactly, although it's possible we would look the same to them. What we've been looking at is the idea that waves can bounce off of what we call 'membranes,' or just 'branes.' They're the walls between the dimensions and we believe that electromagnetic waves, including visible light, can bounce off them, especially where the branes are thinner."

"What do you mean 'thinner'?" Kelly asked.

"The barriers are inconsistent. They're thinner in spots, a bit stretched out, especially if they're overlapping with other branes."

"Kelly can study the numbers later," Joni said. "What's all this equipment for? It must do something."

"We're trying to detect waves that bounce off the branes. The advantage of our method is that it's just normal electromagnetic waves that we are trying to detect, nothing exotic, so it's relatively cheap. We don't need giant underground chambers or cyclotrons or anything like that. It's just a question of trying to filter out all the other waves, which unfortunately make up most of the observable universe.

"Ok," Joni said slowly.

"And hypothetically, we could look through time with it," her father added with a smug little look on his face.

"What?" Joni and Kelly cried out together, and he laughed before continuing.

"Over a hundred years ago Einstein came along and told us that as we approach the speed of light, time slows down for us, even though we can't perceive it while it's happening, right?"

Joni nodded tentatively, having grown up in a house where this sort of talk wormed its way into bedtime stories, even if she never understood it.

"That's why if you spent a year in a spaceship at nearly the speed of light," Kelly said to Joni, "when you got back a hundred years might have passed."

"Right," Joni's father said. "Some of these other dimensions, or the branes around them, may be moving at near the speed of light, even while they may be right beside us along another dimension. So a reflected wave might experience only a second of time, although a century might have passed for us."

"So it lets you see into the future?" Joni asked.

"Well, right now we can't see much of anything. We're pretty happy if we catch what looks like a natural color, although we have had a couple of images. Here, let me show you."

Turning to the console, he flipped a switch, and a large screen on the wall behind the sensor came to life. The girls then watched him type in his password and a few commands and open a program.

"Look at the screen. In terms of actual video, our record is five seconds, but any glimpse is a success. We're building a larger setup in State College which we'll try out when we go up there in a few weeks," he said, opening a file. "Okay, check this out."

The screen lit up with static, a time stamp on the corner dating it from a few weeks prior. A fuzzy image began to appear. It looked like an ocean, choppy waves on a sunny day, but it was like a blurry jigsaw puzzle missing two thirds of the pieces. It returned to static.

"Three of the best images are water. Let's try something else."

Dr. Margulis showed them a few more scenes. One was just a close up of pebbles, which the girls found hard to distinguish from static, and the final one was a rainforest.

"Do you know where any of them are from?" Kelly asked.

"I wish," he said. "Our models predict that we should receive nothing beyond about 8,000 kilometers. We sent the rainforest pictures to various experts, but they couldn't identify any of the species. Want to see it in action?"

The girls said yes, and Dr. Margulis was clearly eager to show off his baby. He yelled at one of his graduate students, "Pat! Are all the units charged up?"

Pat pulled off his headphones and replied, "Yeah, they've been going for about an hour. It should be a go."

"I had Pat set it up, girls, so I could show you how it worked. Watch closely."

The girls stood up to see better. The machines began to hum and the wall screen flickered brightly. Joni would be hard pressed to explain what was different about the sensor block itself, but maybe it sparkled a bit more, as if the ceiling lights were sputtering. And there was a smell in the room, like during a thunderstorm. Dr. Margulis started playing with a console, moving levers back and forth but with no success. Joni found something captivating about the way the machine worked. She followed everything her dad did, concentrating hard on each motion.

"We're not getting anything," he said, "which is pretty common. We've had no luck automating the system."

"The controls look like you stole a soundboard from a rock club," Joni said. "Can I try?"

"'Borrow' is a better word. Sure, go ahead and try, it's pretty much unbreakable. You can think of these levers as controlling different frequencies. Which isn't really what they're doing, but it's a useful analogy."

Joni sat down and began to work the board. Her eyes darted back and forth between the console and the screen, which just kept showing static. She wasn't sure what she was doing, but it seemed right to her as she did it, natural. Something clicked inside her and all her worries about strange photos and secret adversaries slid away. She paused and lifted her hand, as if sweeping the screen clean and then her fingers played across the levers.

The image on the screen changed slightly, with something behind the static. Just as she recognized it as swirling sand, the image cleared and a young woman was running next to a brown wall. The girl covered her face with her hands to block the blowing sand. She stopped and looked around, but not towards the screen. She ran a few more steps and then cowered backwards, until she was stopped by a brown wall. Suddenly a thin man with red hair, dressed all in black, blocked their view of the girl. A moment later, he turned around and Joni and Kelly drew in their breath at the fierce expression on his heart-shaped face. He then walked out of view and they saw the girl, slumped to the ground, eyes unseeing, and blood poring from a gash on her neck.

Then the static returned. The whole scene had lasted just a few heartbeats.

All of them stared at the screen. Joni worked at the controls a bit more, but with no luck.

"What was that?" Kelly yelled. "Omigod, what was that?"

"That was amazing," Joni's dad said, pushing his daughter out of the way. "That's the longest video we've ever captured."

He started rapidly typing on the console, but nothing else happened.

"What are you talking about, dad? She was killed. She was killed right in front of us."

"Huh?" her father said. "What do you mean killed?"

"Were you watching it? Play it again."

The room was silent, as Joni's dad brought up the recording and they watched it, one, two, three times. His eyes widened and Joni saw an expression there she had never seen before. She recognized fear there, more than fear, shock even, but there was a seriousness to him. Redpoll had lectured them about gravitas once, and Joni recognized it here.

"Listen, girls. I…uh…it's time for you to go home. I need to analyze the data and try to figure out what happened. And… I guess, inform the authorities."

"What authorities?" asked Joni. "Where was that?"

"I don't know. That was bizarre. I'm going to have to talk to some people. You go home and we'll discuss it later."

"But dad, what was that? What happened? Who was she?"

"I don't know. I wish I did."

Joni and Kelly stood there for a few moments, but he wasn't watching them, and they walked out of the building and down to their bikes without saying a word.

Their silence continued as they biked home. The vision of the killing made Joni's mystery seem even more

important to her, because lives were in the balance, girls
their age were getting killed. She asked herself, how was it
all connected? What if someone was hunting her down?
What if she were next?

Or maybe, she thought, their little mystery was
totally inconsequential because people were being killed
and here they were playing stupid little spy games, like
kids. She and Kelly were hunting down clues as if it was a
Spirit Week scavenger hunt. Alejandro's papers might be
nothing, just a nerdy tourist with a term paper due. And
she was being a drama queen, while real drama was out
there somewhere, with real heroines dying.

"Joni? I…I don't know if any of that was
connected to you. I can't see how it could've been. But I'm
a little scared."

"So am I."

Once they got home, Joni waited up for her dad,
who didn't come home until she was already in bed. After
a soft knock, he slipped into her room like she was six
years old again and had come in to kiss her goodnight.

"Hey, darling."

"Hi, daddy. What…what happened? Did you
figure it out?"

"No, not really. Only enough that we decided we
shouldn't talk about it, not to anyone."

"Not even to me?"

"Well, no."

"But you are."

"Just a little bit. I know it was a bit traumatic."

"I'll say. Why can't we talk about it?"

"Basically," and he pushed back his glasses at this,
"if we can really use this to see actual events that are going
on somewhere else in the world, it's a little scary. We don't
want it to end up in the wrong hands. But now you've got
to go to sleep. And so do I."

"But…"

"Not another 'but.'"

"But what does it mean? Who was she? Why did they kill her?"

"We'll never know, honey. Sometimes bad things happen."

"But why us? Why did we see it? What did we…what did I do?"

"There was nothing we did to make it happen."

Joni looked skeptical, as he continued, "I mean, how could there be? Go to sleep."

CHAPTER THREE

The next couple of weeks were torture. Joni's dad wouldn't talk about the shooting they saw, except to say that he still had no idea what happened. That left Joni with no option but to keep her own investigation open. She attempted to pry information out of her mom, occasionally eavesdropped, kept wandering the park in search of Alejandro, but all for nothing. He never turned up again. And Kelly was annoying Joni by surreptitiously taking photos of girls around Philly who looked as much like the girl in the photo as Joni did. Lots of photos.

Even Joni had just about decided the whole thing was a mistake, the grainy photo a coincidence and the broadcast in the lab a tragic sideshow. Plus, she was running out of ways to keep Kelly interested, especially with summer break looming. She was finally able to convince Kelly to wait until Joni's dad got the larger machine going at Penn State. It seemed logical that if anyone was spying on their parents' research (that was her working hypothesis), that's when they would strike.

Most summers the families went up to State College for a week or two, part work, part holiday. Anita Redpoll usually met the girls there and took them camping, sneaking in a lot of wilderness survival training— which plants are edible, how to build a shelter, that sort of thing. But Joni planned this trip to be different.

"We need to watch every shadow," she told Kelly, "hear every whisper, smell every odor."

"I'm not going to smell every odor. You can smell every odor. Better yet, let Bramble smell them."

They were sitting at a sidewalk café in the town of State College, the girls and Bramble, where Kelly's father had dropped them on their way to their rental house, with some money for lunch. They were eating tacos and discussing strategy.

"Listen, Joni, I just don't buy it that there's some big network of spies coming here to check out the lab."

"Of course there is. The machine can see people being killed."

"Once. It did it once. Your dad hasn't been able to get a single image since then."

"Once is enough. And when he gets the full setup here going, just wait."

"I just don't think you should get your hopes up."

"I'm not….Duck!"

"What? Why?"

"Shsshh," Joni yelled, pulling her friend down to hide behind the café's small fence.

"What are you doing?"

"Look over there!"

"Where?"

"There! On the motorcycle."

A young man was stopping his motorcycle about half a block away across the street. He turned off his engine and swung his leg over the bike. He took a large phone or small tablet out of his leather jacket and peered at the screen before looking around the town.

"He should wear his helmet," Kelly said. "It's just stupid."

"It's Alejandro."

"Who?"

"Alejandro! You know, the one with the picture? How this whole thing started?"

"No, it's not. I…uh…It is Alejandro. That's weird."

"It's more than weird, Kelly. He's following us."

"What do we do? Should we call home?"

"And tell them what? Let's follow him."

As they watched, Alejandro got on his motorcycle and drove off again.

"I don't think that plan's gonna work so well now. Unless you have another motorcycle."

"Hmmmmm," was Joni's only reply.

"What's your next plan?"

"My next plan is that we watch everything."

"That was your first plan."

"Well, it's still a good plan."

As the girls and Bramble walked the mile or so back to the house, they looked into every alleyway and behind every hedge, even Kelly was ready to believe now in a world of spies and conspiracies. They had been back barely ten minutes, when their mothers told them they were going to visit the lab. So they got in the minivan and drove to the university.

It was a spacious campus, with large trees and clipped lawns. The air was hot on their faces and the lawns were a little brown, due to a recent dry spell. The lab building was much bigger than the one in Philadelphia, white and geometric, like a large cube. Joni's father met them at the parking lot.

He led them all to the lab building, and then upstairs to a room similar to the one in Philly. The types and number of machines were about the same, although the layout was different. Once again, there was the bluish-gray AGA cube, with the weird optical illusion that Joni couldn't help staring at. Standing by the main console was a student, about the girls' age or maybe a little older, wearing jeans and a button-down shirt. He had short blond hair and a serious expression on his pale face. He was leaning over a keyboard, but straightened up as Joni's father called to him.

"Hello, Dr. Margulis," he said, very formally.

"This is Marcus," Joni's father said. "He's doing a high school STEM program here at the university. He showed such a knack for vibrational mathematics that they sent him over here and he's been a real miracle worker.

Marcus, this is my wife, Dr. Margulis, and Dr. Grebe. And this is Joni and Kelly.”

He nodded to the girls and then turned back to his computer before the girls had a chance to say hello.

“C'mon,” Joni's dad said to them all. “I'll show you around.”

The two mothers had lots of questions about the various modifications, most of which went over the girls' heads. After a few minutes, they ditched their parents and wandered back to where Marcus was programming on the computer with rapid-fire keystrokes. He stopped working and attempted small talk, but was not very good at it. Joni would have thought him cute, that is, until he opened his mouth; when he spoke, he somehow managed to be both awkward and condescending. Kelly thought him a touch cuter — enough to give him a little leeway.

“Where are you from, Marcus?” Joni asked.

“A small town in eastern California. You would not have heard of it.”

“So is that a California accent?”

“It is my accent.”

“Oh.” Joni looked at Kelly for help.

“Um, what work do they have you doing here?” Kelly asked.

“You would not understand it.”

“Ooooh-kay, then…Kelly and I better get back to the tour. It was nice to meet you.”

“And you,” Marcus said.

The girls politely refrained from saying anything out loud and strode back to the console, where Joni's father was speaking.

“…and so the main improvement is in the number and power of the supplementary sensors, which should allow us to control the oscillations much more finely. We've also installed speakers and are hoping to get sound.” He looked at his watch. “It will need to charge for an hour.”

"While it's charging," Kelly's mother said, "why don't we join George and Anita out on the patio back at the physics building and help with the barbeque? We can eat, and then come back up here when it's ready."

"Sounds good," said Joni's dad. "You'll join us, of course, Marcus? I'm sure the girls would like to have someone to talk to."

"Of course, Dr. Margulis. I'll just finish up my work."

A half hour later, Joni's mother was grilling, while the girls set the table and Redpoll, who had shown up while they were at the lab, was chopping vegetables. Joni's father, who was forbidden near the barbeque after burning off his eyebrows one too many times, was sitting at a picnic table, drinking a beer. He noticed that Marcus had not joined them yet.

"Joni, Kelly. Go up and tell Marcus to get his butt down here. He's working too hard."

"Well, let him work."

"Now, Joni," her dad looked at her sternly, "Marcus is a long way from home and I gather he's having trouble making friends with the other students in the program."

"Yeah, that's not exactly surprising. He's not a great conversationalist."

"Consider it your little task: teach him how to talk to girls."

"Dad!"

"Joni!" he echoed, laughing at her.

"He's the nerdy kid cliché who can't talk about anything that's not science."

"Sounds like your mom getting her PhD."

"For that," Joni's mom spoke up, "you get the burnt burger."

"Seriously, Joni. Just get him here and be nice."

"All right."

Joni and Kelly stood up and he handed them a security card. The campus was quiet as they strolled back to the building. The guard at the front desk waved them in. They ran up the stairs, but both girls instinctively slowed down as they approached the open lab door.

The lights were off, except for a lamp at the central console where Marcus was working and some flickering from the AGA cube. Redpoll had taught the girls how to walk silently and Marcus was oblivious to their entrance as he stared intently at the monitor in front of him. He then turned to adjust something on a small device connected by a short cable to the main computer. In doing this, he noticed them and flinched, knocking a over a stack of books.

"You surprised me," he said, and picked up the books. He then unplugged the cable with one hand, all the while keeping his eyes on the girls. The flickering from the sensor block died away.

"Um, yeah," Joni said. "We were sent to take you to the barbeque. The food's ready, and dad says you're working too hard."

"We didn't mean to disturb you," Kelly said.

"No problem, no problem. I'll come right now."

Marcus stood up, straightened his shirt, and carried the device he had unplugged over to a desk. He put it inside a drawer and covered it with a folder. He spun around and then walked with Joni and Kelly out the door, locking it behind them.

A few minutes later they were back at the barbeque and everyone dug into the food. Joni's father was discussing string theory with a Penn State professor while Marcus listened in. Redpoll had disappeared. After wolfing down her food, Joni muttered something to her mother and dragged Kelly, still clutching a butter-dripping corncob, around the corner. Kelly swore a bit, but ran to keep up with her as they circled the building.

"What is it, J.?" Kelly asked, as Joni grabbed her by both arms. "What's wrong?"

"Wasn't Marcus acting weird?"

"I dunno. Maybe. Whaddya mean? He was clumsy. He's a weird guy."

"Not that. Did you see the screen on his computer?" Joni looked around conspiratorially. "He had an extra connection set up on the AGA. The screen was different from anything my dad showed us. He nearly jumped out of his skin when we came in. He's doing something with that little machine that he hid in the drawer. I want to check it out."

"Joni! What are you talking about?"

"We've got to get back to the lab! He's probably in league with Alejandro. We've got to see that thing."

"You're imagining it. And besides, how are we going to get in?"

"No problem," Joni waved the security card. "They let us in last time. Who's going to suspect us? There's nothing to suspect. We're just going back to the lab."

Kelly gave a tight-lipped grin and ran after her friend, although too slow for Joni's patience. They skidded to a halt just outside the entrance. They did their best to walk casually past the front desk, although the guard barely looked at them. Once out of sight, they charged up the stairs, swiped the card through the security reader, and entered the lab.

Kelly stood just inside the door, watching as Joni ran around. She sprinted to Marcus' desk, pulled open the drawer, made sure there were no mysterious photos within, and carefully removed the suspect device. Joni was on fire, confident she was about to figure everything out at last. She turned Marcus' device over in her hands, rotating it around. It was the size and shape of a brick, but with gaps on each face where the inner workings could be seen. No wires were visible, but there were silver tubes curving inside. The device had no writing on it, in fact, no visible markings at all. The only part Joni recognized was a USB cable, which she plugged into her dad's computer. She moved the mouse, activating the screen, and switched on the larger wall screen. She sat down in a rolling chair. The monitor started blinking.

"What do I do now?" she asked.

"This is your plan, Joni."

"I know, but you're the techy one. Just get it started."

Kelly sighed, but sat herself on another chair and pushed Joni out of the way. She clicked a couple of icons.

"We need the password, J. Let's get out of here."

"Try 'Bramble.' I saw my dad put it in. He is *so* obvious."

With the screen up, Kelly started typing commands. The machines hummed around them, but the setup here ran more quietly than the Philly lab. The AGA cube began flickering, and the wall screen showed static. Kelly pressed a key and leaned back. The static cleared slightly, but still nothing was visible. The newly-installed speakers emitted a fuzzy sound.

"All right, let's see if this does anything," Joni said, flipping the lone switch on Marcus' device.

On the small computer monitor, the meter readings swung vigorously to life. The static continued on the wall screen for several seconds. Then it cleared some, enough to see shadows before a figure became visible. Joni rolled her chair to her right and started fumbling with the levers, like she had done in Philadelphia. Joni's fingers seemed to become part of the machine, moving independently of her body. Soon the scene cleared and Kelly shouted.

"Joni, it's your dad!"

Joni looked up and saw her dad on the screen, standing over a machine similar to the one that Joni was using. He looked haggard: his hair was out of place and his shirt looked like he had slept in it. He was manipulating something that the girls could not quite see.

"But we just left him! What's going on?" Joni shouted.

Joni's father faced them, but didn't see them. He then squinted a little and fiddled with the equipment. Joni did the same on her end, and the image improved. Another few moves on the console, and they could hear him too, through the fuzz.

"Is that you?" While muffled, they could understand what he was yelling.

"Yes! Dad, how can you be there? You're outside!" Joni was screaming back.

"I can't hear you," Peter replied. "Can you hear me?"

Joni nodded, a full-body nod.

"All right, listen to me. You're in terrible danger. You need to get away. There's still time, but they're hunting for you and you must flee."

"Who's hunting for me? Who? What are you talking about?"

Although he could not hear his daughter, her confusion was obvious.

"I don't know how they found us. But they're after you. Where are you? When is it?"

Joni looked at Kelly and then shouted to the screen, trying to enunciate, "What do you mean? We're at the lab. You're outside barbecuing. Why aren't you outside barbecuing?"

Dr. Margulis was trying to work out what his daughter said. He decided on something and then answered her; "This transmission's on a temporal tunnel…a tunnel through time. What has happened to me hasn't happened to you yet. For me, you and Redpoll disappeared before I discovered all this was happening and then Alejandro went to look for you. But you can't warn me, because you never did. DON'T! Don't try to tell me anything!"

He looked past them and yelled "Redpoll, help her!"

Both girls turned to see Anita Redpoll behind them. She was standing still, staring at the screen. Just then, the transmission started breaking up. Both Joni and her father worked furiously trying to bring it back, but it was gone.

"Damn it," was all Redpoll said. She then gave the girls another surprise, as they stood frozen. This woman, whom they had known half their lives and who was flustered checking e-mail, leaned over Joni and typed something on the keyboard. The screen rewound and then played the transmission again. She watched it through, and then deleted it.

"What's that?" she asked, pointing to Marcus' device.

"We don't know," Joni answered. "We saw Marcus using it and then hide it away. We came back to check it out and then my dad showed up on the screen. What does it mean? What happened to him? Where is he?"

"Your father is enjoying the barbecue right now. I snuck out to look for the two of you. In theory, the AGA can connect different times, but it shouldn't be ready." Redpoll stared at Joni. "You must leave. Come on. Put that thing back where you found it and let's go."

Joni unplugged the device and put it away in Marcus' desk, after which Redpoll examined the rest of the drawer's contents. Kelly ran to the door and peered into the hallway, followed by Joni and Redpoll, whose quick, long strides set their pace as they exited the building. Once out, they slowed down and Redpoll started speaking.

"Listen." Redpoll spoke authoritatively, but from her tone Joni could tell she was planning on the fly. "We're going to get you out of town right now. We'll tell your parents we are leaving a day early for our camping trip."

Redpoll stopped suddenly and looked at the girls, putting a hand on their shoulders. Her voice was calm, but her fingers gripped the girls tightly, "There might be no rush. It might be nothing and, besides, we might be years early for all we know; I've only spoken across time once before."

"What are you talking about?" Kelly asked.

"The transmission must have cut through time and across bubbles. It might be a day or a decade, but your father didn't look any older than now, so it has to be soon. But still, there was something wrong. And how does Alejandro fit in?"

"How do you know Alejandro?" Joni asked.

Redpoll stopped.

"You know Alejandro?" she asked. "How? When?"

"We don't, not really," Kelly answered. "We just met him in Philly and then saw him in town today."

Joni gave her friend a look, warning her not say anything else. She trusted Redpoll, but this seemed to be Redpoll version 2.0 and Joni wasn't sure how far to trust her.

"Well," Redpoll looked thoughtful, "I suppose that explains how your father knows him… or will know him."

"Does dad know what's going on?" Joni asked. "What's he involved with?"

"Is he in danger?" Kelly said.

"He knows nothing yet. Everyone's in danger, you most of all. But I didn't think it would be this soon." She stopped, just around the corner from the barbecue, close enough to hear their parents talking, so she whispered. "We're going to that park that I took you to last year. I should be able to get more information there and I hope, I *hope*, we won't be too exposed. The natural emanations should mask us, at least from general surveillance, if anyone's been able to track you this far. And then I can take you somewhere safe."

Joni grabbed Redpoll's wrist and shouted her whisper, "What are you talking about? Who's tracking me? What do they want with me?"

Redpoll looked Joni straight in the eyes, then at Kelly, then back to Joni.

"I didn't know anyone knew you existed yet, Joni. You'll have to go on the run and I cannot promise to always be there with you. You'll need to find people you can trust. Some people will want to help you and protect you. Some will want to use you. And some will want to kill you."

CHAPTER FOUR

Joni, Kelly, and Bramble piled out of Redpoll's hatchback, parked next to a few other cars at a trailhead, about 20 miles out of town. The girls each carried a backpack, with clothes, a tightly rolled sleeping bag, some food, and other assorted items. They were familiar with the park from previous outings and knew where Redpoll was leading them.

They'd convinced their parents to let them leave right from the barbecue. They were happy to have Redpoll take charge while they tried to process all that was happening. It was good to be doing something active, even if it was running away. Having a plan made it all a little less frightening. But they wish they knew what the plan was.

The area was heavily wooded with beeches, elms, and an occasional hemlock. The girls could also smell pines somewhere near. The ground rose up about three hundred feet in front of them into the park. The hill was lit scarlet by the setting sun, although the forest had passed into darkness. The only noises were a slight buzz from distant traffic, some crickets and frogs, and a trickling stream. Redpoll hoisted her backpack on and strode up the trail without saying a word. With a half-hearted thumbs-up to Kelly, Joni followed. Kelly undid the dog leash and Bramble charged to the front. About a mile up they turned onto a deer path to their left, hidden by a half-fallen tree and soon reached a small clearing next to several boulders. They were still silent as they cut through the underbrush, and dropped their gear.

Redpoll leapt lightly onto one of the rocks and peered into the woods with small binoculars, both south and west. Joni began gathering dry branches and twigs and placed them on an old fire pit. After playing with her lighter for a minute, she made a small flame appear in the kindling, which quickly spread to the branches (Joni was always in charge of fires). Kelly, meanwhile, unrolled their sleeping bags and laid them out near the fire. Joni poured some kibble into Bramble's travel bowl. The girls then sat down on a log near the fire and ate some trail mix, barely speaking, not knowing what to say.

Apparently finished scoping the area, Redpoll hopped off the boulder, walked over to Joni and Kelly, and lowered herself to one knee. The girls had a hundred questions, and they were not particularly happy when Redpoll told them that the truth would take too long to explain and that she had to check on something in the woods. Before going off, Redpoll lifted Joni's pendant off her neck, the pendant she had given Joni years ago. It was dark orange and shaped like a crescent moon, with tiny, silvery threads running through it.

"Use this only as a *last* resort," Redpoll instructed her. "If you're in danger and you have no options left, this may be able to get you out of trouble. Break it in your hand. Make sure the two of you are touching each other. But there's no guarantee that it will send you somewhere safer, just somewhere further out. Now get some rest."

Ignoring their questions, Redpoll ran off like a deer, disappearing into the trees. The girls looked after her and then started whispering, as if the trees themselves were eavesdropping.

"Redpoll just ran deeper into the woods," Joni said. "Where can she be going?"

"Maybe she has contacts."

"In the woods? Is she going to ask the squirrels?"

"I don't know, Joni. She's always been, I don't know, eccentric. But not like this."

"Can we trust her?"

"Of course we can. She's Redpoll. She's always looking out for us."

"I know, but she's obviously keeping secrets."

They paused for a while.

"And how does your dad know Alejandro?"

"Redpoll said he doesn't know him. Not yet. That made less sense than anything."

"Oh…oh…oh."

"What?"

"Let me think, let me think," Kelly grabbed her head. "Yes. It makes sense. Remember back in Philly how your dad said that the branes could be moving at nearly light speed and not at all at the same moment."

"I remember he said a lot of gibberish."

"So in the future, he sends the message and it bounces off the branes in just the right way to go back in time. A 'temporal tunnel' he called it."

"So dad might meet Alejandro tomorrow. Or right now."

"Yeah."

"What's going to happen to him? He looked horrible."

"I don't know. Something."

"And why? Dad said they were after me. I thought it was his work they wanted. Whoever they are."

"Maybe they think you know something."

"I don't know anything. I never have."

Kelly laughed for the first time in hours.

"You know what I mean, Kelly."

"I know. For now, we just have to hide here. Or run. Redpoll will know."

"But I want to *do* something."

The fire was just embers and they were nodding off in their sleeping bags when Redpoll returned. She looked frustrated and all she said was, "Go to sleep." Joni's last sight was Redpoll leaning against a boulder, a blanket wrapped around her shoulders and her eyes drilling holes into the forest on every side.

They were not sure what woke them, but the girls sat up simultaneously and looked around. Redpoll was gone. Bramble was lying where Redpoll had been sitting, head up and paws in front of her, like a canine sphinx. Her ears rose sharply in the air, twitching a little as she faced the woods. She growled, softly. With only a glance between them, the girls put on their sweatshirts and squirmed out of their sleeping bags. They slipped on their shoes and scrambled up onto a boulder. They kept low, in case their silhouettes were visible. Their bodies were tense but not rigid. They were scared but felt ready.

"Remember all those camping trips," said Joni, "where Redpoll would try to get us 'to soak in the environment,' to be aware of everything around us."

"Yeah, it all seemed kinda stupid."

"I guess she was getting us ready for this."

They clenched their shoulders a little as a cool breeze blew by. A low moon in the western sky lit the leaves of the trees and made the forest floor a rippling stage of dark shadows and pale objects, all menacing to the girls' eyes. Joni's watch said four AM. They looked around some more. Kelly reached into her pocket and handed Joni a mint before popping one into her own mouth. Nothing was moving, other than the branches in the wind. Kelly saw an owl swoop between some trees. Or a bat, she thought. Too quick for an owl. Definitely a bat. They kept watching. They kept waiting. Nothing.

"It was probably just a deer or something, Kell. Or a bad dream."

"Then how come it woke both of us?"

"Hmm."

"Hmm, yourself," said Kelly. "Maybe it was Bramble having to pee."

"Who's stopping her?"

Kelly stretched out on the boulder, but kept swiveling her head, like the searchlight on a prison watchtower. Suddenly Bramble was on her feet, ears pressed back against her head, tail between her legs, a ridge of hair raising a stripe down her back. An odor blew by them, filling their little clearing. It reminded Joni of something at the zoo and she was about to ask Kelly the source, since she knew the zoo so well. But just then Bramble jumped to all fours, snarling, her teeth white and fierce in the moonlight.

"Look!" yelled Joni.

Something was moving in the woods, slowly. Something big enough that the girls grabbed the boulder, primed for the shaking of each step of the beast, but the only shaking was from their own bodies. The creature entered a gap, giving them a moonlit view of it. Twenty feet high at the shoulder, it could be a distant cousin of a woolly mammoth, with its bulk and thick fur. However, its tail looked scaly, thick and heavily muscled, going out about ten feet before spreading out into a flat end, like a beaver's. The body was well above the ground; you could set up your tent happily beneath it, happy until the creature decided to sit down. The head was as shaggy as the body. It lacked tusks but made up for it by a profusion of teeth, which its mouth was barely able to contain. Two horns twisted on either side of its head like a bighorn sheep.

"It's gorgeous," Kelly whispered to Joni, who did not share her friend's reaction. Not at all.

The creature took another step and pushed its shoulder into a spruce tree, knocking it to the ground and flattening a few saplings in the process. The girls slid off the boulder and crouched down, near Bramble. The creature appeared not to notice them as it made its way, twenty yards beyond the clearing. It walked almost daintily on its long legs, considering its size and its destructive capabilities. Kelly reached for Joni's hand, their eyes wide, their pulses racing. Suddenly the creature raised its head above its body and roared.

Roared.

Roared in the sense that an angry, angry lion might roar - if it were powered by a jet engine and furious that anything else dared to stand upright. The girls covered their ears and may have screamed; if so, neither heard the other. Trees bent and limbs crashed to the forest floor. The creature bent its knees, reducing its height by almost half, and arched its head back as if to chase away the stars themselves. Then with a shake of its head, it ended with a crescendo, and all that could be heard were wild animals voicing their distress throughout the woods. Bramble broke off her howl. The creature gave a sideways glance at the campers, and then jerked its head in a serpentine manner behind it, where a fresh noise (if the word *noise* has any meaning when there are such sounds in the world) could be heard, like a shrill horn. It whipped its head back and bounded off straight ahead. Where it had been slow and deliberate before, it now was fast and lithe. It had disappeared from sight before the trees knocked down in its abrupt rampage toppled to the ground. With the girls staring down the newly formed path, Redpoll came sprinting from the other direction. The girls just sat there in the dirt, feeling very small and very frightened. Redpoll shouted, as if her ears were still echoing with the noise.

"You must leave, NOW. I don't know who or what brought that thing here, but you have to leave. Can either of you drive?" Redpoll asked, holding her keys out in front of her.

Kelly nodded and took the keys from Redpoll's hands.

"Take the car," Redpoll went on, "and drive to that tiny airport on the other side of the park. You know where I'm talking about?"

"Yeah." Joni's voice was barely audible.

"Go there and hide in the woods until I arrive or send someone. I have to go deal with that creature now. It will attract unwelcome attention."

"But…" Kelly said.

"Don't worry; I won't harm it."

"Harm *it*?" Joni asked. "What if it harms you?"

Redpoll just smiled and somehow Joni knew that the beast had more to fear from Redpoll.

45

"I'll be fine. Just get to the airport."

The girls still stared at her.

"GO!"

Redpoll then ran off after the beast and was gone as quickly as the creature. Joni jumped up.

"C'mon, Kelly. That thing must have been heard for miles."

Joni stuffed their sleeping bags in their backpacks, while eyeing the woods, which were lightening up as dawn approached. Kelly shivered as she stared after the creature, terror and wonder warring in her head and terror winning by a nose. Not until Joni came over and shook her by the shoulders, did she come out of her daze and grab her bag. After kicking some dirt over the ashes, Joni ran back to the main trail. Kelly followed a few steps behind and then yelled at Bramble who came quickly into line behind her.

After a minute's gallop, the girls calmed down a bit and began to talk. Instead of the shock of the situation, or the monster they had just seen, Joni had only one question for Kelly.

"What do you mean you can drive a car? You've had, like, one lesson."

Kelly was five months older than her, and Joni was still bitter that Kelly had not waited for them to take driving lessons together.

"Yeah and I paid attention. Something you could try doing."

Joni made a face, but declined to respond. When they reached the parking lot, they looked at the remains of Redpoll's car and realized that it didn't matter if Kelly could drive or not. The hood was smashed in, where the creature had stepped on it, bursting both front wheels. Hearing cars and sirens approaching they ran to a corner of the lot, behind a self-composting bathroom. Kelly attached Bramble's leash and scratched her behind her ears. A minute later, two police cars tore in, with officers jumping out and cautiously fanning out into the park. A few civilian cars followed in their wake, some full of passengers holding rifles. Finally, the local police chief arrived, holstered her gun, and started barking orders. A young, slightly acne-ed officer ran back down the trail, panting heavily.

"Chief, it looks like a friggin' bulldozer went through there. There's a path, a few hundred feet long at least and twenty feet wide with trees down right and left. No fire or anything. Hogan has the guys looking for any debris. Whaddya think it is, a plane crash?"

"A strange plane crash, with no wreckage. *Something* woke me out of bed, and I live two miles away."

The crowd had reached the police chief and began shouting questions at her. She shouted back, trying to calm them, but they were not taking any of it. Many were on their cell phones, either taking pictures or texting their friends. Joni and Kelly quickly realized the crowd would make good cover. The two girls slipped behind some onlookers, as more cars kept pulling up.

Suddenly, someone tapped the back of both girls' shoulders. Full of adrenalin (and years of Redpoll's lessons), the girls reacted instantly. Kelly kicked out the legs of the boy behind them as Joni grabbed his arm and forced him to the ground, face first. Bramble trotted up to lick his face as he looked up.

"Marcus?" Joni asked. "You shouldn't have surprised us."

"Hello to you, too," he answered and slowly got up.

The girls looked around, but they had been so swift and silent, no one had noticed. Joni gave him a hand, but didn't apologize.

"What are you doing here?" he asked. "What happened?"

"There was some kinda mammoth jaguar thing! It just tore through the forest!" Kelly said, relieved to find a familiar face.

"What are *you* doing here? What's going on?" Joni said, suspicious at Marcus' sudden appearance.

Marcus answered awkwardly, while rubbing his arm, "We must leave right away. The police may ask questions and I do not know what you will be able to tell them."

"What was that thing?" Kelly whispered at Marcus.

"What did it look like?"

"Like a mess of trouble! Thirty feet tall, and shaggy with a flat tail. It took off sprinting through the trees."

Marcus thought for a moment

"It might have been a pismire."

"A pismire?" said Kelly excitedly. "What's a pismire?"

"Yes, a high body with long legs? Herbivores, but skittish."

"That's great, Marcus," Joni said. "Really. I'm so glad you know the monster. But what are you doing here?"

"I was nearby when I detected the disturbance, but I could not determine its nature."

"Why were you here?" Joni asked, her face getting red in anger. "What's so special about this area? What's your part in all this? Where's Redpoll?"

"Redpoll? The woman you left with? I don't know. All I know is that there was an illicit operation of the AGA, after which you suddenly left, and then a pismire shows up. Did you use the machine?"

"We…," Kelly began, but Joni stopped her.

"That's not the question," Joni said. "What are you doing here? Who are you with? Why are you spying on our parents?"

"It's not safe for you here. I've got to get you out of here."

"Not till you tell us who you are."

Marcus hesitated.

"We're not going anywhere with you until you tell us."

He groaned. "I am working for a quasi-government institute that has been monitoring the work of your parents. And…we don't have time for this, Joni. You are in terrible danger."

"That's what Redpoll said," she answered. "Where do you want to take us?"

"There is an airport nearby," he answered. "We can hide there."

Joni stared at him for a moment.

"Let me talk to Kelly for a second," she said.

She pulled Kelly back behind the outhouse, Bramble trotting after them. They spoke in hushed whispers, although no one besides Marcus was paying any attention to them.

"Can we trust him?" asked Kelly.

"No," Joni replied. "I mean, not long term. He's obviously a liar and is still not telling us much. But…"

"But he wants to take us to the airport. Where Redpoll told us to go."

"Yeah. Of course she was lying too, it turns out. And for longer."

"But at least he has some idea of what's going on," Kelly said. "He knew what the pismire was and all."

"Super, Kelly, really super. Maybe you two can go on a date at the zoo once this is all over. But for now can we trust him to get us to the airport?"

"I don't know. Maybe?"

"And then we just have to lose him there."

"How?"

"He doesn't strike me as super effective," Joni waved her finger dismissively. "We dropped him without really trying. We can ditch him, no problem."

"What if we can't?"

"Have I ever steered you wrong before?"

"I have absolutely no way to respond to that, Joni, without crying or slugging you."

"Then let's do it."

The girls walked back to Marcus.

"We'll go," Joni said.

Marcus immediately led them down the road. Once away from the crowd, Joni asked her most nagging question.

"Why am I in danger? Who wants to get me? Why?"

Marcus hesitated before speaking.

"I don't know. My people just told me that you need to be protected."

"Yeah, that's not really helpful," Joni said. "And just who are your people?"

"Your parents are not the only ones developing a device like the AGA. Some have been at it much longer. But your parents have made certain breakthroughs. My institute was working on similar technology when we decided to form a research collaboration with your parents."

Marcus stopped walking momentarily to look at Joni and Kelly.

"Except your parents didn't know we were working with them."

None of them spoke for a bit. The girls were groggy, their bodies crashing as the adrenalin drained from their veins. Marcus was anxiously watching every car and had stopped to try to make sense of a map he took out of his pocket. He fumbled with it and kept folding it in different directions while looking for a landmark. Finally, an annoyed Joni yelled at him.

"Here! Just give it to me!"

She peered at it for a moment and said, "that way."

Kelly took it from her, turned it around and pointed in the opposite direction.

"The airport's a mile and a half that way. But how come we're walking? Why don't we drive?"

"I can't," Marcus replied. "I don't have a license."

"Would you like me to drive for you?" asked Kelly, smiling smugly at Joni.

"Let's just go," he answered.

They set off through the woods. Within ten minutes, they all had scratches over any exposed skin, although Marcus had the worst of it (and was caked with mud, from trying to cross a small stream on an unsteady log – even Joni was starting to feel a little sorry for him). Marcus answered some of their questions in a factual, but not particularly cooperative manner. They asked him why his people (he kept calling them that) cared about the equipment back in the lab, if they had such better technology.

"Well, we don't, not really. We have the benefit of knowing more…how can I put it? More about the nature of the universe. Your parents are trying to learn how the universe works by using their equipment, and my people know better how it works and are designing equipment based on that. But your parents were able to throw their AGA together almost in the dark."

"What do you mean, 'nature of the universe'?" asked Joni, hotly. "Our parents know more about the nature of the universe than anyone. Where are you from?"

"These discoveries have been kept hidden, even from the scientific community. Especially from the scientific community. But even without the benefit of this information, the AGA has as much chance of producing a stable link as any machine out there, some day."

"But Joni's dad spoke to us from the future through it!" Kelly burst out.

"Kelly!" Joni yelled at her friend, who shut her mouth, as Marcus stopped, halfway through a bush he was walking through.

"What message? I could tell that the AGA had been used, but not what happened."

Joni stood up straight and looked Marcus in the eye. "What was that device?"

"What device?"

"The one in your drawer."

"You used it? Did it help? You actuated a working linkage? How?"

"No. You answer my questions. You're the spy. You're the one breaking into my dad's lab, pretending to be a student. So you tell us: Where is that device from? What is this 'institute' of yours?"

"You would not have heard of it. It's what you might call a public-private partnership. We have a government contract to oversee various native technologies. But it doesn't matter. I want to help you. I really do. What happened in the laboratory?"

"Listen, Marcus," Joni said. "I don't trust you. But there's nothing to tell you anyway. We just plugged in your box and I played with controls and my dad showed up."

"How did you play with them?"

"I just played with them! It's not like I had some special trick. Dad could see me but not hear me. He said I was in danger and that I should run."

"And that's all?"

"All I'm telling you."

"Well, I don't understand that at all," Marcus said. "I'd say it had to be a set up, but how could anyone know you would use it and, besides, you should be able to recognize your own father. Either way, we need to get you out of here."

"Is my dad safe? He said we couldn't contact him. Are our parents all right?"

"They are fine. Or were when I left them last night."

They wandered on. The woods were thick with young growth, making the going difficult. Kelly was best at finding their route, although she kept being distracted by animal tracks, interesting birds, and, once, a fox that stared at her for ten seconds.

"Why are we going to the airport?" Joni asked. "Do you have a plane?"

"No," Marcus said. "I don't have a plane. The entire area is a natural nexus and the airport is a good focal point; that's why it was built here. The nexus is also probably what allowed the pismire to get through. We'll meet some people at the airport who can help us."

What people? What's a nexus? thought Joni. What is he talking about? Did Redpoll know about this? What's going on?

"What do you mean, 'get through'?" Joni asked. "What did the pismire get through?"

"Ahh…," Marcus hesitated. "Related to the communication technology is the ability to transfer matter. There are natural confluence locations where portals or gates allow movement from one place to another, sometimes spontaneously."

"No. No. No. That's not the issue," said Joni. "Enough of your crap. I've never even heard of anything like that pismire. That thing didn't just teleport out of Africa or somewhere. What are you hiding?"

Just then a noise rang through the air, a boom or a crash, from the woods, somewhere north of where they were hiking. Bramble barked.

Marcus yelled, "Let's get out of here!"

"What is it?" Joni yelled, while Kelly shouted, "Is it the pismire?"

"No. Run!"

And run they did. The woods were a snarl of fallen branches and hidden pits, so they went in spurts and starts, climbing over logs here, leaping over holes there. Bramble barked a bunch, but outpaced them. Marcus acted like he was in the lead, but he clearly had no sense of

direction and, besides, he seemed to fall into every hole
they came across.

Kelly was helping him out of a mud patch when
they heard sounds of pursuit. There was a growl from
some distance behind them and they heard branches break
as something stepped on them. A large something.

"That's not the pismire," Kelly yelled.

"How do you know?" Joni asked.

"It sounds different. Keep running."

They reached an open stretch in the woods where
they were able to sprint. They sped through a good fifty,
sixty yards and looked behind them. At least the girls did.
Joni saw that Marcus was looking at his watch, checking
the time, even with a monster closing in. They then heard
two crashes, one after the other, but in slightly different
directions. What was following them wasn't an it, it was a
them.

They raced down a hill, still through the trees. The
footing was better here and Marcus was able to keep
upright. They stopped for a moment to orient themselves.
They heard another growl behind them, answered quickly
by a second nearby. Whatever they were, they were getting
closer to each other and to them. The girls were scared,
but kept their wits about them; Redpoll had trained them
well.

"This way," Kelly yelled, and they all galloped
forward and a bit to their left, and then on and on. Minute
after minute. They could hear the pursuit clearer than ever,
footsteps and heavy breathing, although the woods were
thick again and they could see nothing behind them.

Suddenly the trees stopped and they smashed into
a chain link fence. On the far side a swath of grass ten
yards wide turned into a concrete runway. They threw their
packs over. Marcus pulled back a rip in the fence to let the
girls and Bramble through, before snaking through
himself. They grabbed their gear.

Running on the wide-open tarmac, Joni suddenly felt very exposed, although not a soul was in sight. They were on the longer of two runways that crossed each other, near three or four small propeller planes. Marcus ran towards a building, yelling something to the girls. They started to follow him, but as they passed the first plane Joni grabbed Kelly.

"We're not going with him. Redpoll wanted us to hide here and wait for her."

"I'm not hanging out in those woods!"

"Let's hide on the far side. We'll lose Marcus if he comes after us."

"Okay, just let me get my breath first."

As they squatted on the pavement, panting hard, Marcus slowed down and walked back towards them. He then stopped abruptly, as both girls stood up. They all looked back at the fence.

On the far side stepped a creature about six feet high, followed closely by a second. In size and girth they were reminiscent of rhinoceroses, but with no horns. Their only fur was along their necks and it was short and black. The first one reared back on its hind legs for a moment, almost like a bear, and snarled. It put its front feet on the fence and crushed it, walking right onto the runway. It returned to all fours and both creatures lumbered towards the girls, about a dozen feet apart.

Marcus swallowed hard and then motioned the girls to get behind him. The lower jaws of the beasts swung in step with their legs and their lips pulled back to reveal yellow teeth, many broken. The smashed teeth and the scars scattered over the creatures' bodies suggested these beasts had fought their way through more than two young women and an intrepid dog before. The girls walked slowly, scared that a sudden movement would cause the creatures to charge. They were sniffing around, as if looking for something. Joni and Kelly hoped it wasn't them.

Then three things happened. The first and loudest was a screeching of wheels as an SUV with tinted windows drove onto the tarmac and came barreling towards them. The second (which no one noticed right away) was a person appearing under the trees on the far side of the runway. The third (and this one, everyone did notice, no doubt about it) came from overhead. Three more creatures materialized from a bluish haze in the air above them. They seemed colossal to the girls as they plummeted, but merely gigantic as they landed and tucked in their wings. They were like enormous ostriches, nine feet tall, but with larger, crested heads that had larger and sharper beaks. Their powerful legs were covered with yellowish down, but no one noticed, since the legs were already fiercely kicking. And while an ostrich's wings tend towards non-existent, the wingspans of these birds stretched ten feet. The wings were thin, but flexible, so that they could slash with the razor-sharp edges that graced their wingtips.

"Thrashers!" Marcus yelled. "Get in the car!"

The rhino-bears went mad as the winged invaders descended; one stood back, beat its chest and roared, and then smashed down on the wing of the nearest plane. This startled its mate on the other side, who growled and flipped the entire aircraft over. Marcus shouted and took something out of his jacket pocket. He hurled it at one of the thrashers. Sailing through the air, it expanded and glowed like a tiny white sun, sending off shards of orange and red. It exploded in a burst of sound and light right in front of one of the creatures, knocking it back twenty feet, where it struggled to stand, before falling down again and staying down.

Meanwhile, the two other thrashers charged forward and cut off the girls from both Marcus and the SUV, which roared its engine and attempted to ram one of the birds; a quick kick smashed the front corner of the vehicle. Even the windshield was tinted; all that could be seen inside was the deployed airbag. The girls ran in the only remaining direction, towards the far trees. It was then that they noticed the young man standing there. Floating upright in the air next to him was a blue-black, smoky circle, about four feet across.

"Alejandro!" they cried.

"This way!" he yelled.

Joni pulled Kelly towards him.

Behind them, Marcus, who had been knocked down by the blast of his own weapon was shouting, "No! Go to the car!"

While one of the birds pecked at the SUV, the two rhino-bears started moving towards the trees. Marcus had another device out and was circling, trying to position himself between the girls and the thrashers. Joni and Kelly were nearly to the woods.

"Jump through! Jump through!" Alejandro yelled.

Joni gripped her backpack and leapt through the circle. She spun around as Kelly landed beside her. The jagged, pulsing ring began to close and she could still see Marcus in the distance through it. She started yelling, "Bramble! Bramble!" When the circle was about three feet across, floating in midair, a hand appeared from the other side, grasping its pulsating edge. They saw Alejandro look in, suck in his breath, and throw the dog through. There was a golden-brown streak of flying fur, and Bramble was in their arms. The circle closed tight. Joni, Kelly, and Bramble collapsed on the ground and saw nothing but dark and forbidding forest in every direction. A forest they had never seen before.

CHAPTER FIVE

The first thing Joni noticed was the silence. Growing up in the city, there was always noise around. Kids shouting in the streets. Neighbors yelling in their houses. The rattle of the trolley at the end of the block. The yipping of little dogs through screen doors. Air conditioning units all summer long. And the drone of cars, buses, trucks, everything. In the middle of the night you could hear a slight hum from the freeway a mile away. The forest silence here felt ominous, something that at any moment might envelop Joni like a burlap sack and seal her tight.

The first thing Kelly noticed was the noise. A slight wind was blowing through the trees and their branches and trunks creaked, like ancient giants stretching after a long slumber. A brook babbled nearby and water drops fell from the ends of twigs one by one, each drop a soft punctuation mark in a conversation taking place all around them. Crickets and frogs warmed up their voices. There was a quiet rustle in the bushes, betraying small creatures or loose imaginations. She felt that the sounds were trying to herd her, force her in a certain direction, but really in all directions at once, so she remained still.

The first thing Bramble noticed was the stream. She trotted over to it and drank, the water reaching her belly as she waded into it.

Bramble's movement broke the stunned paralysis of the two girls, and they began to look around in earnest. The forest was thick enough above to block the sky, but thin enough below to let them see a good distance. Fallen leaves littered the ground, but more still hugged onto the branches above them. Joni walked towards the brook, as Bramble emerged from it, shaking and smiling. Joni reached down and gave her a scratch, Bramble's wagging tail somehow giving the humans a sense of normalcy.

"Where'd you take us?" Kelly broke the silence.

"I dunno."

"I'm scared, Joni."

"So am I."

They took each other's hand without thinking. Neither of them thought for a moment about staying there. After the confusion and terror of the previous few minutes, they were quivering, still on edge. They needed to keep moving. Find somewhere safe. Find someone who could help.

"Let's follow the stream," Kelly suggested. "It might lead somewhere. Somewhere besides here."

"Good idea."

For the first few minutes it seemed like anything but a good idea. The ground near the stream was either overgrown or muddy and slippery. But by moving into the more open forest, they found they could hike swiftly while keeping the stream in sight. The filtered light gave a dusk-like feel to the area, but they could not be sure of the time. Their internal clocks told them it was approaching noon. In any case, it was warm and they soon worked up a sweat. The ground was flat, with a slight tilt towards the stream, until it suddenly dove down before them at a steep angle. Here they could see some sky in front of them. Joni pointed.

"Let's go over there."

They were at the top of a canyon, its right arm showing some granite, with flecks of quartz sparkling in the sun, while the left was covered with trees. They hopped across a few moss-covered stones in the stream and climbed some boulders to get a better view.

The canyon opened before them, revealing a series of rocky outcroppings ambling into a distant plain. Small hills jutted out from a sea of grass, grass thick enough that miles away they could see it waving in the wind. But what drew their eyes was the road cutting a thin line diagonally across the plain. The road ran straight and true and, even from their vantage point, maybe two hundred yards above the plain, they could see the travelers along it. Many horses, their riders guiding them at walking paces or on gentle jaunts. A series of wagons covered in wood, some on wheels and some sliding smoothly along sleds of some sort. Probably thirty or forty people walked along the five-mile stretch that was visible. But the more the girls looked, the odder it seemed. Some of the horses' bodies stretched more than they ought to and a few seemed to sport an extra pair of legs. And while many of the wagons looked to be made of wood held together with a little rope and a lot of prayer, the sled wagons were clearly something else entirely, somehow levitating in a gentle arc to pass over other wagons.

Closer in was a village of a few hundred buildings. A thin track wound its way up the canyon to a crossing near where they were stood. They must have walked right over the trail as they came out of the woods.

They walked over, warily, into the canyon and read the signpost. The nails holding it together were big and rusty, like old railroad spikes, but the writing was neat, grooved into the dark wood in straight, even strokes.

Oban-bano 25 kilometers →
←Chiliquinn 2 kilometers
Landslide Danger!

"Cool! They use metric!"
"How is that cool, Kelly?"
"Well, it tells us something about them."
"Who?"
"Whoever lives here."
"What? Are they Canadian?"
Kelly spoke hesitatingly, "…no. We're not in our world anymore. This has to be some different plane or

universe or dimension or something. Your dad said something about the possibility of different worlds, although he laughed about it. We can't just be somewhere on Earth, not with horses like that. But they must be connected with us somehow, if they use metric. You know, connected with our world."

Joni was silent for a bit. If they really were in a different world, then maybe it wasn't so weird that a random boy in Philadelphia could have a picture of her dead. And so maybe she was going to die. She supposed she should argue that with Kelly, but somehow she didn't feel like arguing for her death.

Bramble plopped down on a grassy patch, panting. A few birds trilled from the woods behind them. Joni took a swig from her water bottle and passed it to her friend.

"Redpoll talked about bubbles or something," Kelly said. "And Marcus said the pismire came 'through' something. I guess we came through something."

"Do you think there could be more pismires nearby?" Joni asked, looking back at the woods.

"I don't think so…it seems too, I don't know, dry for them. That doesn't make sense. I don't know."

"But there could be other things. We should leave."

"And go where, J.?"

"Chiliquinn," Joni answered decisively, pointing to the village. "It's close. Maybe we can get some information. And a bed."

"And some food. I want something besides a granola bar."

"Okay, let's go."

They started hiking down the canyon.

As the canyon bottomed out, the trail took a wide curve around a thick growth of trees, and Joni and Kelly heard the sounds of people. The girls slunk between the trunks, sap sticking to their hands as they pushed back branches. The growth was thick enough that the girls would not be seen by wayward glances, but they were able to view most of Chiliquinn.

The buildings were mostly wooden, some with stone foundations and chimneys. Several dozen more houses nestled in the woods or sat on small grass-covered mounds. To the girls, the village seemed something out of the old West, with the horses and the rustic buildings and the dry climate; they could even see several men swaggering around like cowboys, with pistols at their hips. Many people were out and about, going in and out of stores and shops, while dozens of dusty wagons kept pulling in and out with more travelers.

Bramble barked at a noise behind them. A company of a dozen men and women came ambling down another trail, chatting away. A woman arguing with a man beside her was pushing a miniature sled, which seemed to be riding on a cushion of air. The group was merry and ignored their two dogs that were barking towards the girls' hiding place. The travelers' clothes did not seem as odd to the girls as they would have expected, considering the floating sleds and the horse-drawn wagons. The clothes were simple, with few elaborate designs. Most people down in the town were dressed in a similar fashion, although many wagon-riders' wore tighter clothes and there were even a few people in t-shirts.

The girls decided to switch up their clothing a bit, to give them better cultural camouflage. They put on jeans and some solid-color shirts.

"We'd better fit in," Kelly said. "It's going to be tough enough to fake our way through this place."

"I'm just glad we got away," Joni said. "After the pismire and those rhino-things, and then the birds, I had no idea what was going on. It was probably easier for Alejandro to send us here than to fight them."

"Yeah, but where did he send us? Is it a trap? I mean, he just appeared, more or less with those thrasher birds, who conveniently chased us right into his hands. And you just did what he said."

"What? Was I supposed to take the rhino-bears for a ride? Or just do what Marcus says?"

"I didn't say that," said Kelly. "But you said jump and here we are, so where do we go?"

"Look, if Alejandro wanted to kill us, he could have just left us for the thrashers. And dad said he was trying to help us."

"I'm not saying he wanted to kill us," Kelly said, "but he separated us from Marcus, who's the only person who knew what was going on since this all started."

"So Marcus is trustworthy? We don't know if anyone's on our side. But Alejandro did get us out of the fight."

"Yeah, but why put us here?"

"Maybe it was the best he could do," said Joni, who then paused before continuing. "I hope they're all right."

"Well, Marcus had his little friends in the SUV," Kelly answered, "and Alejandro had whatever he had to send us here. So, I bet they're both fine. Better than we are at least. But I worry about Redpoll."

Joni thought for a moment before answering.

"I don't know why, but I don't think she had any trouble with the pismire thing. I bet she could have taken care of the thrashers, too."

"Yeah, good old Redpoll. You might be right. But she can't help us now. What do we do?"

The girls talked for a bit, but both realized that their best chance for a meal and a place to sleep was in the village. Enough people were coming and going that they figured they could just slip in with the crowd. They skittered out of the trees and walked into the town, hoping for the best.

The major boulevards of Chiliquinn were made of close-fitting stones but the sidestreets were all packed dirt, sometimes with stone gutters that directed water down to the thin river on the far side. Dogs ran around loose, a couple of them exchanging sniffs with Bramble. Some people nodded politely at the girls, but most of the inhabitants went about their business, walking between storefronts or shuttling in and out of their caravans. As they entered the town, Joni and Kelly examined one of the sled wagons; it had a rich redwood roof, but the sides and bottoms were composed of some kind of plastic or fiberglass. It was almost the size of a bus and rested on two rods or runners, each the width of a fist, which lay two feet below the body of the wagon.

A woman, almost six feet tall with bronze skin, was soldering a panel near the rear of it. She stood up straighter and raised her leather goggles over her close-cropped, light brown hair. She saw the girls, grunted, and then grabbed a rung and swung herself into a storage compartment above her. Joni pointed at the electronic control panel she had been working on, incongruous in a dusty cowpoke town, but said nothing as the woman jumped down, some transistors clenched in her teeth and wearing a roll of duct tape like a bracelet.

They turned around and smelled something delicious emanating from an inn in front of them. They looked through the open double doors and saw a few people eating at tables, one man drinking at the bar, and a woman in an apron behind it. This woman saw their hesitation and yelled to them,

"Come on in, girls, the food's good. Bring in the pooch; I'll pour some water for her."

Her accent sounded foreign to the girls, but not as odd as some Philly accents. They took her advice and stepped into the tavern, choosing a little nook to the right of the door that had windows facing the street. A chandelier with electric lights hung in the center, but oil lamps along the walls lit the room. A few heads picked up when they entered, but then returned to their food and ale. The girls pulled their backpacks up on the booth next to them, trying to keep the familiar close. The woman brought them two water glasses and a wooden water bowl for Bramble. She wore a yellow skirt under her apron with a white blouse on top. Her brown hair, and there was lots of it, was bound on top of her head. She had a bit of grease on her left cheek, although the pinkness still showed through. The girls smiled up at her, hoping she was as friendly as she seemed.

The woman spoke quietly, "So, where ya' two from?"

"I lost my wallet unfortunately, which had our…" Joni began, trying to come up with something believable.

"Where ya' comin' from?"

"Um…um…down the trail, from Oban-bano." Joni hoped she was pronouncing it correctly.

"Uh-huh, I didn't realize there were still people there, thought it was pretty deserted at this point."

"Yeah, well, we were just passing through there."

"Uh-huh. But the bubble's split it in two, hasn't it?" This woman clearly wasn't buying their story, but didn't seem to mind. She sat down beside them, with a conspiratorial look. "You just come across?"

"Across?" Kelly's voice came out in a squeal, causing a look or two in their direction. The woman put a hand on her shoulder.

"Across. Through the barrier. Hopped a bubble. A lot of travelers here do."

"We didn't pop anything…"

"Hopped. Did you come from bubble Earth? The… United States?" she looked at them questioningly, not sure if she was saying it right. "Sounds like, from your voices."

Joni's eyes water a bit as she took a leap of faith or maybe a leap of desperation, "We came through some kind of hole. It was sparkling… We have no idea what's happening."

Both girls started talking at once and Bramble jumped up.

"It's okay, it's okay, settle down. My name's Imbrium."

"Hello," Kelly spoke up. "How did you know we…how did you know?"

"We house travelers here from all over," Imbrium answered. "We're near the bottom of the bubble well, which makes us easy to hop to. A little more work to get out. Now you just relax and tell me what happened."

Joni looked at Kelly and then at Imbrium. She seemed nice, trustworthy in a homey sort of way, but there was something more. In the last 24 hours, no one was who they said they were. Even Redpoll, whom they thought they had known so well, almost family, had been lying for years. Each offer of help just kept steering them to stranger and stranger places. But Imbrium had no stake in them (they hoped), and maybe they could trust her. Joni took the chance.

"Well, we were being chased by these things, these…thrashers."

"Thrashers!" exclaimed Imbrium.

"Yeah, like these giant bird things. I mean, I guess it started at the university, really maybe in Philadelphia. Yeah, we were at home, Kelly and me, I'm Joni by the way, and this is Kelly, and I found this photo you see after I hit a guy with my atlatl…"

She rambled on, with occasional corrections from Kelly, sometimes followed by counter-corrections from Joni. Both girls were relieved for the chance to unload. Sharing, letting someone else know their troubles validated them somehow and Imbrium oozed sympathy. She asked few questions, listening carefully. Finally, Joni took a deep breath before realizing she had nothing left to say and sat there with her mouth still open. Imbrium filled the silence.

"Well, my word. A pismire and thrashers. You two have had quite the adventure getting here, make no mistake."

"Are those creatures from here?" Joni asked.

"Oh, no, no, no. Not native here. Thrashers were from Ebullus Putredinis, according to Menlo at least. Who's not always reliable."

"Putredinis?"

"Oh, a sad land. Ebullus Putredinis is its name now, now that it is gone. When it existed, it had a different name."

Imbrium seemed far away for a moment.

"What happened to it? Was there a war?"

"War? No! Well, yes, I suppose there was, but it's no more because the bubble's dead."

Imbrium looked sad. The girls looked confused. Bramble looked asleep.

"You really don't know how you came here, do you?" the woman asked. "Where *here* is?"

"No," Joni was almost crying, and Kelly would be if she were trying to talk. "Our parents are scientists doing research into…branal," she had some trouble coming up with the word her dad had used, "walls and dimensions and stuff. But they didn't say anything about any of this, and I'm sure they don't know about it either."

"That's all right, honey," Imbrium said, taking Joni's hand in hers. "Most don't know about it in your bubble, I'm told. Earth is hard to get to and it's been officially sealed, so travel there is severely limited, although I've always wanted to. Sealed worlds find ways to explain odd things that happen. Listen, listen, we'll talk later, you just have some food and rest now…what? Oh, don't worry about paying for it. We're not short of supplies here. More food left than years, I reckon. But that's never-no-mind. You just eat and I'll get a room ready for you. Sit tight and try to act like everything is normal. I'm not worried about anyone here," she looked at her customers, "but you might raise questions later when the crowd comes in, although you'll find the locals aren't very nosy. It's going to be okay."

She left like a whirlwind, returning with two deep bowls of a rich soup, teeming with vegetables, and leftovers for Bramble. Before they knew it, she was back with a loaf of bread and a small plate with some whitish butter (the best the girls had ever had), and two clay goblets with some type of juice. Within twenty minutes, they could barely keep their eyes open, and Imbrium led them up a short flight of stairs in the back and down a hallway to a small room with a big bed. There was a washbasin near a window overlooking the back alley and a candle lantern on a small table. They dropped their gear, thanked Imbrium, who was already gone, collapsed onto the soft comforter covering the bed, kicked off their shoes, and were asleep in seconds. Bramble hesitated for a moment before leaping up on the bed and curling into a ball at their feet.

CHAPTER SIX

J oni woke first, in the dark, unsure for a moment where she was. Out the window she saw rose-tinted clouds, and figured it was about eight in the evening ("assuming it's the same time zone as home, which it probably isn't" she thought to herself). She climbed out of bed, eliciting no reaction from her two companions, neither two- nor four-legged. She examined the washbasin in the scanty light and twisted the faucet until cold water came out. After splashing her face, she saw a cup and drank some water. She then went through a thin door next to the sink. When she came out, Kelly was sitting up on the bed, eyes blinking.

"Better?" Joni asked.

"Yeah. Bathroom?"

"In there."

The girls changed into some fresher clothes. So much had happened that it was difficult to believe that they had left Philadelphia just 48 hours earlier. Joni had to look at her watch to make sure it was still only Wednesday.

After a knock on the door, Imbrium came in, "Y' feeling better? Took a nap, did you? Good. The dining room's filling up nicely, a lot of travelers, a lot of traders, so ya' don't have to worry about standing out. There are two in particular, Darl and Menlo, who I want you to meet. They capture large animals that have hopped from one bubble to another and, frankly, they can do a much better job explaining all this to you 'n maybe help you get back. Here's a bone for the pooch."

"Bramble," Joni said.

Imbrium handed the bone to Bramble, who promptly jumped on the bed and started chewing it. Joni and Kelly followed Imbrium through the door and down the hallway. Much of the floor bowed inwards, worn down by many decades of travelers. A watercolor hung on the right wall showing what looked like a large cluster of silver grapes, but as they peered closer the girls saw that each "grape" held a miniature mountain or town or something. One even had a spaceship. There was a mirror at the end of the hallway and Kelly groaned a little at her reflection. That made Joni laugh, her first real laugh in this new world, and she dragged her friend down the stairs.

Imbrium led them through the bustling bar into a small dining room with alcoves built into the walls, each holding tables and benches, all lit by oil lamps. Several larger tables occupied the center of the room and a fire blazed on the hearth, filling the air with a pleasant aroma. On a sideboard were dishes, a few pitchers, some bread, and a block of a dry, crumbly cheese. Imbrium led them to a table on the left, where two people sat, one the woman they had seen working on the wagon out front earlier and the other a man nearly a full head taller with jet black skin and a series of small, silvery scars on the left side of his face. They seemed happily engaged in an old argument; at least the man seemed happy, the woman was scowling a bit.

"The ship is impossible so, *ipso facto*," the woman said, "it doesn't exist."

"But there are so many stories…"

"No. There's one story, told a hundred ways and…"

The woman stopped as she saw the girls and Imbrium at their table. She eyed Joni and Kelly up and down and continued speaking. "This them, Imbry? Take a seat. Menlo, get them something to eat. I'm Darl."

Darl did not offer her hand but moved to the seat on her left so the girls could sit on the bench, while Imbrium pulled a chair over for herself. Menlo gave a big, warm smile and strode over to the sideboard in two, giant steps. He returned with bread, cheese, and three glasses of water that tasted as if they were mixed with a wine (at least for the girls; Imbrium's might have been straight wine). The three adults made some small talk, waiting for the noise in the dining room to return to a more robust level, and they all leaned in a little closer. Imbrium began to tell the girls' story. They corrected her some at first and then, feeling more at ease, Joni took the lead. Somehow, in the girls' minds, these two newcomers were enveloped in the cloud of faith they had placed around Imbrium. They had no particular reason to trust them, or Imbrium for that matter, but they were so desperate for any anchor to help secure them, that they poured forth their story.

Darl and Menlo sat silently as the tale unfolded. The girls had no explanation as to why all this had happened to them; they only knew that it had happened and that they were scared and wanted to go home. While they spoke Imbrium went off to the kitchen and returned with a platter of sausages, some boiled potatoes, and cooked carrots. Joni and Kelly dove hungrily into all of it, while Darl ate only sausages and Menlo only potatoes. The trappers each took a deep draught of their ale and then began to pepper the girls with questions.

"What color was the pismire?"

"Did it have spots? What was its tail like?"

"Was it scared by the noise behind it? Did you hear a whistle like this?"

Menlo whistled six notes, just loud enough that he turned heads across the dining room.

"What did Marcus' device look like?"

"How long have you known Redpoll?"

"What's an Essuvee?"

"Describe Alejandro's gate, the portal he made to this bubble. Was it sharp on the edges or more fuzzy?"

Darl demonstrated with her hands, making a jagged circle through the air.

The girls did their best to answer their questions, for a while. Joni, however, was getting more and more agitated. Staring at the moon through a window above them for a minute, she started shouting her own questions.

"All right, where are we? I'm looking out, the moon's the right shape, in the right place, looks right. You're speaking English; the food's normal or pretty normal. We're not on another planet. This place looks straight out of an old Western, but that guy over there"—here she leaned forward and jerked her head towards some men playing cards—"is using a handheld holographic computer or something. So where are we?"

"And how do we get home?" added Kelly.

Darl again took the lead in talking. "Think of this place as an extension of Earth. Imagine the planet radiating bubbles out from its center, each bubble in a different dimension, each a different size. So they're all in the same place, but not really. You've gone from one bubble, or an ebullus as they're technically known, to another. In your case, from a very large bubble, one of the biggest, to a small one. And one that's getting smaller. The largest ebulli are identical to your bubble in many ways. A few different creatures, some different geography, but essentially the same. Alternate aspects. More like if you took a ship to *Egypt*." (She pronounced it with a hard G and P, E-gip-tuh.) "It wouldn't look like home, but you'd get by. This bubble is smaller, like if strips of your world were peeled away."

Kelly sat there with her mouth making a little "o" and her eyes darting back and forth between the adults, mulling it over in her head, while Joni charged into it, a new mystery to unravel.

"How did it start?" Joni asked. "Has it always been this way?"

Darl answered, "Apparently, although that's the subject of another debate." She gave a look to silence Menlo, whose mouth was already open to argue, before continuing, "Any large body of mass extends into bubbles around itself. Most of the animals and plants are the same between the different bubbles, so there must have always been some migration between them. Your bubble is one of the first ones, at least culturally. That is, most of the bubbles have been populated by immigrants from Earth. But originally, those immigrants traveled across natural rips or portals, without realizing it, and had no way to return."

"It is a lot easier to leave your bubble, than to get back to it," Menlo said. "Which is why this Alejandro was able to send you here, without too much trouble."

"Exactly," Darl went on. "So, for thousands of years, there was only natural leakage between bubbles. People entering a cave in one bubble and emerging in another. Certain places became holy or sacred and sometimes visions were seen, but few people, if any, really knew what was going on. Then about five hundred years ago, a lot more people started leaving Earth and ending up in other bubbles. This might have been because more portals were opening, or maybe because more people were traveling around the Earth. A lot of British ships that were assumed shipwreck ended up somewhere else. That's why most of the bubbles speak English."

"How many portals does Earth have?" Joni asked.

"There are over 100 known ones on land and more at sea," Darl answered. "Your North America has a lot of them, more than the other continents. That's another reason English is so common."

"And while people at first kept thinking it was magic," continued Menlo. "others began to look at it scientifically. A couple hundred years ago scientists in Ebullus Graneas were able to open and maintain a gate to another bubble and they started discovering more of them. Regular gates and portals were set up between many of the worlds. Trade developed and people starting traveling between them."

Menlo took up the explanation, "Because you are so high up the ebullic well, you have influenced the other

ebulli, but there has been little influx to you. I know the…
the…"

He looked at Darl. "Who am I thinking of?
Thousands of years ago."

"The Celts," Darl answered.

"Yes, the Celts. They went back and forth a good
deal. However, their portals were jealously guarded. And
your world had a bit too much of the… fundamentalism.
The zealotry… I'm saying this wrong. Your world tends to
be, shall we say, reactionary. When otherworlders popped
up out of nowhere they were often killed on sight. That's
one of the reasons the Ebulli Council cordoned off your
world, at least for open trade. You officially have an
advocate on the Council. You weren't the only bubble to
be shut off, but you are the largest one. By several orders
of magnitude."

"Which is absurd!" shouted Darl. "Why continue
the restriction? Even when Menlo and I get clearance to
enter to clean up all the crap that's coming through, we
still have to be completely hidden. How will they ever be
ready to join modern society if they continue to be
mollycoddled…"

"DARL AND MENLO," Imbrium quieted the
whole table. "Please, you two… I think we have strayed
from the point. Menlo, if you will continue?"

"Sorry, Imbry. Well, in any case, there are all these
overlapping bubbles, about ninety of them thickly
occupied, with maybe twice that—"

"Or thousands more," piped in Darl.

"…without humans or with only a few. Darl's
right – the science says there should be a lot more, but we
can't find them. Some of the ones we can, like yours, are
huge, while others are the size of baseball stadiums. Your
world is the one with baseball, right?"

"Uh, yeah," replied Kelly.

"Wonderful sport. Anyhow, let's get back to
basics. Imagine a container, filled with a dozen or so *nearly*

spherical bubbles. That leaves a lot of space in between where slightly smaller bubbles fit in. So add those in. But there's still a bit more space for even smaller bubbles. And so on and so on. Am I good so far?"

This last remark was addressed to Darl, who answered, "Well, the container analogy implies there's an edge, but it's a fine start."

"Thank you," Menlo said, with a smirk. "Well, all else being equal, the higher up the Ebullic well, the harder it is to get to using either rips—that's a natural gate that's generally bound to a specific location—or else artificial gates that have been set up. It takes a phenomenal amount of energy to create a gate, unless you can cross from within a nexus, like the one you transported from, or are traveling downhill. A nexus is an area where the barrier between bubbles is weaker."

"'Where the branes are thinner,'" Kelly muttered under her breath at Joni, remembering a conversation in the lab. "Is this where dark matter comes from?"

"Dark what, honey?" asked Imbrium.

"Dark matter. Scientists keep complaining that most of the mass of the universe is invisible, so they call the rest dark matter."

"Exactly," answered Menlo. "The extra mass is all around us, but twisted in on itself."

"There are those who think that all the ebulli were originally reflections of a primal one," said Darl, "perhaps your Earth. Lots of ebulli claimed theirs to be first, while some people think at the center of it all is the original bubble, the primal one, but that the barriers are too thick to pass."

"Or that it collapsed long ago," added Menlo, "consumed by fire or drowned in water."

Darl spoke, "But lately the bubbles have been changing, some growing, but more shrinking. Some of the smaller ones are ripping into each other. No one knows why. Seecanus, the bubble we're in right now, has been very unstable the last few years."

"When I was younger than you, honey," said Imbrium, "my granddam would frighten me with stories of bubbles that shrank to nothing. But now it's happening for real."

"In any event," Menlo again took the lead, "there are a lot of people wondering why the bubbles are changing and what's causing it. There are a lot of factions out there who have something to gain as the bubbles change. That's why I'd like to know who Alejandro and Marcus are. Are they competitors? Are they enemies? And why do they care about you? Describe this Alejandro."

"I can do better than that," said Joni. "I have his picture. I took it at the river that first day."

Joni pulled her cell phone out of her pocket. She punched a few keys, and then handed it to Menlo. Half the image was Bramble, but Alejandro was clear, his head tilting to his right. His nose and chin both looked sharp from this angle and his brown hair tumbled over the side of his face.

"Good," said Darl. "We're lucky that your camera will work here. A lot of technology doesn't transfer. Scientific laws aren't universal across the bubbles."

Menlo then took a small device out of his pocket. The top half contained a screen and the bottom was a keyboard with a jumble of odd letters and numerals. He took a picture of Joni's phone, centering on the image of Alejandro. He then typed on the keyboard and the image dissolved into lines, like a topographic map of a face, before reverting to the original. Nine squares appeared on the screen, each showing a different face. They ranged from a perfectly symmetrical face in the top left corner to an Alejandro with a vivid scar on his right half in the bottom left corner. Menlo swung the screen around.

"Which ones are closest?"

The girls looked at it and Joni pointed out pictures three to six. Darl punched those four and all the photos disappeared, replaced by nine new pictures. The girls removed a couple of the images, and in a minute they had nine pictures, all with slight differences.

"Let's see if there's a match." The frames started flipping through more photos. After about ten seconds, four photos filled the screen. Before the girls had a chance to tell him, he touched the one that was clearly Alejandro. With a glance around the room (only half filled now, as the other patrons had moved to the bar or gone home), he spoke quietly.

"Not much info. Name, Pedro Alejandro Escovar. Nothing before about five years ago. Trained in gates and tips. A bit of an arrest record, from several different ebulli. Mostly disturbing the peace at various demonstrations. Accused of stealing a cop's motorbike in To-linh. Caught trying to put a protest banner halfway up the Ojai Tower in EkPowe. Nothing from the last year. That's it."

"Any record of jumps?" asked Darl, before explaining to the girls, "We can check on jumps from bubble to bubble across any of the commercial gates. That's public record. But not the natural rips, or any private ones."

"Or if he uses an assumed name," added Menlo, looking at his device. "He made a bunch of jumps during his schooling. A few to your Earth…and several one-way trips away from this bubble."

Joni looked confused, "How could he have several *one-way* trips?"

"This bubble is an easy target for beginners, especially around Chiliquinn," answered Darl. "Which is why we're here so often chasing down big game, although this time somebody called us out on a false alarm, still not sure who. If Alejandro were in training, he would practice making his own gates in order to get here. There would be no record of that. But to get to his home bubble he would have to go to an established nexus and that would be registered. Where does he leave from?"

This last question was back to Menlo.

"Out of Nicus."

"That's about 1,200 kilometers away," Imbrium told the girls.

Menlo then asked, "Any photos of Marcus? Okay, well let me look up his name…Nothing."

"Try Redpoll," Joni said, "'Anita Redpoll', I don't think I have any pictures."

Why don't I have any pictures, Joni wondered to herself. I've got thousands of Bramble, but none of Redpoll.

"Let me see." Menlo typed into his device. "Nothing, nothing. Hold on, my system's crashing, something's wrong. Sorry. But nothing was coming up."

"All right," Darl said, "That's good for now. Here's where I think we stand. Correct me if I'm wrong, Imbry, Menlo. The girls' parents are doing research on the bubbles, from a sealed world, although they don't know that. Joni gets a warning from her father, from the future, from a different bubble." Darl looked at Joni. "The time conundrum could only happen if the communication was crossing a membrane; he had to have been in a different bubble. Or will be. Which raises the issue of how they were able to communicate so well across time."

"Or at all," added Menlo. "I've never heard of technology that good."

"Me neither," answered Darl. "Marcus might have been right when he hinted it was a setup. Someone could be using a look-alike. Are you sure it was your father?"

"Yes, no," Joni stammered. "I mean, it looked like him, I thought it was him. Wouldn't I know my own father?"

"Of course you would, honey," said Imbrium. "You stop confusing the poor girl."

"Either way," Darl continued, "this Redpoll woman walks in and shows herself to be a player of some sort. The obvious answer would be that she is responsible for it all and was spying on your parents' work, but it doesn't sound like she did any of that. Instead, she claims to be protecting the girls, and I'm inclined to trust her, at least until we find out more. Why be so supportive for six years, just to then turn on you? On the other hand, she could have sent the pismire. But on the third hand, if anyone were tracing you, the trace should fail once you entered a nexus. Which might just broadcast the fact that you were hiding in a nexus."

Joni and Kelly stared helplessly, more confused then ever.

"But then Marcus shows up at the park nexus and this Alejandro bloke appears at the airport. The only thing Alejandro has going for him is that your father, Joni, said you could trust him."

"He didn't say that exactly."

"Could either one of them arrange a pismire?" asked Imbrium. She then added in an aside to Joni and Kelly, "They be scoundrels, but Darl and Menlo do know their exotic animals."

"They could do it if they have connections," answered Darl. "Pismires are trainable, but they can't do much. And the theradons, the rhinoceros-bear-like things, they're easy to work with. Big teddy bears."

"But then there are the thrashers," said Menlo, his face in a wistful grin.

"And then there are the thrashers," repeated Darl. "No one wants to work with them. No one wants them around at all. No order uses them."

"It's beside the point." Menlo took the lead in the conversation. "Both Marcus and Alejandro were trying to get the girls, but Alejandro sent them here, without anyone waiting. Makes me think he was working on his own."

"Maybe he's just bad at transferring," countered Darl. "It's hard whipping up a gate on the fly, even for a veteran."

"Or maybe, he panicked once he saw the thrashers."

"WAIT!" Joni shouted. "They might both be good, they might both be bad. We don't know. But who are you? Why should we trust you? You haven't told us a thing about yourselves. What side are you on?" Joni sat up tall, with Kelly straightening up beside her, trying to show a united front.

Pause.

Darl spoke, "A fair question. We're telling you to trust no one, yet we expect you to believe us. And I'm not sure what we can tell you, but we won't ask too much of you either, until we earn your trust. Menlo and I work for the Ebulli Council. As Imbry said, our job is to catch animals."

"And occasionally plants," added Menlo.

"…and occasionally marauding plants. All this bubble disintegration means that large animals have been crossing membranes lately. A lot of them. You used to go years between hearing about some animal crossing bubbles. Now it happens every month."

"Like Sally!" shouted Kelly.

"Who's Sally now, honey?" asked Imbrium.

"Schuylkill Sally! In the Schuylkill River a few months ago. She was this big water creature, like a huge river turtle or something."

"You're from Philadelphia?" asked Menlo, excited.

"Yes," answered Kelly.

"Yeah, that was us, we captured her," Darl said. "Still don't know how she got there. The branes are very weak around there, but something still must have drawn her across. She was a cruger, a type of kappa. We've still got her locked up there at that old prison near the river, with someone feeding her cucumbers until we can get her away inconspicuously."

Kelly pointed her finger at her friend, beaming from ear to ear, "I told you I saw her."

Imbrium began laughing and then excused herself to go to the kitchen.

Darl watched Imbrium leave and then spoke again, more conspiratorially, "If I can steer the conversation back a bit… In our various roles, Menlo and I have connections, official and unoffical. It seems like events are coming to a head and that you or your parents are at the bottom of it. And I want to know why."

"But how do we get home?" Joni asked.

"Nicus," Menlo said. "It's the only port that could do it. This whole bubble is easy to slide into, but hard to climb out of. Nicus is a nexus."

"Will you take us there?" Kelly asked.

"Yes," Menlo said, as Darl said, "No."

"I mean, no," Menlo corrected.

"Why not?" Joni demanded.

Menlo and the girls looked at Darl.

"First of all, we're not going directly to Nicus," she said. "We've got an animal to catch out in the mountains. Secondly, you're safer here. If anyone's looking for you, they're not likely to come looking in Chiliquinn. And if they do, Imbry will catch word of it. We'll get to Nicus, ask around, and get the lay of the land. If it seems safe, we'll send a message back here and you can find transport to Nicus."

"That could be days," Joni said.

"Maybe," Darl said.

"Just take us with you now."

"We could help with the animal," Kelly interjected.

Menlo hesitated, but Darl gave him another look.

"It's not safe. I want to know why all this is going on first. We've got to be sure you'd be safe in Philadelphia, before we try to send you there. Someone was trying to kill you.”

“But…” Joni whined.

“The answer is no. Now, Menlo and I are leaving at seven in the morning, so we’ll say our goodbyes now. Imbry will look after you. That’s just the way it is.”

CHAPTER SEVEN

"'T'hat is so not they way it is," Joni said to Kelly, as they walked back to their room, and started scheming. Kelly argued for a while, but ending up agreeing with Joni, just so she could go to sleep.

At five the next morning, the alarm on Joni's phone went off, and she rolled over and kicked her friend. Kelly gave a grunt, but climbed out of bed and into the bathroom. Bramble got a scratch and rolled over on to her back. Joni put some dog food down on the floor and got dressed.

Within fifteen minutes, they were furtively sneaking down the stairs, making sure they didn't run into Darl or Menlo. They did a quick trip into the back alley, for Bramble to do her business and then tiptoed through the dining room and into the barroom. There they found Imbrium standing in the middle of the floor, holding a couple of bags.

"I've some clothes for you, so you fit in better in Nicus and some food for the journey. Now hurry, before Darl and Menlo come down."

Joni and Kelly grabbed the gear.

"How did you know?" Joni asked.

"It was pretty obvious.'"

"Thank you," said Joni. "I don't know how we'll ever repay you."

"Or even just pay you," Kelly added thoughtfully.

"Now don't you worry about it one pip. These clothes are bits and pieces that have been left here over the years. It's times like this when we've all got to stick together. Now hurry up. It's time you were going."

Hoisting the bags, the girls hugged Imbrium goodbye and hustled out to Darl and Menlo's wagon. It seemed to be half stagecoach and half RV. They ran over to the storage compartment on the side they had eyed the day before. Joni opened it and the two of them picked up Bramble and put her inside. They then each grabbed a railing on the side and followed her. They closed the door behind them and waited.

A little light came through a dent in the door. This was augmented by some electronic panels that had a few blinking lights, next to a dozen different outlets, two of which they risked plugging their phones into. They were in a box about three feet wide, five feet tall, and that went back about eight feet, maybe half the width of the trappers' wagon. Luckily it was mostly empty, with a line of tools attached to hooks on the wall and a pile of blankets at the far end. These they spread out a bit to sit on and leaned back on their bags.

They waited about twenty minutes, snacking on some of the food Imbrium had given them, before they heard noises. One of cabin doors up front opened and then was slammed shut, shaking the wagon slightly. As they wondered which trapper it was, they heard Darl loudly swear at something. About ten minutes later, they heard the door open again and Darl and Menlo talking, but too muffled to make it out. They then held their breath as someone fumbled with the panel next to their hiding place. But after a minute, the panel was closed, and the unknown trapper went back inside the wagon. Presently, they felt some sort of engine come to life beneath them and the wagon rose up a few feet.

Bramble barked.

It was short and not too loud, but the wagon settled down with a thump. They heard the wagon door open and footsteps coming towards the back. Joni steeled herself as the door opened and Menlo stared at the three of them. His hand went up to his mouth as he fought back a laugh. Smiling widely, he put one finger to his lips and closed the door. A minute later the wagon rose again and off they went.

Bramble was quiet this time and since the girls dared not talk to each other, they were soon lulled to sleep by the gentle rolling of the wagon as it traveled, floating above the ground. A couple of hours later, it came to a rest again. Joni stirred groggily and then nudged Kelly as she heard the cabin door open and both trappers climb out, their voices getting louder.

"What do you mean we have to stop?" they heard Darl asked. "There's nothing here."

"I thought Bramble might need a walk," Menlo answered and opened the door to the girls' hiding place.

"What…?" Darl began, as she came into view.

She took one look at the girls, rolled her eyes, and walked back to the cabin. Menlo laughed and then helped them out. They were on the side of a paved road climbing through dry, grassy foothills, with taller mountains further up the road. Bramble leapt out of the wagon and went dashing off after a rabbit or two that she had flushed out of the grass. Menlo laughed some more as he led them into the wagon, hauling their bags over his shoulder.

"Don't worry about Darl," he said. "She's a dog person."

And, indeed, looking out the side window, they saw Darl throwing a stick to Bramble in the tall grass. Joni frowned, looking around. Every side of the wagon had several windows, even though there had been none visible from the outside. She went and tapped one. She figured it must be some super high definition video display, but so realistic she expected to feel the wind coming through. The cabin itself was about 30 feet long, twelve feet wide, and everywhere that wasn't a window was crammed with books and tools. There were padded chairs and booths, a sink, and a refrigerator in the back. The equipment appeared high-tech to the girls, although half of it seemed held together with duct tape. Joni thought it all had a woody smell, somehow.

Darl brought Bramble in the main door, told Menlo to "make sure they don't break anything," and then climbed into the front cab area as if she were a stagecoach pilot (if pilot was the word, Joni wasn't sure). In front of her, the area was decked out with a mix of computerized controls and wooden knobs (as well as a hand crank and some kind of pump). It had a clear canopy that could be lowered to protect its inhabitants from the weather. Darl cranked something and the canopy slid back, letting fresh air into the cabin.

"If it's all right with the stowaways, we'll leave now."

"We're sorry, Darl," Joni said. "But we just had to go and we won't be any trouble."

"Why do I doubt that?"

But even the girls could tell she wasn't really mad, just a little annoyed.

Kelly asked Menlo a question, although Darl answered it from the cab while Menlo stowed their bags in various cupboards, "How long until we get to Nicus?"

"About a day. Because of the electromagnetic fields of this bubble, we can't travel too fast without wrecking half the equipment. It's the same field that jams us so we can't just call up Nicus. Every ebullus has different natural laws, so you can't always be sure of what works. We brought the wagon from Ebullus Torghum. There the trip would take about two hours."

"One hour," murmured Menlo.

Darl sighed. "Fine, one hour, if you have the stomach for it. We're at least faster than the horse-drawn ones. Either way, it's going to take longer because there's some cleanup we have to do."

"What cleanup?" Joni asked warily.

"There's a creature holed up in a park about half the way to Nicus…"

"What kind of creature?" Kelly asked. "What does it look like?"

"Um, well it's a hartwig," Menlo answered. "It's big, with a long neck. Like a turtle. Or a cat."

"That makes no sense at all," she replied.

"Well, maybe we'll let you see it. But probably not."

"Hmmmph."

The rest of the day passed in relative comfort. Menlo took one shift at the wheel (really more of a console than a wheel, along with a kind of metal-plated wooden rudder), while Darl tried to read in the back. However, with Menlo driving it soon became so bumpy and the wagon weaved so much that the girls began to turn a little green. When Darl's drink actually fell over, she angrily threw down her book and took over the driving again.

When he wasn't making them nauseous with his driving, Menlo told them about the different bubbles. He explained that most of the ones in the center ("There's no center," shouted Darl from the cab, "the universe is finite but unbounded"), anyway, he went on, most of the ones in the center would look familiar to someone from their Earth, outside of a few details. But the further out you go, the more things change, environmentally, culturally, physically. Even the laws of gravity.

He spoke of an archipelago bubble, mostly ocean, with only chains of islands to make landfall on. These islands stretch for tens of thousands of miles in a series of curly-cues and geometric shapes, only visible from the air. The bubble's inhabitants believe them to be runes written by the gods into the waters themselves. In their Great Pilgrimages, thousands of people set off to sail the entire length, an odyssey of several years, which few complete due to the dangers on the way.

"Whirlpools!" shouted Darl. "Sea serpents!"

"Unfriendly natives with spears and cannons," responded Menlo.

"Or friendly natives with warm beaches and fresh fish," Darl added, "which can be just as hazardous, when you're trying to finish a pilgrimage."

Menlo told them about a bubble in constant winter, so cold that the people live in caves. The caves are heated from geothermal sources and entire ecosystems thrive underground, based off of chemosynthesis rather than photosynthesis. Millions, if not billions, of people live in a perpetual springtime, seldom coming to the surface. The concepts of day and night have no meaning there and their cities are hives of constant activity.

He spoke of the legendary bubbles that, if they existed at all, were in what Darl called "the interstices between the bubbles," the bits left over between larger bubbles. Bubbles where gods and demons walk among men and women. Places where science becomes magic. Or the Dreamworlds, where you could journey to the netherworld to commune with the dead.

"Balderdash!" yelled Darl.

"Balderdash?" asked Kelly.

"Balderdash. Cow patties! I don't buy it for a moment."

"Darl's a bit of a skeptic," Menlo told them.

"I gathered," said Joni.

"And why ask the dead for advice anyway? They just talk in riddles."

"Thank you, Darl," her partner said.

The trappers told them more about the Ebulli Council, the closest thing there was to a multiverse government. About forty bubbles were full members and another dozen were associate members. The Council, its bureaucracy (an administrative staff of tens of millions), and its security forces (millions more) were housed in a small bubble named Ebullus Lengle. Lengle had been discovered a hundred years before; it had unique properties making it nearly impossible to travel there by accident and the entry codes were a closely guarded secret.

Joni soaked it all in. Even on a boring ride through a pretty barren landscape, she was getting her fill of marvels. Kelly asked lots of technical questions, wondering how it all worked, but would occasionally get very quiet, worried about her parents and her self.

They stopped a couple of times, mostly to walk Bramble, as the wagon was fueled and the larder well-stocked. They stayed the night at a town much larger than Chiliquinn stretching out on both sides of a river. Although they slept in the wagon, they wandered around town a little and ate paella at a tavern on the river's edge. As the girls were drinking lemonade and the trappers were sampling the local brew (of legendary reputation, they declared) and Bramble was sleeping at their feet, Joni asked about the park to which they were heading.

"It's the original Cordelian Shrine," Menlo answered. "Although it's run by carnies now."

"What's a Cordelian shrine?" asked Joni.

"A shrine the Cordelias used!" shouted Menlo. "Yeah, I guess you wouldn't know about them. Do you know about Cordelia? *King Lear?* Shakespeare? What do they teach in these schools nowadays?"

"We read *Macbeth* this year," Kelly answered.

"Don't get me started on that. Birnam Wood, my ass. I could show Shakespeare a forest on the move."

"How is this supposed to help us get home?" Joni asked.

"Or to know if we're being followed?"

"Taking a side trip will put anyone off your trail," Darl said.

"No, it won't," Joni said.

"Well, it might. Besides which, you're stowaways! You don't get a vote. We'll get to Nicus when we get there. We've got a job to do."

"If I may get back to my story…" Menlo said, in mock-anger.

"Fine," Darl answered.

"Thank you," Menlo began again. "The Cordelians were these young women throughout history…Wait, that's no good, let me restart. It used to be that some people could use natural gates to see visions, although no one really knows how. And, over the years, there were many visions involving a young woman who could open up bubbles or bring them crashing down. Actually a whole series of different women. Collectively, they're called the Cordelian Chronicles. Once people figured out there was a connection between these different women an order was set up to protect them. The Order of…I'm blanking on the name."

He looked at Darl.

"The Crescent."

"Thank you. The Crèscenters. But another order was set up to kill her, because it could be equally argued that she would be the doom of us all. So they kept killing her or saving her, time after time. But another one would eventually appear. Sometimes she was a queen or a kingmaker or a war leader. That's all ancient history, however; there's been no verified Cordelia in living memory."

"That we know of," said Darl.

"I suppose," said Menlo.

"What are the chronicles like?" asked Joni.

Menlo clapped his hands together, only too happy to share a story or two. Darl snorted dismissively, obviously too familiar with his storytelling.

"Let's start with the first. If we ignore the various apocrypha, the Cordelian Chronicles are composed of about forty visions and around two dozen enactments of those prophecies… If you've got something to say, say it."

This last remark was directed towards Darl, who was waving her hands dismissively. She turned her gesture into an order for more ale from the waitress and then grinned at her partner, motioning him to continue.

"Anyhow," Menlo began again. "My favorite story is that of Mahdeva, which happened in the ebullus of Mumbarum, where I was born, but I suppose we should start with Cordelia herself. Shakespeare himself got the tale from old legends, of which there are different accounts in a half a dozen ebulli.

"So, several thousand years ago, no one's sure exactly when, this land we're in now was the Kingdom of Blydaid. Ruled over by an old king, named Lear or Llyr in most of the legends, who died and left the kingdom to his youngest daughter, Cordelia. Isn't that a beautiful name?"

"It's lovely," said Joni, who was getting almost as annoyed as Darl with Menlo's storytelling. "Get on with the story."

"Well, her older sisters fought Cordelia for the kingdom. Terrible battles. Betrayals on all sides. They made a wasteland of the kingdom. Eventually, she was defeated, but was able to escape with her father's body. She brought it to what is now the shrine. There she opened a gate between the bubbles and led her own daughters and their followers out of this world. Although since no one knew about the bubbles back then, they thought she was a sorceress."

"Sounds like a sorceress to me," Kelly said.

"Six of one," Menlo said. "And supposedly when she left, she cursed the land and it's been barren ever since."

"Where's the moral in that?" Joni said. "I thought she was the good guy."

"It's history. There doesn't have to be a moral."

"I'm not even sure it's history," Darl said, "the way you tell it."

"I wasn't trying to teach anyone a moral," shouted Menlo. "I merely wanted to tell Joni and Kelly the original Cordelian Chronicle. I'm sorry there's no lion with a thorn in its paw."

Menlo then poured from the pitcher the waitress handed him, and the girls watched the trappers argue each other around in circles. After another ten minutes, an exhausted Joni and Kelly walked with Bramble back to the wagon. They were dead asleep when the trappers crept in a few hours later.

They got a late start the next morning, with Darl grumbling to herself in the front cab and Menlo snoring in the back. After a couple of hours, they turned off the highway, under a large arch proclaiming the "Rathbone Wilderness Park: Land of Miracles" in (unlit) neon lights. The gravel parking lot was empty except for three or four vehicles, one resting on levitation rods like the trappers' wagon and the rest on wheels, including what looked like an old Camaro.

"Let me go find the owner," said Darl, climbing out of the front, while the others got out to stretch their legs and let Bramble run about. "I'll see if the two of you can go see the attractions. This place used to be a must-see attraction."

The land around was dry scrub country, with few bushes and even fewer trees. Bleak and dry. Thirty or so small buildings and booths adjoined the lot and crept up a series of low hills on the far side. All the booths were shuttered, awnings folded over and doors padlocked. One of the doors opened and a man came striding towards them. He shimmied through a turnstile that was currently counting no visitors and approached Darl.

The man was nervous, fidgeting as he spoke and absent-mindedly fingering a long rifle. He handed Darl some papers and drew various notes on them. He started to walk towards a gate at the south end of the lot when Darl stopped him and motioned towards the girls. The man then threw up his hands and gave something else to Darl. Darl then returned to the wagon as the owner yelled, "I'll meet you there!"

Darl handed a brochure to Joni and Kelly.

"Here you go," she said, circling areas on the foldout map. "We're going to set up in these canyons here. What they've got is a loose hartwig. They'll only attack if they're cornered. But, as we're going to corner her, it might get dicey. However, they can't scale the canyon walls, so if you stay in this area, you'll be fine. Lucky for you, the pool is the main attraction of the place. I'm sure Menlo could tell you more about it. Enjoy. We'll find you when we're done."

"What if someone's chasing us and they find us here?" Joni asked.

"Then we'll sic the hartwig on 'em," Darl said. "Just get out of here."

The girls complained, especially Kelly, who was dying to see another monster (monsters were fun if you expected them), but there was no gainsaying Darl. The girls could either do some sightseeing, or stay in the wagon. They gave up the fight, grabbed their jackets, and watched the trappers drive away, off to battle their monster. The girls walked through the turnstiles into the park, Bramble charging in front of them.

The place had all the charm of an abandoned carnival. They stood just within the entrance next to a marble statue of a young woman. They were surrounded by booths advertising knick-knacks and tchotchkes of dubious quality and a variety of fried foods, all served on sticks. Joni meandered about while Kelly examined a large map of the park on a wall. Although they saw no one, speakers overhead belted out music, rock music like they might have heard back home, although nothing they recognized.

"Check this out," Joni said, thumbing through the brochure. "There's more about Cordelia. It even mentions Earth. It says that 'Legends of Cordelia and her father are found in dozens of lands across the ebulli (most famously

in the British Isles of Earth), implying a sizable diaspora.'
What's a diaspora?"

"It's a scattering of people around the world. Like
the Jews. Or the slaves from Africa. Don't you pay any
attention at school?"

"No. You know that. Anyhow," said Joni,
returning to the brochure, "you can see the pool where
they opened the gate here. It says it's never been opened
again, even after they figured out how bubble stuff works.
But all sorts of pilgrims and …seers?"

Joni looked questioningly at Kelly who said,
"fortune tellers."

"Thank you…all sorts of pilgrims and seers have
come here over the centuries and seen lots of visions. Both
of Cordelia and other stuff. Supposedly a bunch of the
visions came true, although others were dead ends. Some
ancient seer even made a famous book called *The Scroll of
the Wastes*. Kinda like Nostradamus, I guess."

"How can you know Nostradamus and not know
what a seer is?" asked Kelly, exasperated.

"I've got other things to worry about."

The girls checked their map. The *tereanan*
(translated as "the daughter's mirror" in the brochure) was
located about half a mile to their east. The map strongly
recommended traveling a three-mile route that wound its
way north before heading south again. The map admitted
to the girls, rather reluctantly, that you could instead hike
straight east, up over a ridge, and down again to the
mirror. It even conceded that this was the way Cordelia
was purported to have gone, as she led her people in
retreat from the war and surveyed her kingdom for the
final time. But the trail was marked with a host of warnings
to keep the young, the old, the infirm, the pregnant, and
the lazy from attempting the steep climb. The girls scoffed
at such counsels and strode purposefully to the trailhead.

The warnings proved legitimate. The trail had at
some time in the past been paved with stones, but was

now mostly decrepit wooden stairs and planks. The path started with a steep staircase (the girls counted 144 steps), before going back and forth up a series of switchbacks. The day was getting hot and there was no shade. Kelly drew some lip balm out of her pocket and smeared it on. Some cables ran straight up the hill to some lights and loudspeakers and they could still hear music playing. The girls hiked on.

After what was probably twenty minutes, but felt longer, Joni, Kelly, and Bramble approached the top, which shimmered hazily in the heat. Joni led the way, with Bramble padding slowly behind, panting heavily. Subconsciously Joni picked up her pace to match the rhythm of music coming out of a nearby speaker. The song sang of shining valleys and of shepherds and soldiers and of fountains in the desert and aspects, bright and fair. As she crested the top, Joni breathed deeply, marveling at the view that stretched for miles in all directions.

The ridge she was on extended about half a mile to her left and right, like a shark's fin coming out of the earth. She could see a road at the bottom of the trail and an oval pond or pool beyond it. The pool marked the beginning of a mountain range, which headed southeast to higher and higher peaks. Large, puffy clouds floated across the sky, intermittently illuminating certain areas; as Joni looked at the pool, it caught a thick shaft of sunlight and sparkled and shimmered like a blazing blue sapphire set in a crown, before darkening again. The pool seemed otherworldly to Joni; no, she was already in another world. The pool seemed worldly and all else was strange. She had to struggle to look away from it.

Further east were many small hills, dotted with Iron Age-style forts and thickets of pines and firs. To her right, several small grassy valleys were visible. As Joni admired the view and replenished her oxygen, Kelly joined her and shouted.

"Look! There's Darl and Menlo!"

Joni followed her pointing finger and saw the wagon parked in a nearby valley. The trappers had evidently gotten right to work, because there were already several large fences set up.

"Did they get all that stuff out of the wagon?" asked Joni, incredulously.

"I guess so," answered Kelly. "Menlo said something about the storage trunk folding 'transpace,' whatever that means. It must be bigger inside than outside."

Joni had no response to that, so after a short rest they started down the other side, Bramble following them grudgingly.

Going down was easier and they were soon at the bottom, where the trail joined up with the dirt road, the one less stubborn people used. A signpost pointed the way to the pool. Stepping on the road, a high, shrill sound came from the direction of the valley where Menlo and Darl were, followed by a few, barely audible shouts.

"Let's go see what they're doing, J."

"I wanna go to the pool."

"C'mon on, Joni. We gotta see what this hartwig looks like."

"We can climb over there after the pool," Joni said firmly. "Sheesh! You and monsters."

The pool kept drawing Joni towards it. She was fascinated with it, mesmerized by it, but Kelly thought she was just being obstinate. Kelly followed her friend for half a minute, at which point another wail from the hartwig floated past them.

"I gotta go check this out, J. I'll catch up with you."

Strange, exotic animals were about the only thing that could make Kelly go off by herself. She was too excited to notice how relieved Joni was to be left on her own. Kelly sprinted towards the green valleys. Bramble stared at Kelly for a bit before trotting up to walk at Joni's

side. The trail they hiked on was just wide enough for the
two of them as it threaded its way through thick bushes.
The path took one final curve and abruptly ended in three
wide marble steps. Joni climbed them to look at the
tableau before them.

The pool was perfectly symmetrical and about 40
yards long. So symmetrical that Joni thought it was
artificial, but an informational plate mounted at the stairs
informed her that it was entirely natural. The longer axis
(or what Kelly could have told her was the "major axis")
pointed directly to the beginning of the mountain range,
where a rock wall faced the pool. Low, grass-covered hills
spread around the pool like two arms embracing the water.
They were just high enough to block out any view of the
world beyond, a standing wave of green with only sky
above.

A waterfall emerged from the rock wall, so
smooth, Joni thought it was glass at first. The water came
out of the rock about twenty yards up, before hitting the
pool's surface with just the slightest of ripples. Joni read
more of the plate, which explained that a natural concave
mirror behind the cascade could project a three-
dimensional image onto the waterfall itself, under the right
conditions. The accompanying figures reminded her too
much of science class. Kelly will be sorry she missed this,
Joni smirked to herself. She started walking again.

A path of white stones half-circled the pool, like a
giant horseshoe, with a low, single chain fence along it to
cordon off the waters. The sky was darkening, as more
clouds filled in the patches of bright, blue sky. Joni
stopped at the point directly opposite the waterfall, where
a sign said, "Please do not cross the chain without
approval." Joni presumed approval and stepped over it
onto a patch of scraggly grass. Bramble leapt over the
chain as well and then stopped, watching her mistress.

Right in front of Joni was a finger of rock, leading
straight into the pool towards the waterfall. The rock was

black like obsidian and just below the surface, which explained why she did not see it from above. She began to walk down it. It was several feet wide, but she took each step slowly and deliberately, as if the stone could suddenly teeter; Bramble walked a step behind. Joni's eyes never looked down, only at the waterfall ahead. She could somewhat make out the curved mirror behind the sheet of water, hollowed out by uncounted eons of erosion. She halted in the exact center of the pool, where the rock's surface rose slightly out of the crystal clear water, a dry islet in the water. She looked down, fingering the crescent necklace Redpoll had given her, and saw that the rock spread out a little in all directions, making a circle. The path ended abruptly; two more steps and she would be bathing. A large, thin fish swam leisurely by just below the surface.

Suddenly, Joni blinked as a bright shaft of sunlight broke its way through the clouds, shining on her, a lone figure on the rock. Joni's gaze returned to the waterfall and her mouth gaped.

Her reflection was projected on the waterfall, almost coming out of it. She looked as solid and real as if Joni had a twin sister standing 20 yards away. Joni stared and moved her hand as if to sweep away the curtain of the waterfall. The ever-falling water, coupled with the shifting clouds (although the sunbeam remained firmly anchored on her the entire time), created shadowy shapes around her mirror image. One of these dark shapes came into focus.

"Dad!"

Joni spun around, but there was no one standing behind her, where she expected to find him. She looked back at the falls.

She saw her reflection still, clear as ever, but, no, it couldn't be her reflection because it was talking to the figure of her dad, arguing with him. Her image remained bright and was wearing the clothes Joni currently had on, even though she recognized the scene as an argument the

two of them had fought months ago, over something so
stupid she couldn't even remember what it was about. She
found she could force her eyes to "look deeper" and then
she could see that Mirror Joni was dressed differently, but
then the overall image dimmed. Joni relaxed and the image
brightened again. A wind blew across the water with a
metallic taste to it, and the scene changed.

Mirror Joni was galloping at the head of a group
of horsemen across grassy plains, although she always
remained at the center of the waterfall. The shadowy riders
appeared Asian and, indeed, the deeper image underlying
Mirror Joni (if she concentrated) was Asian as well. Once
again the scene disappeared, and next up Mirror Joni was
riding a chariot and shaking a spear, with mud-caked
soldiers all around her. She stepped out of the chariot and
was instantly in a dimly lit theater. Thirty people sat at
desks of dark marble, staring at her, as if in judgment. This
briefly became a smoky rock club, with her at the mike,
and then suddenly she was in the cockpit of an old airplane
flying towards a wooden ship, burning at night. Then
Mirror Joni was running along the deck of the ship itself,
fire all around her, casting an orange-yellow glow on her
face.

The "camera" pulled back then and the ship and
the sea turned to ice or to crystal and then disappeared.
The image changed and it was Philadelphia from above,
with some kind of shimmering dome centered over the art
museum. Armed troops were marching around in all
directions. A small explosion lit the waterfall up orange.

In the next image, Mirror Joni shone like a golden
statue. She was in a full suit of armor atop a horse,
galloping with cavalry and foot soldiers in her wake. Mirror
Joni halted, drew her sword, and pointed it forward. Her
followers all rushed by, yelling and waving their weapons,
glowing as if lit by flames. The figure of the mounted girl
was lost in the streaming humanity, a humanity that
continually changed between different costumes and

weapons and races, as if a thousand different battles were being waged across history. Finally a few stragglers limped slowly by, and Mirror Joni was walking out of a sandy gulch into an open desert. There was someone with her, but Current Joni could not see who it was. She wasn't sure how long she watched this scene, but Mirror Joni seemed to be walking for hours or days across shifting sands and giant dunes; the seas of sand were so vast at times as to appear endless, but each detail was still vivid, engrained in Joni's mind. She climbed into canyons and followed dry riverbeds, before coming to an oasis surrounded by cliffs, with a bubbling fountain.

As she neared the oasis, Mirror Joni started running and the sand was concrete and Kelly, Bramble, and Marcus were beside her; Joni realized that she was watching her recent history. The theradons appeared and then the thrashers descended from the sky. Joni was watching from behind her other self and could see Alejandro off in the distance, calling to her. Mirror Joni and Kelly sprinted towards him and jumped through his circle, Alejandro throwing Bramble through a second later. As it closed, Alejandro stood where the gate had been, a determined look on his face—determined, but terrified. A thrasher swooped towards him and he gave a defiant cry, but then ducked as a bright energy beam from the side shot the creature down in front of him.

The scene shifted, but remained centered on Alejandro, now in a dark alleyway. His cry continued but became a lament as he knelt down next to a body lying at his feet. Alejandro turned the body over, and Joni saw that it was her. She was covered in blood and her neck rested at an unnatural angle. Alejandro lifted her up and then collapsed over her, his body convulsing with spasms of grief.

Current Joni wanted to look away, more than anything, but couldn't, even as the scene faded. She was shaking, afraid of what else might appear. Another image gradually formed in the cascade. This time it seemed to be a true mirror image: she saw herself standing there, on her rock, in the middle of the pool. But Mirror Joni was standing in the rain, hair plastered to her face. And slowly, Mirror Joni's clothes transformed from what Current Joni was wearing, to a simple dress, once of good material but now tattered. And this time the two Jonis kept looking at each other. Both were shining as if the sunbeam were still on them, although Joni felt that the vision's storm had spread across to the real waters surrounding her.

Then the vision storm lightened and she saw people around Mirror Joni. Behind her two men carried a thin pine box, about seven feet long with a torn blanket or shawl on its top. Next to her a man held a flag up at an angle, both flag and flag bearer drooping. And behind them were multitude upon multitude of people. Men and women and children. Horses and cattle, dogs and chickens. Tired people, waiting expectantly.

Mirror Joni's face betrayed her concentration. She moved her hand as if to sweep away the curtain of the waterfall. Her eyes lit up and appeared to focus directly on Current Joni's. Mirror Joni moved her hands again in an elaborate movement and chanted something. The water in front of Mirror Joni or maybe in front of Current Joni or maybe between the two of them began to froth and boil. The rock upon which the vision of Joni stood (although who is to say which was vision and which was reality at this point) began to grow. It extended straight out from Mirror Joni in the waterfall until it joined the rock on which Current Joni stood, standing firm and solid but jelly inside. The bridge complete, Mirror Joni lowered her hands and the two men with the box, which Current Joni now realized was a coffin, began to carry it towards her. They were halfway across the bridge when all the multitudes surged forward. Only the two Jonis stayed in place, one oblivious to the flag bearer behind her, the other oblivious to the dog standing sentinel at her side.

The crowd poured forward, but Current Joni did not know if she was the end or the beginning of their journey. And, in the way of dreams, she realized that she was witnessing the passing of tens of thousands, the passing of a people.

Finally, it was just her and Mirror Joni again. The storm, real or imaginary, had ceased and sun warmed the faces of both Jonis. Then Mirror Joni blinked and looked across, and two pairs of eyes locked upon each other. Mirror Joni began to walk towards her twin, arms reaching forward, as if to grasp hands or to embrace. Joni, Current Joni, stretched her hand forward as well and took a step.

Bramble howled. Howled and howled. It woke Joni out of a trance, and she staggered and slipped. She was suddenly up to her waist in water and scrambling back on the rock. She climbed back on to hard ground and spun around. All she saw was a waterfall on a cloudy day.

Bramble stopped howling, but across the valley Joni heard a cry and several explosions. She straightened up and ran back to the dry land, took some breaths, and then hurried off to the source of the sound, back the way Kelly had gone. She darted down the path, head spinning, her mind only slowly returning to the here and now. She jogged along the road, until it began to climb. She slowed down, both from exhaustion and wariness. She cautiously climbed the hill and looked out before her.

The valleys she had seen from the peak opened up towards the horizon. The trappers' wagon was a few hundred yards away, parked on a dirt road, with its back open. Darl was standing on its roof, holding a gun the size of a bazooka. Menlo was running in Joni's general direction, yelling something that was lost in the wind. A couple of tall metal poles stood in the ground, but many more were scattered about the grass.

The hartwig lay on the ground in front of Joni, stretching a good twelve yards. Its body was tortoise shaped, but furry and pulsing with each breath it took. Out of its body, four pairs of legs protruded in four different directions, slightly kicking. Most of the beast was neck, a yard thick, with several tranquilizer darts sticking out of it. Its face was vaguely catlike and full of teeth; instead of ears it had small rounded plates halfway around its head. A low rumble came from the hartwig's mouth or belly, Joni couldn't be sure. It looked dangerous.

And there was Kelly, standing next to the creature's head, scratching it right above its eyes, as it panted heavily. She shouted to Joni.

"Isn't she great?"

CHAPTER EIGHT

I t took a good three hours for Menlo and Darl to lick their wounds, clean up the havoc the hartwig had caused, load the beast into the wagon, and pry the negotiated fee out of the park operator. When they threatened to release the hartwig (and the girls still had no idea how the trappers had stuffed the animal in back of the wagon, even though they had watched them do it), they were finally paid. The afternoon was well along when they rolled out of the parking lot, munching on some sandwiches the park operator had sold them.

The rest of the trip was uneventful, as they bounced down through the foothills and into the plains on the other side. Kelly kept talking and talking about the hartwig and how it just threw Menlo and Darl's fences around like toys and how they eventually captured it and wasn't she beautiful and she seemed to like Kelly before the tranquilizers overpowered her, but she *did not like* Darl and Menlo, no, no, no, not at all. On and on she prattled. She didn't even notice that her best friend wasn't listening and hadn't said much of anything since they parted ways in the park.

Joni, meanwhile, was reliving every moment of the waterfall visions, over and over again. Were any real? Were they all real? Which were long past and which could she prevent? Which ones were her and which ones were someone else? Sometimes she could tell in that dream way that although it was her, it wasn't really her and sometimes she wasn't so sure. She made an executive decision to file it all away and think about it when she had time; she was afraid that if she dwelt on the visions, they would cripple her. She wouldn't even tell Kelly, not yet. Soon, but not now. Instead, Joni looked out the virtual window and watched, silently, as they started to come upon farms and then houses.

They reached the suburbs of Nicus a little before sunset. They pulled into an open lot, near the center district. Darl and Menlo wanted to talk with their contacts and headed off abruptly, before the girls had a chance to ask any questions.

The girls waited for an hour in the wagon. Kelly was done talking about the hartwig, but kept wondering about what other animals might be around. They ate some fruit. They looked through the books, which were mostly manuals of different sorts. They played some music on the wagon's stereo (which Menlo had called a "hi-fi"). They kept themselves entertained for a while, once they realized that they could "replay" what they had seen out the side windows and watched the whole trip backwards at a high speed. They figured out how to view archived trips and watched the wagon attacked by a sea serpent as it traveled over an emerald ocean.

"Enough is enough!" Joni said. "I need some air!"

"Joni! They told us to stay."

"They didn't say how long they'd be gone or anything."

"I'm sure they'll be back soon. It's probably just taking longer to find their contacts. It's a big city."

"Whatever. I've been cooped up in this floating hotel room for two days and I'm going stir crazy. I need some air."

"I don't think we should, Joni."

"We'll just stretch our legs. Who's going to know the difference? Ya coming?"

Kelly didn't want to, but she wanted even less to stay by herself. They dressed in the clothes that Imbrium had given them and slid the door open. They locked the wagon and went off into the town.

Where Chiliquinn had been all wood and dirt, Nicus was stone and gardens. Most of the commercial establishments were closed, as least around the wagon. A few residents sat on their porches, but the girls tried to avoid eye contact, although Bramble was happy to sniff anyone who walked near. After about ten minutes, they reached a central plaza. It was large and narrow and had a wide, dry fountain in its center, with a statue of a winged horse emerging from a stone globe. The far half of the plaza was full of noisy sidewalk cafes and pigeons and street performers and the like. But the near side was what drew their attention.

The surface of the plaza was made of large blocks of granite, in a variety of colors, most with waist-high pedestals adjacent that had computer terminals built in. Many people were bustling about, walking to the different pedestals. And then, as Joni and Kelly watched, a glowing circle appeared in the air above one of the squares and three people stepped into it, the circle closing behind them and they were gone. The girls spun around and it kept happening, not always the same size or color, but pop, pop, pop, people were disappearing all over the plaza, and occasionally appearing. A large building anchored one end, from where many people were streaming in and out. Along the side of the plaza a line of taxis and rickshaws waited to take travelers around the town.

They watched, mesmerized, for a while but then decided they had better head back.

"Okay, if we swing down this street, we should be able to loop back to the wagon," declared Joni, over Kelly's objections.

They tried that. It didn't work. They tried a couple of other streets, but they didn't cut through. Then they decided to go back the way they had come, but somehow that didn't seem to work either. After 45 minutes, they sat on a park bench, Kelly very mad at Joni but not saying anything, Joni a little mad at Kelly for being mad, but also feeling somewhat guilty, and Bramble just generally happy being a dog. Ultimately, they returned to the plaza and retraced every step they had taken and finally, there they stood at the wagon door. They punched in the combination, but it did nothing.

"Maybe they changed the combination when they found we weren't here," said Joni.

"Maybe it's open," said Kelly and slid the door to the left.

They unleashed Bramble and walked in. Nearly everything was just as they had left it. Books were still crammed on the shelves. Video screens were still set up as windows, showing the alley outside the wagon's cabin. Menlo's leather jacket was still tossed over a bunk where he had left it. The only real difference was that someone was sitting at the table with a notebook and a steaming cup of tea.

"Alejandro!" both girls shouted, as Bramble ran to him, tail wagging.

Neither girl was scared. Joni was confused, unsure of herself, remembering how Alejandro held her broken body in the waterfall vision, the way he had sobbed; she didn't know how she felt at seeing him now. Kelly knew how she felt and she felt angry. Since leaping blindly through his gate, she had thought she was scared of Alejandro. Yet here he sat and Kelly was just angry, furiously angry. He sat there so complacently, calmly sipping his tea. Joni was angry too, but she wasn't sure whether she felt closer to him after the visions, or more distant.

"I brought some cheese and crackers," was all he said. "Let me slice you some."

Which he did.

"Where have you been?" yelled Joni.

"Do you have any idea what you put us through?" shouted Kelly. "Throwing us into this crazy bubble, not knowing where we were? Not knowing what a bubble was? We could have been killed. We could have gotten lost in that stupid forest for weeks!"

"All right, I'm sorry, I'm sorry." Alejandro stood up and motioned for them to sit down. "I didn't have a choice. You were being chased by thrashers. Those guys were about to capture you. I had to open a link to this bubble but didn't have enough time to direct it. I've spent the last three days trying to track you down from Chiliquinn."

Joni answered, "Forgive us if we don't feel sorry for you."

"You got out of there all right?"

"No thanks to you."

"What happened next? I heard you went with some trappers, but no one would tell me anything more."

"We met some people who helped us and brought us here." Joni again.

"What people? Who were they?"

"You should know! You're sitting in their wagon!"

"¡Carajo! I did what I could. Once you were gone, someone out in the woods shot down the thrashers and that guy you were with hopped in the SUV and drove off, leaving me to fight off two theradons who were angry and scared and not in the mood to talk it out. And then I finally manage to get to Chiliquinn where I nearly get a knife in the gut from an angry bartender, who seemed to have it out for me as soon as I walked in her door. All I know is you went off with two people in this wagon. I followed but still beat you to Nicus somehow. Who are they?"

Joni and Kelly looked at each other. They either had the least reason or the most reason to distrust Alejandro. Distrust, mistrust, untrust. He had literally sent them spinning out of the only world they had ever known. At the same time, maybe he did save them from the thrashers. And Joni's dad from the future had mentioned him, as if his trust were a given. There was something protective about him, an earnestness, a feeling that he was looking out for them, like he was family.

And besides, Joni thought wryly, he's going to cry when I die. I saw it. So that's something. She decided to answer.

"They're trappers. They catch exotic animals that escape across membranes."

"Well, they're probably not short of work nowadays," answered Alejandro.

Kelly asked, "So was Marcus trying to kidnap us?"

"Was he the guy you were with? I'd say so. How did you meet him?"

Joni ignored his question and looked him straight in the eye. "What are you trying to do? Why were you waiting for us at the airport?"

"Redpoll sent me a message."

"What?" Joni and Kelly shouted.

"I hadn't heard from her in six years and out of the blue she texts me four words, 'Go to the airport.'"

"Why did you have a picture of me dead?" Joni asked.

"You got that picture? You weren't supposed to."

"I guess not. What was it?"

"It wasn't you. Is that what you're worried about? You're not dead."

"Why did you have it? Why are you following us?"

"It's complicated," Alejandro paused. "Real complicated. Long story short, there are people after you, people who killed my sister and my dad. And, well, I'd like to stop them from doing it again."

"Who's after us?" shouted Joni. It was bad enough to be running, but even worse not knowing why.

"A man named Matabbi. He's a thug with delusions of grandeur."

"Keep talking. What's his deal?"

Alejandro said nothing for a minute. He walked to a sink at the side of the wagon and grabbed some more crackers and brought them back to the table. While Joni stared at him, Kelly grabbed a couple of orange sodas from the fridge and handed one to Joni. She cracked it open without looking and they both sat down across from Alejandro.

He started speaking.

"Matabbi began as the duke of a tiny ebullus named Atabban. But that wasn't enough for him; he wants all the ebulli. So he married into the royalty of another bubble, and started buying up land in others: farmland, parking lots, stadiums, everything. Made his money in real estate, but then branched out into portal technology about twenty years ago. He has his own standing army and supplies soldiers and weapons to warlords across a dozen bubbles, but it's never been proven. He's basically a crime boss, with legal and illegal business empires across half the major bubbles and he's hungry for more. He's ruthless and has assassins and goons to do his killing for him. He's also a superstitious cretin, surrounding himself with soothsayers and magi and alchemists. And he believes them all. Which is why he's after you."

"What does all that have to do with me?" asked Joni. "I've never met the guy."

They were interrupted right then, by someone trying the combination on the door. They looked out the virtual window and saw Darl with a hooded man in the alley. He then pulled his hood down and the girls recognized Marcus. They stood up, followed closely by Alejandro. Darl gave up on the lock and tried the handle and the two of them entered. Darl instantly pulled a small pistol from her pocket and Alejandro's hands shot up into the air.

"You!" Marcus shouted. "Who are you?"

"Who are you?" Alejandro shot back. "What do you want with them?"

"Shut up, the two of you," yelled Darl. "You, Alejandro, back up against that wall. You, Marcus, sit there." She pointed to a chair and slid another one towards her with her foot, sitting backwards it. She held her gun loosely but kept her finger on the trigger.

"Right now, isn't this chummy? Kelly, Joni, how did he get here?"

"We went for a walk," answered Joni. "We got lost, and when we got back, he was here in the wagon. Tell her."

"Can I trust her?" asked Alejandro.

"Yeah, you can trust her."

Why does Alejandro trust me so much? thought Joni. Who am I to him?

"I arrived in Chiliquinn a couple of hours after you left," Alejandro said. "I made my way straight to Nicus. To keep them away from him."

He lowered his right arm enough to angrily point at Marcus.

"We'll talk about him in a second," said Darl. "You first. Who are you with? Why did you portal these girls here? Why are you hunting them?"

"I'm not with anyone. I sent them here because this guy had thrashers and they were in danger. I'm trying to help them because Matabbi's after them."

And he glared more at Marcus.

"Matabbi?" Darl looked at Marcus. "Did you know Matabbi was involved?"

Marcus answered, "Not until after Joni and Kelly disappeared."

"What are you talking about?" Joni yelled.

"We've run his credentials," Darl said. "Go ahead, tell them."

Marcus looked at Alejandro's face and at Darl's gun and started talking.

"I'm with the Marganus Corporation…"

"Marganus!" yelled Alejandro. "You guys are worse than Matabbi!"

"Please…," answered Marcus, haughtily. "Marganus is the biggest because they know how to do their job. Don't give me your tired conspiracy theories."

"Marganus is strip-mining rainforests in Kemper, running sweatshops in Cenaux…"

"CAN IT," Darl roared, "let's just say that you are both wrong. Continue, Marcus."

"Hmmph. I'm currently doing an internship in Marganus' Portal Technology Division. My father is their lead scientist on transmembranal physics. When the director asked him, he agreed to send me undercover to investigate your parents' research. Earth's a sealed world, and the Corporation has the contract for the trade rights, you see. So, I was sent, just to get a quick read on what they were doing. But their results were amazing, even with their primitive equipment. I reported on this and was told to continue and watch out if anyone else showed interest. Then, these girls show up, bring me to a barbecue, and before you know it there is a pismire and thrashers attacking and then this guy appears out of nowhere. Anyway, once they were gone, I contacted my superiors, who filled me in and transported me here. It was their best guess as to where the gate sent them."

"And that's all you know?" Darl asked.

"Yes." But everyone in the wagon saw his brief hesitation.

Darl turned to Alejandro.

"I'll ask the question again, why are you hunting them?"

"Matabbi killed my father and my sister six years ago. Part of the Walltown Massacre."

Marcus' eyes widened and Darl whistled through her teeth.

"That was never proved to be Matabbi's handiwork."

"It was to me. I had promised to protect my sister and I left her when she needed me. I've spent most of my time since then learning how to make rips and portals and gathering as much information about him as I can, hoping to be ready next time…if there is a next time."

Just then Menlo burst into the wagon. Everyone (except Bramble) had been so engaged in the conversation that they did not even notice him run up to the wagon. He was breathing hard, but had a gun out in a flash as soon as he saw Alejandro. Darl told him to put it away.

"…I was at the depot when I saw one of Matabbi's old henchmen…I followed him to a bar where he met a bunch of other lowlifes. They were talking a lot about nothing, when the first one says something about 'the girl being seen in the plaza.' I ordered a beer and moved closer. They said that Matabbi had some new hot shot psychic, some woman named D'Vico."

"D'Vico!" Alejandro exclaimed.

"You know her?" asked Darl.

"Not personally, but she's legit. She was a failed Cordelian initiate. She's probably pretty good at predictions. And she might be willing to work for Matabbi."

"We've got to get out of here," Darl jumped up.

"Wait, there's more…he mumbled something about Matabbi himself coming and that he was bringing someone special. I couldn't hear the rest, but they were all leaving to go 'watch the action.'"

There was silence for a few seconds, as tears started welling up in Joni's eyes. All the stress and anxiety of the past couple days was getting to her.

"But why? Why are they hunting me? I never wanted to be the center of attention."

"Oh, bullshit!" Kelly suddenly shouted.

"What?" asked Joni, incredulous.

"You just jump into anything without thinking and drag me with you. Even if it's a flaming circle in the air. You can't stay in the wagon for half an hour. But when things get serious, when people are dying, you just want to go home. You want to protect yourself."

"That's not true," Joni faltered under the unexpected attack. "I mean, don't you want to go home?"

"Of course, I do. But are we going to be safer there? Are our parents going to be safe if people are chasing us?"

"I don't know what I want."

"No you don't. You never do."

"We don't have time for this," said Darl. "We have to get you somewhere safe and then work on getting you home from there."

The girls glared at each other, as Alejandro spoke, "Any ideas?"

"Lengle," Darl answered. "They'll be safe there and we can figure out what we do next."

"Impossible!" Alejandro said. "It would take days to process us, even with documentation. These two have no identification and would have to apply for asylum. We don't have time. There's no way to get to Lengle."

"We won't have to go through the official portal," Menlo said.

"What do you mean?" Alejandro said. "How else do we get there?"

"We have special codes," Darl said. "Sends us straight to our kennels. Although if we miss by a few meters we might end up in a gargnoth cage."

"Cool," Kelly said quietly.

Menlo ran ahead to reserve their gates, while Darl got the wagon ready. After about ten minutes, she got it moving and they drove off to the plaza. Joni and Kelly, now not speaking to each other, sat at opposite ends of the wagon and noticed little of what was happening (Bramble stayed in the middle, not taking sides). Alejandro kept looking furtively out the windows, which made the girls nervous, although everything seemed normal. Normal as it could seem, that is.

Darl parked the wagon and they got out, the two girls and Alejandro wearing their backpacks and Marcus swinging his satchel over his shoulder. The cafes were still busy, and a few dozen people loitered on the benches scattered about. Several teenagers sat on the fountain's rim, laughing loudly. After a few minutes Menlo came out from the central terminal and sprinted over to them.

"Marcus, you're set for Portal 10," Menlo scanned the colored squares and pointed next to them, "right here. Plug this in to the accessory port to mask your destination. Get in touch with your contacts, get the lowdown. Send a message to us in Lengle. Everyone else, this way."

Menlo led them over to Portal 11, while Marcus went over to a nearby concrete pedestal; Kelly walked with him, curious as to how it worked. Marcus pressed a button on the pedestal and a metal panel slid down, revealing a miniature keyboard. He inserted Menlo's device, and started punching buttons. Kelly looked back and saw that Menlo was doing the same on the neighboring console. Darl stood guard between them, pivoting around to spy on every corner of the plaza. Still, it was Alejandro who first saw the wiry figure break from the shadows of a building on the southern side and come sprinting towards them.

"Redpoll!" he shouted.

Joni spun around and echoed his cry, running with him towards Redpoll, Bramble following at her mistress' heels.

Kelly probably would have yelled as well, but too many things happened at once. First of all, Marcus got his gate up and running. A large, pulsing green circle appeared, thicker and more stable than the one Alejandro had created at the airport. At the same time, Bramble gave a bark, louder than any Joni had ever heard her give, and everyone ducked down, just as bullets started flying over their heads. Four men had appeared from a flashing portal on the far corner. The two in front were large, well over six feet tall, and alike enough to be brothers, if not twins. Each had beady eyes, a square face, wide shoulders, dark jackets, and even sported similar scars, albeit on opposite cheeks. They also both carried black guns, short and stout, which they were firing. They guarded the two men walking behind them.

The first of these had short blond hair, thinning in places, and his clothes looked expensive, but comfortable. He smiled greedily as he walked towards them, almost licking his lips in anticipation. Joni heard Alejandro mutter "Matabbi," and she stared at her unknown adversary for the first time. Next to him marched a thin, intense-looking man, with red hair over a heart-shaped face. His eyes appeared black to her at first, but seemed to change as he drew closer. He wore a thin backpack, stretching four feet down over his back, and a red coat. He had a few different types of guns at his waist but nothing in his hands.

Joni froze, shuddering. Where had she seen that man before? She had watched him kill someone, saw him slash a girl's throat. But not in the waterfall. She remembered. Her dad's lab in Philadelphia, when she had gotten his machine working. It all came back to her, the blowing sand, the girl's face, and the blood pouring down her neck. And the look in his eyes, like he fed on death. He still had it. And he was looking at her.

"Look out," Alejandro yelled, and tackled her to the ground behind some concrete pedestals near where Redpoll now crouched. Darl was returning fire, while Menlo and Marcus worked feverishly on the gates they were opening. Kelly took cover next to Marcus. Matabbi's guards must have had armor under their clothes, although one of them was down now, clutching his leg. However, the two in the rear kept walking forward. Every bullet flying towards them seemed to stop suddenly, with a momentary flash, and fall to the ground.

Menlo activated his gate, a crimson arch with tendrils of yellow light hanging down from it. He hollered for Alejandro and the girls to get over here, NOW. At that moment a shot from the remaining guard hit Marcus' console and arcs of electricity shot forth from it. A storm seemed to rage in the portal around Marcus and Kelly, who was lying on the ground with her hands over her neck. Marcus' gate wobbled and then began to rotate like a spinning coin. As it did so, it seized Marcus and started whipping him around, sucking him inside its vortex. Kelly's screams could hardly be heard over all the noise, as the gate balanced above her for a moment at a slight angle. Then it fell flat to the ground over her, disappeared with a green flash, and Marcus and Kelly were gone. Joni screamed and started towards where they had been, but Redpoll, crouched on one knee beside her, held her down.

Redpoll then took a small gun from her side, its barrel barely longer than her finger. She squeezed the trigger and, almost instantaneously, a red blaze exploded around the guard and the heart-shaped face man. The second henchman was thrown a good thirty feet and stayed down. Matabbi and his companion were unharmed but their force field was knocked out. Matabbi's companion took a step in front of him, unnecessary as Matabbi cowered behind a stone pedestal. Matabbi quickly pressed something in his pocket and a dark green, crackling energy sphere appeared. He stepped into it and made his escape.

"Coward," Alejandro grunted.

Darl switched guns, as her first was out of ammo. Suddenly another portal opened up and ten more Matabbi henchmen emerged, rolling a machine, thin and dark, about ten yards long, with two men in seats on the back. It had a long metal half pipe, a bit like a long scoop, extended towards Joni and her companions.

Menlo, his fingers still on the console, yelled at Darl to ditch the wagon and jump through their portal, which she did. Alejandro rushed up. Menlo shouted at him.

"Go through! I'm doing all I can to keep it stable. The locking mechanism's been shot through. I need to run it dynamically!"

"You get through!" Alejandro shouted back. "You can lock it from that side. And if I get stuck, I'll use my last emergency gate."

Menlo nodded and Alejandro took over. Just then another explosion hit the wagon and they were all blown down for a moment.

"Oh, crap," Menlo said.

The wagon began shaking and there was a blinding silver flash. The back doors were blown out and walls and fences and boxes seemed to be unfolding themselves out of the rear. Suddenly, with a high-pitched cry, the hartwig sprung out, towering over everyone. Her four pairs of legs emerged from her body and she scuttled over to the fountain. She bent down to drink, was startled by more shots, and then tore the statue out with her mouth, flinging it across the plaza. Matabbi's men swung their new machine towards the hartwig as she approached them. A greenish light seemed to flow down the chute of the machine and then shot out towards the creature. A bright fog developed for a moment and then it disappeared and so did the hartwig, the fountain, and any anything else nearby, including a big chunk of the pavement.

The machine itself was knocked over by the recoil, trapping the gunners beneath. With no one at the controls, the green light shot out again, sending giant sparks in all directions. Small patches of the fog began to appear around the plaza and the surrounding buildings. Most of Matabbi's soldiers were running away.

Menlo yelled something to Alejandro that Joni could not hear and then leapt through the circle and disappeared. Alejandro howled at Joni to hurry, as more shots were fired.

Joni crouched 20 yards away, hugging Bramble close to her behind a pile of masonry. Redpoll was striding forward, cutting off the angles between the redheaded stranger and Joni and Alejandro. She reached behind her and drew a four-foot sword from out of thin air, as far as Joni could tell. The blade was flat, perhaps two inches thick at the hilt and as the setting sun lit it up it seemed on fire. Redpoll's assailant peppered her with two guns now, bullets from the right, light flashes from the left. Redpoll swung the sword as she slowly advanced. She could not have deflected everything, but all the bullets seem to be pulled toward the blade before falling to the ground. The redhead smiled. In a single motion, his guns were at his side and he swung a blade of his own.

Redpoll yelled without moving her head, "Get her out of here, Alejandro! They'll have reinforcements!"

"We need you! I can't save her without you!" he shrieked back.

"It wasn't your fault, Alejandro! We were betrayed. She needs you now. Joni! Go with him."

He steeled himself and looked at Joni, "Joni, we have to leave."

"We can't leave Redpoll alone," she said. "They'll kill her!"

"She'll be fine once you're gone. I don't know how long I can keep the gate going. Run!"

Joni grimaced, grabbed Bramble by the collar, and bolted as fast as she could towards the shimmering arch. Just then, a group of Matabbi's men who had regrouped started firing from the far side of the plaza. Faster than the eye could see, Redpoll had a new weapon in one hand which she fired, creating a sonic explosion that blasted the group back a dozen feet. But not in time to stop one of their shots from hitting Alejandro's console. Joni was in the air, mid-leap, when the gate disappeared with a fizzle.

She landed with a thud on the pavement and looked back at Alejandro.

"Damn it," he said.

He then took something from his pocket and tossed it into the air. It quickly formed a thin and smaller circle floating a few feet above the pavement.

"Jump through!"

"Where does it go?"

"Outta here! Just go!"

With more troops entering the plaza on either side, Joni looked back at the pavement where her friend had been moments before. Was she gone? Was she dead? What happened when a gate went haywire? Eyes filling with tears, Joni plucked up her courage as Alejandro picked up Bramble and they all jumped through. The gate snapped shut behind them.

CHAPTER NINE

K elly screamed as she fell.
And fell.
And fell.

Her screaming faltered, however, as she realized that she was falling upwards, which surprised her, to say the least. She was then further surprised when she realized she wasn't falling at all. She opened her eyes to discover she was lying on a floor. It seemed to be made of steel plates, bolted together and painted over, mostly white with a red trim. She got up on her elbows and looked around; the room was small, maybe eight by ten feet, with no windows and a single incandescent light hanging from the ceiling. It was as bare as a prison cell. Marcus was behind her, slowly getting up and rubbing his right cheek. She scrambled up herself.

"Marcus! Are you all right?"

"Yes," he answered groggily. "I was thrown against the wall, as the gate went berserk. Is my cheek bleeding?"

"No, but it's swelling up some. We should get some ice for it."

"I'll be fine. I just need to shake it out."

As her head cleared, all her memories came flooding back.

"Marcus! Where are we? What happened? Are the others okay?"

"I don't know," Marcus said, massaging his whole head now. "They're probably fine. Menlo had his gate going and chances are they're all off to their little hidden fortress."

Marcus' mood was unlikely to improve until his head felt better. And maybe not then, Kelly thought.

"No. You don't know anything. You saw Matabbi's men. They were outnumbered on all sides. They could be dead."

Marcus sighed and slid back a panel that Kelly had not noticed before. It contained a console similar to the one in Nicus. He fiddled with it for a minute. Frowning, he turned some dials and punched in a few more numbers. He then closed the panel, after removing a foldout map.

"The transit channel is totally wrecked. It would take hours to reconnect it. By which time, they are either away or they are captured. I don't think they'd kill them."

"But how do you know?"

Marcus looked at her for a moment.

"I don't. But Darl and Menlo are exceptional. And my superiors knew about Redpoll. They said if I was in danger and she was there, make sure I was on her side. Either way, our best plan is the original one. I meet my contacts here, find out as much as I can, talk to my supervisors, and then get back to Darl and Menlo in Lengle."

"But where *are* we? What happens to *me?*"

"It's your lucky day. We ended up right where I was aiming for: Earth."

"Earth? My Earth? I'm home?"

"Yes, your Earth. We are still a few thousand kilometers away from Philadelphia, but we are at least in the right country. If it's safe, you might be able to go back."

"I can't go home! I mean, I have to go home, but I need to find Joni first. Joni's always the one with the plan!" Kelly shook her head and looked around at their narrow confines. "But where are we? What kind of place is this?"

"This terminal is constructed of an exotic material that facilitates the transfer between different ebulli. Earth doesn't have many convenient nexuses, so this was set up, last century sometime. It's a way station. It's an easy place for travelers to enter and leave Earth."

"Will they know we're here then?"

"The transfer itself is undetectable. They might be monitoring the gate from the outside, but these way stations are considered neutral ground; otherwise all inter-ebulli travel and trade would fall apart. They are run by a special society of, well… you would probably call them monks. We're totally safe. Probably."

"But where is it? How is it hidden?"

"That's the beauty of it…or it was. When they built it, it was encased in an actual railroad car. The train car existed on its own, for all to see, but the builders wrapped a spatial conundrum inside. That's where they placed this way station. That way all the travelers could be explained away. At least that was the idea."

"What went wrong?"

"Well, no one takes trains anymore. The railroad car that contained the way station was sold."

"What is it now?"

"It's a chili dog stand."

"What?"

"A chili dog stand. In Hollywood. On the Sunset Strip. The best chili dogs around. Come on, I'll show you."

And with that, he opened a door and Kelly was overwhelmed with a whole new array of sights, sounds, and smells. She picked up the knapsack Imbrium had given her from where it had fallen and walked through the opening.

She was indeed at one end of what was apparently once a working train car. Along the left side were a series of tables, set up with rickety wooden chairs with red, upholstered backs. These tables sat at large windows (that is to say, train windows), with a view of a wooden deck and a busy street. On the right side was a line of people, a line that Kelly and Marcus had inadvertently joined. No one seemed to notice them. Further along there were menus on the wall, listing chili dogs and burgers, fries, shakes, as well as typical California options, involving pitas and sprouts. The order counter was about 20 feet long, and backed into an adjoining kitchen car. One woman was taking orders and shouting them out to three cooks behind her. As they walked by, Marcus tried to give a secret signal to a man making chili fries, but had to awkwardly do it a few times before the man noticed Marcus and waved back. Marcus and Kelly walked out the door at the far end.

They sat down at one of the wooden picnic tables, under a large umbrella cooling it from the noontime heat (or what passes for heat on a 72 degree southern California day). Marcus unfolded the map and began giving orders,

"I'm going off for about an hour, maybe an hour and a half. You will stay here."

Kelly stared at him. "What? No. No. You're crazy. I'm going with you."

"Why? Why would you want to?"

"It's either that or sit her by myself, at a hot dog stand."

"Look, it's a beautiful day. Just hang out here and stay inconspicuous."

"Whatever, Marcus. I'm not staying."

"I'm not arguing with you, Kelly."

"Good, because I don't intend to argue with someone working out battle strategies on a 'Map to the Homes of the Stars.'"

Marcus read the title on the map and sighed, "All right, what could possibly happen to you on the Sunset Strip? Just don't go too far. Or try to contact anyone. Or do…anything. Here's a mobile phone. It's base eight, so you won't be able to figure out how to use it, but if you press that and that, you can reach me in an emergency. Just find a store or something and be back here in an hour."

They walked to the sidewalk. The restaurant was on the north side of Sunset Boulevard, the uphill side. Kelly and Marcus looked across to where the streets

dropped away block by block for half a mile into a hazy
Los Angeles. The street bent around the restaurant, as it
wound its way west through Beverly Hills, Bel Air,
Westwood, and all the way to the Pacific Ocean. I see
hawks in L.A., Kelly marveled, as she watched them ride
the thermals, a bit of California country in the heart of
Hollywood. Waiting for Marcus on the boulevard was a
rideshare car, which apparently was thing where he came
from too. He got in, told Kelly to be careful, and held on
tight as the car made a u-turn amidst much honking,
before heading east.

  Kelly watched him leave and then walked off in
the other direction. She opened her bag and took out her
cell phone. Who did he think he was, giving her orders? It
was dead, probably from taking too many pictures.
Angrily, she shoved the phone back in her knapsack and
examined Marcus' phone. The screen was mostly English,
but wrong in various ways. Stranger still was the keypad,
which only got as high as the number "7." She stared at it
for a few seconds.

  "Base eight," she muttered to herself and kept
muttering as she did various calculations in her head. She
tried some numbers. Nothing happened, so she grunted
and tried it again, with slight variations. Still nothing. Tried
again and it rang.

  "Hello?"

  "Mom! Is that you?"

  "Kelly! How is your trip? Are you and Joni having
fun? You're doing what Anita says, aren't you?"

  "Uh, of course. We're having a great time. How
are you? Is everyone okay?"

  "Of course we are, honey. Is something wrong?
You sound worried."

  "No, I'm just tired. Redpoll had us working a lot
today."

  "I'm sure she did. Listen, honey, I've got to run.
Petra's waiting for me at the lab. But if you have reception

later give me a call. Is this Anita's phone? It didn't recognize the number."

"Yeah. She let me borrow it. Uh, mom? Just be careful, okay? I love you."

"Ha ha, I love you, too, sweetheart. It sounds like you need some rest. I'll tell Joni's parents you're all having a great time…honey? Are you there?"

"Yeah, I'm sorry. Tell them that. I…I've got to run. Goodbye, mom."

"Goodbye, Kelly."

Kelly closed the phone and sat on a bench for a minute, pulse racing. Her parents were safe. Whatever had happened hadn't happened yet. Or something like that. And maybe it never would. She jumped up and set off with a bounce in her step for the first time in days. She walked down the boulevard, breathing easier and enjoying herself a little.

She started passing people.

People on roller blades and roller skates. Every cliché in the book, walking down the shiny boulevard. Peroxide blondes with high heels and tiny dogs. Nightclub owners with open collars and gold chains dangling on their chests. Suburban mothers, clutching shopping bags and thousand-dollar purses. Stick-thin men and women, with hollow eyes gazing out into nothing. A team of bicyclists speeding by, sporting AIDS-benefit jerseys. Joggers in matching track suits. Joggers with tight shorts and no shirts. Joggers in khaki pants. Whites and blacks. African-Americans. Caribbean-Canadians. Mexicans. Koreans. Armenians. Thais. Women with full burkas. Punk kids trying to look tough. Punk kids being tough. Tourists. A juggler on a unicycle, with a boom box, playing hip hop. Gun-nut liberals. Pro-choice Republicans. A Marilyn Monroe impersonator running in high heels. A man in a ragged suit and tie screaming about hell and damnation. A long-haired man with a guitar singing about his hour of darkness. Dozens of men and women with dozens of different plastic surgeries. Skateboarders, ages twelve to fifty. Straights and gays. Trans and cis. Men and women and kids shopping and chatting and sipping frozen coffee drinks.

"I'm further from Philadelphia now than I was in Nicus."

She walked on, less worried about sticking out. She did some window shopping and wandered inside a few stores. Prices ranged from suspiciously cheap to stratospheric, often on the same shelf. She got a small, retro handbag ($12, marked down from $35) at a hipster boutique and a sparkling water from a corner convenience store.

She was heading back when she passed a small sidewalk stand, where a man was hawking a bunch of different merchandise. She stopped, eyeing a pair of sunglasses, that had just the right level of Hollywood chic, fabulous but not absurd. She grabbed them and looked at the price, so low they must be either fake or stolen; being a good Philly girl, either was fine with her, so she put them on and admired herself in a small mirror. She was amazed by her own awesomeness. She planned to stun Joni with them, already assuming Joni would make it out okay. Cuz she had to.

"I'll take these," she said, looking closer at the man behind the table.

He was dressed in a suit and tie and his pale skin was accentuated by his thin black beard. He looked more like a banker than a sidewalk vendor. But it was his eyes that arrested her attention; they were green, green like emeralds. Kelly wanted to study them longer, to see if they were just contact lenses, but looked away as he spoke.

"Of course, miss. I do believe they were made for you. Can I interest you in anything else? Sea glass earrings? A hat?"

She could not identify his accent, although it sounded familiar.

"No thank you, just the glasses."

"Perhaps a cd? I have a fine selection of hip hop, rock, dubstep, jazz…"

Kelly was shaking her head no—until he mentioned jazz. Her dad's birthday was coming up soon and he loved jazz (and was the only person she knew who still bought cds). Kelly suddenly desperately wanted to buy him a birthday present, as if to prove to herself that she would be going home soon. She looked over the small and eclectic collection.

"Do you have any John Coltrane?"

He handed her a cd instantly, as if it were already in his hand. The cover was a black & white photo of John Coltrane sitting on a couch with a large saxophone next to him.

"You're in luck. I just happen to have a recording from 1960. It's from a pristine reel-to-reel tape and is the best show he ever did."

Kelly was skeptical, but the price was good, so she bought it, and continued walking. Halfway down the block, she looked back and saw that the man had left, leaving his table unmanned. I do not understand this town, she thought.

She was still thinking that while sitting at a bench back outside the chili dog "train" when Marcus arrived. She smiled up at him, broadly, like California girls do.

"Did you find out anything?" she asked.

He smiled grimly back at her, his face even more pale compared to the tanned hides all around them.

"Not much. There are rumors flying about in the ex-eb community, but no one seems to know what is really happening. State College is abuzz, still trying to figure out the pismire, which they never found."

Kelly's smile faded and her face betrayed her anxiety, as he sat down.

"What's the ex-eb community?"

"Ex-ebulli. Ex-patriot. Citizens from other bubbles, either on business or living here."

"Oh. What do we do now?"

"We go to my world. It's not safe to leave you until we know they aren't hunting for you."

"Why would they be hunting for me? That's what I don't get. What's going on? I mean, why go to all this trouble, just because our parents are developing technology that you all seem to have anyway. Why chase us from world to world?"

"Well, …it's complicated," Marcus looked a little confused and a little less pompous; Kelly thought it made him look nicer. "Very complicated. First of all, your parents' technology goes along entirely different lines than anything ever done. The Marganus Corporation is concerned with any new types of trans-bubble technologies, particularly on Earth."

"Why Earth?" she asked.

"Well…I'm not sure how to say this. Marganus has the rights to Earth."

"What? You own the Earth?"

"No, no, no. But since your world lacks accredited trade channels, Marganus purchased the official advocate proxy. So until you get official status, they have the rights to purchase goods or technology off you. It's all overseen by the Ebulli Council. They can't just steal stuff."

Kelly gave a look at Marcus.

"And you trust these guys? This corporation of yours?"

He had a slight pause before answering, "I always have."

"That's not an answer. At least not a very good one."

"I mean, they're a business. And they're working with the Council. So it's not like they can hurt anyone."

"That's sweet, Marcus. But still not reassuring."

"I trust them enough, okay?"

"Just keep your eyes open. Get on with your story."

"I'll try," Marcus continued, a little flushed, "The crux of the matter is that Marganus, and the Council I might add, monitor any activities that might lead to trans-ebulli contact. So I was sent here."

"But what has that to do with us? With Joni and me? Are we just going to be used as ransom to these people, to this Matabbi guy?"

"No…no. All right. Hmm. Here's the part I don't really understand. I only learned about it the night of the pismire," he paused. "But first, I need to load the coordinates for our next hop. And food. We should get some food. Let's go order."

And with that, Kelly followed a visibly flustered Marcus inside the train car. She puzzled over his behavior. Marcus continually tried to act like he knew more than he did, but here he was clearly…nervous? No, that wasn't the word. It wasn't just that he didn't know what to say; Kelly felt that he didn't want to say it. They rushed by the line of people (ordering a late lunch? an early dinner? a chili dog tea?). Marcus pushed on a wall and somehow swung it around like a revolving door. Kelly followed quickly on his heels, but no one else seemed surprised. Maybe this was normal in Los Angeles.

Back in the small room where they had originally materialized, Marcus played with the panel in the wall. He punched in several numbers, cross-checking them with a handheld computer. Satisfied, he stowed the map away and they dropped their gear and went back into the restaurant proper.

"All right," he said. "It will take a few minutes for that to run. You want a chili dog?"

"I thought you were a vegetarian."

"Well, usually. But these are really good chili dogs."

"I'll just get a cheeseburger. With ketchup and mustard."

Marcus snorted, but said nothing as they waited in line. Once he got to the front, he ordered the cheeseburger for Kelly, a chili dog for himself (with cheese, onions, and tomato) and an order of chili cheese fries to share. The woman behind the counter grabbed a cardboard tray, wrote the order on it, pushed it along, and took Marcus' money. Marcus grabbed some napkins and then took Kelly outside. They had the deck to themselves. Kelly refused to let him dodge the question anymore. Without Joni around, Kelly was forcing herself to take charge more.

"Why are they chasing Joni? It is Joni, right? I'm just an incendiary? Incendiary, is that the word? Accessory? I'm just baggage?"

Marcus paused before answering.

"Yeah, I guess it's Joni. Let me try to explain. But I don't know the whole story and I'm sure I'll get it wrong. But when I contacted my superiors after you disappeared, they told me some of it."

Just then their number was called and Marcus went into the restaurant. He returned a minute later with a tray of food, including drinks, napkins, and plastic forks. He sat back down and started talking while Kelly unwrapped her food.

"You see, I was sent to your world to get some idea of what your parents, yours and Joni's were doing. I got here and it all seemed so primitive at first, but some of their work, especially your mother's mathematics, Kelly, it just…well, it was startling. I was sent to spy, but ended up just being awestruck. I've always been a bit of a math geek, I guess."

Marcus looked thoughtful and perhaps even humble, for the first time since Kelly met him at the university; it made her like him a lot more. He looked at Kelly and then across the boulevard, down over West Hollywood, perhaps imagining he could see the Pacific

Ocean off in the distance. He unwrapped his chili dog and took a bite. And spat it out.

"There's no snap to it," he said. "It's raw."

"What do you mean it's raw?" Kelly looked at her burger. "So's mine. What kind of place is this?"

"Something's wrong. The train's been compromised. We've got to get out of here."

They jumped up, girl and boy, knocking over their benches. Two sedans suddenly screeched to a stop in front of the restaurant; honks filled the air as other drivers veered their way around the two cars. Three men jumped out of one car and a woman from the other. Marcus and Kelly sprinted across the deck and up the stairs to the train, ducking low as a hail of bullets shredded the picnic table umbrellas. The gunfire paused, followed by a cry for them to stop, but they kept right on going. A second barrage of fire followed, but this time white flashes exploded around them. Some hit the railing, sending shards of wood flying in all directions, but, although the train was lit up like a Christmas tree, it remained unscratched. As Kelly opened the door, Marcus went crashing down, clutching his side. Kelly pulled him inside and shut the door behind them.

"Are you okay?" she yelled, watching blood spreading across his shirt on his left side.

"Yeah," he grunted. "Let's get to the control room."

Kelly thrust her shoulder under his right arm and dragged him to his feet. With the noise getting louder outside, she looked around as they staggered to the opposite end of the car.

"What happened?" Kelly yelled. "We didn't hear anything."

A dozen customers or so lay collapsed at their tables or on the floor, their rising chests the only evidence of life within. They half-galloped past the kitchen and reached the end of the car. Kelly began to step over two more bodies, but gave a little screech. These two were clearly dead, lying in a puddle of blood. One was the cook Marcus had nodded to earlier. She recognized him by his face; his body was torn apart. Kelly wrenched her eyes away and started to scratch at the door.

"How do I open it?"

"Here…" Marcus whispered, pressing a knob. The door swung around, just as the far door opened. A man cautiously looked through it, anticipating gunfire, but charged forward as he took in the situation. Kelly pulled Marcus into the room and slammed the door, looking around desperately for a way to lock it. Marcus, meanwhile, lurched over to the buzzing panel and pressed a button. This time, the room seemed to expand all around Kelly to an almost infinite size, before it all went black again.

CHAPTER TEN

J oni, Alejandro, and Bramble materialized cleanly through Alejandro's emergency gate out of Nicus. Cleanly, but unfortunately on the side of a small hill where they tumbled to the bottom. Bramble got to her feet, followed more slowly by the two humans. Joni blinked a few times and looked around, feeling lightheaded. There was a green roof overhead, which turned out to be a canopy of apple trees. The wood was not quite ordered enough to be an orchard, but at the same time a bit too ordered to be natural. If it had been an orchard once, it was no longer one now, as up high the branches invaded each other's space and down below the undergrowth was thick and there were plenty of fallen apples.

"Smell those trees," Joni said, dazed. She picked an apple and gave it to Bramble. "There is something so ...so primal about it. Where are we?"

"I don't know," Alejandro replied.

"You don't know?" Her serenity vanished.

"No. I, uh… didn't have time to set any coordinates. And all the interference in Nicus would play havoc with a cheap one like this."

He looked at the device still in his hand and shook it a little.

"Can they follow us?" Joni asked.

"Maybe. They would have to have sensors in both the coming and going ebulli. That might be possible in Nicus, but I don't know about here."

"Well, let's use your little machine and get out of here and find everyone else."

"We can't. I don't have the codes for Lengle. They're top secret, like, the most top secret. I've been trying to bribe or trick my way in for years. The official portals to Lengle are all encrypted in such a way that if someone tries to hack into them, they just change."

"So, how did Darl and Menlo know it?"

"They've got better connections than I do. But Marcus wasn't surprised that Darl and Menlo knew the codes, which makes me think he's just an idiot. And that's the only reason I'm trusting him."

"You know, Alejandro, when I first met Marcus I though he was one of those nerdy science guys who can't talk to his lab partner."

"Yeah?"

"But you're one of those guys who sets up tables to yell about workers' rights and locally-sourced produce, aren't you?"

"Uh, it's happened."

"I was just checking. If you can't take us to Lengle, just take us somewhere. Somewhere that will help us get home and find Kelly. It's my fault she's wherever she is."

"I can't do that either. It's burned out. It's a one-time device, only good in an emergency. More than I could afford, but still the cheapest one you can get. And besides, gates don't work like that. We have to know where we are, whether this is a one-way nexus, how high the bubble is, all sorts of things."

"So how do we find out where we are?"

"With this," he said, taking something out of his jacket. "Since the physical laws can change in each Ebullus, this machine has distinct sensors to give us a rough reading anywhere."

The contraption was glossy black and about four by five inches, with rounded corners. It had four distinct panels and three different display screens. Alejandro tried the first three panels one after the other with no luck. He then withdrew a lever from the side of the device and pumped it, while fingering the last panel. Again, nothing. Finally, he flipped it over, slid the back cover off and pulled out a spiral-bound book. He began to flip through it.

"A book?" Joni asked. "You have a book?"

"Yes," said Alejandro. "Books work anywhere."

He continued to leaf through it for a few seconds before he burst out laughing.

"You're getting hysterical," Joni said, beginning to chuckle.

They laughed for a minute before quieting down.

"We're not even in here," he said. "According to this our closest match is an all-ice bubble. Probably means they can't trace us, at least."

He kept up a serious expression for a few more seconds before they both broke out laughing again. This went on for another minute or two, as they sat down on old stone wall. Joni's laughs got louder and louder until her whole body was shaking and Alejandro realized she was crying. He stood up and walked over to her, unsure of what to do. He pulled back his hand a couple times, before sitting next to her.

"I just don't know what's going on," sniffed Joni. "I don't know where I am or where my family is, or Kelly, or if she's safe. Or why people are chasing me. Why are people chasing me?"

Alejandro handed her a clean towel from his pack as her sobs subsided and began to talk. He spoke quietly at first, almost in a whisper, and Joni listened, staring at the blades of grass between her feet.

"It's nothing you did, Joni. It's not your fault. Or your mom or dad or anyone. You know how sometimes you can be in the wrong place at the wrong time? Well, you look like the wrong person at the wrong time. The ebulli are a bit like reflections of one another, a little. The major ebulli all have a lot in common. Your world and mine, for instance, are the same shape. All the continents where they should be. And the lines of cultural history have connected a lot. As you get further away the bubbles are more and more different and the smaller ones the most different of all.

"And, to a lesser extent, people can get reflected, too. Not everyone, but some individuals have doppelgangers, doubles in different bubbles or in different times, that they have some connection with. They are not necessarily twins, but they share a bond. It is extremely rare, probably one in millions."

"And I have a double? Is it like reincarnation?" Joni asked, raising her head a little.

"It's not reincarnation, because they can be at the same time. But yeah, you've had many doubles. I'm not sure how to explain this, it's a little unbelievable…"

Joni smiled.

"It's all unbelievable. I can't remember the last time I believed anything. Just tell me."

"Well," Alejandro said, "some of the rips – that's a natural gate – well, the rips can also act a bit like crystal balls, letting you see across a membrane into the past or future of another bubble. It's what your parents are trying to do with their machines, although they don't know that. Only certain people can see these visions, people with what's called talent or sight. And the talent's very rare. And hard to control."

"Can visions be wrong?" asked Joni, anxiously, still thinking about what she had seen at Cordelia's pool.

"Often. Maybe most of the time, or at least they are misleading and difficult to interpret. But of course, no one talks about those. Ever since people have been sharing their visions, certain ones have taken on the status of prophecy. Particularly this one series of visions. They generally deal with war, revolution, invasions, things like that. But the one thing they have in common is that a young woman is seen in all of them. Not always the same woman, although sometimes they are, or at least doubles."

"Cordelias," Joni muttered, starting to put the pieces together.

"You've heard this?"

"Not really. Menlo talked about it, that's all. Go on."

"Okay," Alejandro continued. "The belief is that this Cordelian figure can open or close bubbles, even seal them. Sometimes the visions show the woman leading the revolution, or whatever it is, and sometimes she's just in the thick of things.

"Long story short, these visions have been happening for thousands of years and some of them started coming true. The problem is that you don't know how often they are self-fulfilling prophecies. In certain bubbles, a king would never start a war until he had a Cordelia look-alike to parade in front of the troops. But whether that makes them real is debatable. And maybe it doesn't matter. Most people now think this is all just ancient history. But Matabbi cares. The story is that when he was young his father brought him to a famous oracle who showed him two visions, one where he became the most powerful man across the ebulli and one where he would lose all that he loved. The oracle declared that each was equally true and equally false.

"His father was angered by the reading and had the oracle executed, but since that day Matabbi's been gathering every fortune teller and two-bit psychic he could find. And now it sounds like he's got D'Vico, who's the real deal. She must have been the one who said you were coming to Nicus."

"What about the Créscenters?" Joni asked.

"Did the trappers tell you about them?"

"A little," said Joni.

"The Order of the Crescent is a society pledged to protect these Cordelians. It's an old chivalric order, like 700 or 800 years old. Redpoll's a Créscenter. I'm sure she got away," Alejandro added, seeing the concern in Joni's face. "She's the best."

"This is probably an obvious question, but I take it I am a Cordelia, a Cordelian?"

"Well, they think you are, which comes to the same thing."

Joni and Alejandro were quiet beneath the apple trees for a minute.

"I don't know," Joni spoke up, "but it's a little less terrifying knowing what's happening."

"Really?"

"Yeah, I think so. Maybe not. It's not like I know what to do now, but it makes me think there must be something to do. It makes me feel like I'm in the middle of a story and it's always at this part in a story that the hero thinks that being in a story isn't all it's cracked up to be. But it's so peaceful here. Like we wandered into someone else's story."

Alejandro smiled at her. Bramble snoozed at her feet.

Suddenly something flew over their heads with a shrill "wheeeeeeeeeezzzz" and exploded, showering them with dirt and rocks. They threw themselves to the ground, except for Bramble who jumped up and started barking. They raised their heads in time to see another explosion, a little further off. Thirty or so men and women were charging towards them through the underbrush, about half carrying brown sacks over their shoulders. Some wore green or brown tunics with knee length leggings, while a few had blue jeans on and dark sunglasses. They were pale-skinned and most had long, dark hair, although straw-colored heads were sprinkled throughout. The majority carried swords or long daggers at their sides and many carried bows and quivers. Four of them had rifles over their shoulders. All seemed to be running for their lives.

As they came upon Joni and company, a few slowed down, yelling something like "Arissith! Arissith!" One young man towards the rear, Joni's age or maybe a year or two older, dark-haired with a sliver of beard on his chin, ran to them. He repeated the cry and then yelled,

"Get up! Get up! We must escape these woods! Malfi! Help me with these refugees!"

Another young man of the same age, evidently Malfi, ran back to help. He had a shock of yellow hair and wild eyes. He was taller than his companion and easily pulled Alejandro to his feet. Joni rose on her own.

Suddenly a woman, sporting a rifle and a modern military unifom, jumped behind the first man. As she swung her gun towards him, Joni darted forward and sent a flying kick to her knee, crumpling her to the ground. Alejandro grabbed her gun and whacked her in the head with its butt end, knocking her out.

"Brithwine! Behind you! Use the shield!"

The dark-haired man whipped around and brandished a small shield that Joni had not seen before. She recognized it as a buckler thanks to Redpoll's odd weaponry obsession. It was a foot and a half across, with a red cross on a brown background and a green jewel at each corner. Brithwine knelt down and raised it front of him. There was more noise and an explosion sent debris flying everywhere, except where the shield somehow deflected it, protecting them all. The clearing filled with smoke, as the strangers fled with Joni and Alejandro away from the action.

Joni and the others caught up with the company in a minute or so. Blond Malfi sprinted on to the forefront of the group, while Brithwine stayed at the rear. The ground steepened and the trees changed to pines and firs. After a few minutes the crowd swerved to the left. They seemed to be heading towards a small canyon, but when Joni looked away for a moment, they had all disappeared. Then Malfi stepped out of nowhere into the middle of the canyon's opening and waved them on. They ran past him and suddenly found all the company, sitting on rocks, or lying on the ground. Most were panting for breath and all were quiet. Joni collapsed, as black-haired Brithwine motioned to a few men and then went back to stand by Malfi.

Malfi was making slow gestures with his hands and murmuring softly. Joni realized that the land beyond the canyon's mouth was hazy, as if there were a pane of dirty glass in the way. The general shapes of the trees could be seen through it, but the details were murky and no sound came through. A minute later, about 50 yards away, they saw a large something, then a half a dozen large somethings. They walked in a herky-jerky motion, on two legs, with giant feet. They were over ten feet tall with large round bodies and seemed to have trouble navigating around the trees. Several strode into a sunlit clearing and Joni realized that they were machines. Just then, one of them went berserk, firing flashes of light into the ground near it and then spinning around and tumbling down. Two people crawled out from the wreckage. They were luckier than the machine next to them, which was going up in flames as the berserk machine blasted it. Men and women started jumping out of the other machines, trying to extinguish the fire.

"Jedder, come and watch with us," Brithwine yelled to an older, battle-scarred man who was lecturing a group on the side. "They still have no control over their machines. Yonder one lying on the ground shot up the flaming one and look how they run! They may yet do our work for us."

"Perhaps, Brith," Jedder said. "Still I mark more how their weaponry has advanced in recent months. The fact that they have grown mobile does not bode well for us."

"Ah, Jedder," Brith laughed, "and to think you were the hopeful optimist I once squired to."

"Optimism is not a stratagem, my lord. We were lucky to get all our people back."

"Too true, alas, too true," answered Brith, before turning to face Joni and Alejandro. "And we increased our company by two, two and a hound. Let us get some answers from our new guests."

The two men walked to where Joni and Alejandro sat on the ground. Joni pulled her knees to her chest and scooted next to Alejandro. All smiles had vanished from the faces of the men, whom Joni now comprehended might be more captors than rescuers. Looking around, she saw five archers casually standing in a semicircle behind them with bows drawn. Alejandro, evidently having understood this already, looked determinedly into the face of Brith, his hand next to the rifle he had confiscated, but not touching it.

"Now, young sir and young lady," Brith spoke with an air of command for one so youthful himself, "what causes your trespass into my earldom? I thought you were mine own refugees, when we first came upon you, fleeing the yoke of the oppressors below, but I observe you speak only Ebullic. And indeed, looking well upon you I feel certain that I have not seen you before. I would not soon forget such a lovely damsel. What be your names?"

Joni's face reddened at the compliment, while Alejandro bristled and said, "What is your right to hold us?"

Brith stared into Alejandro's eyes and made the slightest of movements with his right hand. Suddenly an arrow was quivering in the earth in front of Alejandro, from the bow of a nearby archer. He pulled his hand away from the gun and into his lap.

"My right lies in the ground at your feet. Or sufficient right. Be thankful my bowmen and women do not miss their mark. What be your names?"

"Please ignore my friend," Joni spoke, a little quietly at first, but more confidently as she went on. "He's a bit of an ass. My name is Joni Margulis and I come from the Earth bubble, although I just learned about bubbles a few days ago."

"Earth! Really! That's stupendous."

"Yes, thank you. I guess. Say hello, Alejandro."

Alejandro changed his tune, with the arrow still quivering at his feet.

"I am Alejandro Escovar, originally from Ebullus Garstin. Joni and I arrived by chance through an emergency gate, right before you rescued us. For that, our thanks. I extend my apologies for any offense I may have committed, but we have been shot at, chased, and clawed by man, woman, and beast across more bubbles than I can count. So I must ask again by where your authority lies?"

"Ha!" Brith laughed. "A man after my own heart and indeed, my subjects and I find ourselves more often the prey than the predator, is that not so, men?"

Brith cheered with his followers and then continued, "My right does indeed extend beyond this circle, despite the fact I have but seventeen summers to my name. I stand before you Theopolis Brithwine Urthinus Wulfstyn. I am Brithwine the Bear to my enemies and Brith to my companions. It is my singular honor to be the youngest son of the 63rd Earl of Avalon. And unless he returns to us in the body, I stand here before you the rightful liege of this land. My power may not presently be that of my ancestors, but, by my troth, it shall be so again!"

More cheers from the crowd.

"But that day is, methinks, not today and we must be gone from here anon. So tell me truly, what brings you here and what be your connection to those," here he shifted languages, "those *horningsons* in yon valley?"

"Please…sir," Joni spoke hesitatingly, fingering the amulet hanging from her neck and trying to remember how Redpoll had said to use it as a means of escape, "I'm just trying to get home. Some people seem to think I'm someone I'm not and they're trying to kill me and my family and we don't know how we got here or where here is. Or who the horning sons are."

"Yes," Alejandro added. "Where are we? It seems that you are familiar with the ebulli. Which bubble is this?"

"Avalon, my brother! Did I not tell you?"

"You said Avalon is the name of the land, but what ebullus is it within?"

"Avalon is the ebullus itself! A fortnight gallop in any direction will bring you home again. We were a hidden bubble till twenty years ago and remain mostly so today, but I think, by the damsel's expression, that she has heard of us."

"Maybe," Joni answered, trying to figure out if "damsel" was sexist, but deciding she could let it slide. "But I thought it was all myth and stories, Merlin and Knights of the Round Table and all that stuff."

"And so it was to my people when my forebears first came into this land and established the earldom. They believed themselves transported to some legendary realm found in their island's tales. They soon learned their mistake, but the name remained. You can hear the full story at a later time; now we must be off, if Malfi is ready. Malfi! I forgot to congratulate you! This barrier of yours is the strongest, clearest, and fastest of any you have erected so far. Not one of our enemies had the slightest inkling of our hidden perch! A grand hurrah for Malfi!"

Joni thought that this group was awfully fond of cheering, but she joined in as Malfi made a little bow, his mop of yellow hair falling over his face. With the attackers gone, everyone started to get up and the newcomers were glad to see the archers putting their bows away after a look from Brith. He shouted orders to the band,

"Jedder, you lead the front with Gothric and Olyfson scouting the flanks. Malfi, you take the rear and do your best to mask our trail. And you, Lady Margulis…"

"Joni, please."

"Joni. You and your companion will walk with me and regale me with tales of your Earth. I desire to hear all its history and legends."

"That might take a while."

"We march until evenfall," Brith replied and then yelled something in the native tongue. They all strode through the barrier, which melted away at a word from Malfi.

For the next couple of hours Joni tramped through the forest, up gentle hills and down into small vales and then out again. The company crossed many streams and snaked through dense woods. They moved in haste, but with discipline. There was little conversation, but what there was, was light and friendly. Brith marched with Joni, pointing out native flora and fauna, and explaining how his mother's granduncle traded riddles with the black raven of Holcomb on that peak and how his grandfather twelve generations back outwitted the truculent hag of Fawnskin in that cave, and so on. But mostly he asked her about Earth, wanting to know about the land and the smells, about the people and their songs, about everything. Joni soon found herself chatting away, as if she had known him all her life. Brith politely included Alejandro in the conversation, but Alejandro was preoccupied. He kept fiddling with his sensor apparatus, hoping to get it to work and, when that failed, he looked through his guidebook to find any hints about Avalon, but all in vain.

Eventually they reached a gap between two hills. To Joni it looked much the same as the dozens of others hills they had crossed, but the entire throng halted and waited for Brith. He strode forward and, walking straight ahead, disappeared. Jedder and others followed. Malfi, with an impish look on his face, walked over to Joni and Alejandro and waved them on. Bramble sniffed at the invisible barrier, but let Joni pull her through.

The valley suddenly laid out before them was flat and wide, with a series of rocky cliffs on their left, lit orange by the soon-to-be-setting sun. The land was open before reaching thick woods on the far side. What commanded their attention most, however, was all the activity. Blacksmiths beat on anvils, farmers tilled fields, archers shot at targets, warriors sparred, and children frolicked. Hammers rang and wheels creaked and villagers shouted out to one another. Several people ran up, asking news from Brith; he clasped their hands and shoulders, said a few words, and sent them on their way smiling. He motioned to Joni and Alejandro to come with him and they did so, accompanied by Malfi and Bramble.

The four of them walked towards the center of the settlement, where the thickest clusters of tents were to be found. Along the way, Brith stopped and spoke to many individuals working at their tasks, giving them words of encouragement. Most of Brith's companions carried their sacks into a large wooden building, one of the few permanent structures in the valley. Brith kept walking however, and in a few minutes they entered a large pavilion, built on a solid wooden skeleton with canvas sides and top. Over it all, a pennant waved in the breeze, displaying a blue serpent dragon on a tan background.

"Some victuals for our guests," Brith shouted to a boy and girl of eight or so who had jumped up from a table as he entered. "Tell the kitchen to prepare food and drink for four and a bone for their hound. Wait, wait, go fetch Sweeney first and tell him we have fellow travelers whom he will deem most remarkable. And make it food for five then."

"If it pleases you, sir," said the girl, with a long dark braid down her back, "the good Sweeney has gone exploring and will not return until after midnight."

"Well, keep it at four then."

The children ran off through a slit in the curtains and Brith offered wooden chairs to his guests. Malfi went to a large desk that dominated the left side of the room, withdrawing a leather-bound book. He took out a quill and an inkwell and began writing. Servants soon came back with three trays of food, loaves of bread which steamed as they were broken apart, meat still attached to bones (which Joni found stringy but Bramble found heavenly), apples with cheese, and a rich stew. All was devoured hungrily. As they ate, several officers, men and women, came in to make reports about the day's proceedings and the status of the camp. The last to come in was Jedder. He gave a tally of the small arms they had confiscated in that day's raid. But he was mostly concerned with intelligence his agents had gathered about a new weapon their enemies were testing on the tournament grounds.

"That is, if it is a weapon," Jedder said. "My men report that all the top officers have been summoned to a demonstration of some sort tomorrow afternoon. Plus more transported from off-world. They rounded up a bunch of refugees to clean up the arena and a few of our agents snuck in. They report a large device has been set up in the arena but couldn't make hide nor hair of it."

"What of the royal viewing box?" Brith asked.

Jedder glanced at Joni and Alejandro before answering that the box was unharmed. With no further questions he saluted and left. Those remaining finished their meal.

"I am most regretful that Sweeney is absent," said Brith when their plates had been taken away. "It would have been most instructive. Especially for him, I have no doubt. But we will save that discussion for tomorrow."

"Is Sweeney one of your captains?" asked Joni.

"Ha!" laughed Brith, joined by Malfi. "No, if that were true we would be in much more dire straits than we are now. Sweeney is a …what is the word he uses Malfi?"

"An anthropologist," answered Malfi. "He claims to study humans and their condition."

"An anthropologist?" asked Joni. "But who…is he from…?"

"Is he from Avalon, dear sister? No, no. He arrived with the accursed invaders at a time when too many of us welcomed them with open arms. Even I was dazzled by their wonders. But Sweeney was always pure at heart, so we let him stay. It was he who first recounted to me tales of your Earth, although he is not from there. He will have questions of you, I am sure."

"I am sure he will…sir," Alejandro was unsure of how to address the man before him who was his age, but also the ruling monarch of this valley, if nothing else.

"Call me Brith," he answered. "At least in the present company. I was not born to leadership. Upon a time I had four older brothers, all anxious to succeed my father and each one cut down in his prime. But even my father paid little heed to court decorum. Outside of this room, 'sir' will do fine, at least until our land is free again and I have earned a regal coronation."

"Thank you, Brith," Alejandro continued. "Please call me Alejandro. As she told you, Joni has just learned recently of the existence of the ebulli. Like most Earthers, that information was hidden from her. But I have journeyed to many bubbles and have never heard of Avalon. Nor can I find any mention of it."

Alejandro tapped the book that he had been examining.

"Ah, yes, we are a dirty little secret, I have no doubt," answered Brith. "I will tell you the story, though it be so full of gloom and despair, that it may have you in tears by its end. That is, it would, if Malfi were singing it to you. Malfi! Have you spun the tale into song form yet?"

Malfi, who had finished his writing, looked at his lord.

"I am working on it, Brith, in the few precious moments I am allowed. Little of it is in Ebullic in any regard."

"A pity. My poor discourse will have to suffice. Where to begin? Over a thousand years ago, our ancestors, both Malfi's and mine (although through numerous cross-marriages they are indeed one and the same), fought a great and glorious battle."

"If you're going to go all the way back to the beginning," interjected Malfi, "I do have a song for that."

"I know you do, my comrade, and you shall most definitely divert us with it, but tomorrow, tomorrow…Long ago, there was a great battle in an ebullus far, far away. And, depending upon the parentage of the storyteller, one side chased the other, or perhaps both sides were fleeing or all were lost, but the end result of their travels and their travails was that they fell through a portal into this ebullus and established our beloved land. They found it pleasant to the eye and nose, and receptive to the hoe and plough. In addition, they discovered it still contained remnants of what might be called the magic, something that I am led to believe had been lost in their previous homeland. Over time, adventures were had and great heroes were made and we persevered and thrived. In each generation, the tradition was that one member of the ruling family would seek a journey outside what we now term the ebullus, searching for a portal, often with the help of a sorcerer."

"Sorcerer? Joni asked.

"I think that 'sorcerer' does not translate well," Malfi responded. "Scholar might be the better word."

"Scholar then. A scholar who does magic, which is how 'sorcerer' was defined to me, but as it pleases you. Malfi here," Brith said in an aside, "is studying to become such a scholar; he would have long ago ascended to the rank of journeyman, or beyond, if all the masters had not been slain or captured. To continue my chronicle, most of my ancestors' journeys never left the earldom, which was held as no dishonor. Of those that did depart, few returned, hence our partiality to large families. Although my father was the eldest child, he claimed the right to go and none would gainsay him, or so I am told, for this all occurred prior to my birth. Twenty years ago, on the thousandth anniversary of our founding, he departed amid many tears from his mother and sisters and wife, but all needlessly, for he was back within the year. He returned with treasures the likes of which we had never seen. He told tales the likes of which we had never heard. And he brought people back with him, as strange and diverse as his tales.

"My father had great plans for Avalon and few questioned why. We would open trade routes to other ebulli. We would get education and medicine and all the best the multiverse had to offer. We would learn the tongue of the greater worlds. The songsmiths will sing it that the old Earl, my grandfather, was hesitant, but my father built up support amongst our people, meaning nothing but good. When the fever came upon my grandfather, and the new medicines availed him not, my father ascended the throne. Unknown to all, he had built strong ties with an ally, an outsider, like yourselves, but who was an earl himself in his home ebullus. With no one to stop him, my father opened the gates widely and a rush of outsiders entered. We knew prosperity and advancement and soon Ebullic was spoken at the court. My own cradle language was not of my land, a fact that has haunted me since. No offense meant."

"None taken," answered Alejandro. "I'm only a generation or two from the same."

"Although all these persons originally came with the earl's blessing," Brith went on, "soon it transpired that some outsiders did as they were wont to do, regardless of our customs. Having no great knowledge or understanding, our people were easily swayed or overwhelmed by the outsiders. There were several instances that led to rumblings among the folk of Avalon and it came to a head when a young Avalonian man was slain by a high-ranking outsider. The vile slayer posited a claim of self-defense, which was contradicted by all witnesses. Yet with no trial or even an official pardon, the murderer was whisked back to his home world. There were protests and rioting. The outsiders brought forth their own forces to quell them and more of us were killed. You can probably deduce the rest of the story. More soldiers entered and before we knew it, we had an occupying force on our hands. My father led a group to their headquarters, armed, but under a flag of peace. Eyewitnesses say they were slaughtered to a man, with not even their bodies returned."

"That's horrible," said Joni.

"It has been a terrible weight," Brith said sadly. "They commenced giving commands to my people, sometimes reducing them to mere slaves. Many loyal resistors fled to the hills and I have a few thousand under me here."

"It is horrible," Alejandro spoke. "But I don't understand exactly why they should do it. Do you have great wealth or resources?"

"None!" shouted Brith, jumping up and pacing around the room. "Our greatest resource is our people and our strength is our warriors, which they need ten times our number to defeat. 'I am not scared by the paucity of our numbers, nor frightened by the masses of mine enemy,' as one of our earliest chronicles states. Am I translating that right, Malfi?"

"Close enough, but as I remember that battle didn't work out particularly well for your ancestors."

"Pah! Is it not said that we will ultimately triumph over all our enemies and win back what was ours?"

"It will be so," smiled Malfi.

"But why do they continue this occupation?" asked Alejandro. "What do they have to gain from it?"

"It is a question we often ponder ourselves," Brith said, reseating himself and taking a sip of wine, "because clearly they do not have the bloodlust, or take any honor in battle. Fourteen months ago they brought in an entire division of troops, for training purposes. For training! Their weapons barely work here. They have tried scores of different arsenals, with only a few having any measure of success. And those we have stolen for our own use. Goodman Sweeney says that Avalonian alchemy helped them devise better gates years ago and now he postulates that they hope to use the eccentricities of our bubble to make a universal weapon that will strike terror across all the ebulli."

"But they discharged some type of energy weapon in the forest," Alejandro said, "with a good amount of destruction, even if they suffered the brunt of it."

"Yes, it worries me, as does the report of Jedder's brave spies. The outworlders improve by the day. 'Twas good that I had the buckler with me this afternoon."

"What's a buckler?" asked Alejandro.

"Why this, good sir. It has been a protection against all their devilry, so far."

He showed them a leather bracelet on his wrist. With a sudden movement of his arm, the small round shield he had used earlier suddenly appeared out of thin air. Both Joni and Alejandro eyes widened at this display and they examined the buckler.

"That's it!" shouted Malfi.

"What is, friend?" asked Brith, amused by his outburst.

"I have been wracking my brain," Malfi said, "trying to determine what the maiden Joni reminded me of. The legend of the buckler!"

"And what part does it remind you of? Please, please don't sing the whole thing."

Malfi smirked at Brith before speaking.

"When your ancestor, the first earl was forging it and he saw the girl reflected in its surface. Let me see…I would translate it along the lines of 'the damsel of beauty ravished/with eyes of amber burnt/and hair of summer night/beholding aspects, fair and bright' and something about her stare transfixing men."

"'Beauty ravished'?" Alejandro started laughing.

"Alejandro!" yelled an offended Joni. " Knock it off!"

"I'm sorry, I really am," Alejandro said. "I just…never mind. What is that from?"

"It is the story of how the buckler was made," answered Malfi, "and of the sword that once went with it, now lost to the ages. After the first earl retrieved the sword from the lake, old Draco instructed him in the making of the shield. The earl then saw the vision of a girl reflected in its freshly burnished surface. Draco told him that a day would come when a descendent of his would suffer the greatest need of the buckler, whilst the land underwent its darkest hour. And then he would abandon it and give it away to the girl. The story was a favorite of mine as a child and I often drew scenes from it, some of which resembled Joni."

"Who was Draco?" asked Joni.

"A dragon my ancestor found waiting for him," said Brith. "He and the scaled worm fought a great battle. He is the symbol of my house. To conclude my tale: our enemy practices and trains daily in what had been the center of the earldom. Tens of thousands strong. After the initial invasion they have not killed many, but they have imprisoned countless of my people, enslaved thousands, and kidnapped our few scholars, outside of the last apprentice, Malfi here. My people survive as best we can, sometimes raiding for weapons like today, more often just raiding for food. Too seldom raiding to rescue my beleaguered subjects."

"And you say your father was originally friends with these people?" asked Joni. "Who are they?"

"My complaint is not with the people; the soldiers are merely pawns. I would just as soon blame the steel of

their weapons. The true enemy, the one who once posed
as my father's comrade, his name is Matabbi, curse him
forever."

CHAPTER ELEVEN

Kelly found the transport easier this time. She was trembling, but that had nothing to do with transferring to her third world in three hours. She opened her eyes and found herself sitting on a raised platform at the end of a long, dimly lit room, full of several desks, a few threadbare couches, and a lot of dust. Marcus was slumped against a wall to her left. He pushed himself up some and threw a series of switches.

The light, which had been flickering, dimmed for a moment and then came back on steady and soft. It emanated from a strip along the top of the gray walls.

"They should not be able to…to follow us. The transfer…" he took a few breaths and then continued, "is undetectable. But they may guess where we were going."

He sat back down and ran his hand through his hair, smearing a little blood across his forehead.

"How are you?" Kelly asked.

"Not too bad." (Although he looked bad, Kelly thought). He peeled back his bloodstained shirt, contorting his body to look at it. A chunk of wood protruded from his side, above his hip. "Looks like the bullet missed me but a piece of wood ricocheted into my side."

He removed some splinters but left the large piece alone. He coughed a little, which racked his body with pain, and then asked Kelly, "Is there anything…we can use to stop the bleeding?"

Kelly slid open a drawer in a desk near her, but found only papers, maps, and other odds and ends. She went over to her pack and rifled through her clothes. She pulled out a long-sleeved cotton shirt, white with a strip of black flowered design on the front. When she had packed it into her bag just a few days before, it was one of her favorite shirts. Now she just thought it would make a good bandage.

"This do?"

He nodded and she helped him up onto a couch. So this is why Redpoll taught us first aid, she thought. She cut the shirt up, using scissors from the drawer, and then used the sleeves to tie it around his chest. It probably would not ease the pain much, Kelly thought, but hopefully it would reduce the bleeding. The whole room smelled like blood to her. Marcus slowly leaned over to a computer on the desk and started typing. After a minute, he punched the keyboard angrily.

"The communication system's down! I can't contact my headquarters."

"Where are we? This place looks abandoned."

"It is. Probably an old commercial transport gate. I tried to portal straight to headquarters, but they change their location code regularly. This place must be on automatic relay for emergencies."

Marcus swung back to the couch. Too fast, and he had another coughing fit, followed by some dry heaving. The sweat trickled down his forehead, pasting his hair to his face. When he recovered, he looked in the drawer and withdrew a map. Kelly looked over his shoulder at it; it was more origami than a city map. It seemed to contain many distinct maps, or different views of a few, all folded around each other.

"We are here," Marcus pointed at a spot. "And have to get here." Another spot.

"We've got to get you to a hospital, Marcus."

"No. There is an infirmary at headquarters…and besides, all the hospitals in this quadrant shut down long ago. We've dropped into an area called Old Brunswick. A lot of gang activity. None of the locals will help us. We've got to get out."

Marcus was having more difficulty speaking. He kept squinting, as if he was having trouble focusing. Kelly

looked around the room. It stretched about twenty feet
side-to-side and maybe three times as long. There were
storefront windows on the far side, with a security sheet
protecting them that let some daylight through. Kelly slunk
over to them and was able to unlock them. She looked
back at her injured comrade.

"I'm going to check out the neighborhood," she
said.

"You can't...We should go together." Marcus
attempted to stand but fell back down again.

"Yeah, I think it's up to me now." Kelly suddenly
looked anxious, "Will I blend in? Do they speak English?"

"You should blend in fine. And your accent's not
bad. Just..."

He trailed off and Kelly looked at him for a
moment.

"Okay, hold tight."

Kelly scrunched up her shoulders and gave a little
shudder, as she turned the door and then, ducking under a
drooping sign, stepped out. She stood staring a moment,
mouth agape, and then scooted right back to Marcus.

"We're underground!" she yelled.

Marcus opened his eyes and sat up a bit.

"Uh, yes. Esculenta is an underground city. Well,
some of it is domed. The surface is unlivable."

"Give me that map," Kelly angrily said, striding
over to pick it up off Marcus' lap. "...Okay, now this
makes more sense. These are showing different levels.
We've got to get one, two...six levels up, as well as to the
center of town? Any chance I can just call a taxi? I didn't
think so. Okay, I'm taking the map with me. Hold tight."

This time, Kelly was prepared for what she saw.
The street itself was natural enough. Weird, but not too
weird. As different from Philadelphia as Tokyo would be.
Clearly it was a rundown area, but several businesses were
open and there were people on the street (some of whom
glanced at her as she walked out, but quickly turned away

and shuffled along). But about three stories above her there was a ceiling. Some buildings went right into it, while others had rooftops of their own below the ceiling. The ceiling was gray, with a textured finish. There were lights recessed within it, which made a passable daylight, if you did not look up.

Kelly tried to be as inconspicuous as possible as she studied the map and began walking. The light gave it the feeling of a cloudy afternoon day, with rain threatening. None of the buildings had awnings, so she had difficulty sticking to the shadows. In fact, there really were few shadows to speak of, which made it all look a bit two-dimensional, like she was walking in a rather drab comic book.

Kelly didn't know what she was looking for, but knew she better find it quickly. So she hurried along, block after block. She began seeing stores and take-out joints and the sidewalks got busier. In some blocks the overhead lights were fewer or even off altogether; she couldn't figure out if this was intentional, if perhaps nightfall was planned block by block. She briefly entered one of these dark areas, but found it unsettling and stayed in what she thought of as the afternoon and dusk zones.

After a minute or two, she came upon a small "outdoor" market. There were thirty or forty booths, selling vegetables, snacks, clothes, and other sundries. She slunk against a nearby wall and surveyed the area. Sitting on top of the wall next to her was a cat. Well, it obviously wasn't a cat because it was a sleek seventy pounds and its face was more pointed and its claws were bigger and it wore a small pouch on its chest on a leather cord. And a dozen other things. But it had a cat-like appearance and maybe she was worried about Bramble and wished she could ask somebody for help. But she couldn't. So she spoke to the cat,

"Hello, kitty. What do you think I should do?"

"I think you should stop calling me 'Kitty.'"

Kelly jumped back, but recovered quickly (this is not the weirdest thing that's happened to me lately, she thought).

"You can talk?"

The creature looked at her with the utmost disdain and said, "That question I am not going to answer. In regards to your original query, I would need to know more about your current situation and the options available to you."

"Are you from here? This bubble?"

The creature sighed, "We might as well talk about me. It is certain to be a more interesting conversation. No. I am not from this ebullus. I am a traveler. As you clearly are as well, since you did not know that. Although why anyone would wish to travel to this forsaken little world, I do not have the faintest notion."

"Then why did you come here?"

"I was stricken by a moment of unbridled optimism regarding the potentiality of the universe. I determined that my spiritual growth could thrive better *sans* internal bias and so I left my progression up to the winds of chance. I assure you, such optimism has not entered my heart since."

"What do you mean 'progression'? Can you travel? Do you have a way to get out of here?"

"Not a way that you would wish to try."

"But I need help! My friend is injured and we need to get to…" Kelly didn't want to say too much, "center city. And we just dropped into this bubble and I don't know anyone or anything. And I desperately need some kind of transport."

"It's all right, my dear. Calm down. Take a breath. I apologize for my brusqueness. Yes, I can travel but it would not be appropriate for you."

"Why not? I've been thrown through so many holes and vortexes and gates and rips that I don't know if I'm upside down or right side up or what."

"I travel by dying."

"Huh?" Kelly's tears got distracted on the way out of her eyes.

"My species travels by dying. Up to eight times. When we shuffle off our mortal coils, we can then transverse the bubbles, if our will is strong enough."

"Oh."

"Oh, indeed. My name would be unpronounceable by human vocal cords, but you may call me Darius."

"My name's Kelly Grebe."

"Hello, Miss Kelly Grebe. Now, for your own safety and security, I suggest you stand behind this wall for the next few minutes. There is about to be an attack on the market, most likely with a considerable amount of gunfire. I would hate for an errant projectile to hit you and precipitate your own progression from this bubble and, indeed, all corporeal bubbles."

"How do you know there's going to be an attack?"

"I am acutely aware of my vicinity. I observe more than I am observed."

"Did you tell the police?"

"In a manner of speaking. They will arrive soon after it commences, or at least a robotic drone will. But they require an actual crime before undertaking any action. Speaking of which, since your arrival in this bubble was not, shall we say, documented, I assume you have not been chipped?"

Darius' neck (which was also longer than a cat's) stretched to look at Kelly as he said this.

"No, I don't think so. I mean, we just arrived like a half an hour ago."

"Excellent, then you will be safe from the police. The robotic drones will ignore you."

"What?"

"Hush, girl! The game's afoot!"

Kelly squatted down behind the wall, just as two cars came speeding around the corner. They slammed on their brakes, one right in front of Darius' wall, and three men jumped out of each. Momentarily looking away from the new intruders, Kelly realized that Darius had disappeared. But then, once she realized that and began to look for him, she spied the creature again, albeit in a hazy way that she could not quite focus on. The six men in the street brought out their guns and most of the onlookers fled into shops or around corners. The vendors at the booths all ducked down, except for one stall right on the market's corner. A big, burly man inside slapped something and a metal barrier came crashing down in front of the booth. Four of the men began firing at it, while one gunman on each side started to circle towards it. A small metal tube protruded from a thin slot in the barricade and began firing back. The attackers jumped behind garbage cans and cars and anything else they found. Just then, sirens starting going off in all directions. Kelly covered her ears with her hands.

"Now watch," said Darius.

About 50 yards away, over the far end of the market, a ceiling panel opened and a glossy black, slightly flattened sphere about two feet across came out. Within seconds it flew in front of Kelly and then the gunmen all fell to the ground and lay motionless. Peeking around the wall, Kelly could see that the few remaining bystanders were also on the ground.

"What happened?"

"The police drone activated the paralysis circuit in the chips of everyone in the vicinity. You and I are immune, Miss Kelly Grebe. But now you have to get out of here. A foot patrol will be here soon and they will most definitely have questions for you. Go!"

Kelly nodded and began to sprint back the way she had come, but Darius yelled,

"Stop! Miss Kelly Grebe, why do you run?"

Kelly skidded to a stop, "You told me to run! What do you want me to do?"

"Did you not say you wanted transport? There is a car right in front of us. And I noticed that the slack-jawed driver left the keys in the ignition."

"What?"

"Can you drive, Miss Kelly Grebe?"

"Maybe, probably." Kelly stared at the car.

"Then good luck and happy travels." And then Darius leaped off his perch and somehow Kelly never saw him land.

Two minutes later, Kelly burst through the door, overjoyed to see Marcus still somewhat alert. She ran to him and helped him to his feet.

"Come on! We've got to get out of here!"

"Did you find a way to headquarters?" Marcus managed to ask as she led him out the door and to the street.

"Yes, I stole a car."

"What?"

"Just shut up and get in."

She got him into the car then reclined the seat. He didn't move much, just moaned. She felt badly, but there wasn't much she could do. She seatbelted him in, then hopped into the driver's side. A smell of gas, or worse than gas, filled the air as she pulled the car away from the curb.

"Marcus? Can you hear me? Do you know how to get there?"

The only answer was more moans, so Kelly unfolded the map, keeping it steady with her left hand as steered with her right. The signage in the city was shoddy and some of the letters were foreign, but she was able to place herself without too much trouble and head off jerkily in what she thought was the right direction. The most direct path would take her by the market she had just left, but since she had no desire to run into either the police or the thugs she stole the car from, she concocted an alternate route. It looked like there was an expressway or something that went up to the level she wanted. To get there, she would have to take a ramp down to the level below them and then work her way over north by northwest. If the top of the map was north. Which she had no way of knowing.

What am I doing? she thought. I probably shouldn't be stealing cars. I really hope Marcus doesn't die. I hope his guys are the good guys. What if he does die? I'd be driving with a dead guy.

She tightened her hands on the wheel and kept going.

Kelly grew more comfortable driving. It was an automatic, thankfully, and while there were many buttons whose purpose she was clueless about, none seemed to affect the driving. The ashtray was full of cigarettes and the floor was covered in trash, which she did her best to ignore. At first she stopped at most intersections, but the abruptness made Marcus thrash around, so she switched to rolling stops. She found the ramp down (more like a giant tube) and entered it. It was lit by small green lights and as she descended a car came up behind her and started honking. Frightened, she sped up, but as she emerged on the lower level, the car swung around her and disappeared off into the distance.

This level was evidently dedicated to parkland. The ceiling was higher and the lights had a different feel to them, more outdoorsy. There were a few buildings and giant elevators scattered about, but somehow with trees and lawns, all laid out in a systematic, geometrical way. Many citizens seemed to be enjoying what might pass as a sunny afternoon. Kelly hung a left and then a right, following an avenue that traced a long curve past a small pond and a large field where several hundred people were watching two teams play ultimate Frisbee. She saw the tube she wanted ahead of her. She was driving past a row of restaurants when she heard sirens and in her rearview mirror saw what could only be a police car emerging from the tube they had exited. And then a second one.

Kelly wasted no time wondering whether they were after her or not. Panic set in and she gunned it. The drivers in this town were quick to begin with, but Kelly out drove them all getting to the tube, jumping curbs and skidding out in her dash for a way out. This tube was wider, three lanes across. She entered the middle one and put the pedal to the floor and the car flew up the ramp at a steep angle. She passed some large cargo vehicles in the right lane and slowly gained on cars she could see in the distance, even as she saw more flashing lights in her rearview mirror. According to the map in her lap, this ramp emptied into what looked like a giant parking lot or field. Whatever it was, there were no streets listed on it and the headquarters were on the far side, marked in red by Marcus. She turned to him.

"Marcus! Marcus! Wake up! We're going up the Caledonia Tube, but I don't know how to get across to your building. Are you listening?"

"Yeah," Marcus struggled to get upright. "The Caledonia Tube, right. Great. Just go straight across and a little to the left."

"How?"

"You're fine."

Kelly was hesitant, but Marcus wasn't giving her anything else. As he closed his eyes, she kept talking, hoping for a hint,

"Okay. I'm just staying in this lane…ignoring exits to other levels…all right, the tube's widening, Marcus, I think we're near the end. Yes we are, I can see it flattening out ahead…uh…uh, Marcus, there's no road. Marcus, the road just ends what do I do? MARCUS!"

As the car reached the end of the ramp, there was a fifty-yard stretch where the incline became gentler and then the car was airborne and Kelly was screaming. They

were flying through darkness, surrounded by streams of
light moving in all directions. The car arced up through the
air and down again. Marcus reached over, straining at the
seatbelts and punched a green button. A series of new
lights appeared on the dashboard. The car leveled out and
began to fly but was still careening forward in midair at a
breakneck speed. Kelly hung onto the steering wheel for
dear life. The car swerved from side to side, as she fought
to control it. Up ahead a line of vehicles flew across her
field of vision, right to left. The car was headed straight for
them. Grabbing a lever she had noticed before but never
figured out, she pulled back and at the last moment they
banked sharply and rose above the other vehicles.

She breathed a sigh of relief, but then saw she was
heading straight up into a traffic jam floating in space
above her. She played with the lever again and evened out.
Off in the distance, she saw what must be the headquarters
Marcus spoke of, its bright lights and white façade making
it glow like a beacon, as she flew through this dark void.
Marcus had been retching during the twists and turns, but
now drooped unconscious on the seat. She brought her
eyes back to the roadless highway, and swerved around a
few cars.

She was fast approaching the end of the abyss,
when she began to put on the brakes, but with no effect.
Nothing on the console seemed to be made for slowing
down, so she started pressing random buttons, only to get
the radio blaring and the trunk popping open. She aimed
towards a bit of real road between the edge and the
building and said a quick prayer that it would be sufficient
braking room. She hit the road at an angle, with a hard
bounce, and punched the green button again. The car
returned to normal, but was nearly out of control. A few
people on the wide, gentle stairs in front of the building
ran out of the way. Kelly put the brakes on hard and
swung the car off to the left. It skidded right up the stairs,

spinning around as it did so, before it hit a railing and all the air bags went off. Kelly blacked out.

The next thing she knew was that she was lying on a stretcher, outside the car with people all around her. She could see Marcus already being carried inside. A tall man (he seemed ridiculously tall to Kelly from her vantage point) in a white jacket stood over her and asked, "Miss Margulis? Or Miss Grebe?"

Then she passed out again.

CHAPTER TWELVE

The next morning Joni stretched her body on the pallet where she had been sleeping under a pile of woolen blankets. She had slept long and hard, although she woke feeling unsettled by half-remembered dreams; the memory of the night's conversation and the proximity of Matabbi's forces did little to comfort her. She shook that off and took a deep breath; something about this bubble made her feel stronger. No, not stronger, more alive, like your heart beat more heartily or your blood was supercharged. Of course Brith would be the perfect teenage earl here, the embodiment of noble youth. And Malfi would be the best Viking scholar/sorcerer. And she could be the best whatever she was. Vagabond damsel. Virtuous rapscallion. Something like that.

She laughed at herself (which was also easier to do in this bubble), put on some clothes, and opened the tent flap. People were bustling around everywhere, doing their daily tasks, and air was full of aromas of baking breads and sounds of birds chirping.

"It must be ten in the morning!" she shouted to the air. "Where's Alejandro? Where's Brith? Where's Bramble?"

The answer to the last question came trotting over to her, followed by a white-haired man walking vigorously. He wore round glasses, cargo shorts, a well-worn button-down shirt, and hiking boots. If not for his sheepskin jacket and the layer of dirt on him, he might have been going off to watch a baseball game. He spoke first,

"You must be Joni! I'm Dr. Sweeney. You're from Earth! It's a pleasure to meet you."

Sweeney grabbed her hand and shook it robustly.

"Hello," Joni answered, still a little sluggish. "Where is Alejandro? Where is Br…Mr…. where is the earl?"

"They're off scheming ploys and policies with another," he said, waving off to a distant field, where Joni saw Alejandro, Brith, and a few men and women deep in conversation. "The valiant Brithwine was up with the sun and your friend soon found him, wishing to learn more about Matabbi's gates, in the hopes of leading you and him out of this bubble. But back to the issue at hand. Earth! I have so many questions. Let's break your fast and I'll give you a tour of the encampment."

Sweeney led her to the mess hall, another pavilion with an open air kitchen adjoining. Sweeney hardly seemed to stop talking, even when he was asking Joni questions. Instead of being annoyed, Joni found it endearing. Sweeney was just so enthusiastic about everything.

He had been in Avalon for almost fifteen years and was afraid he had "gone native." He came in with the Matabbi-run education program, but had a separate research grant ("my research is still embargoed until this unpleasantness is resolved, but that does allow me more freedom"). When Brith led his followers against Matabbi, Sweeney had stayed with the resistance. "Gathering reams of data, all handwritten, of course, but I wouldn't have it any other way."

But what he most wanted to talk to Joni about was Earth.

"Earth! What is it like to be from there?"

"It's nice, I guess. Have you never been there, Dr. Sweeney?"

"Just use Sweeney, dear, everybody here does. No, no, I was never able to obtain the appropriate permits. So I devoted my career to the micro-ebulli, the smaller bubbles. That's why I was asked to come to Avalon, although it was all very hush-hush. I wasn't told much of anything until I arrived. When I finally publish, it is going to be groundbreaking, groundbreaking!"

"But why do you care so much about Earth, if you study micro-bubbles?"

"Because they are Earthers! The Avalonians. Didn't you realize that? I mean, of course, many ebulli inhabitants are descended from Earthers at one point or another, but most have had so much contamination from other ebulli, that it is impossible to chart the cultural history. Avalon has been utterly isolated for the last millennium. Their history is almost entirely oral, but from what I understand there was a marvelous battle on Earth, and, in the aftermath, combatants from both sides were swept through a natural rip. My knowledge of the regions of Earth involved is somewhat limited, I'm afraid, but I believe the battle was on the Isle of Great Britain and that the invading forces were Vikings. There was a poem about the battle, I believe. How well do you know old English poetry?"

"Uh, not at all. I once saw a movie about Beowulf. I fell asleep."

"Drat. I had hoped. Unfortunately, my digital library doesn't work here and I haven't been able to contact my inter-ebullic associates. But, as memory serves, the Vikings were invading from the Americas and pillaging throughout Europe."

"I don't think it worked that way," Joni said. "The Vikings were Scandinavian."

"That's why I'm so glad you're here! But it is the Vikings I'm thinking of, yes? Naval invaders? Driving ashore in longboats, bloodthirsty, horned helmets, laying waste to farm and village?"

"I think so. I mean, the football team sells it that way. I think maybe they discovered America without telling anyone."

"Ah yes, exactly," Sweeney gave Joni that knowing look that tenured academics give when they don't understand something. "This has been a most providential meeting. Come. Let's take a brisk walk and continue our discussion."

Sweeney took Joni and Bramble all around the valley. He had detailed explanations of all the different tools and diverse farming techniques and kept talking about the "quasi-egalitarian societal structure." Joni attempted to steer the conversation back to the current occupation and what Matabbi was doing, but Sweeney seemed most concerned that the occupying forces were contaminating the native culture.

Nearing the far side of the valley, Joni did finally have some historical questions to ask Sweeney. They were sitting on a tumbledown wall of what Joni figured had been a castle hundreds, if not thousands of years ago, but was now mostly ruins.

"What do you know about the Cordelias, Sweeney?"

"Cordelians! Do they have Cordelian legends in Earth? I had no idea!"

"No, they don't. At least they don't call them that. But Alejandro, uh, mentioned them to me. What makes someone a Cordelian? What can the girls do?"

"You mean when they're not being slaughtered?"

"What? What do you mean?"

"Centuries ago it was not uncommon in some ebulli for boatloads of young women to be rounded up on the suspicion that one of them might be the next Cordelian. And then put to death. But girls kept coming forward. Of course, if they were killed, it proved they weren't a Cordelian, so they didn't need to be killed at all. A bit of a paradox."

"That's awful."

"Indeed, Joni, but long ago. No one takes it seriously nowadays, although I've seen 'Madam Cordelia Tarot Card Parlors' in many an ebullus."

"Why did people want to kill them?"

"Please don't think that most people wanted them dead. But a few did. There was even a society established to root them out. 'The Livonen Brothers of the Sword,' if memory serves. I'm sorry, I don't think I've thought about this since I was your age."

"What did the Cordelias do? Did they have special powers?"

"They varied. Mostly they saw visions and then acted upon them. Think about Jehanne d'Arc, who I know was from Earth. France, yes? She saw visions or heard voices and knew what to do to lead her armies to victory. At least for a while. Now we know that a lot of times when someone had visions, they were seeing into another ebullus."

"So Joan of Arc wasn't a saint?"

"Ha! I didn't say that, did I? Who's to say whom she was talking to? Or who gave her the power to look across?"

Joni thought for a minute.

"Are…were the Cordelias good?"

"Historically?"

"Yes. No. No, morally. Did they do the right things?"

"Aah, a good question. They certainly thought they were doing right. And yes, I think in the moment they always took the high ground. They weren't out for personal profit."

"They sound like they were good," Joni said, more to herself.

"Indubitably. They were the finest of women. But enough of the past! Let's head back to camp and find the handsome Brith and your courageous friend Alejandro. And some lunch. The camp cook makes the most amazing mutton sandwiches, with hot peppers and a secret sauce he swears his great-grandfather learned from a meadow fairy."

When they returned to the pavilion, they found Alejandro, Brith, Malfi, Jedder, and a couple of others seated around a wooden table in deep conversation.

"Joni, Sweeney, come join us," Brith greeted them and was the only one at the table to stand. A woman, who Joni recognized as one of Brith's captains from the night before slid over to provide space for Joni and Sweeney to sit down. Brith continued speaking:

"We were just finalizing our plans. Matabbi's armourers have brought in a new weapon, and we plan to attend the demonstration, uninvited though we may be. Meanwhilst, your companion Alejandro wishes to see one of the transporter gates that the occupiers have established to provide their ingress and egress of our bubble. Along our route to the testing ground we will be able to observe the one currently blaspheming the throne room and he can determine if he will be able to operate it."

"Once again," Jedder interrupted, apparently continuing an earlier argument, "I must protest allowing outsiders to view the throne room through our…spyhole."

"I have already said that I trust these outsiders. I am a good judge of men and women."

"Your father was a good judge of men, yet he trusted Matabbi. But even he never revealed our hidden paths."

Brith looked at Jedder, a mirthless smile upon his face: "Our nation, our world itself, walks upon a knife's edge. You speak to me of traditions. I say, there will be no Avalon left soon to have traditions, unless we start breaking a few when we must. The hour is growing ever darker and while I hope for a bright dawn on the morrow, I can only do what I feel is right in the moment. And so I will take these two through the tunnels."

"Wait," Alejandro interrupted. "Two? No, Joni should stay here."

"Why?" Joni and Brith asked together, the former angry, the latter confused.

"Well, uh, she's just an untried girl…"

Brith answered first, while Joni was still sputtering:

"In Avalon the women fight with the men. And in these times the boys and the girls fight as well. Is your ebullus so backward?"

"Uh, uh."

"Yeah," Joni said. "Is there something wrong with your world, Alejandro? That just sounds medieval, I mean, it really does."

Alejandro glared at her, but raised his hands in defeat.

"Huzzah then," Brith laughed. "We depart in twenty minutes. Galpan here will find some less outlandish clothes for you to wear. Malfi will gather some food for us to eat on the way. Sweeney…"

"Uh…yes, Brith?"

"You're in charge of the dog until we return."

Sweeney looked like he couldn't be happier.

Three hours later, Brith, Malfi, Alejandro, Joni and three of Brith's men-at-arms (actually one man-at-arms and two women-at-arms) crouched in a dank, dirty cellar beneath a loyalist tavern just inside the town. So far, the plan was going just as Brith and Malfi had expected. They had evaded all scouts as they crossed the countryside and then entered the town, while Jedder and his group circled around the city. Once in the tavern, they went through a side door and now Joni was looking around impatiently.

"Why are we here?" she asked. "Where is this tunnel of yours?"

"Soon, my friends, soon," answered Brith, deadly serious. "But I just wanted to repeat myself and make it perfectly clear; this road I will take you on, 'the tunnels of the worm' as they're called, are in the purview of the royal family. It is only in extreme situations that we take our most trusted followers through them. And rightly or not, you and your companion engender that trust. But you must never disclose what you see."

"I would never let down your trust, Brith."

"On my very life," Alejandro added.

"You do well to swear so, my friends, for if you betray us in this, though in all else you be true, it is your soul you will lose. That is the vow of the worm."

They looked hard at each other, before Brith grinned again and slapped Alejandro on the back, dissipating the tension.

"To the tunnels then."

Brith's women rolled a few barrels to the side, revealing a small door, about three feet high. Brith took a key from a chain around his neck, turned it in the lock, and then crawled through, followed by the rest of the party. Alejandro and Joni rose carefully to their feet as someone struck a match. In its flare, they saw Malfi lighting a torch.

They stood at one end of a tunnel, about six feet wide, with a ceiling just above their heads (except for Malfi, who had to stoop), held up with wooden supports and beams, some so old the supports had supports. They walked silently down the hallway and after a minute made a turn to the right. The light from the torch offered little illumination, so that the rest of tunnel, ahead and behind, were hidden in shadows. They came to a sudden halt at a large door, made from thick pieces of wood bound with several large strips of rusted metal. Brith took another key from his chain, and put it into an ornate lock in the door. Malfi grabbed the door by a handle and pulled it towards them. It scraped along the ground, the creak from the hinges echoing down the dusty corridor.

Behind it was another door, smaller than the first. The entire wall was smooth and ivory colored. A thin, black seam along the door's edges was the only thing disrupting the smooth surface, except for a wheel in its exact center and a panel to its right. Alejandro felt the door with his fingertips and knocked on it softly. It felt like some type of metallic alloy, but he could not identify it. It certainly wasn't medieval technology. He and Joni gave questioning looks to each other but said nothing.

Brith put his hand on the panel and three green lights came on, one at a time. He then turned the wheel, spinning it several times around. He pulled and it swung towards him, effortlessly, silently, except for a slight whoosh, as air rushed out. Inside was dark. Brith stepped through and the walls began to glow, spreading down the passage, a passage that to Joni seemed as futuristic as the rest of the ebullus had seemed ancient. Malfi snuffed out the torch on the ground before entering and placed it on a hook outside the door. Brith led the group forward, walking at a faster pace than before. The passage curved gently to the right, making it impossible to see far ahead. The smooth walls were broken up by an occasional closed door and mirrored spheres every thirty yards that Joni thought were probably cameras. The corridor went on and on, with such uniformity, it was difficult to know how far they had traveled, or if they had looped around. After a few minutes, the passage widened for twenty yards. Brith led them up three steps on their left and grabbed the edge of a door. It had a wooden clamp on it to keep it from closing; he slid it neatly into the wall. They all walked inside, and the lights came on instantly.

The room appeared to be a viewing platform, dominated by a giant window or video screen covering the far wall. Joni immediately walked down a ramp to it and tapped the glass, if that's what it was.

"They can't see us from that side," whispered Brith, coming to her side. Then, speaking a little louder, said, "Nor can they hear us."

Through the window they looked down on a long hall, the ancestral throne room, according to Brith. The hall was built of stone and was lit by a series of electric lights strung around the perimeter, although many unused oil lamps still remained. A walkway ran along the second floor, stopping before it reached Brith's spy post. Directly beneath the window were steps leading up to a dais, where presumably the throne must be, although Joni could not see it from this angle.

Joni slid her fingers along the glass and then looked back at the rest of the observation room. It was symmetrical, and rounded on the sides. She and Alejandro strode up to a central platform. Brith remained at the window, looking into the throne room, his back to them. Malfi and the three others were unloading some items they had brought. There were several cots on the floor and boxes of food and drink crammed in various nooks: evidently, Brith's spies would spend nights here, as necessary. Alejandro attention was drawn to a long table bolted to the floor. A tarp lay across it, but one corner had been pulled away. He peeled it back to reveal a computer screen, unlike any he or Joni had ever seen. Where a keyboard would be, there was only another screen on the table, dead to the touch. He examined it from every angle, but could find no identifying characteristics, or even a way to open it up. Lifting the dusty tarp, he saw three more identical computers.

"What's going on here?" Joni whispered to him. "What is this place?"

"I don't know," Alejandro said. "It feels ancient, but I've never seen any technology like this."

"Not even in your bubble?"

"No. But maybe it has something to do with why the bubble is so hidden."

He left her and sidled up to Brith, who stood at the window, an exiled king, surveying the heart of his occupied realm, sizing up his enemy. Alejandro coughed gently, but got no reaction. He coughed louder, and spoke.

"Brith, have any outworlders seen these passages?"

Shaken out of his trance, Brith was himself again as he answered, "Nary a one."

Alejandro grabbed him by the arm and forced Brith to face him.

"Listen to me, Brith. Has anyone from outside Avalon, *anyone*, ever been here?"

Brith straightened up and looked at Alejandro.

"No, Alejandro. The family legend is that the first earl discovered the secret way in the ruins of an ancient castle. My illustrious forefather built the present castle and town to incorporate the passages. And my father, perhaps with a presentient touch, never trusted Matabbi with its secrets."

"Is there only the one entrance?" asked Alejandro.

"No, no. There are several entry points. Also, many locked doors that have never been opened. None know who built them, nor how long they have been here."

Alejandro looked at him thoughtfully, before speaking.

"Matabbi must never know about this. No one must know about this. Not the Council. No one."

"Is this so strange, my friend? Even for you?"

"Yes," Alejandro answered and Joni, who had joined them, nodded. "I wish I could take the time to figure out what this place is. I never heard of anything like it, in any ebullus."

"Another of our hidden strengths!" Brith laughed, jubilant again. "Avalon is forever blessed. But I would gladly trade our secrets for our land returned. Come! Enough of this chatter! Let us examine the hall and see if we can discern our enemy's secrets or the workings of his accursed gate."

Alejandro studied the throne room. The floor was composed of gray stones, except for a white marble pathway running down the middle, with pillars on either flank. Several desks were set up in the center, with electrical extension cords snaking out from a door on the right side. Only one man sat in the hall, lazily typing away. On the far side of the room, was the device that Alejandro had come to see: an open-channel, personnel gate. According to Brith, there was another gate on the outskirts of town, used for larger machinery, as well as people. Alejandro studied the gate as well as he could from a distance and was confident he would be able to operate it.

Just then, the man jumped up and ran over to the gate, where several lights had come on, green and yellow. He then ran back to his desk, where he spun a crank and picked up a phone, yelling something into it. There was a blaze of greenish light from the gate and a new man stepped through it, transported from another ebullus. The visitor scowled, just as three men rushed in through a side door. The visitor barked a few orders at them and one went running back through the door they had just entered.

"Those three unseemly individuals," Brith said, not noticing the stunned expressions on Joni and Alejandro, "are the garrison commander and two of his top officers. I have never seen them so…acquiescent, and indeed, frightened, before. It pleases the heart of this outlaw ruler. But I wonder who the man is."

Before answering, Alejandro watched the gaunt man standing there, red hair falling over his heart-shaped face,

"That is Matabbi's personal assassin. You will never meet a more dangerous man."

"Even with one arm?" Malfi asked, who had joined them at the railing.

"He had both arms yesterday," Joni said quietly, watching as the assassin, with a bandaged stump where his right arm used to be, left the room with the garrison commander.

"That will barely slow him down," Alejandro said, putting his arm around a shuddering Joni. "I just hope Redpoll came out better. I'm sure she did."

There was an uncomfortable silence as Brith and Malfi realized the assassin was the same one who had attacked Joni in Nicus, followed by awkward attempts to comfort them. Malfi explained how well they were hidden here, while Brith was all for charging into the castle and slicing him from groin to neck and splaying his entrails across the tiles. Joni found that sweet for some reason, and gave him a little hug.

"That's okay, Brith. I'll be okay. Let's go off and find this weapon demo of yours. I don't want to wait here to see if he comes back."

"An excellent idea. We will hence forth."

Leaving one of the soldiers behind, the remaining six hurried further down the main passage, still curving to the right. As they went along, Brith pointed out various doors, hoping to distract Joni. This door leads to a trap door in the kitchen pantry. That door leads to the sewers. Those doors lead to a dead end, but in his great-great-grandfather's time allowed access to the prisons, before a roof collapse closed them. The twenty-third earl believed he heard talking behind those locked doors and eventually went mad roaming these corridors. That door leads to a crawlspace that provides spy holes on several bedrooms and council chambers. Although Joni didn't pay much attention, Alejandro walked in a daze, fascinated by all the wonders around them.

Finally, they went through a door on the left, into a small, square room. It was featureless, except for a door on the far side like the one they had originally entered, with a wheel in its center. Next to the door were a few jugs of water and a pile of blankets. Brith placed his hand on the wheel and motioned Alejandro and Joni over.

"Once we make our exit here, we travel through a tunnel 'neath the town, that goes to the tournament arena to spy on the weapon. We will need to remain silent to ensure we are not detected."

Brith spun the wheel and pulled the door open. They found another wooden door behind it, which swung open with a gentle push. They stepped out into a small, stone-lined alcove.

For the next half hour, they walked along at a brisk clip. The majority of the tunnel was an arch of brick or stone, about seven feet high in the center. In a few places, they splashed through shallow puddles and were dripped upon here and there, but it was mostly dry. A thin chimney every fifty feet or so provided sufficient light. Eventually, after a gentle climb, they crawled through a narrow hole to enter a larger chamber, dark, except for some light coming through a high grate. Malfi looked through it and then carefully slid back a wooden panel.

Brith climbed up and through the panel, followed by the others. Joni came last. She found herself in another stone chamber, with several tables and a dry sink. The far side was all boarded up from the outside, with sunlight peaking through a grate at the top. They could hear a crowd of people through the grate, near, but not too near.

"The Royal Box," Brith whispered.

They all climbed quietly onto a table near the far wall and peered through the grate. It was a good height for Joni, although Malfi was the only one so tall that he really had to stoop. Leaning in, she realized they were looking at what must be a soccer stadium, or whatever they played here. Their hiding place was situated behind a medieval luxury box. There were a bunch of broken benches in the box itself, which probably kept people away, but the box was large enough (and open to the elements), so that the six of them had a good view of the field, even looking through the grate.

The stands were all empty but in the middle of the pitch was a crowd of several dozen people. Most were dressed in soldier uniforms, but there was a sprinkling of Avalonian tunics, as well as a few suits and ties. The crowd was facing away from the box towards a large piece of machinery, almost as long as a bus. Two people sat in a cab on one end of it and a long half pipe slid out towards the far side.

"It's like the weapon in Nicus," Alejandro whispered.

"Only larger," answered Joni.

Evidently the demonstration had been going on for a while. There were piles of melted slag scattered across the grass and a whole section of the arena on the far side seemed melted. Someone was making an announcement to the crowd, but Joni couldn't make out the words.

"We have spies," said Brith, pointing out where native Avalonians were carrying boxes and picking up trash, "who will give us the details later."

Suddenly the voice rose to almost a shout and Joni saw the scientist, dressed all in white, striding back and forth with military precision.

"What we have shown you so far," he said, "can be accomplished with conventional weapons. Conventional weapons would do it crudely, prosaically. We have elevated armaments into the realm of poetry. Graceful. Lyrical. Siphoning off energy from existence itself."

There was a great deal of clapping, which he allowed for a minute, before waving the crowd silent again.

"But here we will use the energy of existence to make non-existence. The power of being, in our hands. Today we will test it only briefly, in a controlled environment for the first time. You might wish to step back."

Everyone in the crowd took a step back, while clapping energetically. There was silence as a third man climbed into the cab and put on his goggles. The crowd then took another step or two back. Or ten in a few cases.

The stadium was silent, not even a rustle of wind. Then a faint high pitch whine came from the device, just on the edge of hearing. The whine notched up to a buzz and then to a roar. A greenish light emerged from the machine and flowed down the half-pipe. There was a bright flash and the greenish light shot out to cover a ten-yard swath of the stadium seats, from the edge of the grass to the top row. The whole stadium shook. Several men and women in the crowd fell down, and Alejandro and Joni had to grab each other to stay standing. When they looked back out through the grate, it took a minute to see what was wrong.

"What the devil," Malfi swore to himself.

Part of the stadium was missing. But there wasn't a gap. Two sections of the stands that had been ten yards apart were now touching each other, and the whole arena was slightly twisted. Even the grass was affected. It was like giant hands had squeezed the stadium, scrunching parts of it into nothingness. There was nothing missing, the stadium just had a kink in it.

The six spies stared dumbfounded as the crowd on the field applauded for a few minutes and then began to break up into small groups. Some senior officers went forward to congratulate the scientists running the tests. Joni felt Alejandro twitch beside her and looked down to where they now could see the assassin, standing near the weapon. While everyone else was giving the weapon (or maybe him) wide berth, he was studying it intently. He probed it and stroked it, kneeling on the ground to look into its innards. He did everything but kick the tires. A couple of scientist waited nearby, as if ready to answer questions, but did not approach him.

The assassin stood up and slowly turned around, eyeing every part of the stadium. Joni's companions collectively held their breath as his gaze passed over the royal box. But, as far as they could tell, the assassin didn't notice them. Instead, he snapped his fingers at the garrison commandeer, who came running over like a trained dog. The pair left through a far tunnel, the commandeer scurrying to keep up with the assassin's pace.

As if that was some set signal, the remainder of the crowd quickly dissipated, a few stragglers talking with the scientists. Watched closely by the scientists, eight native Avalonians were wheeling the weapon through the largest tunnel and out of the stadium, while others picked up odds and ends from around the stadium. Joni and the others waited quietly on the floor of their hidden perch, taking turns to keep an eye on the field. Within fifteen minutes, only native Avalonians were in sight. Soon after, those natives still cleaning up began to spread out across the stadium. One approached the royal box, looked around once, and then spoke.

"My lord? Are you there?"

"Is the coast clear?" Brith responded through the grate.

"It is. Marshall Jedder should be arriving soon."

"Excellent."

Upon this information, Malfi lifted some loose boards and crawled out into the late afternoon sun, followed by the others. Brith glanced to the corners of the stadium and then charged down to the field, with Malfi, Joni, and Alejandro close behind.

Up close, the damage from the weapon was just as confusing. An acrid odor filled the area, not strong, but unpleasant. A seam of sorts ran through the grass near where the weapon had stood, only noticeable if you were looking for it. But then it became more evident, as it continued across the dirt track and up into the stands themselves. Seats in the stadium that should be far apart were now adjoining. At points the concrete on either side fused together, as if it were one piece, with maybe just a slight difference in color. In other places, there were cracks and crumbling masonry. Benches were joined at odd angles and the higher the row, the more uneven the melding of the two sides was. Climbing to the back row, they looked over the edge outside the stadium. The seam continued another thirty yards or so. A small building was missing a wall, and half a roof and a row of hedges were jumbled together.

"The devils have brought their sorcery to the heart of my earldom," Brith said, as he looked around. "They will pay for this. My dominion is diminished."

"I'm sorry, Brith."

Joni reached for his hand, but then a loud shout echoed from the north side of the arena. They all ducked. On the north side of the stadium, which was built into a hill, several Avalonians were entering from the top of the stands. Brith let out his breath, recognizing Jedder, and stood up, followed by the others. They strode over along the back wall and soon reached them.

"My lord," Jedder hailed Brith, "Malfi, Alejandro, Joni."

"What is going on?" Brith asked, perplexed. "What happened whereby you forsook your positions? We were to rendezvous two hours hence, unless some unseen danger emerged."

"The troops are gone, sire!"

"What? Explain yourself."

"I exaggerate some. The citadel is guarded yet, but they started transporting out all the training brigades, the infantry, and their infernal mechanical cavalry, sometime this morning. My men have scoured the area, and there is not a Matabbi man between us and our camp."

"What about the town?" Brith asked.

"I would hazard a guess that they have returned to their numbers of a year ago, about six hundred or so. The permanent troops appeared to have been recalled to their barracks for the time being. I sent Sabudan in to converse with our spies."

"This is wonderful!" shouted Malfi. "We must celebrate!"

"Indeed, my friend," Brith answered, "we shall, and soon. But I worry for the poor denizens of whatever ebullus to which Matabbi sends his men. And, lest we forget, the initial garrison kept us at bay long before Matabbi rolled in his extra battalions."

"No, Brith, no," Malfi laughed. "It is not the same. We have become stronger and more cunning. It will not be an easy fight, I grant you, but we will persevere. I will write songs about it that will be sung for a thousand years!"

"You strengthen my heart, good Malfi. You will sing the first part tonight. But I would have us away from here. This place still reeks of Matabbi's foul machinery."

"Before we go," Alejandro said, "I'd like to take a picture of sorts."

Alejandro brought out something from his pocket, the size and shape of a small bottle. He twisted it and the top section popped out another inch or so.

"What is that, friend Alejandro?" Malfi asked, leaning forward to examine it.

"It probably won't even work here," answered Alejandro, "and I don't think you'd understand it."

"Try me," said Malfi. "I have studied a bit of the universe beyond our barbarian bubble."

"I'm sorry…I didn't mean to…anyway, it is sort of a panoramic camera that will record an image of the area in all directions."

"Including above and below the surface?"

"Uh, yes. It will record all objects in a spheroid. Hopefully I can analyze it later and figure out what happened here."

"Does it go beyond the visible spectrum?"

"Yes, in both directions. I'm not sure of the exact frequencies. I won it in a game of Ubilam poker. Double royal flush."

"How does it record the data?"

"Well, if this world had a communications satellite, it would upload the picture and I could download it at my leisure. In this case, it will store it locally. There's not a ton of memory, so I'll just take one."

"Can I help?" Malfi asked.

"Yes. Take the camera and set it up on the wall here. I'll take this reflector to the far wall. When I give a signal, press that button right there."

Alejandro walked across the stadium and up the steps to the far wall. While he did so, Brith and Jedder conversed with the soldiers and sent half back home in small groups. Joni lay down on the wall, waiting with Malfi for Alejandro's signal. He reached the far side in a few minutes, set up his apparatus, and then climbed up on the wall and waved his arm. Malfi pressed the button. It lit up green and started blinking: "Memory Full."

"I guess it worked," Joni said.

"I guess so," answered Malfi.

"Are you all finished?" Brith asked, having strode back to them. "We need to be leaving."

"All done," answered Malfi. "We're just waiting for him."

Malfi pointed to where Alejandro was descending to the field. As soon as he touched the grass, Joni and the others heard a commotion. The echoes in the stadium made it hard to tell its location at first. Then three or four soldiers emerged from a tunnel at the field level. Joni first thought they were natives, but then saw the Matabbi uniforms. Alejandro began to run and the soldiers soon saw him. They chased after him, but he had a headstart of forty or fifty yards.

Brith and Malfi raced down the steps, weapons raised, with Joni just a few steps behind. As Alejandro reached the midpoint of the field, Matabbi's assassin stepped out of the tunnel. He instantly gauged the situation and pulled something from a pocket at his side. He whipped his hand in the air and a second later Alejandro fell to the ground, ropes around his legs.

More soldiers came running from two different tunnels. Alejandro yelled at Joni, "Get away, get away." Brith and Malfi were almost to the grass, when they stopped. Brith hesitated a fraction of a second and started to move forward again. Malfi grabbed him and pulled him back up the stairs. Brith's archers began firing at the soldiers, which slowed them some, but by this point, Joni couldn't even see Alejandro for the crowd of soldiers as she stood halfway down the steps and he lay fallen on the field. Brith reached her and grabbed her shoulder.

"We must fly! We cannot save him now."

Joni couldn't leave, she couldn't. She wouldn't. Brith took her by the arms and then suddenly Malfi hoisted her up and threw her over his shoulder. They ran up the steps and outside the areana to where Jedder had some horses ready. Joni was crying and shouting, but knew deep down that she had no choice. She got on Brith's horse, right behind him.

They took off. They galloped like the wind and, although they heard sounds of pursuit at first, they soon outdistanced their hunters. Ninety minutes of hard riding (although Joni saw little of it through her tears) and they were back in Brith's camp.

The news they brought was mostly joyous and there was much rejoicing. Only those who had set out that day with Alejandro had no heart in it, still thinking of the companion they had left behind. Brith hid it well, having to play the part of ruler before that of comrade. Malfi sang his tales around the bonfire and, if he wept openly, no one wondered, for all the camp was a sea of tears and laughter. But Sweeney knew the truth and let Joni cry on his shoulder.

With the fire still blazing and music still filling the air, Brith led Joni away from the revelry, Bramble at their heels. The stars seemed closer to Joni than on her world, and certainly brighter. They walked towards the cliffs and Brith managed to find a thin path by the starlight and they climbed to top. There was a bit of grass and a cool wind passed over them. They climbed on some rocks and Brith pointed to his capital city, nothing more than a small cluster of lights on the horizon.

"We will get him back," he said, taking her hand in his.

She nodded and the three of them stood there in the starlight, earl, dog, and Cordelian.